maybe one day

SARAH DOUGLAS

maybe one day

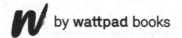 by wattpad books

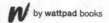 by wattpad books

An imprint of Wattpad WEBTOON Book Group

Copyright © 2023 Sarah Douglas
All rights reserved.
Published in Canada by Wattpad WEBTOON Book Group, a
division of Wattpad Corp.

36 Wellington Street E., Suite 200, Toronto, ON M5E 1C7 Canada

www.wattpad.com
First W by Wattpad Books edition: April 2023
ISBN 978-1-98936-555-7 (Trade Paper OR Hardcover original)
ISBN 978-1-98936-556-4 (eBook edition)

Library and Archives Canada Cataloguing in Publication information is available upon request.

Printed and bound in Canada

1 3 5 7 9 10 8 6 4 2

Cover design by Mumtaz Mustafa
Images © Kevin Kozicki via Offset

For Alex, my home, no matter where we go.

one

JACE

February, the night of the accident

Sitting down on the edge of the bathtub, I shoved my hands in my hair and let out a long breath.

Hayley Donovan had tugged at something inside me, and like a spool of thread, I was unraveling.

All I'd felt since I'd come home for break was a shit-ton of longing and confusion. She was three years younger than me—sixteen—but I couldn't get her out of my head. Her ocean-blue eyes and plump, kissable lips were every guy's fantasy, and I hated that she'd inadvertently become mine. I'd known her my whole life, but it was only now that I was a freshman in college that everything was starting to change between us.

"Are you up here, Jace?"

Hayley's voice was soft, laced with worry, and her footsteps were ominously close to the bathroom door. My body tensed and relaxed simultaneously.

There was a knock at the door, and I couldn't describe my level of fear. I'd come here to escape her, to shut myself away and hide like the fucking coward I was.

Seeing her sitting in Sean's lap, skimming her hands up his sides, and tangling her fingers in his hair, it felt like someone had cut into my chest with a rusty knife. How dare she make me feel this way?

I was pissed off. And jealous. But it was the guilt, growing like a noxious weed in the pit of my stomach, that made drinking tonight pretty much impossible to consider.

I had a girlfriend.

I had no right to be upset that Hayley was . . . kissing someone else.

Music from downstairs blasted, jumping in volume. Hinder's "Lips of an Angel" was vibrating the tiles beneath my worn sneakers, and I almost laughed, because the song couldn't have been more fitting.

All night, I'd hung on Hayley's every word. I'd tracked the gentle movements of her mouth, wanting to press my lips to hers and catch my breath back. She'd stolen it, and I was still trying to work out when, exactly, that had happened.

Hayley had a hold on me, and I was waiting for the awful pressure to stop clamping down on my chest.

"I know you're in there," she said, and I clenched my teeth. "I can see the light under the door. I'm coming in, okay?"

Before I could even respond, she opened the door, and I glanced over at her. Her eyes had me trapped, and she came toward me, not stopping until we were a mere foot apart.

"What are you doing up here?" she asked after a moment of silence. She sounded slurry and tired. "Everyone who's here tonight came to see you."

"Guess I'm just not in the party mood."

The truth was, I just didn't want to see her kissing Sean. I wanted to switch off these damn feelings. I wanted things to go back to how they were, but my body shook with the physical effort it took to ignore her, to ignore the hollowness in my gut.

Hayley crouched between my knees, forcing me to pull my arms off my legs and lean back. I waited for a beat, hoping maybe she'd give up and leave, but she didn't. She never did.

"Why are you being like this?" Her frown deepened, and I focused all my energy on not reacting to her proximity. "Ever since you got home, you've been avoiding me. Did I . . . did I do something?"

You made me want you.

I almost said it, but I clamped my jaw shut and shifted my eyes away. I couldn't look at her.

"Jace?"

The way she whispered my name, the way it came out of her with such desperation and hopefulness, sent a shiver down my spine.

My gaze involuntarily traveled back to her. God, she was so fucking beautiful. How had I only just started to notice that?

Her long hair tumbled over her shoulders like a dark veil, and she had an adorable smattering of freckles on her pert nose. There wasn't a single part of her that wasn't perfect.

"No. You didn't do anything. I don't know. I'm just . . ." I couldn't understand how I was feeling, much less articulate it. I wished I were drunk. Then I wouldn't be so aware of the stupid-ass emotions that whirled inside me.

Hayley nodded slowly, like somehow, she'd still been able to make sense of that. Like she'd heard my unspoken plea for her to drop the subject.

"Do you mind if I stay here with you for a while?" she asked. I didn't miss the sadness that lingered on her pretty face.

Why was I handling this so badly?

Oh, yeah. I had a girlfriend.

My relationship with Zoe had changed since we'd graduated high school—we'd both expected it to. Zoe had been accepted to UPenn because she was Ivy League material, and I'd gone to Delaware because I was . . . not Ivy League material. That wasn't the issue, though. Neither was the hour-long drive it took to see each other on weekends. It was the brunette in front of me, who also happened to be my little sister's best friend.

When I didn't answer, my thoughts elsewhere, Hayley settled next to me, pressing her cheek against my shoulder. The smell of her vanilla-scented perfume wrapped around me like a thick haze, and I couldn't think straight. It felt dangerous being this close to her.

Maybe it was the way those blue eyes stared intently at me, even if I didn't know what they were searching for. It was like she'd always seen something in me. Something worthy. Maybe I was just someone she trusted, could bare her soul to. A guy she'd always think of as a surrogate big brother.

The crushing disappointment of that line of thinking had me drawing in a shaky, surprised breath.

"Don't worry, we don't have to talk or anything. I just need to sit down for a minute," she mumbled, "and I . . . I need the room to stop spinning."

"How much have you had to drink?" I deliberately let my tone switch to disapproving. My sister should never have encouraged her to toss down those tequila slammers. The fumes alone were strong enough to burn your nasal passages.

"I don't know." She shrugged, and that small grin was back. "Does it matter?"

"Underage drinking isn't the answer, Hayles," I said quietly. "Take it from me. It doesn't do shit. Whatever you're trying to escape, it's still there when the buzz wears off."

"I don't need to hear this, Jace." The softness vanished, and a dark look hardened her features. "Tom just chewed me out in front of everyone for coming tonight, then for drinking. I've already heard the brotherly lecture, so you can save it."

"I'm not—" I halted abruptly, and the word *brotherly* dinged in my skull. It felt like I'd been punched. What I felt for Hayley sure as shit wasn't brotherly. "Look, I'm just trying to give you some advice. Take it or leave it. I just think maybe you should reassess some of the choices you've been making lately."

She bristled. "What's that supposed to mean?"

"Well, for starters, it probably isn't the smartest idea to hook up with a guy like Sean. I mean, Sean Pearson? Come on." The response flew out of my mouth carelessly, and I grimaced.

"What's wrong with Sean?"

I told myself that the best thing to do was to stay silent, but another hot streak of jealousy tore through me, roaring back to life. God, I was acting like a preteen. "Uh, let me see." I pretended to think. "Sean's a rich asshole who thinks he can get whatever he wants. You're not sober enough to make intelligent decisions, and yet he feels okay taking advantage of you."

That was 80 percent true. The other 20 percent was about something else entirely. When I'd seen his mouth fused with hers, it had messed me up. It felt like I'd resurfaced from a foggy, dreamlike state, and I was finally seeing everything clearly. I'd known Hayley for seven years. My family had vacationed with her family, shared summers in our small semi-coastal town. We'd grown up together, and I'd never once felt anything for her that wasn't platonic.

But now, tonight, for the first time, I'd wanted to show her what a real kiss was. I'd wanted to kiss her until I could erase the past, until she couldn't remember anyone who came before me. I wanted to know if I was the only one drowning under the weight of how much I wanted her. If I was the only one who felt this way. The prospect of her answer scared me as much as it thrilled me.

"Wow. I must be really drunk."

I hadn't been expecting that.

"I can't believe what I'm hearing," she continued derisively.

"What?"

Hayley watched me for a moment, her eyes narrowing. "Are you jealous or something? Is that what this is?" she asked. "I don't remember you telling Amelia off like this, and she's been kissing boys for a lot longer than I have."

Fuck.

She had me there.

I opened my mouth, then closed it. "I'm not jealous. Emotion has nothing to do with this." It was a douchebag response, and a bald-faced lie, but it was all I had. The thought of her kissing other guys set my teeth on edge. How the hell could I possibly say that?

"Ugh, so you're in one of *those* moods."

My pulse raced like I was preparing for a fight. "What moods?"

"You know," she answered without delay. "Those moods where you run from everything—from the way you feel—even though you're staying perfectly still. You retreat inside yourself, and you don't let anyone reach you. Not me, anyway."

I might've been offended by what she'd said if she hadn't been so goddamned right.

"Why is that?" There was a pause, and then she went on, "I don't think I've ever been able to read you, and I probably never will. You're the definition of a closed book. Why do you always push me away?"

I was speechless. So much for not understanding me. I think she knew me better than I knew myself.

"Christ, Hayles. Usually, my sister's the one who gets all philosophical and shit when she's drunk." I cleared my throat. "I don't know what you're expecting me to say right now. Yes, I push you away. Because I know I do, but I . . ."

She'd picked up on the fact that I was dodging her, especially since I'd come home from college. How was I supposed to tell her that being around her had hot possessiveness coursing through my veins? Or that every time I looked at her, something inside my rib cage seized?

"Is it because I'm Amelia's best friend? Is that why?" Her tone was as grim as her expression. "Because you don't see us having a friendship outside of my relationship with her?"

"No." I scrubbed a hand down my face. If only things were that simple. "You don't get it." *I don't just see you as my little sister's best friend!* I wanted to yell. *That's the fucking problem. You're all I see. Everything I want.*

"But I do," she argued. "I've gotten the message pretty loud and clear. You're not jealous; you're just weirdly protective. You have this warped sense of obligation to be an older-brother figure. I get it. You won't open up to me, you're never going to see me as anything more than Amelia's best friend, and it doesn't matter that I've had feelings for you since—" She swallowed visibly, horror ghosting across her features. "Oh my God . . ."

The words were out there so suddenly, catching us both off

guard, and my heart stopped. I think it actually flatlined in my chest. And then it started to beat wildly—life coming back to me in the form of her deepest confession—as I stared down at the girl beside me.

"What did you say?" I asked before I could stop myself. My voice sounded thick.

I wanted her so badly, and I couldn't have her. But instead of walking away, I fed the temptation. And I let myself pretend, for just a minute, that maybe things were different. Maybe I wasn't with Zoe. Maybe Hayley wasn't Tom's little sister.

In that bathroom, in that bubble of friendship and trust we'd built over the last seven years, it was easy to forget. It was easy to hope for something I'd never have with her.

"I . . . I didn't say anything," Hayley whispered. She squirmed away from me, tucking a dark strand of hair behind her ear.

She was drunk, and I was smarter than this. The alcohol had loosened her lips, and I was taking advantage of that. I wasn't so different from Sean. Disgust clawed at me.

"Bullshit," I said softly. "You have feelings for me?"

Hayley's gaze met mine, and I braced for the shift I knew would happen between us, regardless of her answer. Nothing would ever be the same.

"You have a girlfriend, Jace. How I feel is irrelevant."

I inhaled slowly, trying to compose myself. She wasn't denying it. She had feelings for me too. This wasn't how tonight was supposed to go down. She wasn't supposed to see something good in me. She wasn't supposed to want me back.

Hayley lurched forward and clutched the sides of the toilet, cutting off what would've been my pathetic attempt to let her down. I would never act upon my feelings. I knew all about emotional cheating—thanks to my sister's love of self-help magazines—and this felt scarily like it.

Everything Hayley had drunk tonight made a reappearance, and I wasn't all that surprised. She didn't normally drink, and she and Amelia were partying with all of my friends—most of whom were in college and had built up a decent alcohol tolerance.

I scrambled forward, curving myself around her small frame. Incapable of doing anything more than holding her hair and comfortingly rubbing her back, I'd never felt so reprehensible. I was the idiot who'd let her hang here tonight while my parents were out of town. Tom had told her not to come, but she hadn't listened. And I'd caved when she'd showed up at my house. I shouldn't have.

I cursed under my breath. "I'm so sorry. This is all my fault."

Her skin was hot and feverish, and when she finally sagged back on the floor, I was forced to let go. "Nope, it's the tequila's fault. Tequila sucks."

A chuckle rumbled out from me. "Well, I can get behind that too."

I passed her a clean washcloth, and she cringed. "Oh God, this is so embarrassing."

The vulnerability in Hayley's voice threatened to crack my heart wide open. She had nothing to be embarrassed about. She'd seen me at my worst as well.

"Don't do that." I brushed a loose strand of hair back from her face. Or maybe I just wanted an excuse to touch her again. "It's just me, Hayles."

"I wasn't talking about puking," she admitted, not taking her eyes off me, and it felt like I'd been flayed alive. "I can't believe I . . . I don't even know why I told you that. Well, I guess I do. I'm drunk. But I don't want you to say anything, okay? I don't want this to change us. I'm the one who should be apologizing to you. You're already in a relationship, and Zoe is awesome. I'm sorry. I shouldn't even be here. Can you just take me home?"

I wanted to tell her it wasn't one-sided, that the feelings I had for her weren't disappearing, but I couldn't. She was right. My two-year relationship deserved more. So did Hayley. I wasn't the guy for her. A strangled sound that could've been mistaken for a grunt of agreement came out instead.

"I'll find Tom and tell him I'm leaving," she announced. "He'll want a ride if he's still here. I think you're the only sober person at this party."

Hayley was talking, but I kept my gaze focused on the framed photograph in my parents' bathroom. I took it last summer, right after graduation. The sun had been setting over Port Worth, and the tide was receding. The sand had been glistening orange and yellow where the water touched it, giving the appearance of stained glass. Like life itself, memories were fleeting, and I'd always felt the urge to capture as many as I could. I forced myself to remember who'd been standing behind me back then, arms wrapped around my waist, as I'd taken the shot.

Zoe.

And just like that, I was immediately flooded with more guilt.

Out of my periphery, I watched Hayley climb to her feet and walk out. That put an ache in my chest like no other, but I still couldn't find the words. She'd had the courage to put herself out there, and I'd been too terrified to even acknowledge it.

My next realization pushed the fear and guilt aside, and I welcomed a much uglier, new emotion. I was the asshole hurting her. Not Sean Pearson. *Me.*

two

HAYLEY

February, the night of the accident

Dark roads twisted up ahead, and Jace fiddled with the stereo. Music blasted out of the speakers, and I recognized the song. It was one of my favorites by Five Finger Death Punch. I let my head bop while listening, the cool wind tangling its fingers in my hair. With the windows rolled down and the darkness surrounding us, it almost felt like I was flying, weightless. Or maybe it was because I was still drunk.

Closing my eyes, I savored this feeling. The numbness. The alcohol made everything melt away—my argument with Tom, my imminent grounding. I'd tried to find my brother back at the party, but he was gone. He was probably already home, wrestling with the temptation to rat me out to Mom and Dad, and I couldn't say I blamed him.

Then there was Jace—the only boy, aside from my brother, who could put up with my antics long enough to chauffeur me home. Blurting something about having a teeny-tiny crush on him had been the epitome of stupid, but I was too wasted for the consequences to permeate, fully sink in, and take root. I knew I'd be paying for it tomorrow morning, but right now, my mind was blank.

The town was eerily quiet this late on a Friday night, and I watched as the outlines of trees blur past. Jace's fingers tapped out a rhythm against the steering wheel, and his other hand rested on the stick shift, drawing my attention.

I wanted to keep driving with him all night. I wanted to escape Port Worth, just like he'd managed to. I was hit with the overwhelming urge to reach for his hand—so close I could see the black-and-silver ring Zoe had bought him for their first anniversary—to slide my fingers through his. There was no hope of those things happening, though.

I was still so young: a sophomore in high school. It wouldn't be my turn to leave for two more years. Did that amount of patience required even exist? Not to mention that Jace was taken. How could I have done something so awful? You never told a guy with a girlfriend how you felt. It was part of the Girl Code, and I'd broken it. No wonder he'd hardly spoken to me since we'd left his house. What was he even supposed to say?

That wasn't even the worst part. The silent treatment from Jace was something I was used to. The worst part was, I hardly saw him anymore now that he attended college and lived on campus. I'd thought hiding my feelings from him every day since I was thirteen had been hard. Now, I only saw him once every couple of months if I was lucky. And then when he came home, I almost dreaded it, because that meant he would leave again.

I let myself stare at Jace's profile for a heartbeat too long. He looked more handsome than he had a right to, with his high cheekbones and chiseled features. His chestnut-brown hair fell in waves over his forehead, but his eyes were his most striking feature. They were a steel blue gray, and every time he glanced in my direction, I wished he would see *me*—not just the girl who was his sister's best friend.

But I was willing to bet that was all it would ever be—an ungranted wish. A dumb fantasy.

Jace's truck coasted along the main road. The wheels bumped on a pothole, jostling me in my seat. Cruising toward the interstate, I noticed the first pair of headlights, illuminating the interior of the Chevy. Their high beams were on, blinding, and the music was loud, leaking out of their car and overriding the song that was winding down on Jace's radio. They sat close behind us—too close—but I didn't think anything of it.

"What the fuck is their problem?" I thought I heard Jace mutter, but I couldn't be sure. The wind was strong.

A second later, they blared their horn impatiently.

"I'm doing the limit," he ground out, gaze flicking to the rearview mirror again.

The driver pulled out and overtook us on an unbroken line. They sped past, and I rolled my eyes, barely overcoming the urge to flip them off. At least they weren't tailgating us anymore. They were ahead of us now, and Jace took his foot off the gas, maintaining a safe distance.

My relief was short-lived.

The driver merged in front of us and then overcorrected, causing the car to fishtail, spinning out. A pair of oncoming headlights rounded the corner, gleaming off the asphalt.

A bad feeling pinched my gut, sinking deep.

Jace cursed, slamming the brakes, and I flew forward. His arm shot across my chest, protecting me. My breath left me in a rush, and I instinctively closed my eyes.

We stopped in time, narrowly avoiding disaster—courtesy of Jace's quick reflexes—but the oncoming dark-colored SUV didn't see the smaller car until it was too late. There was a sickening sound—metal colliding, crunching, flipping, rolling.

And when I opened my eyes next, I struggled to comprehend what I saw.

Kaleidoscopic shattered glass filled the sky, falling like snow. There was a long second that seemed to stretch on for an eternity, and then reality rushed back in. It was so silent, and there was a strange, foreboding feeling that changed the atmosphere—that changed everything. All of my senses snapped into focus.

Death had a way of doing that to you—putting things into perspective. It filled the air around me, foul and thick, along with the smell of burned rubber. I could still hear the screeching of the tires as they'd struggled to grip the asphalt.

Jace swerved onto the shoulder of the road, threw the gear stick into park, and flipped the emergency blinkers on.

"Fuck," he whispered. "Fuck. Okay. Here's what we're gonna do. Take my phone. Call 911, tell them exactly where we are and what's happened." He shoved his phone at me, and I realized that his hands were shaking too. "Stay in the car. There's gonna be casualties. I don't know if many people can walk away from something like that. I have to go help."

I blinked rapidly, tears threatening.

When I didn't respond—too shocked by what had just unfolded some twenty feet in front of us—Jace leaned in, his warm palms cupping my face. If it were under different circumstances, butterflies would have been nesting in my belly. "I need you to make this call, Hayles. I'm counting on you. They're counting on you. Can you do that for me?"

Snapping out of my daze, I nodded emphatically. "Y-yeah. I can . . . I can do that."

And I did.

The minute Jace hurried out of the Chevy, I lost sight of him. He disappeared into the darkness, and I dialed a number I never thought I'd need. With trembling fingers, I raised his phone to my ear, but the ringing still sounded so far away.

"Nine-one-one operator. What is your emergency?" A male voice rumbled down the line, cutting through my momentary calmness.

"We need help." My voice cracked. "There's been an accident . . . two cars . . . I—I don't know how many people are hurt. My friend went to see . . . to help. Please . . . please come as soon as you can."

I could make out the sounds of the operator typing in the background. "What's your address, miss?"

I knew this small town like the back of my hand, even when the street signs weren't visible. "We're on Devilbend Road, just before Route 26," I told him mechanically. "Hurry." It was a broken, small plea, but it was all I could manage.

I ended the call and dropped the phone into the driver's seat before the operator could convince me not to hang up, and without thinking, I climbed out of Jace's truck.

I felt useless just sitting in there. I should be doing all that I could, not cowering, scared. Even if I was paralyzed with fear.

My knees wobbled, and I almost lost my balance when I got closer . . . close enough to see the smaller, crushed vehicle in the middle of the road. It was an old, familiar Honda Accord. The bad feeling hollowing my insides worsened. There was glass everywhere, crunching beneath my Converse, and smoke billowed up from the engine, swirling into the night sky.

Jace was up ahead, crouched by the flipped SUV. He was talking to someone, reassuring them, and trying to pry the backseat door open.

My vision blurred as I stumbled over to the Honda, and something ugly and horrible unfurled inside me when I recognized the driver. It was Derek, my brother's loud-mouthed best friend. He'd been at the party we'd just come from. His blond head was hanging forward lifelessly, and there was blood dripping from his mouth . . . so much blood.

Before I could process what I was doing, my thumb was tipping his chin back and my index finger was pressing into his neck. I was trying to find a pulse, even though I was fully aware that it was too late. There was nothing.

He was dead.

Biting down on a sob, I turned away, but not before I caught the twitch of movement in the passenger seat. An uncanny chill burned the back of my neck, almost as if my body already knew what I was about to discover.

There was someone else in there.

When I saw that distinctive black-and-blue letterman jacket—the jacket that was always draped over the couch, a chair, basically anywhere except his closet—everything went numb for the second time tonight.

No. No. No.

I didn't feel sick anymore. I didn't feel brave. I just moved. My feet carried me to the other side of the mangled car, and I almost wished I'd stayed inside Jace's Chevy. Nothing prepared me for the moment I saw my brother, Tom. My childhood sidekick. My flesh and blood.

Cold terror rippled down my spine. Tom's body was pressed up against the dashboard. Worse yet, his head had gone through the shattered windshield. His breathing was labored, whistling strangely, and when those glassy, distant brown eyes locked on mine, I lost it.

I'd never had an out-of-body experience before, but on that road, I think I had one. I was just watching myself, screaming, crying, clawing at the side of Derek's car. It wouldn't open.

"Hayley?" Tom murmured weakly. There was a grunt as he tried to free himself, but he was jammed between the seat and the dash. My reaction was scaring him. "What's happening? Where am I?"

"Don't move," I urged, clinging to my last shred of composure. I couldn't prevent the tears from spilling down my cheeks. I wanted to touch him—be by his side—but the door handle had been swallowed by all of that metal. "You were in a car accident, but help is on the way, Tom. It'll be okay."

The second the words escaped, I wondered if I'd only given him false hope. Jace still hadn't come over. That meant whatever was happening inside the other vehicle was bad, too, and I wanted to vomit again.

"Derek," he called out to his best friend. When heavy silence greeted him, my heart thudded to a halt. He'd come to the same realization I had only moments ago. It was too late for Derek. "I didn't know, Hayley. I swear."

"Didn't know what?"

"After we fought, I hid out in the basement most of the night on Jace's PlayStation, didn't know Derek had . . . ssss . . . mmm . . ." he slurred, his voice sounding funny.

"Tom," I cried, wishing I had superhuman strength so I could lift the roof off the car. "Tom. No! Stay with me."

There was glass in his dark, collar-length hair, but I didn't care. My hand brushed the tangled strands off his forehead. He was still looking at me, still fighting, but I knew he was slipping away.

He dragged in another weak, shallow breath, and his eyes were searching, skittering over my face. He was dying, and I was just standing there helplessly, hopelessly.

I kept running my fingers through his soft hair, trying to comfort him. "You're not alone, Tom," I said. "I'm here, and I love you so much. I won't leave you." They were the only words I could come up with, and I wished I had more. I wished I could take away the pain, or promise that he was going to make it, but I couldn't.

Sirens wailed in the distance, and when I glanced over my shoulder, Jace was walking slowly toward me. Sadness cast his features in shadow. There was blood coating his hands and forearms. I turned back to Tom, still cradling his head, and just like that, in that life-changing split second, the light had faded from his eyes, and he was gone.

He was just . . . *gone.*

I fell to the ground, no longer able to stand, and the gravel bit into my bare knees. I felt arms enfolding me, lifting me, hugging me close, but I couldn't focus on anything anymore.

Tom was dead too.

I'd just watched my brother die, and there was nothing I could do. There'd been a five-minute window, and I'd failed, let him down. My chest heaved, trying to suck in air, but I couldn't breathe.

"Hayley." Jace was saying my name, over and over. I listened to his voice, let it anchor me. He was holding me upright, his body supporting my weight. "I'm so sorry." It took me a moment to register, but he was crying too. He'd never cried in front of me before.

"I should've made sure you stayed in the car. You shouldn't have had to see this."

I buried my face in his neck and clung to his broad shoulders. I wasn't. Sorry, that was. In Tom's final moments, he hadn't been alone.

"T-Tom . . . Tom is g-gone . . . he's dead. I . . ." I couldn't finish.

Among the smoldering wreckage, Jace Hammond became so much more than just my childhood crush and longtime friend. Whether I'd told him how I felt earlier or not, our relationship would never be the same. I'd always be tethered to him for an entirely different and gut-wrenchingly tragic reason.

The way his arms tightened around me conveyed that he understood. "I know, Hayles." He swallowed back another choked sob. He sounded equally broken, destroyed. "I didn't see who was in the Honda at first. I couldn't save them. Couldn't save everyone in the other car. Just one. They were a family."

That only made me cry harder.

Until tonight, I'd never really understood how fleeting life could be, or how something so soul-destroying could happen in so little time.

I had fallen into a nightmare.

And for the first time, I wasn't waking up.

● ● ●

Perched on the back step of the ambulance, I drew my knees up to my chest and huddled deeper into the blanket someone had been kind enough to drape over me.

The chaos and the pain of tonight swept me away and pulled me under. I didn't pay attention to the muted conversation occurring all around me, because I was numb, because I was cold. I was underwater. None of this made any sense.

When an EMT eventually approached and asked if I was okay, I just stared up at her, unable to formulate a response. She pointed to my hand, to all the little cuts and specks of glass that were stuck in my palm, and I shook my head.

Because no, I was about as far from okay as one could possibly get. But it wasn't my hand that hurt. It was my heart, broken in half and lodged somewhere deep in my throat. There was nothing the paramedic could offer to remedy that, though, so I kept quiet while she started picking out the glass from my palm with a pair of tweezers. She didn't ask me any questions or force me to talk to her, and for that, I was forever grateful.

There was one voice that was clear among the white noise. I listened to Jace as he gave his statement to two uniformed officers, standing off to the side. Even though I shouldn't, I wanted him to put his arms around me again. And I wanted to just . . . disappear. But most of all, I wanted Tom to be alive. I wanted this to be some sick, cruel joke.

But when my parents arrived on the scene, their shell-shocked faces convinced me that this was real. This wasn't just my nightmare anymore. It was ours.

My father stepped forward, ruddy cheeks turning pale. His eyes were haunted, red-rimmed, and fixed on my brother's unmoving body.

They were still working on freeing Tom from the vehicle, but I couldn't bring myself to look. I didn't know what I'd been expecting. Maybe for them to haphazardly cover him with one of those white blankets I always saw on crime TV shows, but they didn't. They continued to work on him and a guy who was clinging to life in the back seat of the SUV. His parents and his brother were gone too.

Five people died tonight.

I overheard one of the EMTs saying that despite Tom not breathing, despite him not having a pulse, they couldn't assume he was dead, even though I didn't see how they'd be able to revive him. He'd been gone for at least thirty minutes.

We can't take any chances. With a head injury like that, it's gonna be a traumatic brain injury. Worst case, he could be an organ donor.

Fragmented sentences penetrated the static ringing in my ears, and I wanted to bawl like a baby again. I made a valiant effort to hold the tears at bay. The ache in my chest grew uncomfortably tight. It didn't matter that I knew I was going to be crying for days, for weeks, for months, for years.

Tom was only three months away from graduating, and in a cruel twist of fate, he wouldn't be standing up on that stage. He wouldn't be in the crowd when it was my turn either. He wouldn't get to tell me his secrets, or ruffle my hair, or steal my leftovers in the fridge. He'd suddenly evaporated from my life, and I'd always counted on his presence, his permanence.

The weight of this incomprehensible reality settled over me like a dark, suffocating shadow, and I willed myself to focus on the dull sting of the EMT disinfecting my small cuts. I willed myself to feel something, anything, other than this great loss.

But I couldn't.

three

The early morning sun was casting a golden, heavenly glow on the manicured lawns across campus as I exited Thompson. It was one of the older residence halls at the University of Delaware, and it reminded me of a huge colonial house, except with a flat roof and white trim. As I tucked my swipe card back into my tote bag, I inhaled purposefully. I'd had so long to mentally prepare for this moment—my first day of classes at college—but I still didn't feel remotely ready.

"I'm going to miss you so friggin' much," I told my best friend, who'd been kind enough to call me *and* be my personal alarm clock some twenty minutes ago.

"As if you're not rejoicing right now," Amelia scoffed. Even with her light, singsong voice coming through the phone, it was hard to focus on anything other than the fact that my stomach was flipping around like crazy. "You've been wanting to leave forever."

She was right.

There was nothing wrong with where I'd grown up. Port Worth was a picturesque, secluded little town in Maryland with a tight-knit community; the mainstay of my near-perfect childhood. My life just hadn't stayed perfect for long. Or maybe I'd come to the life-altering realization, earlier than most, that it never was. Either way, being there, it felt like I was living in a town—a life—that didn't belong to me anymore. The need for change had beckoned, and I'd followed.

It also might have had a little something to do with the fact that in such a small town, there was nowhere to hide after tragedy struck my family. No way to forget. For the last two years, living there had been a constant reminder of what I'd had to endure. I knew it wore thin on my parents too. As investigative journalists, they were always hungry for the truth. For answers. The fact that they never found them after Tom's accident—that it really was ruled a DUI—only left them feeling more lost and inconsolable.

Dad retreated. Mom overstepped. And I survived high school.

Even though I could navigate my hometown's back roads with minimal effort, I'd been mapping out the best way to leave Port Worth for what felt like most of my life.

"I am happy," I said, my fingers tightening around the phone. "I just wish you'd come with me."

"*Me?* You know I'm totally leaving the college thing to you and Jace."

My insides churned at his name.

One thing that hadn't changed in the last two years was how I felt about Jace. He'd continued to feature in every one of my girlish fantasies, but I was getting better at ignoring the butterfly that took flight in my chest whenever I saw him. I'd resigned myself to the inevitable. He only thought of me as an honorary sibling. Not to mention, we'd shared a therapist—Dr. Jensen—for months after the accident. None of it exactly screamed romance.

Was I grateful Jace attended Delaware too? Truly. But I felt more intimidated by the idea of seeing him again than the prospect of wandering around lost with some other bewildered freshmen.

"I have no clue where I'm going." Changing the subject altogether felt like the safest option. Frowning, I stared down at the map I'd grabbed from the administrative building last week. "This map is great, but you know I'm directionally challenged."

"I don't think anyone knows where they're going on their first day," Amelia answered, her tone placating. "Listen, Hayley, you're in college now. You've got what you've always wanted. You can move on and reinvent yourself. Don't let anything distract you from that, whether it's finding your way around campus, or dealing with my brother." She paused, as if choosing her next words carefully. Amelia was the first and only person I'd confided in about my feelings for Jace—excluding the man himself. It just never felt like something I could keep secret from her. Jace being her brother didn't top the fact that she was—and would always be—my best friend. "Besides, you can find a new guy to drool over. Maybe a hot football player? Or a brooding artist? Take your pick."

I might have been crushing on Jace for years, but Amelia had always been the boy-crazy one out of the two of us. That worked in her favor, though, because I barely got a second glance when she was standing next to me. I felt . . . plain. A little overlooked. Like her brother, Amelia was beautiful, and in that unfair, "why weren't my genes more blessed?" kind of way. She had long, tanned legs, and silky blond hair, and I was pale and short, with dull brown hair. Not that there was anything wrong with how I looked, but the Hammonds were in another league. Dating scene aside, I held on to her words, repeating them to myself.

This is my chance to start over.

"Thanks, Millie." I smiled. "This is why I need you here. You always know what to say."

"I know," she quipped. "Now go. I'd hate to make you late. Good luck."

Before I could reply, the line went dead. She'd hung up on me. I inhaled another shallow breath, feeling like my lifeline had just been severed.

As I headed down the long stretch of road toward the main campus, a seasonably warm breeze picked up, stirring the hairs that had escaped my ponytail. I tucked the wayward strands behind my ear, scanning my surroundings. The nape of my neck prickled like it tended to when I sensed someone watching me. I wasn't unaccustomed to the stares back home, the heavy feel of eyes on me, but I hadn't expected them here.

I kept walking, fueled by pure determination. I was going to get through my first day of college, sans embarrassing myself or having that clueless freshman look about me. There was no reason for me to be paranoid. I was over a hundred miles away from Port Worth.

Glancing down at the creased map for the umpteenth time, I prayed I wasn't going in the opposite direction. When I spotted the old Georgian architectural-style shops, restaurants, and bars on Main Street, along with the plethora of students milling around, I exhaled in a rush. I remembered it from my tour, and the guide had told me it was close to the Art Studio Building— where most of my classes were this semester.

"Hey there, freshman." I was startled by the fact that someone had just materialized beside me, but it was that familiar, deep voice that really sent my heart racing.

As I turned my attention to Jace, all the feelings I'd spent the summer trying to keep in check came flooding back. He had always been ridiculously tall, coming in at just over six foot three, and I was barely five foot six, but it was like I was only just noticing the height difference between us. I had to lift my chin to look at him properly, and Holy Mother Mary, he was gorgeous. So gorgeous . . . it was pretty much a recurring thought I had whenever I saw him.

He was wearing a faded blue shirt that clung to his broad shoulders and stretched over a ridiculously defined chest. His hair was cut close to the skull on the sides and a little longer on the top, disheveled from the morning breeze, or from running his hands through it. Light stubble shaded his defined, square jaw. But it was those full, expressive lips that always threatened to make me swoon. And damn him, because I was so not a swooner.

I had to wonder how soft those lips were, what it would feel like to be kissed by them—by him. He had this quiet, underlying intensity, and while it had been known to scare the shit out of me, it was still next to impossible to look away.

"Hi," I said, feeling like a nut. I really shouldn't have been standing there, making doe eyes at him like we didn't already have enough of a complicated history. I needed to get a grip. "I—I didn't expect to see you."

He grinned, revealing those adorable dimples. Damn it. "The campus isn't that big, Hayles. Besides, how could I forget?"

"Forget what?"

"Your first day of college." Duh. That was obviously why he'd sought me out in the first place. "You're all grown up. A budding designer. I can hardly wrap my head around it."

"All grown up?" I echoed, teasing him. It was incredible how quickly his presence calmed me, despite my initial reluctance to see him again. "You're only three years older than me, Jace. Not thirty."

I watched as his expression shuttered, as he pulled up that familiar armor. Things were always so measured now, never too friendly, but pleasant enough, and I hated it. The trauma of what we'd been through would always be there, as well as this undercurrent of awkward energy and comfortable intimacy that made my head spin.

"Do you know where you're going?" he asked, gesturing to the map I was still clutching like my existence was contingent on it.

"I think so."

"Lemme see." Ignoring my protests, Jace pried the map from my hands. A flush crept across my cheeks. I'd scribbled the classes I was taking this semester on the side, as well as circled the different buildings they were in. I'd done everything to help prepare for this morning, and it hadn't made a difference. "Ah, you've got Concepts in Design first. I'll walk you," he said easily.

Filled with a sudden rush of gratitude, I nodded.

Walking beside him through Main Street was a surreal experience. It was as if Jace knew everyone. So many people stopped to ask him questions about his summer break, senior year, or his photography. They couldn't wait for him to post the one-of-a-kind photos he'd no doubt take at the upcoming football game.

"I see you're still Mr. Popular." I peeked over at him as he pulled us off onto a cobblestoned path. We started hoofing it toward a tall, brick building in the distance. When our gazes collided, his blue-gray eyes fastening on to mine, I self-consciously glanced away. "You can just point me in the general direction, Jace. I don't want to make you late."

"You won't." His lips formed a crooked half smile. "I'm taking that class too."

His response almost bowled me over, and I desperately tried to control my careening pulse. "Since when?"

"I needed more credits to be able to graduate in May, and I haven't done a design unit since sophomore year." He shrugged as if what he'd just told me was no biggie. "You okay with me being in one of your classes?"

Seeing as I barely had a nanosecond to process this, I managed to recover quickly. Honestly, I wasn't sure what to think about having Jace in one of my classes. I hadn't expected to see much of him this semester. He was a senior, and I was a freshman, and I'd thought that meant we would run in completely different social circles.

"Why wouldn't I be?" I bumped his side with my elbow, a habitual gesture. After so many years of being Jace's friend, I was good at pretending to be cool and composed.

The Studio Arts Building wasn't far from Main Street, so when we arrived and I realized we weren't late, I forced myself to relax as much as I physically could. There was nothing worse than walking into a class after it had already begun, only to have every student in the room gawk at you. And if there was one thing I couldn't stand after Tom had died, it was having a pair of judgmental eyes dissect me like a science project.

Jace motioned to two empty seats at the back of the studio. Relief lightened my limbs, carrying me over to the workbench. As ready as I was to be a college student, sitting at the front was the opposite of appealing. I wanted to keep a low profile and gather my bearings, at least on the first day.

There was a beautiful girl sitting at the workbench already, doodling in her sketchbook, and when her gaze zeroed in on Jace, a bright pink blush spread across her entire face. That was *before* he had even smiled at her. Clearly, I wasn't the only one who could appreciate just how attractive he was.

I pulled out my own sketchbook and a couple of pens before jamming my bag underneath the chair.

Jace ineptly tucked himself underneath the small table, and I stifled a laugh. He sighed in defeat and sprawled out next to me.

"Now I remember why I stopped taking design," he grumbled. "The benches in this studio are miniature."

"Or you're just huge," I fired back before I could think about it.

Jace's hand gripped the back of my chair, and he leaned in closer to me. His low voice triggered a hot thrill when he said, "Which part of me are you referring to, exactly?"

My throat seized up.

"Sorry, Hayles, but you walked straight into that one. I couldn't resist." He chuckled, and the husky sound set off another round of tingles.

As I digested his response, confusion rippled through me, stunning me into silence. He was flirting with me, and I wasn't used to being on the receiving end. I'd begrudgingly observed him wield that lopsided grin with great success throughout high school, and now he was releasing it on me.

What the hell?

It was at that moment a short, auburn-haired girl stopped by our bench. I'd seen her on Jace's social media before—on the rare occasions he posted pictures of his college life versus commissioned pieces or nature shots. She unhooked her earbuds and rolled her eyes at him. "Easy there, tiger. You keep that up and we'll all be swept off our feet."

"Piper. I didn't know you were back from your parents' place already."

"I just got home last night." She sat down at our table, next to the girl who seemed to be tuning us out. "Who's this?" she asked, curiosity sparkling in her eyes as she sized me up in a way that was less than subtle but friendly enough. "Are you finally noticing the opposite sex again, Jace?"

It sounded like he hadn't had any action for a while, and that made me happier than I cared to admit.

"Remind me why I'm friends with you again?" He laughed but didn't answer her question.

I'd known Piper for five whole seconds, but I could already tell she was comfortable with who she was, and she kept her shit together in his presence, completely unfazed. If that were the case, we would get along famously.

"Because I'm a very tolerant person and, unlike you lately, a lot of fun," she declared as if it hadn't been a rhetorical question. God, she was so confident and up-front. I experienced a fleeting burst of jealousy.

"That's harsh." Jace placed a hand over his heart, as if she'd wounded his feelings. It was obvious they were close, with all their mild, good-natured teasing. It occurred to me then that she must be the best friend.

I piqued her interest again. "God, I'm sorry. You must think I'm so rude."

Jace made a noise deep in his throat, which I took as tacit agreement.

"No, not at all," I assured her and did my best to ignore him. "It's nice to meet you. I'm Hayley."

Piper opened her mouth to say something, but before she could, Jace interjected, "She's Amelia's best friend."

"Oh. Yep." She bobbed her head slowly, as if she was privy to something I wasn't. Huh. "He always talks about you and his sister," she added.

Suspicion gnawed at me.

While we waited for the professor to arrive, I watched as more students filed in. I was so excited for the semester to start, to use all the art supplies and cute notebooks I'd bought. I didn't care if that made me lame. As Amelia had pointed out, I'd been waiting a long time for this.

The next person to enter the studio was Owen—I recognized him from Jace's Instagram photos too. He was the opposite of Jace, dressed in a polo shirt and khaki shorts with close-cropped blond hair. He was what my best friend classified as a pretty boy— entirely her type too.

Owen tilted his chin up at Jace in greeting when he noticed him and then picked his way through the small crowd that had gathered in the doorway. There was chatter all around us, people catching up after being apart all summer.

"Hey, man," he hollered as he approached us.

"Owen. Didn't know you were taking this class." Jace stood, clapping him on the shoulder as they both went in for that typical bro hug.

Piper glanced up at the mention of his name, waving halfheartedly before continuing to text on her phone.

"Nice to see you too, Red." He ruffled her hair like she was a small child before turning back to Jace. "Yeah, neither did I until just now. My advisor said I enrolled too late for the other class I wanted."

"Looks like the old group's back together again," Jace commented. "Oh, and this is my friend from back home, Hayley."

Finally, my introduction was upgraded.

One of Owen's eyebrows ticked up. An almost undetectable scar cut across it.

"Hey." I offered him a cordial smile.

"Hey," he greeted, his gaze staying fixed on mine for a long moment before it returned to his friends. "So, are you both going to Levi Brooks's tomorrow night?"

Still distracted by her phone, it impressed me when Piper answered without delay, "Probably." Her multitasking abilities were far superior to mine.

The sharp angle of Jace's jaw twitched. "Undecided. You?"

"Yeah, only because of the free booze, though," Owen said.

"As long as the *only* thing in supply is booze, as opposed to fragile male egos," Piper inserted, keeping her eyes down. "The last thing UD needs is another girl getting attacked."

Confusion swirled inside me, transforming into concern.

The soft scratching sound of the charcoal pencil moving over the paper stopped. The girl who'd remained silent for our entire conversation finally spoke. "Tell me about it. One of my friends refuses to leave her dorm after dark now." Her voice was eerily calm, relaxed, but her words had a tendril of fear curling through me. "Everyone's freaking out, and for good reason."

Before I could ask Piper, or the girl who'd yet to formally introduce herself, about the bombshell that'd been casually dropped on me, the classroom door opened, and the middle-aged, half-balding professor walked in.

"See you later." Owen nodded at Jace, leaving to find a vacant seat.

The man introduced himself to the class as Professor Zimmerman and apologized for being late—not that I think anyone minded much. He was wearing a dark blazer that was at least two sizes too small, starched khaki shorts, and mismatched knee-high socks. He went on to list his impressive credentials and experience within the industry, which quickly outweighed his obvious eccentricities.

For the next twenty minutes, I tried to listen attentively, doing my best to follow the syllabus. When Jace suddenly murmured in my ear, "Do you want to go tomorrow night?" it startled me.

Professor Zimmerman was speaking about course grading, and I looked up from the illegible notes I'd written. For the entire class, I'd barely been able to keep up. Not to mention, I was hyperaware of who was sitting next to me. Jace was so close now that his tanned arm brushed against mine.

"I don't think I was invited."

"It doesn't matter," he insisted.

"I won't know anyone. It'll just be awkward."

"That's the whole point of parties," he said. "Plus, you know me, Piper, and Owen. Just come."

"I'll think about it," I muttered noncommittally.

Jace's lips hitched up at the corners. He dropped his voice to a whisper, and it flared over my skin. "In case you haven't worked it out already, I want you to come with me, Hayles."

My heart stumbled before picking up again, and this time, it beat faster.

I'd only hesitated because I knew that if I agreed to go with him, there was a high probability I would regret it. My track record wasn't exactly stellar when it came to parties, especially ones that supplied alcohol and were frequented by Jace. If that night—my last party—had taught me anything, it could be a disaster of epic proportions. Then again, it was hard to form a single coherent thought when his gaze was latched on to mine.

"Fine. I'll go with you. But I don't drink anymore. You know that. And I swear to God, you better not ditch me for some chick."

His lashes lowered. "I didn't peg you for the jealous type."

"I'm not jealous," I told him as convincingly as I could. I was terrified of where he might be going with this, afraid to hope. "I just don't want to be ditched."

"When have I ever ditched you?" His voice sounded like it was right in my ear again, and I shivered.

He had me there. "I know. I'm sorry. I just don't—"

"Don't want to let me out of your sight?"

"Jace."

"I'm only messing with you." The amused glint in his eyes vanished as he looked down at me, like maybe it'd just occurred to him that I was more upset about this than I was willing to show or say. I knew Jace was just teasing me—something he'd perfected over the years—but I couldn't brush it off. Not this.

If I went tomorrow night, it would be the first party I'd been to since my brother died. That meant something. The accident had fucked me up so badly that I'd boycotted alcohol and most social events.

Beneath the surface, I was still pretty broken. Most things reminded me of Tom, even two years on. My brother had never graduated high school, and here I was, experiencing my first day of college. It wasn't fair.

Jace shifted in his chair, and then his hand rested on my denim-clad thigh, giving it a light squeeze.

I was so acutely aware of his touch—something I'd missed and craved—but I kept my eyes fixed ahead, my features blank. I tried not to focus on the feeling of his big hand on my thigh, but it was a steady pressure and source of strength that grounded me.

He knew where my mind had wandered. He felt sorry for me. That was all it was, I decided.

"College parties are overrated."

I inhaled deeply, shoring up my courage. "No. It's okay, I want to go."

"You sure?" he whispered, withdrawing his hand.

I knew I was.

I hadn't come to Delaware to remain closed off. I didn't want to pass up opportunities like this. This was a chance for me to move on. Moving zip codes wouldn't fix everything. I still had to put in the work, and I wanted to open up and experience life in the fearless way I imagined Piper did. And knowing Jace would be with me . . . it helped.

Whether we were good at talking about our feelings or not, it suddenly didn't seem to matter. What mattered was that he was always there, anchoring me to him.

No amount of distance or time had changed that, could sever the invisible cord that bound us, and I'd be lying if I said I wanted it to.

four

By the time I let myself into my dorm the next afternoon, exhausted from hours of classes, all I wanted to do was collapse into a heap on my bed and dive-bomb into the tub of chocolate chip ice cream I'd been saving in the mini-fridge. I swore it was calling my name.

Instead, I'd tried on my entire wardrobe and wrestled with the dilemma of what to wear to Levi's party tonight.

In the past forty-eight hours, I'd had to tell myself countless times that I was actually here, at the University of Delaware. It still didn't feel real. Probably because for so long, it hadn't been. But I'd kept my promise to myself, and ultimately, to Tom. I'd left my small town; I was making something of myself. I was studying interior design at the college of my dreams. As I'd entered the crowded lecture hall today, I'd glanced out at the sea of unfamiliar faces in disbelief. And when the lights had dimmed, I'd listened attentively, willing my brain to absorb every word. Most of my professors seemed nice. I'd even made awkward small talk with the cute barista at one of the coffeehouses. Might as well add a crazy college party to that list, right?

After much deliberation, I settled on a fitted off-the-shoulder top and my favorite denim skirt.

I was reapplying my mascara, mostly to kill time while I waited for a text from Jace, when I heard a soft rap on my door. My heart sped up. I hadn't been expecting him for another fifteen minutes, or for him to come up to my dorm room, which was looking more and more like Monica's secret closet from *Friends*. Oops.

The bed was unmade, the comforter rumpled and thrown on the floor after my mad dash to class this morning. Worse, there were clothes scattered everywhere, exposing just how much effort I'd put into selecting this outfit—I think I'd changed at least eight times. The wooden desk underneath the small window was the only organized area of my room, storing all of my textbooks and supplies.

Dread filled my stomach as I opened the door, not wanting Jace to see my dorm room while I was still in the very early stages of moving in. I was relieved to find that it was only Piper grinning back at me.

"Hey, I didn't mean to intrude but—you look amazing!" She wiggled her fingers. "Love the outfit, girl."

If it were Amelia, I would've done a little self-indulging spin, but the last thing I wanted to do was make a fool of myself in front of one of Jace's best friends.

"So do you," I enthused.

Her hair was half pinned back, and the loose curls framed her heart-shaped face. She was wearing a jersey playsuit, a studded biker jacket, and a pair of heels I could only dream of wearing, let alone making it five feet in.

"Jace's phone is either having a meltdown or it's dead. It won't switch on. He's saying he charged it, but that's up for debate." She laughed dryly, tucking her hands into her jacket pockets. "Luckily, someone was leaving Thompson when I showed up. Anyway, I'm here to escort you to his truck."

Jace held the title for being the most forgetful person sometimes, so I wasn't all that surprised. I swung the door open farther and gestured for her to come inside. "Sure. I'll just be a sec."

Piper brushed past me, stepping into my cramped single room—thank God I didn't have to share. She glanced around, and I appreciated that her eyes didn't linger on the mess or the stacks of cardboard boxes. Needless to say, I had no motivation left to unpack the last of my stuff.

"Sorry," I said, embarrassed. "I wasn't expecting company."

"It's fine. Believe it or not, I consider this clean. I have a roommate, and between the two of us, you literally can't see the floor." Piper shuddered good-naturedly, like even the mental image was bad enough.

I grinned. "Okay. That makes me feel a tiny bit better."

Piper sat down on the edge of my bed, giggling as she watched me struggle to tug on my lace-up Doc Martens. "Is it too early to ask how you're liking UD?"

"So far so good." I nodded, then scrunched up my nose. "Actually, wait. Maybe you should ask me that next week. I might change my mind when I'm up to my eyeballs in assignments."

"Don't even go there," she groaned. "My body is so not ready for this semester."

I could totally relate. The idea of sitting next to Jace in class each week made me dizzy.

Pushing thoughts of him from my mind, I cleared my throat.

"What are you studying again?" I asked, realizing that although I knew she was in Concepts in Design with us, I knew little else about her.

"Art education," Piper replied, flipping absently through one of the interior design magazines on my bedside table. "I'm really passionate about art, and I've always loved children, so I figured it was a no-brainer."

"That's awesome," I said, glancing back at her before I swiped some strawberry ChapStick over my lips. Teaching was a financially stable career, but I'd never considered anything other than interior design. I was fortunate enough to find my passion early in life, always relishing any opportunity to redecorate my room, and even though it wasn't much to brag about, I'd amassed a decent following on one of my Pinterest boards.

Once I'd hooked in some earrings and located my shoulder bag, I grabbed my keys and took a deep breath. "All right, let's do this."

For the last hour, I'd been giving myself a much-needed pep talk. Tonight would not be a repeat of the last party I attended with Jace. Tonight would be fun and normal. It also happened to be the perfect chance for us to talk, and to put the past behind us, once and for all.

My composure took a nosedive when I spotted him behind the wheel of his pickup truck, parked at the curve. He looked incredible. While I could only see his top half, I knew keeping my eyes off him tonight was going to be challenging.

His hair was styled back in an artfully messy look, and he was wearing a faded gray shirt that made his eyes look even smokier.

"You good?" Piper inquired with a thread of amusement in her voice.

Fuck. I'd completely forgotten that she was standing there, undoubtedly witnessing me turn to mush.

"I'm great." I scraped my hair to the side and smiled at her as convincingly as I could.

Ignoring the way my heart thumped into my esophagus, I reached the passenger-side door as Piper climbed into the seat first. Following her lead, I inelegantly hoisted myself up, trying to keep my skirt from scaling any higher. It'd been so long since I'd been inside his two-door truck, and I was soon sealed against Piper's side, Jace taking up most of the room.

"Hey," he said to me, his gaze drifting over my features. "You look beautiful."

I swore, for a fleeting second, those eyes were dark and unguarded, and I caught a glimpse of everything he kept under lock and key. Confusion poured in, and I wondered if I was imagining it. Honestly, that was mostly what our relationship was now—me, trying to work out if this was all in my head or not. Nothing Jace said or did had led me to believe I was anything more than Amelia's best friend, but I'd seen *that* look only once before.

Blowing out a breath, I reached over to grab my seat belt and buckled myself in. "Thank you."

Jace's attention returned to Piper as he told her to type an address into the navigator on her phone, and I sagged against the seat. I seriously needed to calm down. One look and I was all hot and bothered.

Peering out the passenger-side window, I waited—or, more accurately, braced myself—for the familiar rev of Jace's Chevy. Sure enough, when it rumbled to life, it brought back an onslaught of memories. All the nights he'd followed Amelia and me home when we were too young to drive, but old enough to be out on our bikes past our bedtimes. The worst one—the last time I'd sat in this seat—was the morning we'd cremated Tom. After leaving the service together, Jace had refused to take me home until I'd stopped crying. It had taken two playlists and seventy miles. He didn't say much, like why he insisted on being there for me that day, but those eyes . . . they'd said a lot.

"Is Owen still coming?" Piper asked him, jolting me out of my thoughts. She fiddled with the radio, flipping the station back to country music. Keith Urban crooned through the stereo, and she turned the volume up a little, which I appreciated immensely. Music made all social encounters easier to navigate.

"When isn't Owen mooching beer at one of these parties?" Jace chuckled, accelerating the rattling engine. "He's probably already there."

Piper leaned forward, digging around for something in her bag, and Jace's eyes found mine again. The traitorous butterfly moved from my chest to my stomach. It was ridiculous the way he made me feel. "You ready to go, Hayles?"

And that nickname. God, I'd missed it. I'd missed *him*.

"Totally," I said and hoped I didn't sound as nervous as I felt.

If my heart hadn't already been in trouble, it was now. Being back here, in Jace's truck, it was like a portal, zooming me right back to our past. It managed to feel like home, even when we were both miles away from Port Worth.

• • •

"Can we talk somewhere?" Jace asked, lifting a hand as if to touch my arm, but letting it fall. He motioned toward the empty hallway. Finding some quiet in this old, decrepit farmhouse wasn't such a bad idea, considering it was loud as hell. It'd maybe been ten minutes since we'd arrived, and my eardrums were already ringing.

Music made the thin walls vibrate, and the stench of alcohol thickly laced the air. Sweaty bodies had congregated in the living room, spectating a nail-biting match of beer pong, if the thunderous roaring and shouts of support were any indication.

I hadn't been watching. Unpopular opinion alert: sports were one of my least favorite things.

As I trailed after Jace, he led me farther away from the horde of partygoers—causing my mild social anxiety to rejoice—and up the rickety stairs.

As soon as we reached the landing, he turned to look at me. No one else was up here. The sound of the music was muted, too, and the change was welcome. I didn't enjoy the tense few ticks of silence that followed, though.

"What's up?"

He hesitated for only an instant. "I want to apologize, Hayles, for the way I acted that night, before the accident, and . . . fuck, every night since."

The moment his words fully registered, it was like the ground shifted under my feet and nervousness overtook me. Was I ready to have this conversation with him? We had an unspoken agreement to never talk about it, which suited me just fine. He'd made it clear he didn't feel the same way about me when he never broached the subject again, even after his relationship with Zoe ended.

"And well, there is something I—"

Before Jace could finish, Piper discovered us. A red plastic cup dangled from her fingers, and her brows knitted together in confusion as she sidled up to us, as if she couldn't understand why we'd slipped away from everyone else. At that moment, I became more aware of my surroundings—how dark and secluded it was up here.

"You both look like you could use a drink," Piper suggested, wrapping her arms around Jace and me. "Plus, you're kind of leaving me to fend for myself down there. Is the keg empty, Owen?"

He was standing at the bottom of the stairs, leaning against the doorway of the living room, eyes glued to the game unfolding in front of him.

"Owen?" Piper raised her voice to compete with a Florida Georgia Line song. "Earth to Owen?" Eventually, she stomped downstairs, waving her hand in front of his face.

When I glanced over at Jace, he was smiling, looking like he hadn't just been about to share some deeply personal thoughts. "We'll pick this up again later, okay?"

As much as I wanted to know what he'd been about to say, chances were I probably wasn't ready to hear it.

"Yeah, later."

"Want me to grab you guys a beer?" Piper called out, and we took that as our cue to rejoin the party downstairs.

"Hayley doesn't drink," Jace told her. He touched the car keys in his front pocket, informing us for the thousandth time, "I'm not drinking tonight either."

Piper nudged him playfully, trying to persuade him otherwise. "But we could sleep in the truck bed. Tell me that wouldn't be awesome. I've always wanted to do that."

"Could be fun," he deadpanned. "Maybe when I don't have a shoot at eight thirty the next morning."

"You're such a party pooper," she mumbled, glaring at him as she walked away from us to scope out the rest of the alcohol supply.

There was hardly any room to move, the crowd spilling out into the hallway and pressing in on us. Jace leaned a little more of his weight against me. He was so close that I could have counted every one of his long, dark lashes.

As I tried to think of an excuse to put some distance between us, Owen hollered, "Yo, Hammond! I'm up this round, so you better be watching."

"Don't go far, Hayles," Jace said. He didn't ask me to watch Owen play beer pong, and I wasn't offended. Jace knew me better than anyone here.

Reluctantly, he turned away and headed after Owen, leaving me standing alone. I felt awkward, and my lack of social skills were about to take center stage.

Piper reappeared not even ten seconds later, holding a bottle of beer, and my faith in the universe was semi-restored. She took a long swig. "Did Jace ever tell you how we met?"

I shook my head, taking a seat beside her on the bottom stair.

"I tripped over him in freshman year. He was sprawled out on the green, studying. Who has legs that long? I mean, it's a hazard. I'm lucky I didn't tumble and break my ass." She laughed softly, and I smiled back at her, feeling lighter already. I was glad I wasn't the only one who thought Jace had freakishly long legs. "He said I was accident-prone, and I called him a jerk. The rest is history."

Despite Piper's initial impression of him, she'd quickly realized the same thing I had when I was old enough to recognize it—Jace was pretty amazing. He could be prickly and standoffish, but once you got close enough to him, looked past that rough exterior, it wasn't hard to see that he was selfless, sensitive—entirely my type.

She regaled me with stories about Jace I'd never heard— adventures they'd had at Delaware since becoming best friends.

Her energy and enthusiasm were contagious, and I felt any residual awkwardness between us fade. It was interesting to hear how Jace acted around her as well—the same as he did with Amelia. The teasing and taunting, check. His honesty and protectiveness, double check.

He was like that with me, too, in the beginning, but I couldn't figure out where I stood now. He wasn't my brother, and he wasn't my best friend. We had been friends once, but ever since my drunken confession and the accident, things had changed. I didn't know where that left us.

Piper nudged me with her foot after I'd gone silent for a while. "Tell me something. How long have you had feelings for Jace?"

The question knocked me for a loop. For a few confused, horrible moments, I was rendered speechless. "God, is it that obvious?"

"Not at all. I promise," she reassured me. "I only ask because, well, Jace told me what happened between the two of you that night."

Air snagged in my throat. "What did he say?"

"Enough. But it's not my place," she said, shooting me an apologetic glance. "I'm really sorry about your brother, by the way. I can't imagine how hard that must have been."

I picked at the cracked wooden step beneath me. "Yeah, thanks," I replied. Uncomfortable talking about Tom with her—with anyone, really—I blurted out the first thing that entered my brain. "Hey, what were you talking about yesterday? You mentioned an attack—"

"You haven't heard about Jenna?"

"No. What happened to her?"

"I suppose it was months ago," she murmured. "Jenna was a

freshman. She's a sophomore now. Pretty. Bright. I don't know her very well, but my friend does. Jenna told her she felt like she was being followed all the time, and one night, walking home from the library, this guy pushed her to the ground. He messed up her face, stole her bag, but she didn't get a good look at him. This was in May, right before break. And it wasn't just her. There were other girls—always brunettes—even before that. One reported being groped last semester at a party. Another was being emailed creepy pictures of herself. Everyone's been—I guess we're all just on edge. The president of the university sent out an alert, and campus police are really cracking down on it now. Anyway, it's a good reminder to be careful, to stick together. There are dirty freaks out there."

I swallowed, suddenly feeling nauseous. I almost wished I hadn't asked Piper about it.

Nearly an hour later, when I'd finally worked up the nerve to track Jace down again, it was only to find that a blond had swooped in on him like a starved vulture. I didn't want it to hurt—to put an ache in my chest—but it did.

They were huddled in the corner of the jam-packed living room. She was perched on the arm of the couch, and he was smiling down at her. I hated that I was cataloging everything about their interaction. I was used to seeing him with someone else. For all the years he'd dated Zoe, I'd perfected the ability to shove down the recurrent surges of jealousy. But after he left for college, and after their breakup last year, I guess I was out of practice.

Maybe a small part of me hoped when he saw me again—finally in college, on a similar life path to him—I'd stop being the second sister he never had. And on the really low self-esteem days, the perpetual thorn in his side. Maybe I still wanted things to be different between us.

I turned in the opposite direction, pushing my way through the throng of dancers. Narrowly, I avoided becoming a punching bag as people knocked into me with pointy elbows and other body parts I didn't want to envisage. I made my way toward the kitchen, suddenly overcome with the urge to get stupidly drunk for the first time in two years. Before I could talk myself out of it, I plucked a bottle of beer from the slush of melting ice in the cooler.

I was rummaging through the countertop drawers, trying to locate a bottle opener, when I sensed someone looming behind me.

Spinning around, I saw that an incredibly attractive guy had closed in on me, and I tried not to gape at him. Choppy dark hair tumbled over half of his face, concealing his eyes, and intricate tattoos laced up his pale, wiry arms. They flexed as he folded them across his broad chest.

"What are you looking for?" he asked, breaking the silence. "This is my place."

I flushed, feeling like I'd encroached on his territory, but also because when he'd tilted his head and his hair had fallen to the side, snake-green eyes had slid up and down my body. His intense stare elicited a flurry of jitters in me.

"A bottle opener," I said, finding my voice and holding up the sealed beer in my hand.

"Here." He grabbed the drink from me before I could protest, taking the top of the bottle into his mouth. Intrigued, I watched him, and then I heard a distinct *pop!* He spat the lid out into the nearby trash can.

"Impressive," I commented as he handed me my drink back.

"I know," he said, like a cocky asshole. His eyes continued to simmer from under his thick lashes, deadly and hypnotic. "I'm Levi."

"Hayley," I offered, and took a swig of beer. I winced as the crisp liquid coated my tongue, burned most of the way down, and left a bitter aftertaste. I really hadn't been missing out on much.

"So, you go to UD?"

"Uh-huh. I actually just moved here the other day."

"You moved into Thompson, right?" He was inching closer to me, and I instinctively stepped back, the corner of the countertop jutting into my spine. "No wonder I've never seen you at one of these parties before. What a shame."

There was no denying that Levi was hot, and while I'd been talking to him, I hadn't been thinking about Jace, which was a small victory, but there was something about him—something about the way he almost leered at me—that stirred a horrible, twisty feeling in my stomach. Also, how had he known which building I lived in? Talk about creepy.

"Where's your bathroom?" I blurted out. I didn't really need it, not as much as I needed a reason to get away, but he didn't know that.

Levi tilted his chin toward the door, but his eyes never left mine. There was a strange coldness behind them, and I fought off a shiver. "Just down the end of the hall."

"Right," I said, unnerved as he continued to look at me. "Thanks."

"You can leave your drink here, if you want." His lips curled into a barely there smirk.

"Um." I blinked back at him. Was this guy for real? "No. I think I'll take it with me."

Trying to keep up appearances, I started in the direction he'd told me to go. I shook my head incredulously, replaying Levi's strange proposition over and over—everyone knew you should never leave your drink unattended.

The dangerous curve of his smile, paired with Piper's timely warning to keep my wits about me, caused the hairs on the nape of my neck to rise. But then Jace was sauntering up to me, slinging one arm around my shoulder, and my encounter with the green-eyed boy was immediately shelved.

"Glad you came?" He flashed a grin that made his dimples pop out, and my heart rate picked up. God, I was so screwed. I wasn't sure how much longer I could handle this.

"Sure," I insisted, even though I'd safely pick a night in with Netflix over a rager any day. "Fun times."

Silence.

Jace eyed me, brows furrowed.

I felt wobbly and off-balance, the party atmosphere smothering me.

He mumbled something under his breath that I didn't catch as he reached for me, and I let him. He touched my elbow, pulling me into his chest gently. That was all it took. My whole body tingled, even though I was fully aware that the blond was probably waiting for him in the other room. But then his hand settled on my hip, steadying me, holding me against him, and I couldn't think much about anything else.

"Why are you down here all by yourself, then?" he asked, disbelief and something akin to concern engraved into his face.

"Well, the bathroom was actually my avenue of escape," I admitted with a shrug. "A guy I was talking to kind of creeped me out, and I needed an excuse to get away from him."

His features darkened as he stared down at me. "Do I know him?"

Figuring that anything I said would only add fuel to the fire, I settled for a lie. "I don't think so."

By that point, we'd reached the end of the hallway, and I ducked into the bathroom, grateful for a moment alone. I rested my bottle on the corner of the sink and took several breaths, trying to gather the scattered pieces of my composure. I glanced at my reflection in the small, dusty mirror, blinking back the tears that threatened to fill my eyes.

I'd let myself get into a situation where I felt like I was no longer in control, and my creep-o-meter was still going haywire. Tonight had been a mistake.

Unable to shut myself away in here with these thoughts any longer, I stepped back out into the hallway. Jace was leaning against the wall, waiting for me. I joined him, the cool plaster doing wonders for my feverish skin. The tension dragged out between us until I couldn't take the silence anymore.

"Who's your friend?" The question tumbled out of my mouth. I sounded pathetic, even to my own ears.

"Who?"

I knew it was none of my business, that I really shouldn't care, but it was like my brain had overheated and shut down, which was why I clarified, "The girl you were talking to."

"Hayley," he said my name like a warning.

Hell, I realized I didn't even want to know the answer. Jace was free to talk to and flirt with anyone he wanted. Everything in me recoiled at the thought of him trampling all over my heart again, but as I went to leave, his fingers encircled my wrist.

"Don't go." He exhaled. "It's not what you think. This is why I tried talking to you earlier. I wanted to avoid this."

I stared up at him.

"She's exactly that, Hayles. A friend."

If there was one thing I could always rely on, it was Jace's honesty—sometimes verging on brutal. There was no doubt in my mind, I believed him. "Okay. Sorry . . . This is weird for me. I don't know why I even agreed to come tonight. Everything about this just feels wrong," I said with a nervous, whispery laugh.

"Is that why you're drinking?" Jace let my hand drop. "I didn't know whether to say anything."

"Maybe. I already regret it."

"I'm carrying around a lot of regrets too." His gaze searched mine, his brows threading together. "That's what I wanted to talk to you about."

My next breath hitched in my throat.

"That night you told me how you felt, I was a jerk," he admitted. "I didn't know what to say in response, so I never said anything. I know we lost Tom that night, and it was easy to forget what happened between us after that, but you deserved better."

"*You* were a jerk?" I rasped. "You had a girlfriend and every reason to ignore what I said, Jace. I was drunk, totally railroading you in the bathroom, telling you . . ." I hesitated. Revisiting that conversation would achieve nothing but eternal humiliation. "I know what I said two years ago, and it was embarrassing and stupid, so can we please just keep pretending like it never happened?"

There was a pause. "Is that really what you want?"

Truthfully, at that moment, I had no idea what I wanted. It was more about what I could and couldn't handle.

Before I lost my nerve entirely, I went on, "There is one thing you can clarify for me. We're friends, right? I'd like to think so. I mean, yes, things haven't been the same between us since that night, since Tom died, but I tried, Jace. I tried to be there for you, and you were so determined to shut me out." I was looking at his shirt, not his face. "You always insist on being there for me, but then, when you're hurting, you never let me help you. You keep me in the dark about everything. I still don't know why you and Zoe broke up, and I don't know anything about your new life here, or—"

"I would've thought it was pretty damn obvious."

It wasn't even midnight yet and my temples ached. My brain whirred in overdrive, trying hopelessly to untangle what he was saying.

I glanced up, and I saw the flash of vulnerability crossing his expression, the emotion coming to the surface and then retreating. I suspected that whatever he was feeling, he was trying to contain it behind multiple layers of reinforced steel, and whether that was for my protection or his, I wasn't sure.

For the first time, the possibility of Jace returning my feelings didn't seem so farfetched. I wasn't oblivious, and right now, I was definitely picking up on a vibe.

I took a halting step back. "Well, it's not," I argued, my frustration flaming into anger. "Nothing you do is obvious, Jace. All you've ever done is push me away and be with other people."

The words spilled out before I could stop them.

At that, Jace's mouth compressed. A muscle in his neck twitched.

Immediately, I wanted to apologize. I'd crossed a line. Even if I hadn't, he clearly wasn't the only emotionally unavailable one here. I had a shit-ton of baggage too. But it was too late to take it back, and as the reality of what I'd said soaked in, it lodged like a heavy stone in my stomach.

That was when Piper appeared. This time I was grateful for the interruption.

Awareness returned quickly, and I noticed that a handful of people had stopped in the hallway to listen to my heated exchange with Jace. We'd been gaining an audience. A chill moved down my back when I noticed the figure at the end of the narrow hallway, watching us. In the dim artificial light, it was too dark for me to make out who it was, but something about them, about the way they lingered when others had the decency to disperse, left me wholly unsettled.

"Is everything okay? What's going on?" Piper glanced between both of us, and I refocused my attention on her. She was obviously attempting damage control. As much as I appreciated the gesture, I think we were past that.

"It's nothing," Jace muttered, averting his gaze.

Ouch.

"This is a party," she said, as calm as could be. "You don't want to create a scene, do you?"

Piper went to put her arm around Jace, but he sidestepped her. "Wasn't what I was trying to do." Jace leveled a long look at me, one that confused the hell out of me and nearly brought me to my knees.

And then he was gone.

five

"Are you okay?" Piper asked, eyes wide.

"Not really," I said, my voice coming out in a slight croak.

She nodded, worry pinching her features. "We can leave. Do you want me to ask someone for a ride back to campus?"

"Yes, please," was my immediate response. I couldn't wait to get out of there. "Come grab me when it's time to go? I'm going outside for some air."

I gestured to the fly-screen door at the end of the hall, pleased to see that there was a clear route. Since my conversation with Jace had ended, everyone had regrouped in the living room. And the shadowy figure was nowhere to be found. My whole body relaxed, relieved I wasn't the center of attention anymore.

"I'll meet you out there," Piper told me.

Outside, a cool breeze washed over me. Slowly, I breathed in through my nose and out through my mouth.

My hand shot up and fastened over the locket hanging around

my neck. Tom had given me this necklace for my sixteenth birthday—not long before he'd died—and it was my most prized possession. Engraved on the back of the pendant, written in a small, cursive script: *There's no better friend than a sister.*

The tips of my fingers traced his words—a habit to calm me down.

Although the uneasy feeling had ebbed away, my head still hurt from thinking so hard. I was busy trying to process what had just happened. One minute, Jace and I had been talking, and the next, we'd been on the verge of a weird fight.

The fly-screen door creaked open a few moments later, and I heard the long grass swaying and soft footsteps behind me.

My eyes were still on the cloudless night sky, captivated by the blanket of scintillating stars. How could something so beautiful be suspended above such a horrendous house party?

I'd learned two important things tonight: college parties were overrated, and I really should trust my instincts more often.

"You want the rest?" I held out my untouched beer, under the impression it was Piper, and that she'd found someone we could hitch a ride with. Fleetingly, I hoped maybe it was Jace.

The next thing I knew, I felt a muscular arm snake around my waist, pressing me against a hard, lean body. The stench of beer lingered on his breath, his clothes, and I instantly knew it wasn't Jace—the only person I would've been remotely okay with touching me like this—because he hadn't been drinking tonight.

"No, thanks," a familiar voice grunted in my ear. "But I would prefer it if you didn't run away from me this time."

Spurred by utter shock, I dropped the bottle I was holding to the ground, where it landed with a quiet thud in the grass. My throat constricted, my insides churning harder. I tried to shrug myself out of his firm embrace, using all my strength, but he only pulled me tighter against him.

He reeked of alcohol and cigarettes. The only reason I didn't peg a finger over my nose was because he'd already pinned my arms to my sides.

"Let me go," I spat, trying to free myself from his grip, "or I'll fucking scream."

He dug his fingernails into my flesh, squeezing hard, and I looked up at him over my shoulder. His dark, messy hair hung over his eyes, but I didn't need to see them in order to recognize who he was.

Levi.

His mouth twisted into the same threatening sneer it had earlier.

I knew I'd only just managed to dodge him before, and we'd been in a house full of people. Out here, we were alone, and I was totally defenseless.

"That won't be necessary." He chuckled. "No one will hear you."

A nauseating feeling coiled in my belly. He was right. My cries for help would be swallowed up by the blaring music, by the howls of drunken people. I'd walked too far away from the house. *Fuck*. I should've just stayed put, which was ironic now because it was like my body had frozen under the pressure. My brain was working— screaming at me, in fact—I just couldn't move.

"I've been waiting to get you alone all night," Levi confessed. "How lucky am I? The first party I throw this semester, you show up."

"Levi, stop. I don't want this." My words sounded like they'd been pushed through a grinder.

"I'm sorry, but I can't wait. You're just too beautiful—I have to get a closer look at you." One of his hands landed on my upper thigh, yanking me closer. Disgust crawled up my spine, tingling everywhere he touched. "I didn't think Jace was ever going to let you out of his sight."

At the mention of Jace, adrenaline pulsed through my veins.

I remembered that his truck was parked nearby—that was if he hadn't bailed on Piper and me already. It was a chance I was willing to take. Hell, my *only* chance. There was no way I could go back inside. Grabbing me again would merely be a reflex for Levi if I tried to get past him.

If I could just get my body to goddamn move, I might be able to make a run for it. Even though heading in the opposite direction wasn't ideal, I realized it might be my only shot at escaping.

When I felt Levi's hand push the hem of my skirt higher, I squirmed away, snapping my legs together as tightly as I could.

"Get off me," I begged, my voice wavering.

My body must have finally registered what was happening, how close his fingers were to my underwear—how, at this moment, I would do just about anything to get away from him—because, without any brain involvement whatsoever, I propelled my head back into his chin with surprising force. It collided with a sickening crunch, but I didn't feel it. I hoped I'd at least knocked out a few of his teeth—they were probably already half-broken from opening my beer earlier.

Levi released me on impact. He doubled over, clutching the side of his face.

"You fucking bitch!" he hissed. "I've been nothing but nice to you. I can't believe you did that."

The second it dawned on me that I was free, I sprinted across the overgrown lawn.

Even though my legs felt like they'd turned to jelly, I somehow reached Jace's truck. Relief exploded in my chest, because even though he'd stormed off, he hadn't left me here.

Hastily, I fumbled around in the dark for the door handle on the passenger side, half expecting Levi to reappear and grab me again. With trembling hands, I located the lever. I had to tug it a few times before it finally opened.

Thank God Jace always forgot to lock his Chevy.

Climbing into the truck, I slammed the door shut behind me, promptly locking it and stretching over to lock the driver's side, too, for safe measure.

When I caught sight of my panic-stricken face in the rearview mirror, it sliced through my resolve like a shard of glass. Reality came crashing back in. Not only was I miles away from home, I also didn't know where the hell Jace was, and I don't think I'd needed him more in my entire life.

There was no stopping the tears as they leaked out, coming from a place inside me that was so bottomless and dark. I'd only cried like this once before—the night of the accident. I supposed this was what happened after you'd been plunged so deeply into terror and then had to claw your way back out. I was a wreck, gasping for air.

Fumbling for my phone in my back pocket, I tried calling Jace. It went straight to voice mail. I'd forgotten his phone was dead. Damn it.

Just as I was about to speed-dial Amelia—my emergency contact—I heard a loud knock on the opposite window. My whole body went rigid, and I clutched my phone to my chest, trying to hide the light of the small screen. Fear pounded a wild rhythm through me, and I held my breath, hoping the shadows in the truck obscured me.

The prospect that Levi was peering inside at me, wanting to finish what he started, extracted a low whimper from my mouth.

I nearly died with relief when I saw it was just Jace, his face and cupped hands pressed up against the glass. He squinted inside, trying to locate me in the dimly lit truck.

"Hayley, are you in there?"

I reached out to unlock the driver's-side door. Knowing he'd found me before Levi had, that I was safe, made me cry harder.

"I've been looking for you everywhere, I—"

Jace heard me, saw me, and realized something was wrong. Horribly wrong. He didn't finish. The rest happened quickly. He climbed inside the truck and his arms wrapped around me, crushing me against him until I could feel every inch of his warm body—a solid wall of comfort I found myself sinking into.

"What the fuck happened?"

I couldn't talk. The tears fell faster, soaking my cheeks.

"Someone told me they saw you with Levi." His breath feathered over my collarbone. "Did he do something?"

When I didn't say anything, Jace drew back to look into my eyes. His throat bobbed with a gulp. "What did he do, Hayley?"

I opened my mouth and then immediately shut it. The minute the words left me, there would be no taking them back. No way to know how they would affect me. Or Jace.

His arms loosened a fraction, but I wanted him to keep holding me. I imagined myself curled up in my bed back home in Port Worth—my safe haven—and I imagined being with my parents. I didn't care if that made me weak.

"I swear"—his gruff voice coaxed me from my thoughts, which had begun to spiral—"if he even laid a finger on you, so help me God."

Mustering what little scraps of composure I had left, I replied in the form of a broken whisper. "He grabbed me."

"Did he—?"

"No," I croaked out. Still, Jace's eyes were haunted. The more it sank in, the more I realized it could have been a lot worse. I'd actually been lucky. "He didn't, but he tried. I stopped—I fought back. I was able to get away."

His jaw clenched, and he abruptly smacked his fist against the steering wheel. "I'm going to fucking kill him!"

Anger contorted his face, and I knew I had about five seconds before he flew off the handle. Jace had always been ridiculously protective of Amelia and me, but this was something else entirely.

My fingers locked around his forearm in a death grip—a valiant effort to keep him safely inside the truck for as long as I physically could. "I'm okay. Shaken, but okay. You can't go after him. Do you understand me?"

Silence greeted my question, which forced me to hurl a stern, don't-you-dare look at him.

"Damn it, Hayley. That piece of shit has to pay. You can't just expect me to sit here and do nothing."

"I never said that." I knew what had to come next—who I would've called if Amelia didn't answer. "But if you really want to help me right now, you'll drive me to the nearest police station so I can report it. Putting the guy in the hospital is not going to achieve anything."

Jace exhaled a long, slow breath, like my words had deflated him and his inability to act rationally. "You're right. I'm sorry, the last thing you need is me making this worse. I just hate that he touched you. I don't know what I would do if he'd . . ." He trailed off. "If anything had happened to you."

"Well, it didn't. Nothing else happened, and I'll be fine. As much as I appreciate it, you don't need to protect me."

Jace stared down at me like he was trying to read me inside out, and the air between us instantly shifted, crackling and charging on a molecular level. For the first time in my life—terrible timing and all—he was looking at me the way I'd always fantasized about.

I was suddenly hyperaware of how close we were. Unlike my encounter with Levi, our proximity felt comfortable, *good*. Jace's arm was still around my waist, and his hand was lightly cradling the small of my back as if he wasn't ready to let me go yet. It was like the thought of something happening to me had finally cracked him open, a sudden vulnerability seeping out.

As he tucked a wayward strand of hair behind my ear, his fingers grazed my cheek. Everything stopped, like someone had hit the Pause button. He brushed his thumb under my eyes, wiping away fresh tears. We stared at each other, silently assessing, scarcely breathing.

Jace had never touched me like this before. Not once in the entire time I'd known him.

His eyes dropped to my mouth and lingered there. Any doubt I had about how Jace felt about me faded as I let myself hope.

Just when I thought he was about to say or do something— something that had the potential to heal all the trauma we'd experienced—two bright headlights shone in our faces, and he instantly jerked back, shielding his eyes.

Sheer disappointment slashed at my heart as he pulled away.

The car idled beside us, its engine shuddering before falling silent, and then Jace and I were drowned in darkness once more. He shifted farther away from me on the adjoining seat, clearing his throat. His lashes lifted and his pale eyes sharpened on me.

"Shit, I don't know what I—"

I braced myself for the speech I was about to receive, but it never came. Jace stopped short, noticing that Piper had stepped out of the car that had parked next to us.

Sliding my gaze in her direction, I squinted out the windshield as she said something to the driver of the other car before slamming the passenger door shut. She approached the truck, and Jace elbowed his door open. The overhead light flicked on, and the instant Piper spotted me, her shoulders slumped.

"Oh, thank God. I couldn't find you. I got my roommate's friend to drive me around the property. No one had seen you since you went outside earlier, and I heard something about Levi, that he—"

"I'm okay," I interrupted, but it couldn't have been further from the truth.

I wanted to take a scalding hot shower back at the dorm, crawl under the covers, and never surface again. Not only had Levi just tried to attack me, but I also had absolutely no idea what was going on between Jace and me. Both were contributing to my mounting anxiety.

"I think Hayley and I are going to head out," Jace told her. "Do you have a ride back to campus?"

Piper nodded and leaned into the truck. She stretched over Jace until her hand reached my leg, which I'd been jiggling up and down. When she squeezed it, something indecipherable flashed in her hazel eyes. "If something *did* happen, I hope you're planning to report it, but there's no pressure. I'm here for you, and so is Jace," she said softly. Piper eased out of the truck, a thin-lipped smile ghosting across her pretty face. "But I'm sure you already knew that."

"Thank you," I said, meaning it. "And I think we're going to do that now. Right, Jace?"

"Right," he confirmed quietly. He turned to his best friend. "Don't worry about it. I'll take care of her."

"I know you will." She dipped her head. "See you later."

Piper must have picked up on the tension radiating off both of us because she barely stayed for a minute. She mouthed something to him before heading back over to the other car. I watched in silence as they drove past us, a cloud of dust kicking up as the car sped off down the gravel track that led from the farmhouse to the main road.

There was a beat of awkwardness, and I didn't know what to say. Naturally, I was nervous, and when I was, I babbled. A lot.

Jace knew that too.

"So, do you think we should go to the police station now? Or should we just, like, go in the morning?" I asked, my voice rough with restrained panic. "Maybe I should sleep on it . . . but it's probably better I get it over with, right? I mean, what would you do?"

"I would report it tonight, if it were me." A shadow slid across his profile. Then a soft, tentative smile replaced it, catching me off guard. "As adorable as you are when you're nervous, Hayles, you don't have to be. I know what you're doing, and you don't have to fill the silence. It's just me."

My cheeks flushed. "I know, but I don't know how to be around you right now, and I feel awful about our fight earlier. You know that I didn't—"

"I know. I feel like shit too." He sighed, closing his eyes. "But let's just focus on you right now."

I ignored the way my heart faltered a little at his words. "Okay." I nodded as he turned the engine on, buckling myself in. I didn't move over to the passenger side of the seat, not wanting to waste the opportunity to stay close to Jace. His denim-clad leg was touching mine, and I needed human contact. I needed *him*.

I took his advice and enjoyed not having to speak just for the sake of it. We lapsed into a comfortable silence. As glad as I was to be leaving the party behind, the realization of what I was about to do weighed heavily on me. Fidgeting with my fingers, I kept checking the illuminated clock on the dash, wishing I could freeze time and stay in Jace's Chevy forever.

"You good?" he asked, hooking a right as we neared the local police station. He'd clearly picked up on the fact that I was losing my cool. Not to mention, my head was really hurting.

"Yeah," I lied, and then I reminded myself that this was Jace—the boy I'd harbored feelings for since I was thirteen. And technically, he was that one person who I should try to be honest with. I looked away, blinking back more tears. "Actually, no. Not good."

I was impressed that I wasn't totally breaking down in front of him. Usually, all it took was for someone to ask me how I was doing—always when I was visibly scrambling to keep it together—to rupture my resolve.

"I can't imagine what you went through," he ground out. "As difficult as this is, I know you can do it. You're the strongest person I know, Hayles."

"I don't know about that," I whispered, shifting my gaze out the window, away from him again. He was becoming increasingly difficult to look at. Aside from his ridiculous good looks, the expression on Jace's face was so sincere, so revering, it made my insides hum.

"I do," he said in a no-nonsense tone. His faith in me was palpable, and that helped my dwindling confidence, the festering self-doubt. "I know you'll get through this."

The parking lot at the police station was practically empty this late at night, but the fluorescent lights inside the building and the dark figure behind the desk indicated that they were always open.

For a moment, I wasn't sure I was ready to report this. A sudden wave of nervousness swept over me, and my stomach clenched. I needed to focus all of my brain on what was about to happen, on everything I was going to have to tell them.

Levi would probably get away with it, anyway. And what happened if he tried to hurt me again when he found out I'd gone to the cops? Worse yet, what if he succeeded?

Every fiber of my being wanted to run, to avoid reliving the fear, to avoid having to verbalize everything. The moment I did that was the moment it would be real. I couldn't take it back.

I told myself that while there was no guarantee that Levi would be charged, the thought of him doing this to someone else terrified me more, especially if they weren't able to fight him off.

My mind made up, I went to open the passenger-side door when Jace's hand found mine in the darkness of his truck. Our fingers intertwined, and his thumb smoothed over my skin in a rhythmic circle. Nothing had ever felt so right.

His eyes, a hazy swirl of gray, narrowed slightly as he studied me, *really* looked at me. "I'm here, and I'll stay as long as you need me to."

Understanding burgeoned in that instant. I realized that it wasn't about being ready to report it. Truthfully, I might have never been ready to do that. What mattered, what made all the difference in the world, was that Jace was here—just like the night of the accident—and he wasn't going to leave me.

six

Tension had been knotting my stomach since we'd arrived at the police station, and it only tightened its grip as we were processed and escorted into a private interview room. My hands were shaking, but it wasn't because I was cold—Jace had ransacked his truck earlier, giving me an old pullover to wear. I inhaled deeply, willing the woodsy scent of his cologne to ground me. The ceiling fan whirred noisily above us as we waited for the officer to return.

"You can do this," Jace assured me, currently occupying the chair beside me. He was making a really difficult situation more bearable—again—and I was eternally grateful. Under the harsh fluorescent lights, it was easier to see the concern that had settled into the striking lines and sharp angles of his face.

"I want to go home," I whispered, lowering my gaze to the untouched Styrofoam cup of coffee that had been placed in front of me.

My response did nothing to ease his worry, but I didn't have the energy to pretend I was handling this well. I felt numb from top to toe. Jace reached over to squeeze my hand. This was obviously hard for me, but I understood that it wasn't easy for him either.

Making a formal statement was official and scary, but there was no point where I genuinely questioned what I was doing or saw it as a mistake. Making a formal statement was also something Jace and I had done before, together. After talking with the police when my brother had died, there was a morbid familiarity with the process we were about to embark on for the second time.

As I waited for the officer to return, I twisted my fingers tightly, almost cutting off the circulation. As calm as I was trying to be, there was still a god-awful tightness snaking around my torso, suffocating me, until I couldn't suck in a breath deep enough. I wanted to get this over with.

When the door finally opened, I straightened in my seat, ignoring the sting of pain in the base of my skull—where I had cracked it on Levi's jawbone.

"Sorry for the holdup." The officer sat down in front of me, and I registered the polished name tag on her uniform with R. BEDFORD engraved in big block letters. She was a tallish woman, willowy, with short black hair. The shadows beneath her eyes suggested that she frequently worked the night shift. "So, Hayley, again, my name's Officer Bedford, and I'm going to ask you a few questions now, just so we can establish what's happened and work through things from there. Is that all right?"

I nodded.

"Fantastic." She unzipped her leather folio and flipped to a new page in her notebook. "When you're ready, it would be great if you could describe what happened, when, and where, as that will paint the clearest picture for me."

Swallowing the lump that had built in my throat, I forced myself to meet her eyes and tell her everything in as much detail as I could remember.

Jace bristled beside me when I got to the part where Levi's hand had pushed my skirt up. I was certain he would've ended up between my legs if I hadn't stopped him, and I felt like I was going to be sick, my brain unable to shake those final moments.

"Thank you for all of that information, Hayley," Officer Bedford started, holding my gaze sympathetically. "Given that we already know who the assailant is from the name and description you've given us, formal identification procedures shouldn't be necessary, which is good."

I tensed, and so did Jace, his forearms resting on the table. Whatever she said next would determine how they were going to handle this.

"But it's too early to tell in the investigation if the defendant will be charged. He may only receive a warning, but if there's enough evidence to prosecute, if he has a criminal history or an arrest warrant, there might be a court hearing and . . ." It was then my brain decided to totally shut down. I forced myself to at least appear like I was listening.

Only two thoughts drummed into me repeatedly: *I'll have to tell my parents*, and *What am I going to do if Levi confronts me about this?*

Nervously, I tugged at a loose thread on the sleeve of Jace's pullover.

Officer Bedford must have detected my unease because her eyes flickered to Jace. "Is there someone Miss Donovan can stay with tonight?"

Although the question wasn't directed at me, it was about me, and I felt the need to respond. "Um, well—"

"She's going to spend the night with me, ma'am," Jace told her, cutting me off.

Holy hell.

It was incredibly inappropriate that my heart did a little cartwheel inside my chest, especially considering the reason that I needed to stay with him. In an attempt to downplay his offer, I told myself that spending the night at Jace's apartment meant absolutely nothing. It would be just like it had been all those times I'd slept over at his house when we were younger. This was no different.

Except . . . Amelia wouldn't be there. I was going to be completely alone with her brother—just like the night we'd lost Tom and he'd stayed with me.

Jace wasn't interested in hanging around after the interview was over. He thanked the officer, and I gave her a timid wave.

A shiver traveled through me as we stepped into the parking lot. The temperature had dropped since the last time we were outside. I climbed into Jace's truck and buckled up, my head tipping back against the seat as my eyes fell shut.

When Jace didn't start the engine, the silence stretching around us, I turned my head to look at him. He was staring out the windshield, his features guarded.

"Listen, uh, I really don't have to stay over tonight," I breathed the words before I could think better of them. "You can just drop me back at the dorms."

There was a pause, full of hesitation. "Is that what you want, Hayles?" A feeling of déjà vu washed over me. They were the same soft-spoken words from the party. "I don't know if now is really the time to be a martyr. Let me help you. Please."

"I don't want to impose . . ." I figured he only felt obligated because he knew there was no one else. The last thing I wanted to be was a charity case. Again.

"You're not," he answered without missing a beat. "You're coming home with me, end of discussion."

I couldn't argue with that. And most important, I didn't want to.

He cranked the engine, and it hummed loudly, overriding the sound of my heartbeat thumping in my ears.

"Are you hungry, or do you want to just head back to my place?" Jace asked as his fingers spun the dial to turn the heater on.

"I don't have much of an appetite," I said, which was true. The events of tonight had blended my insides to a consistency that felt a lot like watered-down soup.

"Of course." He shook his head, his eyes softening. "Stupid question."

Speaking of stupid questions, I let my curiosity get the better of me. "Do you even have a spare bedroom?"

"No." Jace's forehead crinkled, as though it had only just occurred to him too. "But I've got a decent couch that I can crash on."

"Great," I agreed lamely, and relief trickled in when he finally shifted the truck into drive.

God forbid if we had to sit here any longer, exchanging small talk.

Wrapping my arms around myself, I eyed him closely while he navigated the empty streets, music playing softly on the radio. His jaw was doing the rigid thing, and even though I couldn't see his expression, I felt it—the tension ratcheting up between us. When you grew up with someone like I'd grown up with Jace, you learned their tells. He was in a shitty mood.

I gathered the courage to ask, "Are we okay? I mean, you're

not actually giving me the silent treatment right now, are you?"

"That's not what I'm doing." His lips twitched at the corners. "I just don't have anything to say."

"Really? I'm not just some girl, Jace. I know you. I know when something isn't right. You're being . . . different."

He didn't respond.

What a surprise.

Jace looked both ways, even though the traffic was light at this hour. He pulled out onto the main road, and we were soon flying along, heading toward his apartment complex.

"I don't want to get into this. Not tonight."

"Well, that's too bad, because I do," I said, sitting up a little straighter. "I'm tired of not talking to you. We used to have real, meaningful conversations, like, all the time. You helped me more than anyone else did when Tom died. I miss you, and I miss hanging out. Not because I'm Amelia's best friend, or because you're her brother. We used to be really close, Jace. I miss that."

His tone dropped a level and held meaning. "I know. I miss that too. All the times I'd hear you in the background when I'd call Amelia, and we weren't really talking . . . yeah, that was hard," he admitted. "Because I do like you, Hayley, and I'm attracted to you. I think that much is obvious."

The thirteen-year-old version of me felt like doing a victory dance up until I detected that there was an unspoken *but*, which made my heart plummet.

"I just . . . don't want you thinking this is something it isn't," he said slowly, carefully, like he'd thought about this often. "I'm here for you, always, but I'm not looking for another serious relationship— you know that. And even if I were still into meaningless hookups, you mean way too much to me to ever cross that line."

Well, shit.

It took a second for my brain to register what had just happened, what Jace had finally dared to voice, what he'd probably been wanting to say to me since I got to Delaware. Eventually, the words sank in, and I wanted to crawl inside myself.

Even though he'd admitted that we shared a mutual attraction, apparently that was as far as it went. There it was again—his unfailing brutal honesty.

Tears sprang to my eyes, and I squeezed them shut. When I opened my mouth, nothing came out. There was nothing left to say. And with that, the awkwardness of the decade settled in.

• • •

As Jace and I rode the elevator up to his apartment, I tried to piece together how this night had even happened. My first college party wasn't supposed to end with me filing a report at the local police station. Obviously, I couldn't catch a break.

When my phone chimed in my pocket, I was happy for the distraction. There was a burning behind my eyes that I still needed to get under control.

I read the text that had just come through from Amelia: *WTF! ARE YOU OKAY? Jace called me from the police station and left a message. I know it's late, but if you want to call me, I'm still awake.*

My vision tunneled, the walls of the elevator seeming to close in on me. So that was what he'd been doing when I'd headed straight for the nearest bathroom, feeling sick to my stomach. After we'd been called into the interview room, Jace hadn't let me out of his sight.

"You told Amelia." My voice came out as a whisper.

He looked at me, his frown deepening. "Was I not supposed to?"

I hadn't even had the chance to think about whether I was going to tell my parents tonight, let alone Amelia. "You could've at least asked me." My voice rose as my frustration peaked. "Maybe I didn't want to tell anyone yet."

"Shit, I'm sorry. I just thought—" Jace averted his eyes and ran a hand through his hair. "I don't know. I get that it wasn't my place to tell her, I just don't know what to do. I don't know how to be here for you."

The problem was, I wasn't sure I really believed that. At one stage, he'd been my favorite person to turn to for support for a reason. Now, it felt like he just didn't want to deal with me anymore.

Jace unlocked his door, and I brushed past him, entering the dark, quiet apartment. He flicked the entrance light on, illuminating the entire length of the hallway. The walls were decorated with framed photographs—mainly nature shots, which were Jace's specialty. He'd always been a talented photographer; committed to seeing the world through a lens. When I was younger, I couldn't remember a time when he hadn't carried a camera with him. Amelia and I had been his loyal subjects until he'd taken his photography more seriously.

My gaze jumped around the sparsely furnished foyer and living room before landing on him again. He closed the door and dropped his house keys into the little tray.

The minute I went to speak, he folded his arms across his chest, his biceps stretching the cotton sleeves of his T-shirt.

"Let me have it," he said, sounding the tiniest bit insecure if I was reading him correctly. His eyes, a sad, stormy gray, confirmed I was; any anger I'd felt was immediately snuffed out. Cracks were appearing in his mask of indifference. "You're looking at me like there's this long list of things you're dying to say. How else did I fuck up tonight?"

Without warning, something inside me snapped clean in two, like splitting kindling. I couldn't do this anymore—couldn't contain the heartache that was threatening to pour out of me.

"Not you, Jace, *this*—all of it—is fucked up," I clarified, my voice cracking.

He swallowed, his Adam's apple bobbing.

"I'm constantly living in fear," I told him on impulse. "I was so scared tonight. Scared of Levi. Scared that the argument we had would be the last time I spoke to you, like the argument I had with Tom was the last time I spoke to him before . . ." A heaviness knotted my insides, and I bit back a sob. I couldn't even finish that sentence. And the worst part was, I knew I'd only glimpsed a fraction of what my brother must have felt when he'd seen those headlights.

"This is my fault," Jace said, resigned. "I invited you to the party tonight. You wouldn't have been there if it weren't for me. Fuck, I didn't mean for any of this to happen. Seeing you like this, Hayles, I can't stand it." He reached out his hand to me, but I stepped back, needing to leave at least three feet of distance between us. Having Jace in close proximity never ended well for me.

I noticed his fingers were trembling, and another slash of guilt tore through me. He'd tried to stonewall me a lot over the last two and a half years, but you could only outrun something for so long. I knew this because I was trying to escape something, too—my past—and these days, I could feel it catching up to me.

I wondered if moving out here had been a mistake. I'd sworn up and down that Jace had absolutely nothing to do with my decision to go to Delaware, but at this moment, I was suddenly aware of how much he had. There were other great colleges where I could study design. I'd chosen UD for its art program, yes . . . but if I was being honest with myself, I had also followed him here. And was Jace enough of a reason to stay?

"Please, don't call me that anymore. Don't confuse me," I said, trying to push my emotions back down. "And the way you held me in your truck at Levi's, don't do that again either. Not unless it's going to mean something, like it would for me."

I clamped my mouth shut, heat crawling up my neck. Jace blinked, taken aback.

I might as well have just told him I loved him. And I was thinking maybe I did. Nothing else explained this deep-seated ache.

"It's late. I should go to bed," I announced. I thought I'd learned my lesson by now—not to share things with him I really shouldn't.

Shifting his light, unnerving gaze to mine, he said, "Okay."

I looked away and suppressed a sigh. We were so bad at this. "Do you have a spare toothbrush I can use?"

"Yeah," he responded, gesturing for me to follow him. He led me farther down the carpeted hallway. "There's an unopened one in the first drawer."

He was keeping his distance, eyes wary, as I walked past him and entered the small bathroom.

I sucked in a deep lungful of air, and my vision swam with black dots as I took note of my reflection in the mirror. I looked like an extra from a low-budget horror film. Now that I wasn't so numbed by the emotional trauma, the reality of what had almost happened to me tonight was sinking in. I wasn't sure whether to laugh or cry that it was always Jace who was dragged into my tragic bullshit. Still, he never bailed. That was more than a lot of people could say.

As I stood there, my thoughts churning, Jace spanned the

bathroom in two effortless strides. His hands enclosed my shoulders. "C'mere. Sit down," he ordered gently, steering me toward the toilet. Stretching behind me, he placed the lid down so I could take a seat, and then grabbed a clean washcloth from the cupboard.

"You've been through a lot, Hayley. Let me take care of you." There was a pause. "Besides, your mascara is, uh, well . . . down to your chin. You're kind of a hot mess." Jace chuckled, a deep, rich sound that never failed to elicit a thrill.

"I know," I mumbled, burying my head in my hands. "I look so gross right now."

"Nah. Not possible."

My insides practically melted when I peeked up at him again to find him running the cloth under the steady stream of water. I couldn't help but wonder how many other girls he'd taken care of like this. Were Zoe and I the only ones who'd seen this side of him? The sweet, tender, loving guy that was buried under that hard exterior. The guy who was now making a habit out of wiping down my face after I'd hurled . . . or, in this case, bawled my eyes out.

Tuning out my halfhearted protests, Jace pressed the hot washcloth against my face, and I held my breath. He finished up by wiping the mascara under my eyes. Warmth surged, dipping low in my belly.

"You didn't have to do that," I pointed out as he stood back up, opening the drawer to grab me a fresh toothbrush.

We shared a look I would never forget, like it was more powerful than any words we could've exchanged at that moment. I didn't know how I knew he was prepared to do just about anything for me, but I did. And how was I supposed to move on when the reasons to love this man were staring me in the face?

"It's nothing. Amelia asked me to do it once when she was in rough shape. Sorry I don't have makeup remover shit. Here you go," he said gruffly, handing me a loaded-up toothbrush. "Is there anything else I can get you?"

"No, I'm fine. Thanks."

Silence fell between us for a while as I brushed my teeth, rinsed my mouth, and got ready for bed, but Jace never left. He hovered in the doorway, our gazes meeting ever so briefly in the mirror. It was almost like he knew I didn't want to be left alone.

Once I was done, I crossed the space between us without my brain explicitly telling me to. My heart was the culprit.

A flash of momentary surprise flickered across his face when I stretched up onto my toes and wrapped my arms around him, drawing him into me. Oh, good Lord, that was one hard chest. But even if I hadn't seen Jace's expression, I knew the hug I'd initiated would've caught him off guard. Believe it or not, Jace was the affectionate one in our friendship—if you could even call it that. I was officially clueless about what we were anymore, but right now, I didn't particularly care.

Slowly, he leaned into me, dropping his chin into the crook of my neck. His fingers trailed up my spine in a smooth, comforting gesture.

"Thank you for looking after me," I said, gripping the back of his shirt, "for letting me stay. It reminds me of the last time you slept over."

"Same." He exhaled, his warm breath raising the tiny hairs on my body. "I'd do anything for you, Hayley. You know that. And when I say I can't be what you want, I'm not telling you that to hurt you or as a cop-out. I'm just not the guy for you."

I swallowed away my sadness. Oh, how I wished he were.

The hug only lasted ten seconds or so before I pulled back, my sense of self-preservation kicking in.

Among everything else that had happened tonight, a different kind of feeling had been brewing, and I hadn't been able to shake it—the slow burn that was threatening to consume me. It was spreading now, lighting up every part of me, because I'd just realized that I wasn't at risk of falling in love with Jace anymore.

No.

I *was* in love with him.

I couldn't pinpoint the exact moment it had become so much more—the start of my senior year, the night we'd lost Tom, the morning he'd revealed we were in the same class and unleashed that dimpled smile again—but the knowledge that I was in love with Jace sang at me, over and over again.

This wasn't crush-love, not anymore. This was real, I-want-to-be-with-you-forever love, terrifying and true.

It wasn't smart. And it certainly wasn't going to be easy. But despite all of this, somehow, I'd always known I'd never had a hope in hell. Falling for Jace was inevitable.

seven

Planting my elbow on my desk, I propped my chin on my fist and blew out an exasperated sigh. I'd been trying to study all night, and I was fairly certain I'd just reread the same paragraph for the fifth time.

In the hallway outside my dorm room, I could hear the high-pitched voices of two girls talking to a guy who lived a couple of doors down, punctuated by the sounds of their shrill laughter. I was surprised anyone else was even here. It was a Saturday night, and I'd locked myself away like some sort of recluse, but that was mainly because I didn't have anywhere better to be. College was already kicking my butt, even after I'd taken Professor Zimmerman's advice and meticulously mapped out a study timetable.

It wasn't until I'd started to pack my things up, planning to move to the shared common room in the hopes it was a little quieter down there, that I discovered the crumpled-up note. It fluttered to the floor after slipping out of a random page in my textbook. I glimpsed slanted, messy handwriting, and struggled to decipher what it said.

You're so gorgeous, I wish you were mine.

My initial reaction was surprise, assuming Jace had written it, but the more I thought about it, the less that theory made sense. I didn't recognize the handwriting, and it wasn't his style. Whatever he wanted to say, he'd just come out with it. That meant I was left with one question: Who else could have gotten close enough to slide a note into my textbook without me noticing? The admiring words didn't exactly give me a warm, fuzzy feeling either. I promptly ditched the idea of heading to the spacious common area tonight in favor of hiding out in my dorm room.

Tapping my pen against my desk, I willed my brain to concentrate, to not think about the note, but it was like the words were blurring together. My mind was elsewhere, zooming back to Levi. The night I couldn't wait to forget still wouldn't leave me alone. I recalled the way he'd smiled down at me, like he was oh-so-pleased with himself, then the feel of his hands on me, wandering inappropriately.

Firmly pushing those thoughts of Levi aside, I glanced out the small window in front of my desk. It was a dark, moonless night, and I didn't know what time it was anymore, just that I still had a lot of reading to do—research for a big interior design project I was working on in one of my other classes.

It had been two weeks since I'd stayed over at Jace's, and I hadn't heard from him except for the brief interactions we'd had in class.

I'd texted him once, asking if he, Piper, and Owen were interested in getting together to study, but he'd never responded. There'd been nothing but radio silence. And when he was a no-show to Concepts in Design yesterday, I'd felt a prickle of worry. I'd automatically assumed the worst. He was dropping the class, and for some unknown reason, never wanted to speak to me again. Clearly, jumping to conclusions was my specialty.

It wasn't until Piper had come over to my workbench and revealed that he was back in Port Worth for a photography gig this weekend that I'd realized maybe I was being a little irrational. Besides, he didn't owe me an explanation.

I hated feeling bitter and twisted, but it was obvious he was ignoring me. I thought I'd handled the whole "I can't be what you want" speech with impressive maturity, but I also knew not to confront him about going MIA on me. The future of our friendship was on shaky ground as it was.

It wasn't easy to be just friends with someone you couldn't help but want more with, especially considering we'd already laid it all out there on the line. I wanted to be with him. He didn't want to be with me. End of story.

Yes, he'd admitted he was attracted to me, but whatever he felt didn't run deeper than that. His feelings couldn't, otherwise they would have been enough to overcome whatever reluctance he had about being in a relationship. And it didn't matter how many times I told myself that I needed to forget about him—to give up on the idea of us being together. As much as I wanted to move on, it wasn't that simple. There was so much shared history between us. Imagining a future without him was proving impossible.

Lost in my surging thoughts, I jumped a little when my phone buzzed on my desk. Amelia's name flashed on the caller ID, and my lips twitched at the image saved to her contact. It was a photo of the two of us pulling goofy faces at the beach bonfire she'd dragged me to last summer.

I slid my finger across the screen, accepting her call. "What's up?"

"Just thought I'd check in. What about you? Did you just get back from a run or something?"

"No. Why would you think that?"

"You sound breathless, like maybe you were hoping a certain someone was borrowing my phone."

"You're hilarious." I barked out a humorless laugh. More like exhausted from battling constant anxiety. "So, was there a point to this conversation?"

"Ooh, feisty."

"I'm just over it," I said, attempting to sound neutral.

"Why? What happened?"

I wanted to lie to her. Not because I didn't want her to know, but because I knew how complicated this whole situation was. Instead, I found myself telling her the truth. It was going to drive me nuts if I didn't get it off my chest. "I'm either trying to distract myself from thinking about Levi, or I'm in class, or I'm studying, literally every waking hour. And I think your brother is avoiding me again." I left out the part about finding the note, unsure what to think.

"First, I'm so sorry about the creep." She spoke low, just above a whisper, and the sound of her window creaking open caused nostalgia to unfurl inside me. Growing up, whenever we'd needed to have a deep and meaningful conversation, Amelia had always climbed out onto her rooftop. The walls of her house were paper-thin, and I appreciated her still taking precautions. "But I'm incredibly proud of you for reporting it, Hayley. You know I'm always here if you want to talk about that night again. Second, that's understandable; classes have only just started. It's going to take a minute for you to get on top of everything. Third, my brother is not avoiding you. I wasn't kidding before, Jace borrowing my phone to call you is a possibility. His phone's broken."

"His phone's broken," I echoed. "Right. Makes perfect sense."

"Come on," she scoffed. "You didn't really think he would just ignore you?"

"Are you seriously asking me that? After Tom's funeral, he avoided me like the plague, and we both know it."

"That was different. Plus, you didn't exactly try to fix things either," she said quickly. Her instinct to defend Jace was both admirable and infuriating. "You know my brother wouldn't recognize a good thing even if it punched him in the face. He's always been slow on the uptake."

"Well, there goes that plan," I joked.

Amelia laughed, and then I heard Jace's deep voice in the background. My heart flipped over. Uh-oh. If that wasn't my cue to get off the phone, I didn't know what was.

Then there was nothing but silence, and I suspected Amelia had put me on mute.

When she came back on, she sounded uncharacteristically wary. "Hey, um, listen," she started. "Jace wants to talk to you. Is that okay?"

I hadn't been expecting that.

My stomach tumbled over itself.

"Sure," I croaked out.

More silence ensued, and my knee bounced impatiently. Tying myself into knots was stupid, but I couldn't help it.

A moment later, Jace's voice rumbled down the line. "Hey, Hayles," he said. Damn it. The nickname was back, and it made my pulse spike. "I'm sorry for not telling you I was leaving—my phone's busted."

I stayed quiet, waiting to hear what he'd say next.

"I had to come home to shoot a wedding for the McAllisters. You remember Drew and Amy, right? They were in the year above me. Anyway, how are you? Everything okay?" he asked, his voice dropping by at least an octave.

"Yeah, I guess." I bit my lip.

"You sure?"

One question nagged at my conscience, and I had to know either way. "Did you, uh, leave me a note in my textbook?"

His response was immediate. "No. Why? If something's going on and you need me, I'll come back. You've just gotta ask."

"I'm managing, I promise." I almost told him to call me again tomorrow, to check in with me later in case I had an entirely different answer for him, but Jace wasn't my boyfriend, and I was used to surviving on my own.

He exhaled raggedly. "Okay. That's good. I should be back by Monday morning for class, but if I'm not, I was hoping you'd cover for me."

My stomach plummeted like a shot-down missile. Jace had only wanted to talk to me about school.

"So, uh, I'll see you," he breathed.

Everything felt so awkward now. Stilted.

"Yeah. Bye, Jace," I mumbled as he disconnected the call.

• • •

I couldn't even remember falling asleep last night, but I must have, because the sound of someone banging heavily on my door woke me up.

As I slowly sat up, I noticed my loose-leaf notes sprawled out over my comforter, and I pushed a textbook with surprisingly sharp corners out from beneath me. My laptop had slid off me, wedging itself between the wall and my bed. Luckily, the lid was closed, and it was still intact.

I'd given new meaning to the term *study animal*.

My eyes peeled open, all grogginess dissipating when another pounding knock made my door rattle.

"I'm coming," I muttered, untangling myself from the blanket. "There's no need to wake up the whole freaking floor."

I swung my legs off the bed and winced, a sharp, stabbing pain lurching in my shoulder. I really needed to speak to the resident advisor about replacing my sorry-ass excuse for a mattress.

Dawn streamed in through the gap between my curtains, and I hadn't the faintest idea who would be here this early on a Sunday morning. A small part of me wondered if Jace had driven back late last night, or if someone had broken the news to my parents about the attack. Marching me back home would most likely be their knee-jerk reaction—which was why I hadn't told them yet.

"Who's there?" I grumbled.

When I heard Levi's distinct laughter—the same hair-raising sound from his party—it wound around me like a python, squeezing the air from my lungs.

Thompson was always locked to nonresidents. Had someone buzzed him in?

I didn't even want to consider what would've happened had I not already been paranoid enough to start locking my own door. The reality of the situation slammed into me with the force of a freight train. Although it was a lot sooner than I'd expected, Levi must have found out I'd reported him to the police.

"What do you want?" I asked, keeping my voice tight and controlled.

"Why don't you open the door," Levi taunted, "and ask me that to my face?"

His words pierced my gut, and I almost stumbled back. Closing my eyes, I swallowed against the wave of nausea that rose in my throat, the strange burning sensation growing in my chest. My whole life was back home. Even Jace was over a hundred miles away. I was totally alone.

After a few moments, my delayed fight-or-flight response kicked in. My brain rallied and drove my feet forward. Snatching my phone from where it had been charging on my bedside table, I dialed campus police, a number I'd had the foresight to save in my contacts after orientation. They said they would dispatch two officers who were close by. Then I called the only other person I could think of.

"Hello?" Piper answered almost instantly, and I was thankful for small mercies. The fear I felt retreated ever so slightly.

"Piper—" My voice broke on a shuddering gasp. I struggled to speak quietly when I tried again. "Levi's here . . . outside my dorm room. I'm so sorry, I didn't know who else to call. The police are on their way, but Jace isn't—"

"Holy shit," she whispered. Guilt pricked at me as I acknowledged that I was literally dumping all of my problems on her. "I'll bring Owen, in case he's . . ." Piper trailed off nervously. "We'll be ten minutes, tops."

"Thank you," I said in an agonized rush before she quickly hung up.

I crawled onto my bed, crossing my legs. Grabbing my pillow, I hugged it close to me, my vision blurring with angry tears. As much as I hated Levi, I hated what he was trying to do to me more. He was trying to frighten me, and it was working.

When the door groaned against the weight of someone pounding it again a few minutes later, I held my breath. I wasn't sure if it was the police officers, Jace's friends, or Levi.

"It's just us." Piper's voice shook me from the anxiety that had been gripping me.

With newfound enthusiasm, I sprang from the bed and threw the door open.

She took one look at me and paled, fear carving her features. Whereas Owen straightened, eyeing me like he was afraid I might fall apart at the seams.

"Was—is he still outside my dorm?" I craned my neck down the empty hallway, tension clinging to my bones.

I couldn't believe the commotion hadn't set off alarm bells for any of the other first-year residents within earshot of my room. Then again, I wouldn't be surprised if I was the only one in Thompson who wasn't nursing a killer hangover this morning.

"Lucky for him, he wasn't," Owen stated, lips thinning. "He's gone."

Relief pressed a sigh out of me, weakening my hold on the door, which was the only thing keeping me upright now that the adrenaline had faded.

Piper opened her mouth to say something, but Owen stepped out from behind her. His fingers ensnared my wrist, tugging me forward.

"Let's go," he said without preamble. His expression was serious and strange—nothing like the guy I'd met on the first day.

"I'm still in my pajamas!" I pointed out incredulously. "Plus, campus police will be here any minute. I can't leave yet."

He released his hold on me, a faint blush staining his cheeks. "Fair enough." He cleared his throat. "Sorry."

Piper tossed him a look, then her gaze swung back to me. "I think what Owen meant to say is, once you've gotten dressed, given the nice officers the lowdown, and packed an overnight bag, *then* we'll go."

At the prospect of having to rely on these people—people I barely knew—I hesitated in the doorway. Trusting them was a nonissue; they were Jace's closest friends. I was only wary of dragging them into my mess. It didn't feel fair to them—they didn't owe me anything.

"As much as I really appreciate you guys coming over here, I don't want to involve you more than I already have," I explained, brushing a dark strand of hair out of my face.

"You're a smart girl, Hayley, which makes what you're saying even more stupid. No offense." Piper winced a little. "I know we haven't known each other for very long, but I already consider you a friend, and friends don't let each other deal with this shit on their own."

I flushed to my hairline, especially when Owen grumbled in agreement. "Thanks. I know. I just didn't want to—"

"Let's cut the crap," Owen interrupted, startling me. "I'm just going to say what everyone's been thinking. God, he'll probably kill me for this, but"—he swiped a hand through his short, blond hair—"look, we're already involved, like it or not, because it's pretty damn obvious to everyone—well, everyone except Jace— that he's into you. And even if you both continue to keep denying it, running from it, whatever the hell you're doing, we all know it."

The conversation I'd had with Jace the other week sprang to mind, and I was suddenly too scared to acknowledge what Owen was saying. Because if Jace truly had real, deep feelings for me, that meant there was something else holding him back. And while a relationship with anyone was hard, being with a guy who wasn't willing to be honest with me was doomed from the start.

I shifted my attention to Piper, silently searching for confirmation, and she nodded weakly.

"But more than anything, I'm just looking out for number one, because as much as Jace will be fucking pissed when he hears about what's gone down this morning, it'll be nothing compared to the regret that will haunt me for the rest of my life if I bail on you, and something happens. I haven't got room for that on my conscience. Understand?"

I knew he was right. There was nothing worse than having regrets—knowing your actions had consequences and being reminded of them every single day. I couldn't have argued with Owen, even if my life had depended on it.

And looking back, I guess it kind of did.

eight

"So, what are you going to do?" Piper eyed me as she shoved another cherry Twizzler into her mouth.

For the entire drive back to Owen's studio apartment, I'd asked myself the same question. I drew a complete blank every time.

I was still trying to figure out where to begin when it came to the whole having-a-stalker thing, but I was strangely calm, all things considered. Then again, maybe I hadn't had enough time to digest the enormity of what I was up against. It was all so surreal. The note that had probably come from Levi, his unwelcome visit, the fact that I was now seeking refuge at Jace's friend's house. My conversation with the cops had left me shaken as well. I wasn't the only girl on campus shit like this was happening to, and that was extremely unsettling. Finding out I would have to go to court to file for a restraining order while my case was still being investigated wasn't the way I wanted to start my day.

A few seconds and a deep inhale later, I dragged my attention back to her. "I honestly have no clue," I admitted, fiddling with the edge of the placemat on Owen's oak table.

A headache clamped around my temples, the mixture of a lack of caffeine and mental exhaustion.

I knew I had to tell my parents—I just didn't want to have the conversation over the phone. I could tell them I wasn't cut out for college. If I wasn't at Delaware anymore, Levi wouldn't be able to bother me. But my insides twisted at the thought of him running me out of town. I wasn't a coward, and I'd only just gotten here. Most important, though, I refused to give up on my studies—my long-standing dream. Nothing was ever easy, but that just made it even more rewarding. I was determined to stay, to graduate, to get to spend my days decorating and brightening people's spaces. I knew the value of a cozy, safe place to heal, to find yourself again.

"All I know is, I can't go back to my dorm. Not right now," I continued, an odd lump swelling in the back of my throat. "But I can't just crash here on Owen's couch. I don't want to be a burden. And I barely know him." *Or you*, my brain added unhelpfully.

Piper chewed the sugary goodness slowly, her eyebrows knitting together. "You two have more in common than you think," she said after a pause. "That's why he's been acting so weird today. Owen's sister—"

We both tensed at the sound of the sliding glass door opening. Owen stepped inside from the balcony, lowering his phone and slipping it into the pocket of his khaki shorts. Something was off about his expression, and I immediately went on high alert.

"That was Jace." His eyes darted between Piper and me.

Judging by the way campus police had combed through Thompson earlier, I knew what had happened would be common knowledge to most people by this afternoon. I'd called Jace and left him a voice message on the way here, grateful he'd texted me his new number after we'd hung up.

Last night, I hadn't wanted him to make a mad dash back to campus, to swoop in and rescue me like I was some damsel in distress over what could've been a creepy, albeit harmless, note, but things had changed since then.

"Has he calmed down at all?" asked Piper.

I crossed my legs at the ankles, needing an excuse to prevent them from bouncing up and down restlessly.

"Nope." Owen grabbed a beer from the fridge. It wasn't even midmorning. He cracked the top off the edge of the counter, wisps of cold air floating up the neck of the bottle. He took a long, slow swig, like the conversation we were about to have demanded something to take the edge off. "Who wants to hear that some weird dude is stalking your girl? He understands how serious this shit is. He knows he needs to be here, and you need to file that restraining order. Don't make the same mistakes I did."

Sympathy gathered in Piper's eyes, although I wasn't exactly sure whom it was directed at anymore. Owen was obviously speaking from personal experience, and given what Piper had just hinted at, it had something to do with his sister.

"I don't think it's a good idea for you to stay with me tonight either," he added, filling the silence. "That, uh, didn't go over too well."

My stomach bottomed out. *Great.*

The caveman routine wasn't attractive, and I hoped Jace wasn't about to start acting like a jealous boyfriend. Especially when he claimed to have no interest in that title. Effectively, I'd been friend-zoned. Nothing justified his overprotective behavior. If I wanted that, I'd have called my father. I honestly just wanted the emotional support from my longtime friend when I'd reached out to him earlier. When it came to that—being there for me without question—he'd never let me down.

Piper gave a quick shake of her head. "See. This is why I usually stick to dating girls," she said to no one in particular. "Jace is turning mixed signals into an art form. How are you not together already?"

She had a point, but I hadn't worked hard to change the trajectory of our relationship either.

I couldn't exactly tell them the truth. That for the last few years, I'd had bigger issues to deal with, like cremating my brother. For a while, Tom's loss had consumed me. No amount of counseling, cute outfits, materialistic purchases, my monthly *Architectural Digest*, or boys—not even Jace—had been enough to make me feel even a fragment of happiness. Nothing had mattered. Nothing had made me feel *anything*, not back then.

I still had a long way to go, but I never wanted to lose myself like that again.

And I'd learned the hard way that not having Jace in my life was so much worse than not having him in the way I wanted. Death had a way of changing your perspective like that.

"Right person, wrong time?" I gave them my very best one-shoulder shrug. None of this felt blasé in the least.

Satisfied, Piper twirled a lock of auburn hair around her finger, and her gaze trailed back to Owen. "Did you explain to Jace why she couldn't stay at my place tonight?"

According to Piper, her roommate was unstable at the best of times, but she hadn't been in a hurry to give me any more details.

"Jace knows," Owen said, amusement flickering in his eyes. "Which is why he's driving back now."

Piper choked on a laugh. "Isn't the wedding he's supposed to photograph happening this afternoon?"

Inhaling through my nose, I leaned my head back on the top of the chair, focusing on the exposed beams in the ceiling. My thought process was twofold. First, Jace was ditching work? Things were already complicated between us. I wanted him to come back, but I would have been fine with his friends for the day. And second, I decided that someone up there was hell-bent on making my life difficult lately.

"Jesus," she muttered under her breath.

"Okay, well, that's just—I don't . . ." I fumbled for words, speechless.

Owen frowned at me. I knew I wasn't making sense, but then again, none of this was. "All I'll say is, you're fucking with his head, Donovan. I've never seen Jace act like this in all the time I've known him."

"I second that," Piper agreed, growing pensive. She scrunched up the candy wrapper in her hands. "Not only are you here on campus now, but also you're a catch. It's only a matter of time until you find someone else. I think it's driving him a little nuts."

I wasn't sure what to say to that, momentarily stunned.

"I don't get it," she said, sighing. "I don't get why you're not dating."

Jace's desire to be single was a total mystery to me too. Out of my peripheral vision, I felt Owen watching me, and I got this feeling he knew more than he was willing to let on. That he understood Jace in a way that Piper and I didn't.

The urge to shut this conversation down rushed through me. I really didn't want to talk about this—about him—anymore. Baring my soul to his best friends wasn't exactly my idea of a good time.

"You know what Jace is like." My voice was surprisingly level considering my heart was pounding off-kilter. "He has no interest in a relationship. Not with me, anyway."

Owen gave me a weird look, like I was seriously failing to see something. Then he quirked a brow and mumbled, almost inaudibly, "I wouldn't be so sure about that."

● ● ●

Thinking back on everything that had happened this morning made my stomach hollow, but a degree of numbness had settled over me. I was curled up on Owen's sofa under a ridiculously soft throw blanket, nursing a mug of hot chocolate, and watching an old episode of *The Vampire Diaries*. It was only noon and the sun was yet to reach its highest peak, but sleep still beckoned. I was longing to stretch out in my bed back in the dorm—something I thought I'd never say.

Piper had left a little over an hour ago, and Owen was at the library on campus, claiming he had a paper due midweek. I had the distinct feeling that their impromptu departures were the result of a hidden agenda. Owen didn't exactly strike me as the kind of guy who had a close relationship with the student library. Not that I wasn't grateful they'd made themselves scarce. With them gone, Jace and I wouldn't have an audience. But that also meant until he arrived, I was alone with no distractions.

It had been two weeks since we'd had a meaningful conversation, and I wasn't sure what to expect when he got here.

One thing I was sure of was that I really needed to explore the option of dating other guys. I had to move on from him, for good this time, if he couldn't offer me what I wanted.

Pressure built in my chest when it occurred to me that maybe I wouldn't be in this position if I hadn't dragged my feet so much every time Amelia had tried to play matchmaker. Coming from such a small town, single guys were slim pickings, but now that I was in college and trying to be more social, there was no excuse anymore.

But regardless of whether I found a boyfriend or not, I couldn't keep depending on Jace. That wasn't fair to either of us.

I cut those troubling thoughts off and tried to sidetrack myself by focusing on Ian Somerhalder's six-pack.

Good God, I'm lame.

My thumb paused over the remote when I thought I heard something move outside Owen's front door. I flicked the TV on to mute. All that greeted me was silence.

Explaining it away as hearing things, I pulled my gaze from the entrance. Remembering my phone was switched to silent on the armrest beside me, I picked it up. I hadn't been obsessively checking it. The dread that knotted my insides about Levi and this entire situation outweighed the need to see if Jace had been trying to contact me.

When I hit the screen, revealing two text messages from him, it shouldn't have surprised me—I should have known he'd be checking in.

Halfway back to Delaware. You good?

I'm downstairs. Be up soon.

The knowledge that he was here did stupid things to my composure. The last text had come through over five minutes ago—ample time for him to park his truck, climb the stairs to the second floor, and knock at Owen's door.

The unmistakable rattle of keys in the lock resonated in the quiet apartment. For a split second, I'd thought it might be Owen coming back, but then I saw Jace's familiar outline and exhaled.

He lingered in the doorway, his intense stare latching on to my face, and the duffel bag slung over his shoulder dropped to the floor with a soft thud.

I pushed myself into a sitting position, suddenly self-conscious.

With the curtains drawn over the large windows, the faint glow of the muted TV illuminated Owen's entire apartment, and there was no avoiding the look of utter devastation Jace wore, like someone had kicked a puppy in front of him or taken a flame-thrower to all his framed photographs.

Something in me coiled tight, and I pushed the comforter aside, feeling hot all over. Bringing my knees up to my chest, I waited for him to say something. A moment passed. More silence. The anticipation was slowly killing me.

"Hey," I managed.

"I left as soon as I could." His voice was deeper, rougher than I'd ever heard it, and I shivered involuntarily. "I had to see for myself that you were okay."

Although he was still standing in the entrance, the space between us felt like it was shrinking.

"Well, aside from being pretty freaked out, I'm all right. You didn't have to rush back here," I replied. "As much as I appreciate it, I know you had work. I would've been fine."

"I know. I guess I just didn't like the thought of you spending the night at Owen's." Jace scratched the back of his neck. "He's one of my best friends, and I trust him with my life, I just—it bothered me."

I opened my mouth, then closed it. I had no idea how to respond to that. I knew him well enough to know this was all coming from a place of concern, but he was also being way too overprotective for my liking, and confusing. I didn't have the emotional reserves for this.

"It's not like I want to be here, feeling this way," I said, a tad defensively. I climbed to my feet and walked toward him, noting his pinched, somber expression. "It's embarrassing, being stuck on Owen's couch, having nowhere else to go." My voice unexpectedly cracked, and I inhaled, trying to regain my composure. "I can't go back to my dorm room because Levi might still be around. And you weren't here. So, tell me, Jace, what other option was there?"

"Fuck. I'm going about this all wrong." He closed the distance between us in one stride. Tucking me against him, he hugged me and let out a shaky breath.

I froze.

"I don't mean to act like an ass. I was just so worried about you. Honestly, I don't think it would have mattered where you were staying or who you were with; I just needed to be here," he murmured, and I practically melted into him.

"Hmph. Well, thanks for coming back," was my muffled reply. "You should've led with that." I hugged his waist tightly and pressed my face into his shirt. I got another whiff of him, the familiar, comforting scent of his cologne filling my lungs.

"What did the cops say? What are they doing about Levi?"

"I need to file for a restraining order while they try to gather more evidence," I told him. My unease was back, growing in intensity. "You might be able to corroborate my statement, but no one saw him grab me that night or show up at my dorm. It's all just circumstantial right now: my word against his."

"I hate that you have to go through this again. It's fucking bullshit."

"Mm. Surely one traumatic-as-hell event is enough."

"Are you hurt?" he asked, and I shook my head, feeling his second sigh of relief. "Hayley, please, for my own sanity, when shit like this happens, I need you to answer my texts. When I didn't hear from you just now, I—"

"Hang on a minute," I croaked, pushing my hand against the hard ridges of his chest. "I don't *need* to do anything. You were gone. I left you a message this morning. I told you about Levi, even though I've hardly heard from you over the past few days."

My expression must have been pretty damn fierce, because Jace let go of me, his entire posture changing.

"Not true," he stated. "I spoke to you last night before I organized a new phone. After what went down at my apartment the other week, I wasn't just going to ignore you." His voice lowered to a husky whisper. "But I know. I wasn't here. I feel like fucking shit about it."

"That's the point, though. I'm not your responsibility, Jace. You shouldn't feel guilty about living your own life. Besides, you're always showing up for me when it counts, which makes this so much harder." I looked away, swallowing. "I used to think that there was no harm in pretending our . . . connection didn't exist, but now that I've moved here, it's too much. Nothing about this feels casual anymore. We both know things haven't been the way they used to be for a long time now."

He didn't deny any of it. "I care about you, Hayles. Please, don't shut me out. Keep talking to me. I just . . . I need you. You've been there since I was just a kid."

My muddled head tried to make sense of what that meant, and as my thoughts whirled, they automatically drifted back to the night Jace had told me he wasn't interested, that he didn't do complicated. However, here he was, blurring the lines between friendship and something more.

"What am I supposed to say to that?" I asked, my gaze moving back to him. "You keep blowing hot and cold, Jace. One minute, you're saying you don't want to complicate things, and the next, you're doing that all on your own." A warning siren went off in my head, but I didn't listen. "And there was absolutely no reason I couldn't have crashed at Owen's tonight, aside from your misplaced jealousy, that is."

A loaded minute of silence passed.

"You're right," he said quietly, and my stomach flipped. "I could barely think straight when Owen told me you planned to stay the night. Felt like I lost something I never really had. How messed up is that?" His steely blue eyes were storming with something I couldn't identify. "Even though I don't quite understand it, it doesn't change the fact that when I look at you now, I see a hell of a lot more than my baby sister's best friend."

Whatever I'd expected his response to be, it hadn't been one fueled by such fierce honesty. There was something in that tone—a combination of fear, but also a degree of powerful intensity—that erased any shadow of a doubt.

Jace felt this too. It wasn't just me.

It was next to impossible to gather any semblance of calm when he was looking at me like that, like he was considering whether to hightail it out the door or to take a step closer. His stare was unnerving, like I had been stripped bare and he was seeing everything there was to me.

Ever since I could remember, Jace had always had that effect on me. All it took was one discerning glance and he knew every little thing I was feeling. But, like that night in his truck, I was getting glimpses of what he was hiding underneath too.

"What exactly are you saying?" I asked, needing to know what was happening here before rational thought escaped me.

Jace didn't reply. Not verbally, anyway.

He hooked his fingers into the belt loops of my jeans and slowly pulled me against him again. His other hand reached out and cupped my face. The way he was touching me was the furthest thing from platonic, and my heart, Lord, my heart was going crazy.

I watched as his gaze jumped from my mouth to my eyes. I was so caught up in the feel of Jace's hands on me that I barely noticed he had backed himself up against the nearest wall in Owen's living room.

"What are we doing?" I gulped, a tantalizing mixture of nerves and excitement fluttering inside me.

I waited for Jace to change his mind, to release his grip as soon as reality settled in. But those heavy-lidded, pale eyes seared into mine, and when he spoke, his voice was gravelly. "What we probably shouldn't be doing."

White-hot lust distorted some of my thoughts, but my mind still spun high with confusion.

Jace leaned in, his thumb brushing my bottom lip. "This okay?" Maybe he expected me to do the same—to put an end to whatever was about to happen. Or maybe it was because he knew the last time a guy was this close to me, it hadn't been consensual. I cut that line of thinking off as quickly as it popped into my head, refocusing on the moment I'd been dreaming about for so long.

Remembering I still hadn't answered him, that he was waiting for me to give him permission, I nodded.

Instantly, I knew Jace was going to kiss me. I knew exactly where this would lead, and I chased after it, hoping I was right.

His head bowed a little, the stubble along his jaw rubbing

deliciously against my chin. About a thousand different emotions swamped me as his lips brushed mine for the first time, feather-soft, sweet. Infused with shock, I barely had time to register the feeling before he was drawing back, and I missed his touch immediately.

Unfulfilled desires crashed through me, and I went up on my toes, holding on to his broad shoulders for leverage, and then, much to my relief, my mouth was back on his. This time, there was nothing tentative or questioning about the kiss. It was desperate and shattering—a release of years' worth of pent-up sexual tension and longing.

A low moan escaped the back of his throat, and the sound reverberated against my lips, making me shiver. Jace deepened the kiss, his tongue sliding into my mouth, tasting me. Devouring me.

The push of his solid chest against my breasts, the feel of him nudging my legs open with his knee, had lightning zipping through my veins. I felt like I was sparking to life beneath his touch, seconds away from combusting.

I'd fooled around with a couple of guys before, but it never felt like this.

Note to self: *this* was what kissing someone you loved felt like. Nothing bad existed here. Only unfamiliar lightness, a distinctive warmth. Our bodies were fused, and Jace's mouth molded to mine perfectly, like he'd been born to do this—to hold me and kiss me so thoroughly, to make me feel sexy and wanted.

My arms skated up his biceps, over his shoulders, and slipped around the back of his neck. Every square inch of him was corded and strong. It was so easy to press against the entire length of him, leaving little to the imagination.

Despite lying awake at night, fantasizing about this moment for an embarrassingly long time, it occurred to me then how badly I'd wronged Jace. I hadn't done him justice. At all. He was so beautiful, crafted by a master hand.

Jace's tongue danced along mine, a lick of heat, and I was catching on fire. Melting away. I gasped when he pulled my bottom lip between his teeth.

His hands moved from my waist, sliding down to palm my ass, and tendrils of pleasure coiled in my belly. With slight pressure, he ground me against him. The friction was intense, almost taking me over the edge.

"Damn it, Hayles," he whispered, mouth moving against mine. "You feel so good."

As if to prove his point, his erection lined up against me. My breathing constricted.

Holy shit.

In the corner of my mind, I knew we should slow down. Things were escalating faster than a speeding bullet, but what my body needed and wanted was something entirely different.

When his lips moved over my neck, placing an open-mouthed kiss where my pulse was hammering crazily, I found my voice again. "Jace," I rasped out, tangling my fingers in his soft hair—something I'd had the urge to do every day for the last five years. So worth the wait. "We should—"

The apartment door swung open suddenly, and my eyes widened. We jumped apart, and I welcomed the cool air that flooded every place he'd touched and kissed me. Both of us were breathing hard.

"Ah, shit, sorry. I didn't mean to interrupt anything," Owen said. "Should I . . . ? I can come back later."

I didn't need a mirror to know that my face was turning an unattractive shade of red.

Straightening, Jace slipped out from between the wall and me, shoving his hands in his pockets.

Another twist of embarrassment stirred as I watched Jace's reaction, the tension that poured into his body language. Surprise and confusion marked his expression, but that was quickly replaced by something much, much worse. Something I didn't even want to comprehend flickered across his face. It looked way too similar to regret.

"Nah, man," Jace said in a deceptively casual voice, like dry-humping one another against Owen's wall was no big deal. "It's fine. You don't have to do that. We were just about to leave."

I nodded, tamping down a stream of curses. Gathering my phone and my bag, I tried to keep my cool, but one question continued to beat at me like a drum: *How can I possibly spend the night at Jace's now?*

nine

The drive to Jace's apartment was about as fun as I imagined eating glass would be. At one stage, I'd even considered jumping out of the moving vehicle if that meant I didn't have to endure the awkward silence anymore.

My knuckles hurt from clenching my fists—from holding back everything I wanted to say. The last thing I wanted was to get into a heated argument while Jace was behind the wheel.

The silence only thickened as we rode the elevator up to his floor. When I mustered up the nerve to give him another sidelong glance, Jace's profile was stoic. No surprises there. The thin line of his lips was a stark contrast to earlier, yet I could still feel how they'd adeptly moved over mine. That kiss had changed everything. He'd officially taken a piece of me—a piece of my heart—and I'd handed it over so willingly. But now, the memory of that kiss felt tarnished, and I hated the stab of disappointment that came with it.

When we reached the door to his apartment, something in Jace finally seemed to shift. His gaze met mine, and although all emotion was gone from his face, his eyes betrayed him—they usually did. Digging into the pocket of his jacket, he withdrew his set of keys.

He held them out to me. "Here."

That one word dropped between us, like a gigantic pebble that rippled the quiet. I had this sinking feeling I'd take an awkward car drive over the conversation we were about to have.

I blinked. "You're not coming in?"

"I'm not," he said. "I know exactly what happens behind that door, and I won't do that to you or me."

When I stubbornly refused to take the keys from him, Jace exhaled and pushed past me. He unlocked his door and then he stepped back like he couldn't get away from me quickly enough.

"You're just going to leave?" I asked, disbelievingly. "Don't you think we should at least acknowledge what happened at Owen's?"

I knew I was only adding yet another layer to my possible mortification, but my mind was reeling, trying to understand what on earth was going on.

Until less than an hour ago, I'd put my heart and hopes on ice. Now I wasn't so sure. Not after Jace had just kissed me like his very life depended on it.

"I can't stay," he murmured, features softening. "Not now. Not when we'd already decided that this can't go any further, and it still can't."

The awful sting of rejection lashed me.

It felt like I'd been dangled over the edge earlier, and now I was free-falling, only to discover that Jace had no intentions of being there to catch me. For the first time, I felt let down by him.

"You mean when *you* decided?" I challenged, my anger rising. I refused to be continually rejected with zero explanation. "It's okay, I get it. You want me, just not nearly enough."

Jace's jaw twitched. "It's not like that, Hayley. I just can't do this."

"I don't think your dick got the memo."

He choked on a cough. "Well . . ." Jace's lips turned down at the corners. "What do you expect? You already know I'm attracted to you. Shit, anyone with eyes can see that you're fucking gorgeous. But that doesn't mean that this can lead anywhere. We've always been better off as friends."

I quelled the overwhelming impulse to punch him in the throat.

Better off as friends?

I tried to swallow that statement, but it tasted like acid, burning the entire way down. That was what I'd been trying to tell him back at Owen's—we weren't capable of friendship, not anymore. We'd left that turnoff behind years ago. It was too late.

I averted my gaze, pride spurring me to hide the tears that pricked my eyes. "Then don't kiss me," I shot back. "You know I've always liked you. Hell, I told you how I felt two years ago. Everything you've ever said to me has been honest . . . or so I thought, until you kissed me. You don't kiss someone like that and then claim you're better suited as friends. You just don't, no matter your reasons."

Jace recoiled, his eyes flaring darkly. "I don't—" He stopped, inhaling through his nose. His shoulders sagged in defeat. "You're right."

I expected to be satisfied with that answer, but I wasn't. I felt empty as his admission hung there, suspended between us. Emotion clotted my throat like a plug, and I couldn't speak.

"Hayley," he tried again. "I'm sorry that—"

"I don't want you to apologize. I want you to . . ." I trailed off, frustration punctuating each of my words. It was then I finally understood. Nothing he said, no apology in the world, could fix this. Whatever Jace's logic was, it didn't change the heart-wrenching fact that he didn't want to be with me. He didn't want a relationship. And I wasn't willing to settle for less than that. "Forget it."

Detecting that the fight had drained out of me, Jace rocked back on his heels. "I should go."

"Please, don't leave." My arms were hugging my chest, holding myself together.

His lashes lifted, his features pinching in anguish.

"I need you, Jace. Whether we like it or not, we're practically family. You can't go. You didn't drive all this way just to leave me on my own, did you? I'm scared, and the last thing I want to be right now is alone," I reluctantly admitted, ignoring that familiar tug—the crushing weight of heartache. "I understand what you're saying. I do. You wish the kiss didn't happen. It was a mistake. Nothing else is going to happen between us. Message received, loud and clear. But that doesn't change the fact that Levi is still out there, or that you're my closest friend at Delaware. It'd really help if I knew you were in the other room."

I waited for him to respond, half expecting him to argue with me, but he didn't. "Of course I'll stay," he said quietly, then sighed. "I don't know what I was thinking. I guess I was just so focused on . . . dealing with what happened back there, between us, that I kind of forgot about everything else."

I had quite the opposite problem: I couldn't forget. Lately, my mind was so caught up in the attack, or my brother's death.

Spending another night with Jace—a ridiculous amount of time with him again—jogged a memory loose, and it knocked so loud on my subconscious, I had to let it in.

"Are you awake?" Jace's voice found me in the darkness. He hadn't spoken for a solid thirty minutes, and I figured he'd finally fallen asleep.

I was. Even though I was exhausted from the night's events, sleep was physically impossible.

Tom was gone—something I still couldn't even comprehend—and I was a hollow, empty vessel. Stuck here without him, it felt like things would never get better in this world, or the next. If reality was my nightmare now, I wanted to stave off sleep for as long as I could. Imagine how much worse my dreams would be.

Jace was lying on the air mattress next to my bed, the one I stored in my closet for whenever Amelia stayed over. It was late, and he'd insisted on spending the night while my parents were still at the hospital, so I'd let him. For reasons that escaped me, he wasn't at Zoe's, getting her to play the comforting, doting girlfriend. He was in my bedroom, silently reliving tonight with me. The numbing force of everything was weighing me down, drowning me, and I was too tired to come up for air.

I heard the distinctive rustling of sheets, and then Jace's voice was closer. "Remember something good, Hayles. I know it's hard, but you have to try," he murmured, and I recognized that heavy, heavy tone. He sounded exactly how I felt. "The first thing that pops into your head. Don't overthink it."

I stared up at the ceiling. My mind raced back through the years. I wasn't sure if Jace was trying to distract me, calm me down, or both. Either way, it was working.

"I'm four years old. Tom bought me a Berger cookie on his way

home from school," I said. My newfound smile wobbled, then fell. "They were my favorite, and he knew that. Every week without fail, he'd save up his allowance and get me one." I brushed a few stray tears from my cheeks and pressed my face into my pillow. Childhood memories with Tom no longer made me feel happy anymore. Another fucking injustice. I was so close to sobbing or screaming uncontrollably, but Jace was here, and I couldn't.

I sensed the change in him as soon as he realized I was crying again—the opposite of what he'd set out to achieve. "Hayley." His voice, deep and low, felt like a forbidden caress. "Shit. I'm so sorry. What can I do?"

Hold me, I wanted to say. Never let go.

Instead, I breathed out, "You're doing it." This was exactly why I had to keep it together. If I fell apart, and Jace caught me, I'd never forgive myself. I'd never trust him again either. He had a girlfriend, and how he acted was important to me. Integrity mattered. Always. "Your turn. Keep distracting me. Tell me something, something nobody else knows."

"Let me think." It was eerily quiet again as he decided what secret to let me in on. I was desperate for a change in subject.

"I haven't always wanted to be a photographer," he eventually told me.

I shifted onto my stomach, peeking down at him. "Really?"

"Is that so hard to believe?"

"Yeah, a little."

Moonlight spilled in through the gap in my curtains, a sliver of dappled light in my dark bedroom. I could make out Jace's silhouette, the way his brows threaded together. Even through tears, I could see the arm that was tucked beneath his head, his makeshift pillow.

My hair tumbled over my shoulders as I leaned forward, resting *my chin on top of my hands. The position I was in allowed me to admire Jace without him knowing. He was so handsome—so easy to look at—but the depth of emotion I normally felt for him was missing. Watching my brother die had been equal to carving my heart out and handing it over to Death himself.*

"What did you want to be?" I asked, mildly intrigued.

I always liked talking to him—the real, unguarded Jace—more than my best friend's brother who might've attended all our family dinners but was so good at putting up a front and feeling out of reach.

"Growing up, I wanted to be a surgeon," he said, tone devastatingly gentle and certain. "I wanted to use my hands in a different way. I wanted to save lives. I wanted to make a difference, but I wasn't smart enough. I knew I'd never get into medicine, so I went with photography, because I was good at it, because it was safe." A sigh shuttered out of him. "I've never told anyone that. Never even admitted it out loud."

His words cycled over and over in my head. "If it's any consolation, you kind of did." I forced out the words. "You saved a life tonight. I know it's not the same, but it counts."

Jace's eyes snapped open, fixing on mine. "I can see you, you know," came his loaded reply. It was like he was daring me to look away, to be the one who broke eye contact first. Dangerous territory, my brain warned. He was slipping past my emotional walls, all my usual barricades and defenses, and I had to keep him out.

Without unlocking our gazes, I said, "I'm just trying to figure you out." After he came home from Delaware for Christmas, he was different. "I mean, I know you, duh, but I—"

"You've changed too," he admitted. "You're not the same girl I remember when I left for college."

Holding his stare burned like I'd been lit on fire, turning my mouth to ash, and I looked away. His whispered response was like a nuclear bomb, intent on reviving my dead heart, but I couldn't let it—I couldn't let him. Dealing with my grief while I was numb was hard enough.

Instinct told me it was time to shut this conversation down, so I huddled under the covers and said, "Good night, Jace."

"G'night, Hayles."

Pushing the old, intimate memory aside, I followed Jace into his apartment. Even though I'd asked him to stay here with me tonight, I needed space. Starting tomorrow, I'd put some distance between us. Focus on meeting new people and making new friends I could come to rely on. It was the only way forward from here. If we kept this up, it would completely destroy our friendship. I didn't want that. I didn't want to lose anyone else I loved.

Jace locked the door, then shrugged out of his jacket, saying nothing for seconds that felt more like minutes. Unable to take the excruciating silence any longer, I wheeled around in the hallway and opened his bedroom door, wide enough for me to slip inside. Feeling his eyes on me the entire time, I started to shut the door behind me. I hesitated when the door was only open a tiny crack, enjoying the fact that I was hidden from view.

"Jace?"

"Yeah?"

"Thank you for staying." On the cusp of raw, utter heartbreak with nothing left to lose, it made what I was about to do so much easier. "For being here."

"Of course." I heard him collapse on the couch, then the sound of him kicking off his boots.

I wasn't finished. "While I appreciate everything you've done for me, you're off the hook now," I told him, forcing my voice to remain level, unaffected. "We both know this needs to stop."

I didn't wait for a response. The door closed with a soft click behind me, and I slumped back against it, grateful for the barrier.

• • •

By the time dawn rolled around, I was already wide awake. Sunshine crowned the skyline, filtering through the window of Jace's bedroom, and I crouched down, cramming my toiletries back into my overnight bag.

The determination to have cleared out before he woke up was what had forced me to haul ass out of his bed this morning. Otherwise, I was certain I could've stayed there all day, making quick work of consuming my weight in ice cream and feeling sorry for myself.

It hadn't helped that Jace's heady scent clung heavily to his sheets, making it dangerously easy to pretend we'd spent the night wrapped up in each other. But we hadn't, and a fist tightened around my heart as I remembered last night. God, that kiss . . . and then our conversation, which had made it abundantly clear it would never happen again.

I'd bawled like a baby last night—quietly, ugly. Having nursed a broken heart before, I knew how to piece it back together, but the splintered fragments were stuck too deep in my chest. I had to put on my big-girl panties and accept that it wasn't going to stop hurting any time soon. Just like Tom's absence, I'd learn to live with it.

Hooking my bag over my shoulder, I tiptoed down the narrow hallway of Jace's apartment and checked that I hadn't disturbed him on the couch. I could still hear him snoring. *Phew.*

As I was leaving, it occurred to me that this was probably the last time I'd be here, and my insides coiled into a complicated little knot. The elevator pinged, the doors sliding open before I could second-guess what I was doing. Thankfully, it was empty. I stepped inside and halted in my tracks, drawn by my reflection in the all-surrounding mirrors.

Wincing, I saw that my dark hair had spilled out of the bun I'd secured it into last night, and unforgiving shadows had already developed under my eyes. Swinging my gaze away with a soft curse, I absentmindedly retied my hair away from my face.

Once the elevator had begun its descent, I inhaled several deep breaths. It was barely eight in the morning, yet my head hurt like someone had drilled a nail through my temple. The lobby was quiet except for the low hum of the air conditioning, and I kept my head down as I ducked out of the building.

Remembering that I was stranded here without a car, I fished around for my phone in my bag. I considered calling an Uber to take me back to campus, but it seemed stupid to stand around waiting for one when I could speed-walk it in ten minutes. Fifteen, tops.

With that thought circling around, I coasted onto the sidewalk, my shoes scuffing on the pavement.

A second later, my phone vibrated in my palm.

Maybe it was Amelia finally returning my missed call. I glanced down hopefully, but my grip loosened when I saw the caller ID.

Mom blinked on the screen.

Apart from the occasional text, I hadn't spoken to my parents since I'd moved out here a few weeks ago. Even when I was still living at home, our conversations usually consisted of small talk at best. I was honest enough with myself to admit I was mostly to blame for that.

After Tom died, everything changed. I was so consumed by his death, plagued by lingering flashbacks of the accident, that I felt alone. It didn't help that the fun-loving, laid-back parents I'd grown up with were now people who erred on the side of caution and sought to wrap me in cotton wool.

I'd already lost my brother, and I was losing them too. So, at sixteen, I'd pushed them away, hoping the distance would diminish that feeling, the dull ache behind my rib cage.

"Honey, I didn't wake you, did I?" my mom said after I'd shakily hit the Accept button.

The sound of her warm voice cut through the sadness that had invaded my core. I was silent for a moment, swallowing back a rush of unexpected emotion.

"No, I've been up for a bit." That was the understatement of the century—I'd hardly slept last night. "Is everything okay?"

There was a pause. "Your father and I were talking . . . and we think it would be best if you came home."

Shock rippled through me, and I pressed my phone closer to my ear. Maybe I hadn't heard her correctly. There was no rationale behind why she would've said something like that.

"What?" A frown pulled my brows together. "Why?"

My parents had been less than thrilled when I'd announced I was moving to Delaware, but they'd still paid for my tuition and wired me my regular allowance. They'd never once discouraged me from studying, particularly when they knew Jace attended UD too.

"We got a call from campus police, following up on a report you made yesterday," she told me, and I stiffened. It felt like liquid metal had been tipped down my spine. "They wouldn't tell us what it was about, just that they were checking over the details you'd provided them. What's going on?"

My posture, my grip on the phone—everything in me—relaxed a tiny bit. She still didn't know. Good. My mom shouldn't have had to find out from the police. I should have said something sooner. I fought the urge to tell her everything right then—even what had happened last night with Jace. It didn't surprise me that the first person I wanted to confide in about boy troubles was Mom. It had always been that way between us, before the accident. But I knew the best thing I could do was to not talk about Jace—to not think about him at all. It was time to tie it up in a neat little bow and forget about what had happened between us.

I exhaled tiredly. "I'm sorry, Mom. I just didn't want you and Dad to worry about me. It hasn't, uh, been the smoothest start this semester, but I'm okay."

I would not cry. Not on the sidewalk, not in front of the strangers who passed me by, and not over this.

"We always worry about you, honey. We want you to talk to us. Come home. Just for a couple of days. This has been going on for too long. You need to stop pushing us away and blaming yourself. We miss you and love you so much." The vulnerability in her voice startled me, tapering off at the end like she could hardly get the words out.

For the first time since Tom's death, I wasn't filled with trepidation when I considered her offer: to let them be there for me again.

And it wasn't just because I didn't have anywhere else to go.

It was because I knew I was lucky to have parents who cared too much, as opposed to not nearly enough. Perhaps they were unduly protective, but I was the last person in a position to judge how they'd coped—how they'd chosen to rebuild themselves after our family had been torn apart. I certainly wasn't the same person anymore either.

With my free hand lifting to knead some of the tension out of my neck, I murmured, "Okay, Mom. I'll come home."

ten

While being back home in Port Worth was a relief, it also meant confronting all the feelings I'd been running from. It was all too easy to remember when you were surrounded by the remnants of everything you'd been trying to forget.

The dusty piano—not played in two years—tucked away in the corner of the living room.

The empty seat at the dining table.

How visibly my parents had aged.

I'd missed them more than I ever thought I would. Despite trying to heal on my own, I was hit with the overwhelming revelation that I wanted them to hold me until I felt better.

The smell of my mom's world-class baking—the delicious aroma of cinnamon and sugar—followed me as I left the kitchen and walked down the carpeted hallway. On my way to stow my bags, I stopped at the door to my brother's bedroom. It was always closed, and I'd never been able to summon enough courage to set foot inside. Not even the morning of his funeral.

I wasn't sure how long I just stood there, working to draw enough oxygen into my lungs, but it felt like someone was tugging at an unfastened, invisible thread, and suddenly I was unraveling.

My hand grasped the brass door handle of its own accord, and then, somehow, I was walking forward, stepping inside.

I moved slowly, my heart breaking all over again as I scanned Tom's room. The bags slipped from my arm, disregarded. It was like a time capsule, preserving all memories of him. His bedroom looked the same, and it set my teeth on edge.

His wall shelves were filled with awards, ribbons, and trophies, and a copy of *The Catcher in the Rye* was still on his nightstand. He'd been reading it for school, and I noted the bookmark sticking out, only halfway through.

Tom had never gotten to finish it.

Just like he'd never finished his senior year.

I stopped in front of his desk, spotting an old framed photograph. It was a picture of the four of us from one of our family vacations to Florida. We were standing at the end of a pier, all laughing. I knew if happiness could ever be captured, it was in that image.

It had been so long since I'd heard my parents laugh.

Whirling around, I dug my palms into my eyes and sat down on Tom's narrow bed, the mattress dipping under my weight. I was hardly breathing, too consumed by the anger that welled up, surging hotly in my veins.

God, I wished my brother had never climbed into Derek's car.

Then I wouldn't feel so completely alone.

I could practically see Tom scooting next to me on the bed, spouting brotherly advice. I would have told him about Levi, and he would've done everything in his power to protect me, to make me feel safe. Then he would have threatened to take Jace's ass down for sending me mixed signals.

All the emotions I'd tried to subdue bubbled up to the surface, spilling over, and I made a loud, strangled noise. I pressed my hand over my mouth, struggling to stay quiet as my composure smashed into tiny little pieces.

When I heard the sound of footsteps approaching, I felt suffocated.

As my parents entered the room, my gaze traveled across their faces, and it was like looking in the mirror. Both of their expressions were contorted with grief and something close to hope—everything I felt.

"Are you okay, Hayley Bayley?"

It was my father who spoke first, his deep voice, and that cringe-worthy childhood nickname, reaching out to me.

Swallowing the barbed wire that had lodged in my throat, I didn't think about my response for once. "I don't know what I am anymore," I admitted, hoping my voice sounded steadier than it felt.

A couple more moments passed, and then Mom sighed. She placed a hand over her chest. "Oh, honey. You can always talk to us."

The bed shifted as my dad sat beside me, and the next thing I knew, he pulled me into his side in a one-armed embrace. "I know how hard it is, being here," he murmured, chin resting on my head. "But this is a good thing. Tom wouldn't want you cutting yourself off from our family any longer."

The guilt was even worse now, a heavy, crushing knot in my esophagus. "It was *my* fault, Dad. If we hadn't gotten into an argument at that party, if I'd gone looking for him sooner, if—"

"Stop. It wasn't your fault. You've tortured yourself long enough," he cut me off, voice stern. He hesitated a split second, then added, "So have I."

My eyes widened. My dad didn't talk much about Tom, or about the accident—not like my mom did. For a long time, he'd retreated so far inside himself that I couldn't have reached him even if I'd wanted to. He was never the same after he'd seen my brother, lifeless, trapped in that car. Knowing it was too late, that there was nothing he could do, was the same reason I was so fucked up. I realized at that moment just how similar my dad and I were—from how we'd mourned Tom to how easily we'd blamed ourselves.

"You think I don't have regrets?" He drew back to level me with a long, meaningful look. "Derek was a nice kid, sure, but he was always up to no good. I should've picked my son up. As his father, I should've . . ."

My heart thumped painfully. I bit my lip to keep from crying all over again.

"You *both* need to stop torturing yourselves," my mom spoke up, her own tears falling freely. She sat down on the other side of me, arms engulfing us both. Her fingers touched my dad's arm and squeezed. "It was an accident. And even though we will never fully understand it, I know one thing. He wouldn't have wanted his death to come between us like it has. He'd want us to heal this rift."

She was right.

Hope flickered through me, brighter than ever. Even though I'd lost my brother, and now Jace, I knew I shouldn't have doubted that I'd always have my parents to lean on. We were still a family, even with Tom's gaping absence.

"Maybe you can come back some other weekends to visit, when things at school settle down. We'd love that, wouldn't we, Andrew?"

Dad grunted his approval as he stood back up, and I swore he sneakily wiped under his eyes.

Despite being so overwhelmed, I was still able to smile and nod at my mom.

After two years, all it had taken was one honest conversation. One moment, an outpouring of emotions. *When all else fails, Hayley. Just be honest and tell them how you feel.* Dr. Jensen's words came back to me without warning, a heavy blow. I couldn't help but wonder why I'd been so afraid of taking her advice, to reconnect with my parents and bring up that fateful night. Maybe shutting them out had been a way to subconsciously punish myself. In a rush of startling clarity, I knew I'd been going about this all wrong. I needed my parents. I needed their support and love and forgiveness to heal, to move on from that night. And it was okay to want that.

"Now, tell me, why were the police calling us? I'm trying really hard here not to think about the worst-case scenario," Dad said, hands on his hips. "Is there something going on that your mom and I should know about?"

At that, my stomach lurched.

Leaning back against the pillow on Tom's bed, I stilled my racing pulse and thoughts.

It would be so easy to lie to them, to continue with this ruse that everything in my life was better now that I'd moved away, but I couldn't. I *wouldn't.* And even though I predicted the consequences of what I was about to tell them, a worse fate would greet me if I ignored the signs that I wasn't safe at UD anymore.

"Yes," I replied, squaring my shoulders. "There's something I need to tell you."

Concern flitted across their features. My dad seemed like he was about to say something, but with a glance, Mom silenced him.

Before I could change my mind, I dragged in a shallow breath and told them everything.

• • •

"I'm surprised your parents haven't placed you under house arrest yet," Amelia started, her face the very picture of disbelief. She'd been applying a thin layer of lip gloss in front of my bedroom mirror while I'd recounted the entire conversation I'd had with them. "Although I have to admit, this time, I think they have every right to be worried about you. What happened is a big fucking deal."

Confiding in my parents about everything that had occurred with Levi—the attack, reporting it to the police, and then him showing up at my dorm two weeks later—had been mostly therapeutic.

Despite their anticipated reactions, relief had still swamped me. I knew that the only way I could face this was head-on, and I wanted them to support my decision.

It wasn't until they'd insisted that I defer from UD and move back to Maryland that I'd almost regretted telling them.

My parents had been wanting me to let them in for years, to share my difficulties with them—Tom had always been my closest confidant. Yet, only hours after I'd shown up yesterday, they'd showcased the reason why it was easier to just keep things hidden.

But my parents were just trying to protect me. I kept telling myself that and tried to see it from their perspective.

"I think I spent over an hour just convincing them to let me stay at UD." I laughed in spite of everything. "The only way I got them to agree was if I moved back here again. I'm going to take my classes online next semester."

Done pouting in the mirror, Amelia spun around and slanted me a sympathetic look. "That's not much of a choice, is it?"

"Nope." Shifting on my double bed, I tucked my knees to my chest. "But there's no way I'm postponing my studies, Millie. It's my only ticket out of this place."

"Not necessarily. You always have two options." She pulled her blond hair into a loose ponytail. "I mean, I'm still patiently waiting for some hot, rich bachelor to whisk me away on his boat. Why do you think I work full-time at a jewelry store?"

"Good luck with that." I snorted. "Maybe you can ask him if he has a twin brother."

She lowered herself onto the bed beside me, nudging me with her elbow. "See, that's the spirit. Keep looking at the glass as half-full, not half-empty. This whole situation isn't so bad. It could be worse."

"How? Besides having to commute to Delaware, I've gone from tasting pure freedom to haggling for my curfew to be pushed back an extra hour." I groaned, lying back to stare up at the ceiling. My heart spasmed in my rib cage when I detected the faint outlines of the glow-in-the-dark star stickers Tom and I had been a little heavy-handed with in elementary school. My voice barely a whisper, I added, "This is exactly why I wanted to leave."

"Would you rather I say that you're right? That this *does* suck donkey balls?" When I gave her my best withering glare, a small smile tugged at the corners of her mouth. "That's what I thought. Look, Hayley, just remember, this is only temporary. I'm sure there'll be an update on the investigation soon. Better yet, that little freak will be held accountable."

"I'm not holding my breath." My attention shifted to my window, and I watched as the wispy clouds drifted in the sky. I imagined them absorbing all my worries, then carrying them away. "I don't know, I just have this feeling they won't have enough on Levi to charge him."

Her response was immediate. "Have you filed for a restraining order?"

That was the question I didn't really want to think about. When I returned to Delaware, the first thing I planned to do was march myself down to the courthouse, but it was still a big, intimidating step. A heavy feeling settled over me again, and I buried my face in my pillow.

"Not yet," I mumbled. "But I will. As much as I love you for what you're trying to do, I want to forget about it—about all of this—at least for today. Can we please talk about something else?"

I tried to dispel the horrible dread and disappointment that swirled inside me, particularly when I thought about how I was going to be driving to UD at the crack of dawn, starting tomorrow, for all four of my classes.

I'd wanted to stay home for the entire week, but when my professors had attached a massive amount of coursework in an email, explaining that I'd have to make it all up in my absence, I'd reassessed the idea. There was no way I could afford to miss any more classes. This early in the semester, I didn't want to fall behind or spend the rest of it trying to catch up.

Amelia frowned. She had that troubled look in her gray eyes that I'd gotten so used to seeing over the last two years. "Fine, I'll drop it, but I swear to God, you better not retreat into your shell or something. I'd never know what to do if you did that to me," she went on, lips thinning with concern. "Just promise, whatever happens, you won't freeze me out."

"I promise. You should know by now that'll never happen. Normally, I'd be falling apart with everything that's been going on, but I'm not. I'm okay." When Amelia shot me a disbelieving look, I was quick to add, "Really. I am."

A shadow of worry passed across her features, but it was so fleeting I wondered if I was seeing things. "All right." She jumped to her feet, heading straight for my wardrobe. "So, does this mean we can go back to talking about my birthday now?"

"Only if you stop squirming like you're in pain whenever we do. Just ask me whatever it is you want to ask me."

"Geez. I almost forgot how blunt you could be," she commented and stopped flicking through what few items of clothing I'd left behind when I'd moved into my dorm room last month.

"Only with you."

"Well, as you know, my party is next weekend. I can't imagine how awkward it'll be for you to see my brother so soon"—she paused, grimacing—"but you're going to come, right? You're not going to bail?"

Tiny hairs on the back of my neck prickled at the mention of Jace.

After returning home, one of the first things I'd done was fill Amelia in. I felt bad, always changing the dynamic between us. We were so far now from the trio who'd grown up together. Probably because we hadn't always been a trio. Long before Tom had died, we'd been an inseparable group of four. Up until high school, it had been that way. First, the boys stopped spending as much time with us. Jace and Tom were only one year apart in age, so Amelia and I had lagged behind. Then they stopped spending as much time with one another. Nothing happened. They just grew up, drifted apart. We weren't all those same carefree children anymore. But my friendship with Amelia hadn't wavered once in those nine years—strong and steady.

And then there was the minor detail of me falling for Jace along the way. It was that simple and that complicated.

I'd had no choice but to disclose that Jace had kissed me. It was the catalyst that had prompted our big, awkward confrontation. Without it, none of it made sense.

Amelia had given me the standard scrunched-up face of disgust as I'd brought her up to speed on everything. I'd spared her the intimate details of our hot, and insanely stupid, kiss the other night, of course, but I'd told her what she needed to know: Jace and I were over before we'd even begun.

And even though it felt like someone had dropped my heart into a food processor, I knew the solution wasn't to completely avoid him—whether that was at school or at Amelia's birthday party. It would only make this process harder, more dragged out.

"Millie, you're my best friend. Nothing could stop me from going, not even having to see Jace," I said. "Plus, my life feels like it's about to get even more complicated. I could use some fun."

Amelia grinned, pausing in my doorway. "I know. I haven't wanted to say anything, but you've kind of been killing my vibe lately."

"Oh, hardy har har." I threw the pillow at her retreating form.

A tug of warmth pulled at my chest as her laughter echoed down the hallway. "See you after my shift," she called out.

Maybe moving back home next semester wouldn't be the worst thing in the world.

eleven

Every muscle in my body constricted when I entered the art studio the next day. My gaze met Jace's, and I was disappointed to find a schooled lack of expression on his striking face.

I sucked in a soft breath and tried to calm down.

It didn't help that I was already beyond tense, having come straight from the courthouse. That probably hadn't been the smartest move. Filing for a restraining order? Yes. But coming to class immediately afterward? Not so much.

I needed caffeine, to call my best friend, and to decompress. But that would have made me late for class, and I'd missed too many already.

Amelia had stayed with me on the phone the entire time I'd sat out in the parking lot of the courthouse, trying to work up the nerve. I didn't let myself look at the large, Romanesque building for too long, or focus on the way the surrounding evergreen trees had seemed to sway ominously. Three stories high, the courthouse towered over all the other buildings in town, with large pillars in front. Etched in stone at the top of the courthouse was a motto: JUSTICE AND TRUTH WILL ALWAYS PREVAIL.

Normally, I wasn't much for prayer, but I hoped the big guy upstairs made good on that. I'd officially filed for a restraining order against Levi. And it had taken a serious amount of willpower to not run back and grab the papers after I'd exited the clerk's office, fearing all I'd done was make everything worse. Under no conditions could Levi approach me, or set foot in Thompson again. That was considered my residential property.

If I could get through that experience, I told myself I could get through sharing a class with the guy who'd rejected me not once but twice. I straightened my shoulders, putting on my brave face.

Jace was lounging behind the closest workbench to the door, sitting with Piper and Owen, and even though he only had on a navy sweater over jeans, he still managed to look like he was modeling for an ad in *GQ*.

I knew that the next time I saw him was going to be difficult, but this was hitting me way harder than I'd expected. Seeing him now, it was so much easier to remember the way it had felt to be in his arms, the soft texture of his hair beneath my fingers. My lips tingled as I thought about the kiss for the umpteenth time. And when I noticed Jace was clean-shaven, I couldn't help but mourn the loss of his stubble, recalling how good it had felt grazing my—

I winced internally.

Nope. Not going there.

Jace's gaze remained laser-focused on me, those smoky, blue-gray eyes boring into mine. There was an unmistakable flicker of hope in them when he saw me take note of the empty seat beside him.

My skin flushed under his intense stare, but I forced myself to walk past him, offering him a small nod of acknowledgment because I wasn't a total bitch.

All the other chairs were taken, aside from one at the very front of the room next to a girl with curly black hair. Wishing I'd stayed home again today, or that I could suddenly develop the superpower to turn invisible, I stopped at the front workbench and wedged my tote bag in between the table leg and the chair.

"Hi, I'm Hayley." I smiled down at the dark-haired girl, who was busily flicking through her sketchbook. "Can I sit here?"

"Oh, hey." She tipped her head back to look up at me, and her eyes were the coolest color I'd ever seen. They were amber with darker flecks of gold near her pupils. "Sure thing. I enrolled late in this course, so you're actually saving me from looking incredibly pathetic and alone right now."

I laughed as I slipped into the spot beside her, tugging out my books and a pen. I was so ready for this class to be over—my motivation for today was nonexistent—but Professor Zimmerman was still setting up his briefcase, notes sprawled out in a disorganized heap.

"My name's Eden, by the way," she told me, booting up her laptop. Then she spun on me. "Listen, I'm going to do something totally embarrassing now, so promise me you won't judge. I've read that sharing things about yourself is a good way to break the ice. I mean, that sounds legit, right? I thought maybe you'd like to know three very interesting facts about Eden."

Okay, I officially like this girl.

Anyone who spoke about themselves in the third person was automatically considered a friend.

"Where were you when we had our orientation session?" I

smirked. "You would've loved all the awkward 'turn to your partner and get to know them' activities."

"Oooh." Eden's eyebrows shot up. "That's like dirty talk to me."

Grinning involuntarily, I prompted her, "So, tell me, what are these very interesting facts about Eden? I'm dying to know."

"Well, obviously, I'm also a freshman," she started rambling. "I have an unhealthy addiction to painting my nails. Don't ask me why. Oh, and don't be frightened by the life-size Ryan Gosling pillow in my dorm room if you ever come hang out. You can't say I didn't warn you."

"Oh my God, you can get one of those?" I gasped. "Why am I only hearing about this now?"

While Eden and I sat together throughout the class—snickering when Professor Zimmerman couldn't find certain handout sheets or exchanging sidelong glances when he lost his train of thought as he preached about the principles of design—I forgot all about Levi and the restraining order, which had been at the forefront of my mind all morning. It was the longest I had gone without thinking about Jace too. I'd even quelled the urge to turn around in my chair to see if the pair of eyes I felt searing into the back of my head belonged to him.

Suffice to say, Eden was heaven-sent.

Now that I was giving myself some space and time to move on from Jace, I'd lost my connection to Piper and Owen—the only other people I'd gotten to know at UD. I'd reverted to being friendless again, almost a month into the first semester. Meeting Eden, knowing someone else in this class, caused a wave of gratitude and relief to rise. That feeling intensified when we compared schedules and discovered we also had Technical Drawing together.

The minute class ended, I said goodbye to her and raced from the art studio like I was trying to outrun a fire.

Tightening my grip on the strap of my bag, I threaded my way through the students who had gathered outside the room, waiting for their next class.

Cutting across the quad, I headed back toward east campus. In my periphery, I noticed a dark-haired, hooded figure with rolled-up sleeves and arm tattoos falling into step beside me—a little too close—and I picked up my pace.

I'd been on edge all morning, convinced Levi had seen me entering or leaving the courthouse. It made sense he would confront me again.

His footsteps grew closer, and I felt my throat tighten as I got ready to scream. His shoulder jostled mine as a crowd of students overtook us, and I swore he was about to break his usual MO by grabbing me in broad daylight, somewhere so public. Maybe he'd push me to the ground, like he'd probably done to poor Jenna. Panicking, I kept my head down, hoping if I ignored Levi's presence, he'd evaporate like a ghost. But he didn't. He matched me, stride for stride. Anxiety had me in a stranglehold.

As I neared the cobblestoned path that led to the library, I heard a voice call, "Hey, Chris! Over here, man. What took you so long?"

Breathless, I watched as the dark-haired guy to my right, who upon closer inspection, looked nothing like Levi, glanced up from his phone and waved to his friend. Because I'd stopped walking, pulling back in fear, he practically slammed into my side as he changed his trajectory.

"Shit, sorry. Didn't see you there," he apologized, his brown eyes sliding toward me and then moving away. He kept walking, indifferent.

It wasn't Levi.

It had never been.

Exhaling, I glanced over my shoulder, scanning my surroundings. Preoccupied people milled all around. I wasn't drawing attention to myself. I wasn't in danger. No one was following me. It was just nerves, paranoia. Dark-haired guys with tattoos weren't exactly a rare species at Delaware, and I suddenly felt silly.

I'd completely come to a standstill, fighting to regain my composure, which allowed Jace to catch up to me. Had he noticed my freak-out?

I was happy he'd come after me, that he wasn't just going to ignore me for the rest of the semester, but that didn't mean I was over what had happened between us last week. And it certainly didn't outweigh the fact that I was living in perpetual fear again.

"You okay?" he asked, frowning. "What's gotten into you? Why'd you take off so fast?"

"I thought I—" Shaking my head, I stopped short. Nothing had happened. Levi hadn't been there. It was just my imagination, playing tricks on me. "I have another class."

My answer seemed to mollify him. "We need to talk," he said, conviction ringing clear in his voice.

Our last conversation replayed in my mind and that familiar ache spread through me. Being alone with Jace and rehashing everything we'd said that night was something I'd hoped to avoid until Amelia's birthday party.

"Okay." I dragged my eyes up to his, my heart rate slowly returning to normal. "I'm listening."

"I've been thinking a lot about everything you said." He took a tentative step closer, expression serious. "I don't think one slip-up should ruin or change our friendship. We can get past this. We always do."

A slip-up? Was that what we were calling it?

It made it sound like he'd tripped and fallen onto my lips, accidentally kissing me senseless. That might've happened in some of my favorite K-dramas, but in reality, I wasn't prepared to accept that.

It took a bit for my tongue to form the words. "I can't. I can't keep doing this. Being friends with you is too hard." *Being friends with you isn't enough.*

Jace readjusted the messenger bag slung over his shoulder and looked away, jaw tight. When his gaze finally crawled back to mine, he said, "So that's it, then? There's nothing I can say that will change your mind?"

There was.

A simple *I think I'm in love with you, Hayley. I can't believe I haven't been able to see who was standing right in front of me all along* would change everything, but I kept that crap to myself.

"No," I answered. Going back on everything I'd said wouldn't only be humiliating, it would be a mistake. "I think we still need to give each other space. See you later."

Ignoring the guilt that scraped at me, I pushed past him, making it all of two steps before he caught my arm.

"C'mon, Hayles," he pleaded. His touch seared through the thin material of my cardigan, sending warmth right into my veins. "Don't do this. Under normal circumstances, I'd leave you alone, but I can't right now. I'm worried about you. I never wanted—"

"That's the point, though," I interjected. "You and I, we don't want the same things. At first, I thought you might come around.

I mean, you'd been a relationship kind of guy before, but you and Zoe broke up ages ago, and I kept waiting. I'm done waiting, Jace."

He remained silent, his throat dipping as he swallowed.

"We've known each other for so much of our lives," I continued. "You will always mean something to me. Tom died, and you were there. Maybe you thought you had to replace him, maybe that's all I am to you—a pity project—but that's never been what I wanted. I always tried to be there for you when you were hurting. There was even a time I confided in you more than anyone, more than Amelia, and you've had so many chances to do the same, to let me in. But you didn't. You don't."

Despite his drawn-out silence, Jace didn't run in the other direction, which made this even harder. It was like he always had one foot in, one foot somewhere else.

His fingers slid down my arm, curling around mine, and I concentrated on not reacting. "Yes, you were there for me when my relationship with Zoe ended, but to be fair, I wasn't going to put meaningless shit on you when you were barely keeping your own head above water. Tom was gone, and we both know you weren't coping."

I winced. My grief for my brother was always being dragged to the surface, and I didn't want to talk about it—*think* about it—for just *one* day.

"I don't talk about Zoe because I'm over her, and I have been for a very long time." Jace's chest rose with a heavy breath. "But the main reason I don't talk about it is because then I'd have to admit to myself, to everyone, that my relationship with her didn't fail just because we were miserable, it failed because I was with the wrong person."

"The wrong person?" I repeated. I needed to make sure I wasn't imagining what was happening here, in the same way I'd imagined Levi walking next to me less than five minutes ago.

"I stayed with Zoe for a lot longer than I should've." The vulnerability he was radiating was slightly unsettling. He'd obviously been doing some major soul-searching since the last time we'd seen each other.

"I appreciate you fighting for our friendship, I really do, but I'm still upset and confused. I don't understand why you're constantly pushing me away," I told him, feeling the familiar sting in my nose, the twinge inside my rib cage. "I just don't think this is going to work. We don't want the same things."

Fear shimmered across his face. For once, Jace was an open book, and I was devouring every page, every sentence, he was letting me read. "That's not true. I may not be good at communicating how I feel, but I'm trying. Surely, you know, this isn't friendship, Hayles. We haven't been just friends for years," he confirmed, voice gruff. His entire focus was on our entwined hands, and I was suddenly aware of what we must've looked like, standing in front of the ivy-covered building, talking honestly about our feelings. Something Dr. Jensen had only managed to get us to do twice—both times in her office. Our therapist would be so proud. Even though this wasn't the declaration of love I'd been holding out for, Jace was right. He *was* trying. This was more than he'd ever given me. "I know I don't deserve you, but you're too important to me to risk losing. Give me more time. Please."

When I didn't shoot him down immediately, Jace pressed his lips together, tempering a smile. Those two gorgeous dimples appeared, forever taunting me. "Well, I better let you get to your next class." He dropped my hand and took a step back. "I just . . . I had to tell you that. It was what I should've said after that night, when you had the courage to say how you felt. Or outside my apartment last week, after I kissed you. I'm sorry it's taking me so long. I'm sorry I keep pushing you away. Most of all, I'm sorry I didn't choose what I already felt back then over what I had with Zoe. I'll always regret it, but I wasn't ready. And I can't exactly apologize for that, Hayles."

I blinked, startled by his heated confession.

Jace didn't wait for a reply. "See you around," he murmured, stuffing his hands into his pockets as he walked away.

The warmth in my heart lingered for a long time after he left, because it felt like I was finally getting a peek into the life, a future, I'd always wanted for myself.

twelve

"She's here! My best friend's finally here!" Amelia shouted, her singsong voice carrying over the party, and before I knew what was happening, she was wrapping me in a body-crushing hug.

It was the weekend after Halloween, and her house was packed like she'd posted the invite to her socials or just everyone she knew in Port Worth. People were everywhere, gyrating on the makeshift dance floor, making out on the couches, and gathering around the pool table that was in the corner. Club music blared from the in-wall speakers, causing the floorboards to reverberate beneath my heeled boots.

Amelia's tight embrace was practically cutting off my oxygen supply, but she continued to cling to me, unfazed. She hugged me like we'd been apart for years, not hours—I'd been over earlier this afternoon, helping her set up.

"Struggling to breathe over here," I wheezed.

She mumbled something incoherent and giggled.

Pulling out of her viselike embrace, I registered the silver tiara, sitting slightly lopsided on top of her head, and the empty champagne flute glued to her hand. Her simple black dress was riding dangerously high, and those gray eyes were hazy and unfocused when they met my own. It took me all of three seconds to conclude that the birthday girl was already drunk, and my smile inched wider.

"You're late," she whined, and her words were slurred. "You were supposed to be here over an hour ago. I had to start without you."

"I can see that." I snickered. There were dozens of bottles of alcohol open on the kitchen counter, next to various mixers and discarded red plastic cups.

"Jace was looking for you earlier," Amelia informed me.

My heart tugged in two different directions. I'd spent the whole day caught between being thrilled and nervous at the thought of seeing him again.

Bumping into Jace around campus, sneaking glances at him in class over the last week, had proven difficult. After our last conversation, it'd taken a lot of self-control to not fling myself at him or ask that he share more of his feelings with me every chance I got.

Trying to be the picture of perfect calm, I straightened and made sure my tone was devoid of any emotion. "I need a drink." Then quickly clarified, "A nonalcoholic drink. Sorry, Millie. Levi's party was the first and last time."

Just saying his name out loud had my stomach sinking lower than the floor. Even though I'd taken out a restraining order, I still felt like I couldn't let my guard down.

"Don't apologize, I get it." She winked, linking arms with me.

"You're not here to get drunk; you're here to celebrate and have fun. There's a difference."

I didn't object as she began steering me toward the kitchen. Navigating our way through the throng of sweaty bodies, I noticed several guys checking me out with forthright interest. I hated the twinge of disappointment I felt when I realized that none of them were Jace, and then I wanted to kick myself for drawing comparisons between him and other guys. The last thing I wanted to do was obsess over him like a lovesick puppy tonight, but it was better than the alternative—obsessing over Levi and his whereabouts. I knew he was the only person who had the potential to destroy my happiness and this new life I was trying so hard to create for myself.

Squeezing past a group who were in the middle of an intense round of Never Have I Ever, we sidled up to the kitchen bench.

Amelia stabilized her weight by leaning against the granite countertop, grinning. "Take your pick. We have Coke, sweet tea, or my personal favorite"—she wiggled her eyebrows—"root beer."

Not only was she not pressuring me to drink, but she was also willing to make light of the fact that I wasn't going to be catching up to her drunk ass tonight. Another reminder that she was the best friend I'd ever have.

"Root beer it is," I replied without a beat of hesitation, reaching for an unopened can.

Feigning party spirit, I popped the tab and took a long swig, the sweet, carbonated liquid burning my throat. It beat the hell out of regular beer, that was for sure, and I felt totally proud of myself. It was a win-win in my books.

Amelia's light-colored hair brushed her shoulders as she leaned closer and said in my ear, "We're going to go dance in a sec. But before we do, I want you to come with me, 'kay?"

"*Okaaay.* Now I'm curious."

She tugged me back into the living room, and I was immediately hit with the smell of sweat, alcohol, and cheap cologne.

There was loud chatter, competing with the volume of the thumping music and raucous calls of encouragement from the spectators who swarmed around the game of pool. I skimmed the crowd, wanting to know where Jace was. I still hadn't seen him yet, and despite reminding myself that I wasn't here for him for the five millionth time, I wondered if he was going to spend the entire night dodging me.

Amelia's voice filtered through my thoughts when she hissed, "Also, why didn't you tell me you'd met Owen? That guy is so *fiiiine.*"

I swallowed a laugh or a choking sound. It was hard to tell the difference as the music had scaled to lethal decibels.

Then we were approaching Piper and Owen, who were standing near the doorway that led out to the Hammonds' wraparound porch, and a niggle of guilt ensnared me. I hadn't noticed they were here.

Piper looked up and spotted us, smiling broadly. "Hayley! It's so good to see you," she greeted, offering me a quick hug.

Owen slid his baseball cap around backward, and his gaze smoldered as he stared down at my best friend. "Amelia. Hey. Thanks for saying yes when Jace asked if he could bring some friends along."

I bit down on my lip, unable to hide my amusement as I watched Amelia's entire body flush.

"It's no problem. The more the merrier." She waved a dismissive hand, then her attention returned to Piper. "She's here, as promised. Did you want to—"

"Right, of course. I was hoping to talk to you about something, Hayley," Piper said, before flicking an unsure glance up at Owen. "Actually, we both were."

"Is this about Jace?" I asked, my apprehension heightening. He was the biggest thing we had common. "Because if it is, I don't know if I want to hear it."

Amelia let out a big sigh. "I tried telling you guys. This isn't her problem."

Scratch that. The apprehension I'd felt was nothing compared to the huge, icy ball of fear that was now forming.

"Why? What is it? I'm not happy about how things are between Jace and me right now, so after this, can we please just—"

"That's the thing, neither is he," Owen ground out. "He's skipping classes. He was supposed to present his portfolio, and when Professor Martinez threatened to fail him, he just walked out."

My mouth fell open, but I couldn't make a sound.

"I know Jace. He hasn't worked this hard just for his GPA to take a hit now. Not only that, he isn't returning our calls. I didn't think he'd even show tonight," Owen continued, undeterred by my stunned silence. "Whatever happened, whatever he's working through, it's taking a serious toll on him. Don't get me wrong. I'm not saying he's your responsibility, but maybe you could talk to him? He isn't listening to any of us. I'm worried. We both are."

I didn't know how the heck to interpret any of that. Last week, Jace and I had spoke outside of the library and it hadn't gone that badly. It didn't make sense.

"We did talk. After class," I revealed. "Are things great between us? Not really. But they've been worse. It doesn't sound like this is about me."

Owen's blond eyebrows drew together. He didn't respond.

"I don't understand." The confusion in Piper's voice spoke for itself.

Jace iced people out sometimes. I knew that. But this was a wake-up call that it truly wasn't a reflection on me. I never should've listened to the awful voice in my head that whispered I wasn't trustworthy or good enough. He was shutting everyone else out too.

I shifted my weight. "Where is he? Have you seen him tonight?"

"Last I saw, my brother was up in his room," Amelia told me, but concern creased her features. "Should you really be the one to go looking for him?"

"Yeah, it's okay. I'll talk to him."

At the same time, Owen said, "It has to be her."

Choosing not to read too much into that, I left them all standing there and went in search of Jace. I did a quick scan of the living room—just in case he'd ventured downstairs—and stopped in my tracks when I spotted him, talking to a group of people I vaguely recognized from high school and nursing a bottle of beer.

He was so tall and broad-shouldered; it was never hard to pick him out of a crowd. He was wearing Doc Martens, dark jeans that hugged his legs, and a black sweater that stretched across his chest. The urge to slip it on and breathe in his scent was strong, which reminded me that I still hadn't returned the pullover he'd lent me. Most nights, I wore it to bed, especially when I was missing him or worrying the nightmares might come back.

I nodded at a couple of people, who smiled and waved at me as I walked over to him. Someone must have been in the middle of changing playlists, because there was a rare break in the music that had been blaring from the speaker system.

Jace heard me approaching, and he turned around, shifting his attention to me. His conversation with Leslie—a girl who'd been in Tom's year in high school—skidded to a halt.

"Hey," I greeted them.

"Hey," Jace returned easily. He seemed okay. Not the train wreck Owen had previously described. It might have had something to do with the fact that I was pretty sure he was half-drunk. I could feel his eyes on me, sliding down my body for a millisecond. "Nice boots."

"Thanks." Our gazes collided beneath the dim lights, and I felt every hair on my arms stand on end.

"No way." Leslie shook her head in disbelief. She was wearing a pink bralette and a skimpy pair of shorts. I wouldn't have gone to sleep wearing so little clothing, let alone ventured out in public. But she was able to rock that outfit in a way I never could. "Jace and I were just talking about you, weren't we? Gosh, I feel like I haven't seen you in forever. How long has it been?"

My smile fell a little. "Two and a half years," I answered, referring to Tom's funeral. That was the last time I'd seen a lot of the people who'd been in his social circle. It wasn't like he and Leslie were good friends. After his classmates graduated high school, they'd moved on. I understood that was how grief and loss worked. Most people eventually forgot. It was nice to see Leslie now, but the sadness was still there, lingering beneath it all, because seeing someone from my brother's past reminded me that he didn't get to grow older. He didn't get to live a life beyond high school. That was something all the other seniors in Tom's year had been able to experience—aside from Derek.

As I thought back to that night, my vision tunneled like I had blinkers on. Taking a breath, I glanced up at Jace and tried incredibly hard to focus on the guy beside me and not on the sharp needle that pricked at my chest.

Jace must've sensed it, because before the panic could completely set in, his hand rested on my lower back. It was a comforting, warm pressure, radiating through the thin material of my dress. It helped me reach for calm.

"I hope you know I never spread those rumors, Hayley," Leslie said, sounding a little despairing, and dread crept in. "I heard them, and God, they were just cruel. I don't think Tom was responsible for killing that family. That might've been other people's opinion, but it wasn't mine."

Her words were an echo of everything I'd had to endure. The main reason I'd been so desperate to escape our small town—and most of its people. I knew the devastating things that were whispered about Tom all too well. I'd spent so long trying to defend my brother, then eventually, tuning them out.

"Leslie, it may have been two years, but it's always too soon to say shit like that," Jace was quick to reply, his voice coming out low and harsh. "What the fuck?"

She blanched. "Oh my God, I'm sorry! I've had way too much to drink tonight, and I didn't mean—I was just trying to—"

"You think Hayley needs reminding?" A new voice chimed in, one that I didn't recognize, and my insides hollowed sickeningly. That question triggered another wave of anxiety. "Nah. She knows. Those boys were driving drunk. They killed innocent people. I can think of another word for them. It's not about having an opinion. It's the cold, hard truth."

"Don't speak ill of the dead, jerk," a red-haired girl who wasn't Piper snapped.

A dull roaring sound filled my ears, drowning out the noises of the party. For a long moment, I couldn't move at all. Everywhere I went, the accident seemed to follow. Strangers were listening, weighing in on the circumstances surrounding Tom's death again, and it was just too much. I couldn't breathe, and I started to edge away, needing to disengage from this situation. I tried to ignore the emotion that clawed its way up my throat, suffocating me. I thought I'd made progress, that I was finally doing better, but everything was happening at a dizzying speed.

I took another step back and someone knocked into me, elbowing me in the side, and it sent the liquid in my can spilling all down my dress. I gasped as cold root beer soaked me, but I barely caught the muttered apology. Besides, I was too focused on trying not to have a visible breakdown.

Cradling my spilled drink, I turned to Jace, and he grimaced. His face reflected myriad pained emotions. He knew exactly where my head was at, what I was going through. I knew the accident still haunted him sometimes, but it was different for me. It always had been.

"Hayles, wait up." He followed me, swearing softly under his breath.

"You should be ashamed of yourselves," Amelia scolded, but I was already leaving them all in my proverbial dust. "What are you still doing here? Get the fuck out! You're not welcome anymore."

I didn't stick around to see how the rest of it played out. I just wanted to be left the hell alone.

Stumbling down the hallway, I shoved my way through the crowd, walking toward the front door. The thick air and the faint smell of cigarette smoke was nauseating. I needed to get out of here. Right now. Before I did something embarrassing, like cry in public over it.

Reaching for the front door, I shot outside, a chill rolling over me. The temperature felt like it had dropped by about ten degrees, and I shivered in my damp dress, but I didn't turn back. Not even when I heard Amelia and Jace calling after me.

I knew the minute I stopped running, I'd break.

• • •

It was a quarter past two in the morning when my phone chimed on my nightstand, but I wasn't asleep. Slowly blinking my eyes clear, I peeked at the lit-up screen.

It was another text from Amelia: *I'm so sorry, Hayley.*

She'd left my house not that long ago, and yet she'd already texted me twice, apologizing. I'd lost count of how many times she'd told me she was sorry in such a short amount of time.

I shook my head, smiling faintly. *Don't be. I'm the one who's sorry. I hope I didn't ruin your birthday*, I typed back.

A few seconds later, her reply popped up. *No way! Spending quality time with my bestie? Best birthday ever!*

Relief poured through me.

Shortly after I'd driven home, Piper and Amelia had come over to check on me under the guise that her party had turned into an out-of-control rager. Honestly, I think everyone had cleared out not long after I'd left. When it became apparent that Amelia wasn't planning on leaving my house, and Piper was her ride, the three of us had settled on watching a movie together. It was so nice to just hang out with them and raid my pantry for snacks, to be reminded again that I had such incredible friends.

It had been so kind of Piper to drive my best friend over. She clearly knew that Amelia was the most important person in my life—her brother a very close second.

Rolling over, I buried my face back in the pillow and expelled a quiet groan. I needed a distraction, something to pull me from my bleak thoughts.

For the last hour, my brain had been whirring relentlessly and replaying the same scene of Jace's hand, landing on my lower back. The heat and certainty in his touch. Then what Leslie had said, dumping a bucket of ice over the fuzzy feelings I'd felt. The memory of everyone watching me, the same morbidly curious look on all their faces, had my stomach churning.

Fumbling around in the darkness, I switched on my lamp. Light flooded my room, and my eyes took a minute to adjust. Needing to focus on something else, I crawled off the bed and over to my desk, reaching for my laptop. I still had the season finale of *Yellowstone* to—

Creeeak.

Shit. It was the typical, creepy opening-door sound, and I bristled.

Except, in this case, that was impossible, because my bedroom door was unmistakably shut.

Creeeak.

The noise came again, and I jumped about five feet high. Obviously, my house was haunted, or I was hearing things. Either way, both outlooks were equally concerning.

Out of the corner of my eye, I noticed my European-style windows scraping open farther in the wind, which was currently rattling the house. Frowning, I stepped closer and inspected the latch.

"I swore I closed you before I left," I whispered to myself.

Carefully, I placed my palms on the windowsill and peered out into the night. The seasonably cool breeze knotted my hair as I scanned my front yard. The dense foliage surrounding my house stirred, the tall magnolia tree swaying, but other than that, there were no other signs of movement.

It wasn't until I was about to draw back from the window that I heard heavy footfalls and the crunching of dry leaves.

My pulse jackknifed.

There was someone lurking outside my bedroom.

How the hell could I fall asleep now?

My phone vibrated on my nightstand again, but this time, it droned on for longer. When I realized it was a call, not another text from Amelia, I slammed the windows together, flicked the latch, and dove for it before it went to voice mail. At that moment, I didn't care who it was, just as long as there was someone else on the other line to prevent me from completely freaking out.

"Hello?" I inhaled sharply, not even thinking to check the caller ID beforehand.

"It's me. I wasn't sure you'd answer." Jace's deep voice rumbled through me. I couldn't express the relief I felt, or the way my heart squeezed. "I thought maybe you'd be asleep. I'm, like, five houses away."

My breathing faltered. "You're on my street? Are you walking over? Have you seen anyone around?"

"Whoa. What's with all the questions? Are you okay?" His tone was low, strained. "And yeah, I'm walking over. There's no way I'm driving anywhere tonight. I'm tanked."

"No, I'm not okay," I responded. "My window blew open, even though I remember shutting it, and I heard someone outside my bedroom. I think—"

"Hey, slow down. It's okay. I'm here. Can you let me in?"

"Uh-huh," I spoke quietly as I tiptoed out of my bedroom. Even though my parents were out of town for the weekend—like his—I needed to keep a low profile, particularly if someone thought my garden made for the perfect hiding place.

As I crept out of my room, the moonlight filtered through the skylight above, illuminating the foyer and providing just enough light for me to reach the front door without tripping over or bumping into anything.

Steeling myself, I unlocked it for him.

Jace was standing on my porch, and I couldn't resist studying his profile, the flutter in my stomach amplifying. One side of his lips curled up when he turned to face me.

"Hi," he exhaled.

I pulled my phone away from my ear, disconnecting the call. "Hi," I said, keeping my voice neutral.

"I couldn't see anyone outside, Hayles."

Unable to shake the feeling that I was being watched, paranoia practically crawled over my skin. "Are you sure?"

"I'm positive. If there was someone else here, they're long gone now."

Hearing those words sent a small wave of relief rippling through me and eased some of the tension in my neck. I murmured thanks and opened the door a little wider.

We stared at one another, the air between us growing thick.

Jace's eyes darkened as they raked over my face, my chest, my bare legs, and then back up to linger on the lettering of my sleep shirt, which read: HOTTER THAN HELL.

His grin was spreading.

It wasn't until I followed his gaze down that I realized he probably wasn't even reading the printed text. At all.

My nipples had pebbled in the cold, pressing against the thin material, which pretty much hid nothing. And aside from that old T-shirt, all I had on was a pair of cotton sleep shorts.

A shiver ran up my spine, reacting to the heated way he was looking at me. My body felt like it had been scorched, dangled above an open flame.

Folding my arms across my chest, I asked, "Why are you here, Jace?"

"Because apparently I can't stay away from you."

Holy crap.

Just hearing that set the butterflies off, and they swarmed my stomach.

"You weren't answering any of my texts, and I was worried about you. The usual." He leaned in as he said it, and the faint smell of alcohol clung to him. His pupils were dilated, almost covering the blue-gray of his irises. He might have been able to speak coherently, but I could tell he was drunk. "Can I come in?"

Wordlessly, I stepped aside, praying this wouldn't be added to the pile of Hayley's Dumb Decisions.

He followed me inside, stumbling as he struggled to remove his boots. He tucked them beside the entrance, and I locked the door behind us. Even though I automatically felt safer in Jace's presence, I double-checked that it was definitely locked. Then I gestured for him to follow me, our footsteps silent as we padded into my carpeted bedroom.

I was busy trying not to listen to the inner voice that was screaming at me, *Jace freaking Hammond is in your bedroom again!* If I gave in to that—the knowledge that the unattainable guy I'd fantasized about for the last five years was here this late at night because he just "couldn't stay away from me"—it would've been all too easy to lose this "logical, cool-headed" vibe I was trying to exude.

Walking across my room, I opted to stand over by my bookshelves, aiming to put as much distance between us as possible. Being close to Jace only made my senses spiral, clouding rational thought—undoubtedly the worst thing that could happen right now.

"Do you have to be all the way over there?" He sighed, thrusting a hand through his hair.

"Yep. Here's good."

Jace sat down on the edge of my bed, bowing his head as if bone-weary. There was a beat of silence as he sifted through what I guessed were some seriously heavy thoughts. When he glanced up at me through thick lashes, my knees felt strangely weak as I stood there. It was as if the mask he wore was finally slipping. His openness was staggering, and I knew at that very moment, Jace had dismantled those walls that always snapped back up whenever I got too close.

"I'm sorry," he started. "For so many things, Hayles. For always needing to apologize for something. For what those people said to you tonight. For not coming over and checking on you sooner. I don't know, I guess I'm trying to give you space, because that's what you said you wanted."

What I wanted was to go to him, but I continued to wrestle with the impulse.

"You don't need to apologize for anything. You have been giving me space," I acknowledged. "Thank you. And for what you did tonight, Jace. Standing up for me. You always do."

He studied me intensely. "Do you still want space?" There was a lot going on behind his eyes. None of which I could read. "Because I'm fighting every damn instinct to be here, with you. I don't know how much longer I can do it."

"What does that mean?"

"It means this whole time, it's only been you," he said, voice rough at the edges. "Because even when it hasn't, it's still been me, trying not to want you."

My heart pounded; every inch of my skin was hyperaware. The breath I'd been holding leaked out of my lungs at Jace's heartfelt admission—something he'd been doing on the regular lately.

I opened my mouth, but he got in first. "When Leslie brought up the accident tonight, and I saw your face drop, it killed me, baby. Ever since we lost Tom, it's been there. The need to protect you, to be the person you turn to for support. And if I'm being honest, even before then, I've wanted to be that guy for you."

When I didn't respond, still trying—and failing—to absorb what he was saying, his throat worked on a swallow. "I've been going out of my mind since we last spoke, because you were right. Right about everything. I wish I'd been honest with you from the beginning, that I hadn't tried so hard to push you away. Things would've been different. The guy I've been lately?" There was a pause. "Let's just say, if Tom was here, I think he'd have landed a punch or two on me by now."

"Maybe." I couldn't help but smile sadly. It wasn't a question. He definitely would have.

"I miss him."

"I know. I miss him too."

"Tell me, how much did you have to drink tonight?"

"Ah, I might have lost count." His lips curved, causing the adorable dimples in his cheeks to sink in. "But I'm not just saying all this because I'm buzzed. I know I'm gonna lose you for good if I don't man up and tell you how I feel, if I don't offer you more."

"Jace . . ." I choked back the emotion lining my throat.

"No, it's okay. I need to get this out," he said, sitting forward. "Tried to drown it out by drinking tonight, but I haven't been able to stop thinking about you. How you felt against me. How easy it was to get lost in you."

Despite my valiant efforts, my body overrode my brain, and suddenly, my feet were moving toward him.

"I thought maybe after that night, after that kiss at Owen's, I'd be able to get you out of my system—as if it were that easy. I tried to convince myself it could be enough, but it's not. It never will be. I've wanted you, Hayles, for a long time, and I'm done fighting it," he ground out. "I'm done trying to ignore the way I feel about you. I'm done being scared."

I sucked in a shaky breath when his warm hands grazed the bare skin on the backs of my legs. His touch was like an electric current, sending a jolt of lust and sizzling awareness through me.

"Say something," he urged, his voice gravelly and thick. "Even if it's just to tell me to leave."

Jace's fingers dug into the soft flesh beneath the curve of my ass, and he drew me in even closer. I was now standing directly in between his knees. His gaze swept up over my body, totally owning me.

By some miracle, I managed to get out, "I don't want you to go, and I definitely don't want space."

Putting some distance between us was the only way I could deal with how much I love you, I was scarily close to admitting, but there was no way I could confess something like that to him—not yet.

"Oh, yeah?" He arched a dark brow.

"Yeah." I nodded jerkily. "I think we've given each other more than enough of that."

Lacing the fingers of one hand in Jace's hair, I gently tilted his head back. The vulnerable expression I was rewarded with almost knocked me off my feet. Our eyes locked, a tangle of emotion and longing, as I placed my other hand on his hard shoulder.

And then I bent down to kiss him.

thirteen

I woke up the next morning before my alarm, almost like some internal clock anticipated that I'd roll over and find Jace gone. It was early and the sun climbed the hills on the horizon, crossing my face as it filtered through my bedroom window.

When I felt Jace shift behind me, the front of his warm body sealing against the back of mine, my stomach swooped. This had to be a dream. After five years of discouraged wishing, dreams were all I'd known when it came to moments like these.

I let myself sink into his embrace, reveling in the feel. His breath fanned my neck, softly stirring the tendrils of my hair, and I suppressed a shiver. His arm lifted, curving around my waist as he tugged me closer, pulling me into the circle of his body heat.

I inhaled as it dawned on me that this was oh-so-real. With my body pressed to his, I could feel him hardening against me, even through the denim of his jeans, and my eyes snapped open in a rush.

"Jace?" I gasped out.

"Mm-hmm?" he mumbled sleepily.

"Are you awake?"

Everything in me tightened when his palm dragged down my belly.

"Maybe," he answered, kissing the sensitive spot behind my ear.

My brain short-circuited as his fingers toyed with the elastic band of my cotton sleep shorts. I bit down on my lip, a surge of delicious heat spiking through me. Barely able to form a coherent thought, I blurted out the first thing that came to mind, "Thanks for staying last night. For being here."

Jace stilled behind me. "Where else would I be?"

The silence gaped between us, and I could practically hear the cogs turning in his head.

Oh God.

Fear slammed into me as I realized it was probably the wrong thing to say. "I know, I just—"

"You thought I'd have left by now?" Jace guessed. Even though I couldn't see him, I felt unease coming from him. Nothing was buried too deep or hidden away. Not anymore.

My throat closed up as I nodded.

There was a long pause, then he exhaled slowly. "Damn. We've gotta change that."

"We do?" I asked dumbly.

"Can't have you thinking I'd just up and leave." He dipped his chin into the crook of my neck, his husky voice drifting over my skin. "Not after last night. Not with you."

We hadn't done anything last night aside from kiss and talk before we'd eventually fallen asleep, but I was glad sex wasn't a requirement for us to feel closer—more connected.

Jace rolled abruptly, hauling me with him, and before I could blink, I was lying flat on my back. The corded muscles in his arms rippled, his biceps flexing as he hovered above me. When he aligned our lower bodies, it fed the fire that was always building between us. The fire that had been burning for years.

"I've wanted this—us—for a long time. The last thing I want to do is something that might ruin it."

The pressure of him straining behind his zipper left little room for doubt about just how much he wanted this. My brain ran a million miles an hour, attempting to sort through my jumbled, sleep-deprived thoughts.

"I'm glad we're on the same page," was my genius and somewhat breathless response.

Jace's eyes were fervent, ablaze with something I couldn't identify—an emotion I had never seen in them before. He cupped my face in his hand, his thumb smoothing over my cheek. Then he inched closer, his lips seeking mine. At first, it was soft, unhurried, and then the tenor of the kiss changed. It reminded me of the night at Owen's apartment—going from sweet to frenzied in an instant—and I tried not to moan when his tongue brushed against mine. Desire swirled around us like a brewing storm.

Tangled in the intensity of Jace's kisses, I curled my fingers in his hair, holding him close, but it still wasn't enough. I pressed against him, trying to assuage the need that pulsed between my thighs. My shorts were a thin layer against the rough scrape of denim, and a sharp burst of pleasure pulsed through me.

Jace seemed to like that, too, because there was a rich, deep sound that shook him.

"Fuck," he spoke in an undertone, wrenching his mouth from mine.

Levering up enough to tug at the hem of his T-shirt, he lifted it over his head in one fluid motion. Enthralled at the sight of Jace shirtless, I drank him in. The urge to reach out and touch him was strong, and I was done fighting against it. The heels of my palms slid down the hard ridges of his abs, my stomach clenching as I unashamedly explored his warm, tanned skin.

The guy was freaking gorgeous, and I still couldn't believe he wanted me too. I must have been wearing a look of awe, because Jace chuckled quietly, suspended above me in all his bare-chested glory.

"Now you understand how I feel," he rasped, not a hint of indifference to be found anywhere. "I can barely concentrate on anything when I'm around you. And when I'm not around you, I can't stop thinking about you. I feel like a fucking preteen."

"Sounds like you've got yourself some out-of-control hormones."

"Something like that." His laughter tickled my ear as he settled more of his weight on top of me. "You have no idea how many filthy dreams I've had since you came to Delaware, Hayles. I jerk off to the thought of you most days."

Holy mother of God.

Nervousness and arousal warred inside me. "I don't—I've never . . ." I faltered for a beat, and it was impossible to stop the flush that spread down my neck.

Great. My reaction made it sound like I'd never seen, or touched, a dick before. I wasn't completely inexperienced. There'd been two guys I'd messed around with, but when it came down to it, I just couldn't go all the way. I hadn't been ready, or maybe I'd known they hadn't been the right guy, and it was worth holding out for the right one.

Jace drew back, features tightening as some sort of emotion flitted across them. "Hey, I don't expect sex, okay? I would never pressure you into anything you didn't want to do. And aside from me not wanting to rush things, it'd be pretty much impossible when there's so much history between us. This isn't just physical. This is different."

It took a moment for my brain to grasp what he was saying, and then my blush deepened. "I know. I'm sorry, you just took me by surprise. You're more experienced than me, and I—"

His mouth descended on mine again, effectively cutting me off. "You don't need to apologize." He punctuated each word with a kiss. "If it makes you feel better, I've never felt anything like this before with anyone"—he tucked a strand of hair behind my ear—"and that's what has me so fucking terrified. I never want to do anything that might jeopardize what we have."

He was implying that he hadn't even felt this way about Zoe, and well, that made me feel downright giddy.

"I'm terrified too," I said quietly. More so of the things I couldn't control, not necessarily when it came to being with Jace, but I needed him to know he wasn't alone in this.

"Don't be," he told me in a whisper. "You know you can trust me, Hayles, just like you can trust that things are going to be different between us from now on."

"I know."

Nothing about this moment—waking up in Jace's arms—was familiar. We were navigating very new, uncharted territory, but I loved that we were already losing sight of our past and everything that'd held us back from giving this a chance.

My heart rate kicked up when Jace kissed me for the third time this morning. Yes, I was counting. But unlike the other kisses we'd shared, this one was achingly tender, filled with everything unspoken. Hope and happiness flashed through me, zipping through my veins, as he held me like I was something to cherish. I knew some people waited an entire lifetime for that feeling.

Kissing Jace topped my list of favorite things to do. I slid my hands over his muscled shoulders and into his hair again, wanting to keep him in this bed with me, now and always. Splaying my legs on either side of him, I got comfortable. The tips of my breasts grazed his chest, almost tightening to the point of pain. It felt like every inch of my body was on fire, smoldering beneath him like an ignited ember.

Jace's strong hands gripped my thighs, rocking me against him, and I practically whimpered at the friction.

"Please, touch me," I pleaded, too turned on to be embarrassed.

Just because we'd agreed to keep sex out of this, for now, didn't mean that we couldn't fool around a little. Jace touching me had been my primary fantasy since I'd been old enough to recognize it for what it was—lust. Hot, unmistakable lust.

"I know, baby. Let me get you there." He reached down, fingers slipping between my legs, dipping slightly, and everything in me liquified. "Like this?"

There was a good chance I wasn't even breathing anymore. I let out a shallow hiss, the remaining air leaking out of my lungs. Clutching the comforter, I writhed as his knuckles brushed over my most sensitive area. Of course he was teasing me, drawing this out. More heat flooded deep in my core, the ache intensifying as he tugged the stretchy material of my underwear aside and the tips of his fingers skimmed over the very center of me.

Holy shit.

"Jace." His name escaped from my lips, a breathy whisper.

Oh God. This was really happening. And it was happening with Jace. All traces of doubt dissipated when his fingers played over me again, his touch and pressure just right. It felt so damn good, almost overwhelming.

After years of imagining what it would feel like to be with Jace, for him to kiss and explore my body like his sole purpose in life was to worship me, I didn't have to imagine anymore.

"Fuck," he grunted, placing a kiss against my pulse point. "You're so wet."

His thumb found my clit, circling my bundle of nerves, and I was certain I was going to spontaneously combust. Everything in me was so focused on what he was doing to me, the riot of sensations he was making me feel. Then he eased a finger inside me, and I couldn't think at all.

Jace continued to kiss me—slow, deep, drugging—as his deft fingers brought me to the brink of ecstasy. Tension coiled in my stomach, a pressure that had me chasing relief. My hips rocked against his hand, craving more, and I swallowed back a moan.

"You're so beautiful." His voice was guttural, hot in my ear. "Never thought I'd get to see you like this."

I glanced up at him, our gazes locking, and I felt my heart do something funny in my chest. His eyes glimmered with need, fueling the flames that slowly licked over my skin.

He slid another finger in to join the first, pushing in and out of me. My nerves sparked and jumped, ready to explode. When the palm of his hand found just the right spot, and he worked me a little harder, faster, I almost lost it. My head kicked back against the pillow, so close to release.

"That's it," he said, his breath hitching slightly. "Let go for me."

Hearing Jace talk to me—the knowledge that he was watching,

that he liked what he saw—spurred me on. It was too much. The whole world felt like it was suddenly falling away, shattering into tiny shards. The knot that had formed in my belly unraveled, and I arched off the bed. I came with a sharp cry, shuddering through the strongest orgasm I'd ever experienced.

Thank God we were home alone.

Body trilling with a tingly, sated warmth, I peeked up at Jace. He was grinning a barely restrained grin and looking at me in a way that did insane things to my heart. Insane, stupid things. Everything about him swamped my senses.

My plans of going slow with Jace had taken a perfect swan dive out the window. I went to flick the button on his low-hanging jeans, wanting to return the favor, but his hand covered mine, preventing me from undoing them.

"Hayles . . ." The half smile disappeared, but his eyes softened. "Don't."

I blinked several times. "Why not?"

"Because I always told myself the first time this happened, the first time I got to touch you like this," he explained, expression suddenly serious, "it needed to be about you. Not me."

"*Now* you're going to be a gentleman?" I asked, voice light, teasing. "You don't have to be. I want you to feel how I felt."

Honestly, thinking about what we'd just done had me more turned on than I'd ever been in my life, so it didn't help when he leaned into me again, sealing me against his side.

"Trust me, I already do," he assured me, and his lips brushed mine in a slow, tantalizing sweep. "You have no idea what it felt like to wake up next to you this morning. It's taken me a long time to get here, but I know I'm finally where I should be."

• • •

I couldn't contain the smile on my face as we stopped in to see Amelia later that morning. I almost slipped in the sea of discarded beer bottles and plastic cups that littered the floor tiles in the kitchen, but I was still smiling—the afterglow of a good orgasm, I guess.

Jace steadied me before I lost my balance, his hands landing on my waist.

"Shit," he said with a soft chuckle behind me. The heat of his palms felt sublime on my skin, and my brain instantly started playing in the gutter. All I could think about was how talented those fingers were, how badly I wanted him to touch me again. "You all right?"

His voice snapped me out of my lust-induced stupor, and I managed to nod. "Yeah. Thanks."

Amusement flashed in the depths of his eyes, like he knew where my thoughts had gone—the effect his proximity had on me. As hard as I tried to appear calm, my pulse betrayed me, pounding erratically.

When someone cleared their throat, alerting us to the fact that we weren't alone, Jace's arms dropped from around me.

My gaze landed on my best friend, perched on a stool at the island bench, her head lowered over a bowl of untouched cereal. She was the epitome of hungover.

Amelia took one look at us, her eyes narrowing. "It's about fucking time," she griped. "And no, don't mistake this as an invitation for you to gross me out with the details. I'm already feeling sick to my stomach this morning."

I cataloged her reaction—the good-natured teasing—and exhaled.

"Shut up." Jace smirked, striding over to her in a few quick steps and ruffling her blond hair. "Oh, and you're officially nine-teen today. That's cool."

I carefully navigated my way over to them and pulled her in for a hug. "Happy birthday, Millie."

Surreptitiously, I wrinkled my nose. The odor of booze and smoke still clung to her, and she'd clearly slept in her dress last night—it was askew, twisted around her small frame. Scanning her face, I saw that her gray eyes were puffy and bloodshot. Her mascara was smudged, too, staining her cheeks.

"I know, I know. I look like a piece of dried vomit. After Piper dropped me home, I might have kept the party going for a teensy bit longer than I should've. But you want to know what occurred to me last night? This is my last year as a teenager. Like, how the hell did that happen? My life's over," Amelia groaned miserably. There was a soft thud as her forehead connected with the granite countertop.

"You can't be serious," Jace commented. When she raised her head and fixed him with a glare devoid of any levity, he mumbled, "Wow, okay, way to make me feel old."

"Newsflash, you *are* old." She scowled at her brother.

Beside me, Jace sighed.

I rolled my eyes, more than accustomed to their constant bickering. Their relationship was nothing like mine and Tom's had been. Even though it was obvious they cared for one another deep down, they always butted heads and fought over the most insignificant things. Occasionally, whenever it got bad, I was tempted to say something, to remind them that they should stop taking each other for granted. I mean, some of us didn't have any siblings at all. But, for the most part, I knew it was in my best interest to stay out of it.

Not to mention, when I thought about it for long enough—drew too many comparisons between their relationship and how my relationship had been with my brother—it hurt in the worst possible way. Because I didn't get to share birthdays with Tom anymore. I didn't get to receive funny memes from him or update him on my day. I didn't get to make new memories with him. No, I was left with flashbacks. Spliced fragments of our past. Most days, there was little choice but to think about the final interactions we'd had. While we'd rarely fought, we had the night he died, and over something so pointless.

I'd spent the last two years of high school trying to let go and heal the brokenness inside me. Truthfully, I was still working on it.

More memories started to creep up the back of my neck, and I was momentarily transported, sucked back in time.

Spinning the dial on my combination lock, I ignored the whispers in the hallway, then the silence followed me like a lingering shadow. Adjusting my baseball cap, I pulled it down at the bill, hoping to remain as inconspicuous as possible.

My biology notebook was exactly where I'd left it last month, next to my planner. The last time I'd touched it, scribbled half-assed notes in its pages, I'd been distracted, way too excited for Jace's party . . . and Tom had been alive.

I gnashed my teeth together, tears rushing to my eyes. I knew it was going to be hard, coming back to school, but this was so much harder than I'd anticipated.

Getting my AP English books out for the first period, I tried not to think about the vacant seat that would greet me in my upcoming student council meeting. I tried not to think about the fact that Tom and I were supposed to be giving a presentation next week, but a lump still swelled in my throat.

Walking down the corridor, I could feel everyone looking at me. Baseball cap or not, I couldn't hide. I forced myself to lift my gaze, maybe find some normalcy, some reprieve. But all I saw were sympathetic, prying eyes, and I wanted to disappear.

Amelia sidled up beside me at that moment, her strawberry-blond ponytail wagging back and forth. She looped her arm through mine, and I let out a sigh, sweet relief trickling in. I hadn't seen much of my best friend lately, but that hadn't been for lack of trying on her part. She'd been texting, calling—supporting me from a distance—because that was what I'd said I needed.

I hadn't wanted to see her until I felt better. I hadn't wanted to be a burden. But no part of me was beginning to feel better, and I honestly had no idea if that day would ever roll around.

"How are you?" she asked softly, then winced. "Sorry, dumb question. Don't answer that. I just . . . I don't know what to say. I don't know how to help. I can't imagine what you're going through. None of us can."

With Amelia by my side, no one tried to come closer or talk to me. She was like a human shield, and I was beyond thankful. I couldn't deal with the insensitive questions or heartfelt condolences. Not when I still couldn't understand this myself.

"It's fine. I don't mind if you ask me that," I told her. "I just don't want to have to try to explain anything—why he's gone, why I can't sleep, why I can't bring myself to eat—to anyone else."

I'd already revealed more than I intended to, but it was the truth. I was hardly functioning. A total mess.

"Do you want to come over after school?" Amelia offered as we scaled the stairs, heading to class. "We can just hang out, skip homework, and watch a movie or something?"

"That'd be nice," I admitted, grateful she wasn't letting me push her away.

I dreaded returning to a house that was so empty. My dad locked himself away in the garage at night, then went fishing before dawn. Mom had only come out of her room one time yesterday, which was once more than me.

"Have you heard from Jace?"

I hadn't spoken to him since he went back to Delaware. Jace was the only other person who had the power to dull this ache, and he'd left. He was over a hundred miles away now, weeks into his second semester. The only decent sleep I'd had since the accident was the night he'd stayed over. Without him, I'd been plunged into perpetual darkness.

"Not really. We talked on the phone last weekend. He's not doing much better than you."

It was a cold comfort.

Concern twisted her beautiful features. "Seriously, what can I do, Hayley?" Her eyes searched mine. "Whatever you need, I'll do it."

It was a nice sentiment, but there was nothing that could truly help me. That was what made losing someone so uncomfortable and difficult to navigate.

I was silent for a few moments, unsure how to respond.

"Another stupid question, duh." Amelia's voice sounded small, and I hated the defeat I heard in it. "There's probably not a lot I can do, right?"

"You're my best friend, Millie," I said, halting in my tracks. The throbbing in my chest had increased so much that I had to take a slow, deep breath. "I don't expect you to take my pain away. Nothing will do that, not even the meds Dr. Jensen wants to put me on. Just support me, like always. That's . . . what . . . you . . . can . . . do."

It wasn't until Amelia pulled me into a tight hug that I realized I was crying. More accurately, sobbing all over her.

"*God, I'm so sorry. I loved him too,*" *she murmured, squeezing me.*

People were watching, pausing, whispering, all around us, but I couldn't bring myself to care anymore. I focused on the feeling of her arms around me, the smell of her signature lavender and rosemary shampoo tickling my nose.

"*He deserved better than this,*" I choked out.

My brother deserved more. He shouldn't have had to die to pay for his best friend's mistake. He didn't deserve to have his name leaked to the media. It'd been dragged through the mud, like he was the one behind the wheel, driving drunk.

Even a month later, the accident was plastered all over the local papers, headlining news channels. Updates on the sole survivor's condition filtered in every few days—a boy who'd been identified as seventeen-year-old Aaron Holt. He was still in a coma, but he was alive.

When I managed to compose myself and muster up the courage to walk into class, it was no surprise that not even Amelia could shield me from my new reality, not forever. I had to learn, somehow, to handle it. The pity that would be eternally etched into the heavy lines of my teachers' faces. My wide-eyed peers, who didn't know whether it was ruder to look at me or to look away. Every time I entered any room, I was reminded of who I was—the poor, nameless high school girl the news anchors kept referring to. I'd become a story, an ending steeped in tragedy—the sister who couldn't save her brother.

The clink of metal broke into my thoughts, yanking me back to the present.

"Are you gonna finish that?" Jace asked, pointing to the uneaten bowl of Lucky Charms in front of his sister.

"Nope. Go for it." Amelia shook her head, dropped the spoon again, and slid it toward him.

"Great. I'm starving," he announced before proceeding to wolf down the cereal. He grinned around a spoonful of Lucky Charms, and I almost laughed.

"You want some?" Jace swallowed another mouthful.

Pressing my lips together, I tried not to smile. "No, thanks." I refocused my attention on the kitchen, remembering the state it was in. Last night must have been wild. "When are your parents due back? Shouldn't we try to clean this place up?"

Amelia squinted at the clock above the stove. "Oh, fuck. They'll be here any minute now." Springing into action, she knocked over a few bottles in the process, and they all clattered on the tiles. "Jace, can you check upstairs? It shouldn't take you long. No one really went up there last night." She paused, as if trying to sift through her memories, and a flush of red crossed her smooth cheeks. "Yep. Should be fine. Hayley, you're with me."

I half laughed, half choked at the drastic change in her demeanor. It almost felt like she was a sergeant conducting drills or something, and her no-nonsense attitude was slightly terrifying.

She began scooping the trash into a huge plastic bag, and I don't think I'd ever seen anyone so frantic.

I frowned. "They knew you were throwing this party. I'm sure they'll—"

"I sort of didn't tell them," Amelia interrupted.

A confused sound huffed out of me. "What?"

"Don't act so surprised, Hayley. You know my parents aren't that awesome."

"For once, we actually agree on something," Jace muttered, placing his empty bowl in the sink.

I glowered at him because he was not helping.

If their parents really didn't know about the party, they were going to be in for one hell of a shock. The entire downstairs was trashed—God only knew what it looked like upstairs—and there was no way we'd be able to clean everything up before they got home. Their house would make the perfect set for a deep-cleaning service commercial.

"Do you remember when I asked them if I could have a big graduation party at the end of senior year?" Amelia gave her brother a pointed look as she tidied. "Dad turned it into an hour-long lecture about how we need to stop using alcohol as a crutch to improve our social skills. So, yeah, I rest my case."

Maybe she had a point. Judy and Geoff Hammond were pretty old-school, but they were also the kind of people who wouldn't hesitate to give the clothes off their backs to a stranger. They were like family to me too. After Tom had died, I'd found myself drifting away from my own parents and inadvertently growing closer to them, the result of spending most of my time after the accident hiding out at their house.

With a squeak of horror, Amelia's voice scattered my thoughts. "Did you hear that?"

"That's probably them," Jace said dryly, folding his arms across his chest. An amused smirk tugged at his lips.

As if on cue, the jingle of keys sounded outside the front door.

I helplessly watched the slideshow of emotions that passed across Amelia's face. I was even more glad I hadn't been drinking last night and that I'd left early. I didn't want to be included in this.

When the click of the latch came only moments later, followed by noises that were somewhere between shock and outrage, I couldn't say I was all that surprised.

"Fuck, I'm in so much trouble," my best friend whispered, her grip on the plastic bag tightening until her knuckles whitened. "It was nice knowing you both."

fourteen

According to my new friends, attending a football game was a rite of passage for any freshman. Over halfway through my first semester at Delaware, I thought I'd done well to avoid one up until now. Jace was booked to photograph the Saturday game against our school's biggest rival, and Owen and Piper had insisted I tag along with them. Despite my protests—I'd rather tiptoe over hot coals than watch any sport for an extended period—they hadn't taken no for an answer.

If I truly wanted to fit in and simultaneously bond with my peers, apparently it was by cheering the Titans to victory from the stands, followed by getting wasted at the party tonight in their honor. Fortunately, they hadn't expected the latter from me. I had nothing against football, it just wasn't my idea of a good time. The only reason I hadn't bolted out of the stadium the second we'd arrived was because Jace had greeted me with a dimpled smile and a loaded-up plate of cheesy nachos—he knew, while I wasn't a fan of football, I was all about eating.

"Best part about football games," Piper agreed after she'd retrieved a soda and french fries. Owen was too busy devouring his hot dog to even come up for air.

We hadn't been sitting for long before we all stood for the national anthem. As the broad-shouldered players took the field, I could see flashes of white, navy, and red jerseys. I inhaled the smell of freshly mowed grass, liniment, and oily fast food. The loud ambience of the game took over after the Titans' first kickoff, and I hated to admit it, but I could kind of see the appeal—keywords: *kind of.*

Watching a home game with the people who'd welcomed me with open arms this semester, who were also supporting me through a scary time, was the least I could do. The three of us were quiet for a while, just eating our snacks and drinking soda— although I was pretty sure Owen's was beer. The crowd roared so often that getting drawn into a real conversation wasn't possible. People all around us cheered and booed, and I felt myself getting more immersed in the lively atmosphere.

Still, I was more interested in watching Jace as he worked than the players in tight jerseys, who were either grunting at each other or chasing after a leather ball. I spotted him by the edge of the field. It wasn't hard, considering he was wearing a bright vest with PHOTOGRAPHER printed across the back. He was crouched down, capturing all the action. The camera he was using looked more like a telescope, and I bit back a laugh. He even had a small tripod and a second digital camera slung over his shoulder. Clearly, his gigs paid well.

"Do you go to all the games?" I asked Piper at halftime, sipping my can of Dr. Pepper. The Titans were in the lead by a touch-down, and the cheerleaders and band were about to start their halftime show.

"Nah. Maybe four or five a season. Always the championships if we make it," she said, grinning. "Jace gets us great seats, so it'd be a waste not to."

I nodded in response.

While I knew next to nothing about football, I could appre-ciate how close to the field we were. Sitting in the first few rows, near the fifty-yard line, was incredible. The only other time I'd gone to any kind of sporting event was when I'd been in the nose-bleed section at a Baltimore Orioles game. I'd been in elementary school, Mom was on a girls' trip, and I'd had no choice but to go with Dad and Tom. The players had been so far away, I'd had to squint.

Smiling at the memory, I recalled how obsessed my brother had been with baseball. Being here felt like forging a new connec-tion with him, and after two years of looking for ways to honor him and feel close to him again, I hadn't been expecting that.

Just when I'd started to relax and find all the rabid fans amus-ing instead of annoying, I felt it: someone was watching me.

Stiffening, I glanced over my shoulder, scanning the crowd. My stomach burned with a mixture of fear and anger. I hated the fact that I was searching for Levi. But, most of all, I hated the power he wielded over me.

"Are you okay?" Piper spoke directly in my ear, capturing half of my attention. Concern settled into her expression.

The cheer routine had ended, and I couldn't recognize any-one in the rows behind or ahead of us. I exhaled a ragged breath. Everything about this situation was making me paranoid. Of course I'd feel eyes on me every now and then. I was in a jam-packed stadium with at least a thousand spectators.

"Yeah, I think so." Frowning deeply, I tried to concentrate on slowing my careening pulse.

The sun was setting and the stadium lights flicked on, illuminating the field. The third quarter was about to start. All the players were in a huddle, listening to the quarterback call the play. Jace was still on the sidelines, getting all the atmospheric shots. Then he pointed the camera my way, as if sensing my gaze on him. Piper and Owen posed, and I waved. He grinned and waved back. The reminder that Jace was only a few feet away, that I was in a very public area, shielded by a sea of people, soothed my worries.

Despite the short-lived panic I'd felt, I ended up enjoying my first football game. The Titans won by three points, maintaining their well-deserved winning streak, and it was surprisingly easy to get swept up in the postgame celebrations.

"I got a great shot of you guys," Jace said when we'd made our way over to him. A sharp chill was in the air, and I snuggled into his side, soaking in the heat from his body.

"Let's see," Piper said, her face full of excitement. "I really need a new Tinder picture."

Jace rolled his eyes but complied. It took him a minute to find it. He sped back through hundreds of photos, then passed the smaller camera to her at the same moment the Titans' coach asked him a question and he stepped away.

Piper stared down at the screen for a beat, then her lips curved up. "Damn. We look good. Here, wanna see?"

"Sure." I took the camera from her. Owen had left in search of a bathroom, and Jace was still chatting with the coach. It was just Piper and me, standing near the field, admiring his photographic skills. No wonder he'd been hired by the team years ago. I was sure if he wanted it, he'd have a future as an NFL photographer in the bag.

As I studied the picture of the three of us, my throat closed up. Even though I was outside, I couldn't get enough oxygen. My hands began to shake. "How—does this thing zoom in?"

"Don't ask me. Digital cameras may as well be high-tech space equipment."

"Can you see him? Or am I just losing my mind?" My voice had a grating tone I'd never heard before, and I practically threw the camera back to Piper. I was amazed I didn't drop it.

She glanced down at the screen once more and paled. Her ramrod posture confirmed that I wasn't imagining it. I vaguely heard "That sick motherfucker," but I was too focused on trying not to vomit, on controlling the bile that bubbled up.

"What's going on?" It was Jace, finally rejoining us. There was no mistaking the flicker of unease in his blue-gray eyes.

The blood rushed in my ears, and suddenly it was that morning in my dorm all over again. Everywhere I turned, Levi was infiltrating my life. I couldn't speak.

"Can you zoom in? Three or four rows back, directly behind us," Piper told him. The way she spoke in choppy fragments made me realize I had every right to be afraid.

"Why? I mean, yeah, I can. You're lucky I used this camera." Jace was talking low, thumb moving in a circular motion. His voice tapered off abruptly.

Then his gaze locked with mine and his jaw clenched.

I didn't need to see the photo again to know what he'd found. The image had already been branded into my brain. Initially, all I registered was Piper, Owen, and me smiling, cheering in the stands, but it had quickly blurred, like it was out of focus. It was overshadowed by the person standing behind us, blending into the crowd, watching me.

What haunted me most? It was everything I'd imagined, feared with every fiber of my being, down to the fine details.

Scuffed leather jacket, hands stuck casually in the pockets. Baseball cap, concealing short, mussed black hair. That perverted smirk permanently carved on his face.

Even though I'd only seen him a handful of times, I'd recognize him anywhere.

Levi.

• • •

A frigid gust of wind blasted me in the face when I pushed open my car door on Tuesday morning, chilling the tips of my ears. Grateful I always packed light—my notepad, drawing pencils, and sketchbook—I slung my tote bag over my shoulder and exited the parking lot.

It was my first time on campus since the game, and honestly, the urge to turn around or just keep driving had been strong. Seeing the Delaware turnoff on the highway, then the ominous ENDLESS DISCOVERIES slogan on the sign at the edge of town, felt like returning to a horrible place I never wanted to visit again. But technically, I was safe. Safer than I'd been in a while. I wasn't ignoring every ingrained survival instinct I had, because not only had Jace promised he would protect me—no matter the cost—we'd also shown the photograph to Officer Bedford. The police were finally holding Levi for questioning. He was locked up and would be for another day, at the very least. Apparently breaching a restraining order was something they *could* prosecute him for—which was why they'd strongly encouraged me to file for one—unlike the assault charges they were trying to make stick. Still, I hated that Levi was ruining this. College was something I'd been looking forward to for years, and it was supposed to be the best time of my life. A chance for me to start over. Instead, it felt like I'd stumbled into something darker and more dangerous than anything I'd had to deal with back home.

Other students hustled to their classes all around me, and the knowledge that Levi wasn't one of them made me feel better. I exhaled heavily, relaxing a little. As I headed toward central campus, debating whether to grab a coffee from Bean Alive, the little indie café on Main Street, I heard someone call out my name.

Pivoting on my heel, I turned to see Eden fast approaching. The hollows of her cheeks were flushed from the cold wind too.

"Hey," she said, falling into step beside me, and I hunkered deeper into my knitted sweater. "How was your weekend?"

Internally, I grimaced. "Uh, yeah, it was pretty good, thanks." The lie came out easier than the truth. "What about you? What did you get up to?"

"Oh, you know, the usual." She waved me off. "Studied until my brain hurt, pigged out on a whole bag of peanut butter M&M'S, and watched *Crazy, Stupid, Love* again, just so I could appreciate all that is Ryan Gosling."

Shaking my head, I laughed. Ironically, it sounded way better than my weekend. "Is it bad that I still haven't seen that movie?"

Eden stared at me, brows raised. "Yeah, I don't know if I can be friends with you anymore."

I sighed dramatically, adjusting the strap of my bag. "Then I guess you don't want the notes I took for you when you missed the last class."

"Forget what I just said. You're the best."

I grinned, and she grinned right back.

"Did you hear about the frat party happening on Greek Row?" she asked after a few seconds, tucking a jet-black curl behind her ear. "Apparently it's going to be huge."

The abrupt change in subject caught me off guard. "No, I haven't." I supposed that was what happened when you didn't live on campus anymore. Levi had obliterated my newfound social life. I swallowed back the bitterness that was clawing its way up my throat.

Looping her arm through mine, Eden said in a singsong voice, "Well, I don't know about you, but I'm one hundred percent going. I need to balance out all this study and stress with some well-earned fun. And oh my God, the guys. Talk about eye candy."

That got a smile out of me. "Those frat boys won't know what's hit them."

"Too right," she agreed, squeezing my arm. "Are you planning to go?"

I frowned slightly. "What night is it?"

"The first Friday back after Thanksgiving break, which is perfect. It gives me a couple of weeks to figure out what Reese's deal is."

Reese was the hot ginger she hadn't shut up about recently. According to Eden, they'd been exchanging texts and sidelong glances in her elective psych class. I was happy for her, and even happier that she felt comfortable sharing personal details with me.

"Well, I, for one, still think he's into you. And I usually head back to my parents' house for the weekend, so I probably won't be there." I kept my response vague. Parties and I were like water and oil, we didn't mix well. I also wasn't sure I was in the mood for standing around awkwardly again, pretending to have a good time.

We started up the wide steps to the building, and I couldn't resist looking over my shoulder. Apparently dealing with this weird, paranoid crap was my new normal. The idea of probably having to face Levi in court soon slipped into the crevices of my mind, only adding to my anxiety. Seeing him any sooner than that was too much to bear.

"You okay?" Eden asked, watching me with concern.

"Yeah," I lied, snapping out of my stupor.

The art studio was nearly full, everyone filing in with renewed enthusiasm and interest. One of our assignments was due today, and our Thanksgiving break started this weekend. I swear there were so many unfamiliar faces, people I hadn't seen since the beginning of the semester. So typical.

We made a beeline for one of the bigger workbenches, squeezing through narrow gaps as we edged our way down one of the rows.

"Do you think Professor Zimmerman will be here soon?" Eden planted her elbows on the table and rested her head in her hands as if she were worn out already. "I might take a quick power nap. I stayed up way too late last night."

I wrinkled my nose. "Honestly, I doubt it. He can barely keep track of the time."

Sure enough, we were running ten minutes late, and Professor Zimmerman wasn't here.

Ducking down to rummage through my bag, I pulled out the materials I needed for this class and thumbed through my notebook. I scanned over the messy scribblings I'd jotted down last week, in the rare moments my brain let me concentrate.

"Morning, gorgeous," came a deep voice that rumbled through me, and I felt it all the way down to the tips of my toes.

Jace slid into the empty chair on my right, and I was struck speechless, which was a new thing for me. And it wasn't because he was here, sitting next to me, it was because he'd called me gorgeous so casually in front of Eden.

"Hi," I said, the word coming out in a breathless tumble.

His lips curled up like he knew the effect he had on me, and then his eyes shifted to acknowledge Eden. "Hey, I don't believe we've met before."

She straightened in her seat, her posture going rigid. "Uh, yeah, I mean, no . . . we haven't. I'm Eden," she said, giving a little wave.

On my other side, Jace leaned in closer to me, smiling at her. He placed his hand on my thigh, the simple gesture managing to speed up my pulse. "I'm Jace."

"I know," she said, and then her eyes popped wide. "It's just— well, I'm fairly sure everyone knows who you are. I mean, you're kind of—" She swallowed. "Why am I still talking?"

"Don't worry about it," he assured her, chuckling.

That was one of the things I loved most about Jace. Even though he had a face and body that looked like the gods had sculpted it, he never had an ego trip about it.

"Anyways, it was nice to meet you," Eden muttered under her breath as she flipped through her design portfolio, looking conveniently busy.

I'd had years to get comfortable around Jace, to work through my nerves and be able to talk to him like a normal person, but it would have been a completely different story if I'd only just met him. It was easy to see past his tall, good-looking exterior when I'd known him for half my life. I could still remember all the afternoons he would tug on my braids and wheel his bike home with me. I think I'd been the only girl who'd thought the braces to correct his overbite were cute, or that his Pokémon card collection was anything but lame. Since then, we'd continued to forge a friendship that wasn't based on looks and would exist even when our siblings weren't in tow.

Jace's dark lashes lowered as he set his notebook and pen down. "Want to grab a bite from Russell after this?"

Out of the three dining halls the University of Delaware offered, Russell had quickly become my favorite. "Sounds good."

"You're welcome to join us," he added, turning his attention to Eden again.

"Thanks," she said, pausing to mull it over, "but I better not."

I frowned.

Before I could think too deeply about the reason behind her answer, Jace's hand moved to my lower back. "Have the cops said anything new?"

I shifted in my seat. Eden could probably hear our conversation, and I didn't want her to know about any of this. She'd one hundred percent run in the other direction. "No. They haven't." His touch was warm and strong, and I channeled my nervous energy into him. "Can we talk about this later?"

"Sure." There was a beat of silence. "My parents invited you to spend Thanksgiving with us," he said. His words—the kind offer— wrapped my heart in warmth. "They've made reservations at this new restaurant that's opened not far from home. I said I wasn't sure what you wanted to do this year, but I told them I'd ask."

The doors of the studio swung open just as I was about to reply.

A professor who wasn't Zimmerman—a woman I'd never seen before, wearing a gray pantsuit and heels—entered and approached the front of the room. She didn't greet us immediately. Instead, with her back to us, I watched as she wrote the instructions for today's class on the whiteboard. Then she turned around and waited dutifully for the chorus of chatter to drop off, hands clasped in front of her body. It didn't take long; her entrance and severe demeanor garnered several curious eyes.

"I'm Assistant Vice President Briggs," she announced, her pert features screwing tight. "I'll be replacing Professor Zimmerman today. He is otherwise engaged."

There were some indiscreet scoffs and snorts of amusement.

"I know you have a written assignment to turn in at the end of this class, and that it's worth almost half of your grade," she went on, tone authoritative and unperturbed. "So, I strongly suggest you overlook Mr. Zimmerman's absence this morning, follow the directions I've written for you carefully, and use your time wisely. Good luck."

For the next hour, I managed to concentrate on passing Concepts and not on potentially having Thanksgiving dinner with the guy next to me—a guy who might or might not be my boyfriend. Things were finally different between us and yet we still didn't have a label. My brain was kind of struggling with that. Jace hadn't brought up the whole girlfriend/boyfriend thing, and I didn't know if I wanted him to.

After class, we met up with Owen and Piper and headed to Russell for lunch. I opted for one of their healthier options, loading chicken, steamed vegetables, and rice onto my plate. Any junk food I ingested tended to sink like lead in my stomach. Jace ordered a massive hamburger I'd have needed to tackle with both hands.

Eating lunch with the three of them in the dining hall, poking fun at Assistant Vice President Briggs, and talking over the assignment we'd just submitted, had made it easy to pretend I was having an ordinary college experience. Like I'd stepped into an alternate reality where Levi, the attacks on campus, and my brother's death . . . none of it existed.

It wasn't until thirty minutes later, when Owen and Piper left to go to their next class, and Jace and I joined the line for takeaway coffees, that he was free to say what I sensed he'd been holding in all lunch. "You sure you're okay?"

Shrugging, I reached into my purse and pulled out my debit card. "I think so. I mean, no closer to a nervous breakdown than normal. We've already gone to the police, given them multiple statements. We're doing our part. Let's let them do theirs."

"Maybe so, but I feel like I'm on edge most of the time. Afraid of what else is gonna be put in our path. I hate that we're always dealing with morbid, life-threatening shit." He exhaled harshly. "I'm so fucking sick of it."

My surprised gaze climbed up to his, and those blue-gray eyes were suddenly all I could concentrate on. The Jace I was used to— the very picture of calm—was nowhere to be found.

"Do you want to skip class?" I blurted. "Or not. It's probably a dumb idea. I don't know, I was just thinking, if you wanted to, we could get out of here. Go for a drive. Talk about . . . stuff. I like it when you talk to me, Jace."

"That so?"

I nudged him with my elbow, resisting the urge to glance in his direction again. "You know I've always wanted this. Us, being open and honest with each other."

"In that case, let's ditch," he answered, voice gruff and low. His arm encircled my waist, drawing me up against his solid chest and back into his orbit before I could blink. "I want you to spend Thanksgiving with me too. I feel better when you're close, Hayles. Always have. Then I don't have to worry about you. Feels like all I do is worry lately. I'm exhausted."

A thread of guilt wormed through me at hearing that, but I nodded and tried to keep things light. "Count me in."

Wordlessly, Jace moved his finger under my chin, tilting my head up, and his mouth found mine. He kissed me, and it was no short peck on the lips. Leaning into him, I enjoyed this public display of affection a little too much. People were probably watching us, rolling their eyes as they walked past, but I didn't care. More important, he didn't appear to care either.

My heart was a drumbeat, thundering out of tempo, as Jace pulled back and his words took root deep inside. I was clearly destined to spend Thanksgiving with the Hammonds, too, which was why I agreed to go with him rather than studying for finals, even though they were steadily approaching, or freaking out some more about the dark, unsettling happenings on campus.

It was like a switch had been flicked somewhere in my brain because the way Jace was talking, how he was acting, he *felt* like my boyfriend. And I think knowing he was ready to be by my side—that he had no intention of going anywhere—made it easier for me to shut everything else out, at least for a little while.

Like Jace always vowed, he'd protect me. And as long as he was around, I knew I was safe.

fifteen

Days slid into a week, and as the semester kicked into a higher gear, the workload nearly doubled. I was still getting up an hour and a half earlier every morning to commute to Delaware, but I hadn't seen Levi on campus since the football game. Even so, I'd made sure I was never alone, and always in public. I wasn't taking any chances.

And when I'd called Mom earlier in the week to let her know I planned to spend the Thanksgiving break at home, she'd been ecstatic.

I wasn't about to break our annual tradition: Mom would cook *way* too much for the three of us, I'd help her get the sides ready, and Dad would be in the garage, sorting through our street's food drive donations for the local charity. This year was no exception. In fact, it was the first Thanksgiving that things had felt relatively normal versus just going through the motions. My smile hadn't been forced, and I could enjoy myself without the pang of guilt that usually followed. It would never stop hurting—my brother's absence—but our family dynamic was slowly returning in imperfect pieces, and while things would never be the way they used to be, I knew that if I wanted to move forward, I had to let go—*really* let go—of the past. Spending most of the day with my parents also meant they weren't as disappointed when I'd told them I had dinner plans.

Jace and I were headed to Pavilions—a fancy restaurant twenty miles outside of Port Worth—to meet up with his family to celebrate. The Hammonds were the only people I knew who preferred to dine out on turkey day.

Ironically, the closer we got, the more my appetite was rapidly abating—not that it had been all that strong to begin with after the feast I'd had only hours earlier.

Tension had crawled into Jace's Chevy after he'd reversed out of my driveway, and it'd nestled uncomfortably in the space between us ever since. Studying Jace's profile in the darkness, I noted the muscle flexing in his jaw and the way he was white-knuckling the steering wheel.

"Is everything okay?" I asked, frowning. "You seem kind of distracted."

"I'm fine," he told me, but his lips slipped down at the corners.

"Are you sure?"

As we rounded the curve, his truck bounced roughly over a pothole in the uneven road.

"Nothing's wrong, Hayles." There was a glimpse of his easy, laid-back grin, then it disappeared. "We're good."

Despite Jace's efforts to reassure me, I wasn't convinced. There was something off about his shuttered expression, the way his brows furrowed together. He felt a million miles away.

Fiddling with the locket around my neck, I tried not to concentrate on the fact that he hadn't greeted me with a kiss when he'd knocked on my door earlier. The ringer on his cell phone had gone off—his mom letting him know they were on their way too—and he'd suddenly seemed stressed out. His shoulders were rigid as he'd walked me to his truck in silence, his hand lingering by the small of my back like he was making a concerted effort not to touch me.

Deep in thought, I tried not to let the panic eat at me. "You're not changing your mind about us, are you?"

Jace's steely gaze swung to me. "No. Not for a second."

Relief hummed through my system, the newfound fear I'd felt dissipating.

Turning his attention back to the road, he murmured, "I'm sorry, I'm just keyed up about Levi, and now this dinner. I don't know. My head's kind of all over the place, but not when it comes to us, you hear me?"

"I hear you," I echoed, warmth blooming in my chest.

"I know I've acted like an asshole in the past"—he cast me a sidelong look, and even in the shadows, his blue-gray eyes danced with emotion—"but like I said, I want to be with you, Hayles. More than I've ever let myself want anything. That's not going to change."

His straightforwardness startled me. Then he was reaching for my hand in the darkness, threading our fingers together, and placing it in his lap with emphasis.

My eyebrows shot up.

I loved being around *this* Jace. The guy who didn't feel like he had to hide behind a mask of indifference. I knew he had trouble opening up to people—articulating his emotions. For years, I'd been stonewalled and shut out, but now he was letting me in, showing me everything I'd glimpsed, and it had been worth the wait.

"I want to be with you too," I whispered, becoming Captain Obvious's trusty sidekick. Because let's face it, I'd been about as subtle as a hand grenade when it came to my feelings for Jace. He responded by sweeping his lips lightly across my knuckles. It was such a simple gesture, but it was sweet enough to make me feel like I was moments away from melting into a pile of gooey nothingness. The lump that had formed in the back of my throat was hard to speak around when I added, "Which is why you better hold up your end of the deal tonight."

"Yeah?" He smirked, interest piqued. His eyes met mine, sharpening as they roamed over me, filled with pure desire. The thick, gloomy cloud that had been hovering around him seemed to dissipate a little. Mission accomplished. "Remind me, what's that again?"

As shyness threatened to streak through me, I told myself that Jace had already given me the most amazing orgasm I'd experienced in my entire life. Not only that, he'd made it abundantly clear this past week that he planned on doing it again. I had no reason to feel embarrassed. "Hmm. If I'm remembering correctly, I believe it had something to do with me being naked in your bed tonight."

The rough catch in his voice was hands down the sexiest thing I'd ever heard. "Damn it. If you start talking like that, I'm going to have to pull over."

I shifted in the passenger seat, my insides starting to heat and tighten in response. I stretched over to his side, placing a kiss on the corner of his mouth. "It's good we've got this whole patience thing on lock then."

The sexual tension that laced the air was verging on suffocating. Jace was like a drug, and I was slowly becoming addicted. The raw need to feel him kissing and touching me again had long since seeped into my bloodstream. But it wasn't lost on me where we were in time and space—speeding down a dark stretch of road—and the impending Thanksgiving dinner that required our full attention.

Now that I knew what it was like to have this with Jace— intimacy, understanding—I didn't want to lose it. And I certainly didn't want to rush this or risk doing anything that might mess this up. The emotional connection we'd forged after almost a decade was more powerful, more consuming, than the heady attraction that burned between us. I liked that this wasn't just about slaking our physical needs. It was more.

For the rest of the drive, I concentrated on the feeling of Jace's rough, calloused fingers gripping mine. The weight of his hand was heavy, secure, and yet, I knew what we were doing, what we were building together, was still so fragile.

Ever since Tom had died, I'd developed this horrible habit of expecting to lose the people I loved. It would be a difficult fear to conquer, but I was determined to place my trust in the universe again, to keep my self-sabotaging tendencies at bay. To believe, somehow, in the promise of a better future, and to hold on tight, even when it tried to elude me again—and it would, because nothing worth having, nothing worth fighting for, stayed in reach for long.

• • •

When we strolled into Pavilions fifteen minutes later, stopping at the hostess's desk, Jace stood beside me and touched the small of my back. My nerve endings tingled from the contact, feeling his warmth through the thin material of my long-sleeved dress. I lifted my gaze to his, and the intensity I was met with made my breath fall short. The tension had returned tenfold, radiating from his body, and it dug its talons into me, refusing to let go. What was I missing here?

Concern overrode any other thought. I shifted closer to Jace, murmuring, "Hey, whatever's going on, I'm here."

Some of the anxiety dissolved from his eyes. "Yeah, I know, baby," he drawled. "Thanks."

The hostess appeared and guided us past a crackling fire, well-stocked bar, and into the dining area. Amelia waved at us both, relief flooding her expression as we wove our way through the upscale restaurant.

Jace lowered his six-foot-three frame into the plush booth, fishing out his wallet and keys and setting them on the table. "Sorry we're late," he said gruffly.

I slid into the seat next to him, sitting directly across from his parents. "Hi, everyone." I raised a hand in greeting, self-consciousness bubbling up inside me.

Judy beamed at me, then moved her gaze to her son. "It's fine, honey. We haven't even had the chance to look at the menu yet." Her voice was light and airy. Unfazed.

Granted, the restaurant was packed, and when I scanned around, it seemed like they were understaffed. It was Thanksgiving, after all. There was an ample amount of noise, laughter, and chatter ringing out from other neighboring tables, and surprising crowds of people continued to stream in through the sliding glass doors. If I was being honest with myself, I was partly grateful for the distraction. It meant I wouldn't have to navigate or fill any uncomfortable silences.

At that admission, my stomach dipped. I hadn't been able to shake the feeling that I was fifth-wheeling the Hammonds' family dinner. I knew Judy and Geoff loved and accepted me like a daughter, but I still felt pressure. Jace and I were together now. Everything about this was uncharted territory.

Amelia kicked me beneath the table, drawing my gaze to her, and her gray eyes narrowed on me. She leaned over, whisper-hissing low enough that only I could hear, "Do you know what's up with Jace? He's been acting weird ever since my party."

"No clue," I told her honestly. "But I'm working on it."

With a slight frown, she picked up the menu to study it, but she didn't say anything else.

I slumped further into the booth, feeling confused and agitated all at once. Focusing on this dinner and finals had kept me distracted from my real problems—a feeling I was grateful for—and I reminded myself of that as I glanced between Jace and his family.

Not wanting to interrupt the flow of conversation, I reached for my glass and swallowed a gulp of cold water. Turning my attention to Jace's dad, I offered him a small smile.

"So, how's school going, Hayley?" he asked me, and I appreciated that he was touching on such a neutral, easy subject. "Keeping you busy?"

"You could say that. I've got a couple of assignments due soon, then finals next month. I did okay in my midterms, so I'm really hoping for good grades." I exhaled wearily, feeling my stress levels climb at the mere mention of everything that was on my plate right now. Maybe not such a safe subject in the end. "It's hard work, but I'm really enjoying it."

"I'm glad." There was a pause. Geoff nodded slowly. "You're lucky you've found something you enjoy and want for yourself so soon. It takes some of us most of our professional lives to get there." His hazel eyes took on a faraway look, and I didn't miss the heavy meaning of his words.

Before I could reply, the waitress materialized beside our table, and we were all ordering food and drinks.

Halfway through dinner, Jace had still barely said anything to his parents. Or to Amelia. Or to me.

The silent routine was never a good sign, and I could tell that he was waging some kind of internal warfare.

Peeking over at him, I found his expression carefully blank, like it had been since we'd gotten here. Sure, he was always pretty impassive, but I had the sneaking suspicion that whatever thoughts plagued him were truckloads of bad. He never acted like this without a reason.

I tried to nod and smile as Geoff insisted on staying for dessert, but it felt more like a grimace. The prospect of having to sit here any longer, conversing in meaningless table talk, sent another wave of reluctance crashing through me.

I blinked back into awareness when Judy shifted in her chair. "All right, so there's no easy way to say this, and there's no point putting it off any longer," she declared. At first, she focused all her attention on her husband, and he put his arm around her, rubbing her back soothingly.

Amelia and I froze, exchanging a brief glance of mirrored turmoil, and I felt Jace bristle beside me.

Judy paused long enough for our desserts to be delivered.

She swept her golden hair behind her shoulders as she leaned forward, facing us once more. "Geoff and I have made a decision that is probably going to come as a surprise to you, but please know, your father and I haven't made it lightly. This is something we've wanted to do since we were your age, and it feels like it's the right time now that you've both finished high school."

"Why does it feel like you're only having this conversation with me?" Amelia's eyes, cold and accusing, swung to her brother, then to me. "Do you two already know about this?"

Jace tensed again.

The fine sheen of sweat that dotted Geoff's forehead didn't escape my notice.

"I have no idea what's happening right now," I said, feeling the need to clarify.

Was this why Jace's mood had been off all night? Because he'd been steeling himself for this conversation?

Jace was silent for so long that I didn't think he would speak. "I knew, okay?" he admitted. "But could you just let Mom finish before you start with the dramatics? This is why people find it hard to tell you stuff sometimes."

"Oh, I'm sorry. I didn't realize having an emotional reaction was a bad thing." Amelia chuckled humorlessly, and I couldn't help but cringe. "You might only like to share your feelings about, uh, anything, once in your lifetime, but I'm not like you, Jace. And I'm okay with that. Please, Mom, continue."

I tried to concentrate on the uneaten slice of chocolate ripple cake in front of me and not on the fact that these siblings—two people I loved so dearly—clashed so often. The urge to say something—to reveal how badly I would give *anything* to have *my* sibling back, that I'd never treat him this way—overwhelmed me, but I knew I couldn't do that. This wasn't about me.

"It's not even that big of a deal in the grand scheme of things," Jace added, his voice losing some of its hard edge. "It's good, Millie. Keep an open mind."

There was a strained pause, and Geoff chimed in, "Thanks, son. Appreciate that." He steepled his fingers, pondering his next words. "We planned to tell you both at the same time, but I guess things don't always work out how we want them to. Jace came home early and met the Realtor we'd hired. They were in the middle of an appraisal. It wasn't something we were trying to keep from you, sweetheart."

"We're at a restaurant," Amelia pointed out. Her gray eyes were shining with unshed tears, and she blinked fast, as if she was trying to stop them from falling. "Why are you doing this here?"

"Because, honey, tonight should be a celebration. We're not getting any younger. Life, as we all know, is so short," Judy replied, and I concentrated on not reacting or reading too deeply into that. "Your father and I, we . . ."

"We've decided that it's time we grab life by the proverbial horns; do the things we've always wanted to do," Geoff supplied when it was apparent his wife had momentarily lost her nerve. He studied his daughter from behind his wire-rimmed glasses. "As much as we love you and will always be here for you, we think you're both old enough to take care of yourselves now."

A smile crept over Judy's features, and she reached for her husband's hand. "You know it's always been our dream to travel around Europe in one of those motor homes, and well, we're going to make that happen. No more excuses," she rushed on with a newfound thrill. "Your father and I have decided to retire and sell the house."

Amelia's shell-shocked gaze flicked back in my direction, then never left. All communication was through her eyes, and I knew she was ready to go cry somewhere. I recognized the need to escape and flee a situation all too well.

While I knew this news wasn't all that ground-breaking for me, my best friend's whole life hinged on that house, on her parents. What they were doing must've felt like a betrayal, or at the very least, a transformative shift in her world. I knew grief and change were always relative, and they didn't come with a manual. Navigating any loss was like driving without a destination. There were plenty of blind spots and pit stops, and the darkness was there sometimes, following you like an ominous storm cloud in the rearview mirror. It made it easier when you had other people in your car, a support system to turn to for directions, or just to pass the time as you slowly got better at never knowing what was around every corner.

Amelia was always there for me, a constant source of love and acceptance, and I was more than ready to place myself in the passenger seat for once, to help her navigate this.

sixteen

Shortly after midnight, my phone chimed, and my stomach took a pleasant tumble when I registered the name on the lit-up screen.

It was Jace.

You awake?

The knowledge that we were under the same roof crackled through me like an electric current. I was a coiled live wire, too antsy to fall asleep. His text did nothing to ease the heightened awareness, the endless pull from the invisible tether, I felt.

After we'd left Pavilions, I'd stayed the night at Amelia's. The two of us had binged the Die Hard series and consumed our weight in gummy bears, just like old times. My best friend had curled up at my side, her hot tears soaking through my sleep shirt. She'd apologized for crying over it, but I'd reassured her it was okay. For years, she'd been the superglue that had held me together—long before Jace had entered the picture—and I wanted her to know how important her friendship was to me. It was something I'd never sacrifice, take for granted, or lose sight of . . . but I was also human. If ever I'd had the overwhelming urge to slip out of her room, tiptoe down the carpeted hall, and crawl into her brother's bed, it was then.

Chewing my bottom lip, I typed in and sent: *Unfortunately. Can't sleep.*

Within seconds, I got a message back. *Same.*

I tried to think of a casual response and came up empty.

Another text popped up on my phone, vibrating my palm. *Meet me outside at the spot?*

A slow, curling heat flickered in my belly.

Amelia snored beside me, dead to the world, and I momentarily struggled with guilt. My loyalty to her demanded that I stayed put, that I didn't go to him, but then I reminded myself of two things: She knew about Jace and me. Better yet, she was cool with it. I had no reason to feel like I had to sneak around or choose between them.

Easing out of her bed, I used the light of my phone to illuminate my path. Fumbling around in the darkness, I shrugged on a puffy jacket from my overnight bag, wiggled my toes into my sheepskin boots, and quietly closed the door behind me.

I paused outside Amelia's bedroom and forced myself to breathe. For a nanosecond, a small part of me contemplated retreating and face-planting into her bed, blaming this on sleep-deprived insanity. But I'd wanted to spend time alone with Jace over the break, and I'd wanted to figure out what was bothering him—if it truly wasn't about his parents. It felt wrong to pass up on this opportunity.

Stepping out into the cold night, I gathered my hair into a messy ponytail and crossed the Hammonds' manicured lawn.

Nestled in the branches of a wintry, leafless oak tree, I saw the old treehouse, its white panels glowing iridescent in the moonlight, standing out in the shadowy backyard. The darkness . . . the way my footsteps were silenced by the gust of wind that picked up . . . unsettled me, and I walked faster. Even if Jace was that safety zone for me, where nothing bad existed, I wished I'd told him to meet me in the kitchen instead. That was where normal people crossed paths in the middle of the night when they couldn't sleep.

"Up here," I heard Jace call from the top.

An exhale tumbled out of my mouth, my shoulders sagging a little. Tucking my phone into my pocket, I curled my fingers around the metal rungs of the ladder I'd scaled at least a thousand times. Before I could second-guess myself, I started to climb, muscle memory thankfully taking over. When I reached the platform, I accepted Jace's hand and let him haul me up.

"You good?" he asked, frowning slightly.

"Yeah." I hugged my jacket tighter around myself, glancing around. Everything was still the same. Smoothing my hand over one of the low-hanging branches, I traced the *J.H., A.H., T.D., &* *H.D.*—our proud, scribbled initials—carved into the wood. A sad smile tugged at my lips, my mind caught up in the ghostly memories of a long-ago past. "Wow. It's been years since I've been up here."

"Me too. I wanted somewhere to think. Then I got up here and, I don't know, I realized I didn't want to be alone after all," Jace admitted, casting me a long glance. "I'm not going to lie—I'm kind of impressed, Hayles. You made that climb look easy."

"You're an asshole," I said, laughing. "It's creepy as hell out here. I seriously regret not telling you no."

Jace lowered himself to the floor, and I settled beside him, gingerly scooting forward until my knees were dangling over the edge. I could see everything from this height, the shingled roof of his childhood home, to the faraway city lights, twinkling on the horizon.

"Well, I'm glad you didn't." Jace's shoulder bumped mine, and I held his gaze, inhaling slowly.

Being in the treehouse was like being in a time warp, transporting me back to a collection of moments when life was simpler, easier. Everything about this was reminiscent of our childhood—the summer nights the four of us would hide out here together, playing make-believe, stargazing, and dreaming—and yet nothing about our late-night tryst felt innocent.

Despite the intense family dinner we'd sat through, and the fact that I'd chosen to sleep in Amelia's room afterward, not his . . . it all just melted away when Jace pulled me into his arms. I nestled against him, letting the warmth of his body soak into mine as I closed my eyes and rested my cheek against his chest.

"We should probably talk about earlier," he said, his voice rumbling through me.

"Yeah, we probably should."

"But I'm kind of all talked out, you know?"

"I know."

For what felt like an eternity, we sat in companionable silence, listening to the ethereal calls of a nearby owl that echoed in the sky, and the sound of our breathing, short and shallow. My thoughts were blissfully empty for a while, until my brain eventually drifted back to everything that had happened tonight. I couldn't help but wonder, again, the reasons for Jace's changed demeanor—quiet, serious, moody. I mean, he was never a ray of sunshine, but something felt off.

I withdrew, just about to ask him, when he turned to face me.

"Do you remember the last time we were up here?" he asked. This close to him, his eyes were crystalline. "Back when we were just friends."

I nodded. "It feels like a lifetime ago."

"Exactly. It might be why it took me so long. You've always been there, and I . . ." He broke our eye contact, looking off into the distance.

Never in my life had I been so laser-focused on Jace's profile. I wanted to absorb everything he was about to say and commit it to memory.

"I thought it was about being ready for another relationship, but it's not. It's about being ready for the *right* person. As rough as my breakup with Zoe was, she wasn't the right person for me," he revealed. "I'm not saying it won't be hard, us being together. I'll probably piss you off sometimes, struggle to talk about the shit that matters, but you're it for me. You're my person. Probably have been ever since you pushed Payton Reynolds over on the playground."

A surprised laugh escaped me. "Oh my God, I can't believe you saw that. You've never told me that before."

He shrugged. "Of course I saw. You stood up for my sister. Payton had been bullying her since the second grade, and no one was brave enough to go to bat for her, until you. Even when I was twelve, I knew you were a total badass. I mean, you offered to trade your first-edition Pokémon cards with me. You were one of my closest friends growing up. I've always cared about you, Hayles, but something changed over the years. I don't know when it happened, but it did."

The flutter returned to my chest. For a guy who didn't enjoy expressing his thoughts and feelings very often, from where I was sitting, he was tremendously good at it.

"What I'm trying to say is, I wish I could go back and tell myself not to run scared from what I felt for you. I had a chance at being with you a couple of years ago, and even though I was with Zoe and not really in a position to start something with you back then, I didn't take it. I've been regretting it ever since," he went on, his voice gravelly and deep. "So, yeah, I want this—all of it—with you. And I'm not going anywhere, so I need you to stop thinking that I am, okay?"

My breath stuttered. "Okay," I whispered.

He was right. I needed to have more faith in him—us—and get back to the hopeful romantic I was pre-accident.

Satisfied, half of Jace's mouth tipped up, that dimple I loved finally popping. His low-lidded gaze dropped to my lips, and the air around us seemed to thicken and become charged, heavy. I leaned in out of instinct, closing what little distance was left between us.

Jace might've kissed me back, but it was me who deepened the kiss and took control. My tongue touched his, tentative and urgent at the same time. There was no fear, no pain, and no thought of chancing rejection. Not in the shelter of his old treehouse. Not after everything he'd said.

My hands skated up Jace's biceps and looped around his neck. I needed to be closer than this, to feel every inch of him against me. We seemed to communicate on some unspoken level, because the next thing I knew, his hands were settling on my waist, tugging me into his lap. His back muscles were tight beneath my splayed fingers as I rose, feeling my bare knees graze against the wood, and my other hand slid into that dark, shaggy hair. Drawing back, he blinked up at me, and I straddled him, another rush of power surging through me.

"Sometimes, I still can't believe that we're doing this," I admitted. "That I get to kiss you whenever I want."

Jace groaned when I ground my hips down on his. The friction was heavenly. Maddening. His hardness pressed against the sensitive spot between my legs, and reflexively, I rocked into him again. Burning arousal swept through me, an unmistakable drumbeat, growing louder and louder, until it was all I could hear. I suddenly understood why Amelia always made such a big deal about this—finding someone you could be physically intimate and emotionally vulnerable with.

I cradled the sides of his face, welcoming the prickly tickle of stubble against my palms. "Since we're being so honest tonight, I should probably tell you that I've fantasized about this for an embarrassingly long time."

He sighed, and I swore I heard relief. "That makes two of us, Hayles."

"And then there's that. My nickname." For as long as I could remember, Jace had been the only person to call me that. Maybe thinking it'd symbolized something, all those years ago, was a bit of a stretch, but still, it had only ever been his term of endearment for me and no one else's, and that meant more. "It makes me feel like I'm yours."

"You are mine," he said simply. "Have been ever since that night at Owen's apartment."

And then his lips were capturing mine, unrelenting and sweet. He knew exactly how to angle my face, how to tangle his fingers into my hair, how to make every part of me ache—the best kind of ache.

In the several seconds that followed, Jace helped me tug my jacket off, then my shirt. His knuckles grazed the undersides of my breasts, raising tiny bumps across my skin. When his hands skated up higher, cupping me through the white lace of my bra, a whimper rolled out of me.

He kissed the valley between my breasts and each swell, setting every nerve ending on fire, and I swallowed another moan that probably would have embarrassed me. He expertly unhooked the clasp of my bra, and I felt the cool air rushing against my chest. Self-consciousness crawled over me like a shadow, but I refused to cover up. I liked the way he was looking up at me a little too much. It went so much deeper than lust or desire.

I shivered at the first sound of his voice. "You're so goddamn beautiful."

If someone had told me at the start of the semester that I would be half-naked in Jace's treehouse on Thanksgiving break, I probably would've said that they were insane. But here we were, and the reality of it settled around me.

"You have no idea how long I've wanted to see you." He exhaled through his nose. "All of you."

Moving farther from the edge, I eased back, my puffy jacket acting as a makeshift blanket. I got comfortable, tracking the trajectory of Jace's hands as they explored my body. His mouth lowered to the tip of my left breast, his breath warming me. I cried out when his lips closed over my nipple—a hot, wet kiss as his tongue languidly flicked over me.

Jace moved his mouth from one breast to the other, and I made a happy humming sound, little darts of pleasure zinging through me. Gradually, he began his descent, peppering open-mouthed kisses over my rib cage, then past my navel, and finally, over the flare of my hips. My heart pounded an unsteady rhythm. When Jace's hands smoothed over my thighs, fingers digging in just a little, I was dizzy.

"God, I love the way you feel. So soft and smooth and perfect." As his touch—his mouth—drifted closer to where I most craved it, a strong pressure built, clamping down deep inside me. "You'll never know how much I want you right now."

I went to say something, to reassure him the feeling was mutual, but his big hand disappeared under my shorts and any coherent thought I had vanished when his fingers slid over the seam of my underwear.

"I want to make you come again," he said, voice rough. "I have to see you, feel you, taste you. Are you gonna let me?"

Swallowing hard, I managed a jerky nod. Because seriously, what girl said no when they were at the mercy of Jace and those wicked fingers?

"Thank fuck," he growled. "I'm dying here."

In a stuttered heartbeat, he'd stripped me bare, all patience and finesse forgotten.

His hand returned between my legs, and a spiral of heat twisted low as he grazed my slick wetness. Sensation careened through me as the pad of his thumb found and teased the spot that had stars flashing behind my eyelids.

Slowly, he pushed a finger inside me, then two, and my hips moved restlessly in small circles. I needed more. With Jace, it was never enough.

That pulsing ache intensified as he positioned his head between my legs, the scratch of his stubble tantalizing against my inner thigh.

He looked up, eyes hooded. "Trust me?"

"Always," I whispered. My chest seized, a mixture of nervousness and anticipation.

A second later, his breath heated me where I was most sensitive. If I wasn't lying down, I probably would have keeled over.

There was a prickle of insecurity—being naked while he was still fully clothed—but simply knowing that it was Jace was enough to scatter any fear. In fact, it had every muscle in me drawing tighter and tighter. So, when he replaced his fingers with his tongue—the first time anyone had ever done that to me—it seared my skin and wrung a gasp from my mouth.

I'd never felt anything like this before. Glancing between my legs, I'd never seen something so dirty and yet sweet. New, exquisite sensations flooded me, and I reveled in them, wanting more and more, but I also couldn't help but squirm away, not used to their intensity. Strong hands gripped my hips, and Jace yanked me closer to his mouth, holding me in place, devouring me.

"Oh my God," I moaned, letting my head fall back.

While Jace had started out slow, almost leisurely, his lips quickly turned hard, hungry. His tongue worked me to the brink, circling me. My legs started to shake against his ears, the pressure building, and I sank my fingers into his hair, tugging him closer. I didn't want him to stop, but I knew I was close.

His breath fanned my clit as he exhaled, then sucked, and release charged through me at a blinding speed. My vision blurred. The whole world went white. The aftershocks of pleasure eddied through my entire body, leaving no corner of me unaffected. I was rescinding my previous statement. *This* was the most intense orgasm of my life.

And maybe it had a little something to do with the fact that I'd also just allowed myself to be so vulnerable with Jace, too, shedding the last of my defensive armor.

I heard him whisper something in my ear, staying with me until the shivers abated.

When I finally blinked my eyes open, it was to find Jace staring down at me. The way he was looking at me was better than any fantasy I'd concocted in my head. He was looking at me like I was the center of his universe. Like he wasn't sure this was real either. The warmth and closeness of him washed over me as something dislodged inside my chest, a myriad of emotions rushing in.

The last time Jace and I had been up here together, we'd still been forming what I'd like to think was a pretty epic friendship. We'd played an integral part in each other's young lives . . . but nothing compared to this, to how our dynamic was changing. My childhood had ended at sixteen, and I'd lost that girlish hope that I would have that romance-book or fairy-tale ending. A lot of stuff, my wants and dreams included, hadn't mattered until recently. Choosing to move away from Port Worth, relinquish control, embrace the unknown, and fall in love was me finally reclaiming that power.

Jace made it easy to be that person again. Every day I was with him, I was reminded of who I used to be, of what we'd always been to each other, and of the future—the fragments of a life I used to glimpse: *us*, happy, together. And as usual, he offered all this while expecting next to nothing in return.

seventeen

"Y'all seem cozy." Piper's lips curled into a delighted smirk. She looked in Jace's direction, who was closing in on us, carrying two cups of coffee from Bean Alive. "Did something happen, like, between you two over the break?"

The unexpected question caught me off guard, and my silence was all the confirmation she needed.

"Oh my God. Spill!" she practically squealed, interest flaring in her eyes. "You have about twenty seconds before he gets back here to tell me everything."

I might've been waiting for this day for what felt like forever—to finally say I was Jace's girlfriend—but right now didn't feel like the right time. Not with everything else that was happening. But I couldn't exactly lie to Piper. I was an open book.

Besides, it would've been way too hard to deny it—to claim that nothing had shifted between us over the Thanksgiving break—when Jace had been showering me with affection all day. In class, his hand had never left my thigh, and when we'd been walking through campus, he'd draped an arm around my shoulder, pulling me into his side. And just a few minutes ago, before he'd left to fetch us coffees, his lips had brushed the shell of my ear, and he'd whispered, "Have I mentioned how incredible you are? I'm so fucking lucky."

My stomach and heart had tried to out-flutter each other.

This had understandably earned a curious glance from Piper, eyes flicking up from the book she was reading, but Owen had continued to sleep on the lawn, his baseball cap twisted forward to shield his face.

The temperature had increased by at least ten degrees since this morning, the sun filtering through the trees and beating down on us as we'd eaten lunch near the quad. With winter just around the corner, we were all enjoying the last of the sunshine.

I peeked surreptitiously over at Owen, praying he wasn't awake. This wasn't the kind of personal information I wanted him to overhear. Subjecting him to the heated make out session in his apartment had been more than enough. "Well, we've kissed a couple of times and—"

"I knew it. The way he looks at you," she said, fanning herself with her book. "Like, wow. You don't see that every day."

Pushing my sunglasses farther up the bridge of my nose, I asked, "See what?"

"Don't act like you don't know what I'm talking about," Piper deadpanned. "That boy is crazy about you, I swear. I've never seen him—hey, Jace! How's it going?"

I winced.

"Good? You saw me, like, five minutes ago." He shook his head, amused. Then he passed me a steaming cup of coffee. "Be careful, it's hot."

"Thanks." I grinned, taking a tentative sip. Caffeine was about the only thing that was getting me through this semester, especially all the driving back and forth from Port Worth to Delaware.

Jace sat down beside me again, and then he leaned back, stretching out his legs. He balanced his coffee on the grass, somehow managing not to spill any.

A breeze picked up, scattering the fallen foliage and stirring my hair around me. A comfortable silence had descended between the four of us. There was no doubt in my mind that Owen was out cold, and Piper had returned to her well-worn copy of *Persuasion*, seemingly oblivious that Jace and I were there.

With both hands wrapped around the cup, I took another sip, admiring the dark orange leaves. It was like I was only just starting to pay attention to my surroundings because, suddenly, I was overcome with the prickly feeling—a feeling I hadn't missed—that someone was watching me.

When my gaze instinctively zipped over toward the student services building, I caught a glimpse of someone standing half-hidden behind the bulletin board. Dark jeans and grass-stained sneakers captured my attention first, and then they moved slightly, the person coming directly into my line of vision.

Oh my God.

Fear rocketed through me at breakneck speed.

Levi stood there, those vacant eyes locking on mine like a missile.

Even though it was a beautiful day, I felt like I'd been sealed in a freezer, immediately going cold and numb all over.

I couldn't breathe. Not when he was staring at me like that. And when he had the nerve to smile at me, it ripped the remaining air from my lungs.

My hands shook, sending the scalding coffee I was holding sloshing into my lap. "Shit!" I yelped, shooting forward.

My reaction must have freaked Jace out because the next thing I knew, he was tugging on my elbow, forcing me to look at him. "Are you all right? What the hell just happened?"

I heard Piper's voice in the background, sounding equally confused, but I couldn't tear my gaze from Jace. His eyes were intense and full of concern, grounding me.

I sunk my teeth into my bottom lip, trying to prevent it from trembling. "Don't look, but . . . I think Levi's been watching me."

Ignoring my request, Jace wheeled around to scan the quad. Then he straightened, spotting him. "What the fuck?" A tendon in his throat ticked.

It was only then that Owen sat up, blinking through his sleep-induced disorientation. He flipped his cap around backward and climbed to his feet. "What did I miss?"

"Levi," was all I said, but it was enough.

Owen's features turned to stone. "Where?"

"Over by student services," Jace told him. "He's still just standing there. He knows I can see him. It's like he's baiting me or something." He opened and closed his fists.

Apprehension flooded my system. "Don't, Jace. I don't want you to say anything to him. Don't go anywhere near him."

"I agree. Not when that dude has, like, zero boundaries whatsoever. We don't know what he'll do," Piper commented. "Have you heard from the police yet? Have they given you any updates on the case?"

"No. Nothing about the attack. The court hearing is soon, but that's to do with him breaching the restraining order and being too close to me at the game. Not the case. I don't understand.

Why won't he just leave me alone?" I voiced my questions, even though I was fully aware that none of them had the answers.

What *was* clear: Levi needed help. For his sake—and my own safety—I really hoped he got it.

"Make sure you add this to your testimony," Piper said. "We'll be your eyewitnesses. This is like, what, the third time he's been watching you? What a fucking creep."

"It's gonna be okay, Hayles," Jace breathed, giving my arm a reassuring squeeze. "This will all be over before you know it."

I cuddled into him, taking comfort.

This whole thing with Levi was venturing into territory I hadn't been prepared for. A shiver skated down my spine, my eyes inadvertently wandering back to him over Jace's shoulder as I thought about this.

Levi's head was tilted to the side, assessing me. I was a safe distance away, but it felt like he was standing right beside me—his presence all encompassing. That smirk inched wider, like he was totally getting off on this. Reveling in it, even. And now there was absolutely no doubt in my mind, this guy had serious problems.

The longer I stared at him, and the longer he stared back, I realized something. Something unsettling and unexpected. His dark hair, those green eyes, that sly, sadistic smile, they were merely features, but his face . . . it looked vaguely familiar, like I'd seen him somewhere before. I just couldn't remember where. It felt like trying to recall a memory from my childhood—buried too far down for me to retrieve.

I forced myself to take a deep, slow breath, to focus on the sounds around me and the smell of espresso that tickled my nose. Everything was spinning out of control, but I knew from experience that engaging with anxious thoughts—trying to quieten them—would do nothing to alleviate the way I was feeling.

"Okay, that's it," Jace declared, sensing my inner battle. "I'm gonna go over and—"

"And what? Have it out with him in plain sight? I wouldn't do that, brother," Owen ground out. "Technically, Levi's allowed on campus. Restraining order or not, he's a student at UD, just like the rest of us. If you go over there and things get out of hand, all you'll do is screw up the investigation. Keep ignoring him. He'll get what's coming to him." There was an unfamiliar hostility in his voice, a razor-edged hardness that made me flinch.

Jace's brows lowered, knitting together. A thoughtful look crept into his expression. "Yeah. Let's hope you're right."

• • •

I could hardly sleep that night. Staring at the ceiling—a solar system of faded glow-in-the-dark stars—I tossed and turned until I'd cocooned myself in the blankets. As ridiculous as it sounded, a small part of me had honestly thought after the police had brought Levi in and ultimately released him that he would be done toying with me. But Thanksgiving break was over, he was back, and so, too, was the fear of closing my eyes.

If I was asleep, I couldn't protect myself. If I was asleep, I couldn't control where my brain went. Dr. Jensen had pointed that out a dozen times—my need to always be in control of my emotions or any situation that made me feel threatened. Unfortunately, knowing the reason behind my insomnia didn't make it any easier to manage.

Minutes or hours later, I must have eventually drifted off, my body caving in, because the next thing I registered, I was sitting in a passenger seat. I didn't need to look to my left to know who was driving.

Jace.

He always was.

Everything about this scene was heartbreakingly familiar. The deserted, never-ending road that stretched out before us, and the moon, suspended dangerously low in the sky. I was trapped inside a weird, unidentifiable car—it wasn't Jace's Chevy. There were never oncoming headlights—or any other cars—but I was forced to relive losing my brother over and over again. Each time I had this nightmare, it was the same. I'd even learned to stop peering out the passenger-side window, knowing I was condemned to pass Tom every few miles. He was always standing on the edge of the road, like a forgotten hitchhiker, flagging me down. Even though I could move my head and make eye contact with him, I could never talk or grab the wheel. I was frozen, forced to drive past him, never slowing down, on a loop until something woke me up. It was my personal hell.

Something about the nightmare I was having tonight felt off, though. I could sense the change—a presence that had never been there before.

"Behind you."

It was the first time Jace had addressed me. Each time I had this nightmare, I wondered if he'd even known I was there.

Unnerved, I moved my gaze to the rearview mirror. I expected to find the back seat empty—I'd checked it countless times before—but again, something about this nightmare was different.

Sure enough, there was a dark silhouette sitting behind us, watching, silent. A scream rose in my throat, but shock, paired with the fact that I was incapable of talking or making any sound during these recurring dreams, choked it back down.

At the very least, I wanted to look away, to press my hands over my face, to *wake up*. But I couldn't do any of those things. I could only stare in the rearview mirror and catalog every detail my brain slowly revealed to me. At first, I saw the outline of his face, then the blood, trickling down the side of his mouth, as he lurched forward, hands gripping the back of my seat.

I noticed the stark contrast of his skin against his hair, like chalk on a blackboard. His eyes were missing, hollow, as he turned to face me in the rearview mirror, as if only just realizing I could finally see him.

"Help me."

My heart was beating so loud in my ears, I was surprised I even heard it—the garbled voice. A voice I'd recognize anywhere. It haunted me, even when I wasn't asleep.

I gasped awake, bolting upright and pulling air deep into my lungs.

I hadn't had a nightmare in over a year, and the coincidence that Levi had reappeared the same day they'd returned—that he was suddenly starring in them—wasn't lost on me.

An icy chill snaked down my spine, raising the damp hair along my neck.

This whole time, I'd thought my nightmares were my subconscious trying to process the loss of my brother. Not once had it occurred to me that maybe I wasn't looking at this from the right perspective.

Maybe it wasn't Tom who was in danger this time.

Maybe it was Jace and me who needed saving, and no matter how many times my brother tried to warn us, he couldn't get us to listen.

eighteen

"You ready for this?" Eden touched my arm, her red-lipsticked mouth stretching into a grin.

It was supposed to get rid of my doubts, but instead reluctance jammed in my throat. I almost told her I'd changed my mind, because as I ascended the stairwell to the Alpha Gamma Rho frat house, the small voice in my head shouted, *Go back!* The nightmare had returned after a year of escaping its grip. That meant something, I was sure, but so did entering this recent personal growth phase.

The court hearing was in just a few weeks, and Officer Bedford had told me that they'd had undercover officers working with the university to protect girls like me all semester. Not only did UD have a duty to care for its students, the last thing the university wanted was to start losing enrollments. According to her, the cops were good at blending in. That information didn't make me feel better, but it did at the same time. Mostly it helped to know that law enforcement was well aware and on top of everything that was going on. Assuming Levi was responsible, and he wanted to avoid being charged with a long list of criminal offenses, he would stay away.

I didn't want to live in fear or press pause on my life. I shouldn't have to. And I refused to let one nightmare set me back. I'd realized the next morning how deluded I was if I honestly thought Tom was trying to communicate with me through a dream. This was just my grief, paranoia, and stress, all looking for a reliable outlet.

"Yeah, I think so." I gave her a barely there nod.

"Listen, Hayley, I know you're only here because you're meeting Jace after he gets off work. I'm not offended. It's cool. You can ditch me—just make sure I'm with Reese first," she explained with a wink.

Hearing her say that, I winced infinitesimally. Her voice might have carried that usual carefree pitch, but a smidgeon of guilt blossomed in my belly.

Approaching the giant glass doors and the loud music that pulsated behind it, I squared my shoulders and mentally gave myself a quick pep talk.

I can totally do this.

The only thing worse than facing Levi again was letting him get in my head. He didn't deserve to have that kind of power or control over me. I should be able to go to a frat party with my friend and hang out with Jace without having to worry about the consequences.

I stepped inside the overflowing house, soaking it in. The party atmosphere was alive and beating, a tangible thing. Drunk college students were everywhere, swarming the hallways and crowding the rooms, making it much like a maze as we maneuvered through the house.

Eden led me deeper into the mob of rowdy frat boys, and her hand squeezed mine as we tried not to get separated in the chaos.

"Tell me if you see Reese anywhere," she said, referring to the guy who'd invited us tonight—he was a member of this frat—as she stood on her tiptoes.

"You're forgetting that I've never met him before," I replied dryly.

Everywhere I looked, I saw people dancing or kicking it. Like a deer caught in the headlights, I took in the party, the sea of faces surrounding me. I didn't recognize anyone.

Scooting back a little, I managed to avoid being bulldozed by two girls who were screaming insults and drunken accusations at one another.

Completely normal.

"I hope we don't have to stand here for much longer," Eden murmured, inching closer to me. "This is so awkward."

I nodded in agreement and fired off a text to Jace, telling him I was here, then shoved my phone back in my purse.

We'd drawn several curious stares, but no one was approaching us. I wasn't sure if that was a good thing or a bad thing.

At that exact moment, a familiar voice rose over the loud music, calling my name, and I saw a flash of red. Thank God. My gaze landed on Piper. She found us in the crowd and gestured for us to follow her. The only person I knew here, up until five seconds ago, was Eden—except for Reese, whom I'd still never laid eyes on before.

I discovered that frat houses were seriously huge as Piper led us farther down a long hallway with wooden arches and paisley carpeting. Venturing into a slightly smaller living room, we wove our way through the throng and settled by a green felt table. The music wasn't as deafening here, which meant that having a conversation was possible.

"I'm glad you changed your mind and decided to come." My red-haired friend drew me into a hug.

"Thanks for rescuing us," I said, stepping back. "Have you met Eden before?"

"No, I haven't. Nice to meet you." Piper's smile widened.

Eden lifted her hand and waved back.

"Do you guys want something to drink?" Piper asked us.

As always, the idea of alcohol made my stomach churn. Eden and I were quick to shake our heads, but a girl who'd dragged herself away from a group of dancers sidled up to us at the same time and said yes. She introduced herself as Madison and explained that she was also a senior majoring in education. She and Piper were fast friends.

"How are your classes going?" the petite girl asked as Piper went to fetch drinks.

"Good, I think," I told her, holding up my hand to show my fingers were crossed. "We'll see. Still waiting on a grade for a big term paper."

Piper returned with two Jell-O shots and passed one to Madison, keeping the other for herself. I stared down at the sweetened drink in her hand, wondering how the hell she was going to get it out of the tiny glass.

"Ever had one of these before?" Piper asked me, her lips twitching in amusement. "They're my preferred poison."

I shook my head.

"All you have to do is run your tongue around the rim so that you can loosen the Jell-O from the plastic," she instructed.

In one fluid motion, Madison tipped the shot back, showing us how it was done. "Word of warning. These things will knock you on your ass if you're not careful."

Yeah. I'd learned that lesson the hard way.

There was an appeal to staying sober at parties. Those Jell-O shots looked dangerous.

"Point taken. I don't want to—"

"Eden!" a distinctly male voice called out. "When did you get here?"

I turned my head as a cute guy with wavy auburn hair sauntered up to us. He was wearing a letterman jacket and cradling a red plastic cup in his hand. The shortness of Eden's skirt only briefly caught his attention, and even then, I glimpsed nothing but healthy desire, unlike half of the other sleazy guys that had been shamelessly checking her out since we'd arrived.

He was already making a good impression.

Eden fidgeted next to me. "Just now."

"'Sup, Piper, Madison," he said, acknowledging them.

Before Piper could reply, a girl wearing spike heels interrupted us, tears glittering in her dark eyes. There was no time for any official introductions, but I guessed this was Piper's infamous roommate, Beth. And she was leaving, apparently.

"I'm out," she announced, shooting Piper and Madison a look that spelled trouble. "I didn't sign up for this shit. It's too soon."

The perma-smile melted off Piper's face. "Fuck, I'm sorry. My roommate. I have to go," she apologized.

"And that's my cue too. Sorry. Beth's my ride," Madison said, giving Eden and me a cursory glance as she watched her friends exit the room. "It was nice to meet you both." Then she bolted after them, leaving Eden, Reese, and me.

"Frat parties." Eden gave a quiet, humorless laugh. "Never a dull moment, right?"

An awkward silence thumped by, and then Hot Ginger's eyes fell on me. "Who's your friend, Eden?"

"Reese, meet Hayley," she introduced us, grinning outright in no time. "Hayley, this is Reese. We go way back."

"You could say that," he said with a crooked smile, looking down at her.

When she leaned into him, brushing her arm against his, he didn't back away, and I felt a sense of victory on her behalf. Reese was definitely into her, and something told me he was interested in more than just a meaningless hookup—what these parties typically boasted. Then again, their familiarity might have had more to do with the fact that they'd known each other for a while.

"It's nice to finally meet you. Eden's been telling me about this guy she's—" I ground to a halt midsentence as she elbowed me in the ribs. Hard. "So, Reese, what's your major?"

He chuckled and slid his free hand into the pocket of his jacket. "I'm majoring in criminology."

"Oh, wow. That's awesome," I responded, genuinely impressed. "I love a good whodunit story, but I don't think I'd be cut out for that line of work."

"Mm. Hopefully I've got what it takes."

As much as I nodded and tried to appear fascinated by what his plans were after he graduated—he was a senior, like Jace—I found myself peering past Reese's shoulder, overtly scanning the crowd. It didn't take me long to find who I was searching for, considering he was almost a head taller than most of the other guys here.

My heart inflated as I spotted Jace.

It was almost criminal—ha!—how attractive he was, wearing a pair of faded jeans and a blue plaid shirt. His hair was messy and tousled, toppling across his forehead, and the stubble shadowing his jaw made him look older, kind of rugged.

Beside him was Owen, slightly taller but no less good-looking. He was the same kind of good-looking as Jace, but he didn't give off the level of intensity that Jace did . . . or have those blue-gray, soul-searching eyes.

"I'm gonna go say hi to Jace," I told Eden, momentarily distracted. "You don't mind, do you?"

She firmly shook her head, humor swirling in her eyes. "No, not at all. Go for it."

I turned back to where Jace was, about to walk over, when I saw a stunning brunette sashay up to him and glue herself to his side.

Jealousy shot through me, and I skidded to a stop. In Jace's defense, he wasn't even paying her a lick of attention as she got her flirt on, but the irritation was still there, building inside me.

I pretended to be cool and composed as I watched him talk to her, as he didn't hesitate to shrug out of her manicured embrace. Her face contorted into a scowl, and a rush of relief swept through me, but I still hung back.

I was nervous about going over to him. I just couldn't work out why.

"What are you waiting for?" Eden urged softly.

"I don't know."

As stupid as it sounded, I was waiting to see if he'd notice me first.

Several seconds later, as if hearing my thoughts, Jace's eyes darted in our general direction. His smile was all for me. I guess I had my answer. Owen nudged him and leaned over to say something. Jace nodded in response, deposited his beer on the bookshelf, and approached me with purposeful strides. Practically every girl in the room turned to admire him as he made his way over to me, a huge grin in place.

"My night just got a hell of a lot better." His husky voice lit up every nerve in my body, and then his hands were cupping my face. "Thanks for meeting me."

I figured I must have been imagining the heated way he was staring down at me, those lead-colored eyes molten, but then Jace did something totally unprecedented.

He leaned in and kissed me in front of everyone. And this wasn't the dining hall, filled with strangers who'd mostly had their backs turned. Here, we had an avid audience.

My body melted into his when his mouth descended, covering mine. There was nothing low-key about this kiss. This was not a hey-how-are-ya kind of kiss. It was the type of slow, drugging kiss that left you intoxicated and barely able to think straight.

His fingers threaded through my hair, tugging me flush against him, and I could feel the wild hammering of his heart beneath my palm. With a groan, he angled his head to deepen the kiss, and his tongue tangled with mine. I did my best not to concentrate on the overpowering lust that sizzled through me, the heat that raced up my neck, and then, before I knew what was happening, he was pulling away.

Holy hotness.

I resisted the urge to adjust my halter top.

Jace casually slung an arm around me and jutted his chin at Reese. "Crawford, how's it going?"

I doubted that there was anyone on campus Jace didn't know. Not to say I wasn't grateful that we could forget the formal introductions and the small talk.

Eden stopped shifting nervously when it occurred to her that her new beau and Jace knew one another too.

"Pretty good, thanks, man." Reese smiled, clapping him on the back.

"Whoa, that was some hello," Eden choked out.

A silent laugh brewed in my chest, but I couldn't bring myself to look at her, knowing what little semblance of composure I had would take a nosedive the minute I met her wide-eyed gaze.

Beside me, Jace murmured, "Remember what I told you the other day?"

My brain officially needed a jump start. I couldn't comprehend the first thing he'd said. All I could think about was that kiss, and the fact that quite a few people were still blatantly staring at us.

"About wanting all of it with you," he prompted, and those adorable dimples appeared.

A flood of warmth spread through me, and the conversation we'd had in the treehouse last weekend moved to the forefront of my mind.

Somehow, I was able to keep my voice sounding impressively unaffected when I said, "I remember. So how was your day?"

"Good. Wish we shared more than one class, though. I missed you." My heart rate picked up speed. I loved how easy things were between us—the comfort and security his words provided, they enveloped me like the best kind of hug. "I know you didn't feel like coming out tonight, but I'm glad you did. Been looking for an excuse to see you all day."

A goofy smile took up most of my face. "I missed you too."

"Professor Martinez gave us our last assignment for the term today," Jace revealed. "It's portraits, my least favorite."

"You're so talented, and you've taken photos for the Titans since freshman year," I pointed out. "You'll kill it."

"Thanks. That's not why I'm telling you, though. I actually wanted to ask you for a favor." Instantly, I picked up on the nervousness rolling off him in waves. "I wondered if—can I photograph you?"

My breathing went shallow as I stared up at him. There was something so intimate, so touching, about his request. It settled in my chest like a warm fire, burning brightly. "Of course. I mean, gosh, I don't know, Jace. I might be able to help you out. What's in it for me?"

"Hmm. Let me think. A hot date with yours truly." He spoke close to my ear. "I won't be able to take my eyes off you the whole time, literally. Imagine what it'll be like when I can finally put the camera down and touch you."

I pursed my lips, stifling a laugh, but I'd be lying if I said I wasn't interested. "Tempting stuff. You've really got it all figured out, huh?"

Jace's hand traveled down my spine, sliding dangerously low, and another jolt of heat seared through me. "When it comes to you, yeah."

At that moment, I was so stinking happy, it honestly felt like nothing could bother me, or burst this loved-up bubble I'd wrapped myself in lately.

Clearly, the universe thought I needed a reality check, because as I turned back to our friends, I detected a blur of a shadow—a dark outline—outside the nearby window. I blinked and it was gone. It was probably just the branches of the cedar trees that lined the frat house, I reasoned, but it was enough.

Even though Jace was chatting to Eden and Reese again, their voices loud as they competed with the music, I struggled to focus on what they were saying. Being here still had me on edge. I hadn't seen Jace since the nightmare I'd had, and we'd promised years ago: if either of us started having them again, we would tell the other person.

I knew what I had to do.

"Jace, can you come with me for a sec?"

"'Scuse us," he said.

I pulled Jace away from them, and we slipped out the back door into the cool night.

The air was easier to breathe out here, the music quieter. Even though there were a couple of people already out on the deck, smoking, I knew it was the best place to have this conversation.

Jace moved closer, the scent of him enveloping me like a thick haze. "If you wanted to take me somewhere quiet to have your way with me, all you had to do was ask."

He was being cocky and flirtatious, and ordinarily, I would have enjoyed it, but right now, I had to tell him the nightmares were back before I lost my nerve.

"Sorry, not that kind of rendezvous," I clarified, and he halted midstep. Placing my purse down on the folding table, I leaned back against the railing and released a tired-sounding breath. "I know I always ask you to be honest with me, so that's why I have to talk to you. I need to tell you something."

"Okay. What is it?"

The night sky above Alpha Gamma Rho house was a deep purple, and dark, odd-shaped clouds blanketed the stars. Casting my gaze to the hedges and rocks surrounding the in-ground pool, I forced myself to say, "I had a nightmare last night. This is the first one I've had in, like, a year."

"Your nightmares are back?"

I chewed on my lower lip. "It's not a big deal, right?"

While Jace hadn't battled insomnia after the accident, he'd often wake from his own blood-soaked nightmares. It was yet another thing we'd had in common.

"Hey. C'mere." Jace engulfed me in a warm bear hug, and honestly, his timing was pretty perfect. "It's whatever you want it to be, okay? I'm just glad you're telling me about it. Last time, you hardly said anything."

Drawing back, I studied his profile, noticing that the shadows under his eyes had become darker, that his shoulders always seemed tense lately. This was eating him up too.

I'd told him. That was enough. I wasn't in the mood to burden him any more than I already had.

"I know I brought it up, but let's just have one night where we don't think about Levi, my brother, your parents moving away—any of it," I suggested. To my amazement, he was already looking down at me with infinite tenderness and understanding. Something in me threatened to crack open, but I managed to get a handle on the outflow of emotion. "We're at a party. We should at least try to have fun."

His eyes narrowed a fraction of an inch. "You sure you don't want to go? We can."

"No," I told him. "I don't. I just want us to be a normal couple for one night."

"Okay. I'm down for that." He nodded. "As long as you remember that you asked for it."

I blinked at him. "Asked for what?"

There was a beat of silence, and then Jace was hooking an arm around my waist. He bent down, tossing me over his shoulder as if I weighed nothing more than his camera bag.

"Oh my God!" I squealed, gripping the back of his shirt. "What are you doing? Put me down."

"No can do, babe." Jace chuckled, and his forearm braced the backs of my thighs. "Operation take-your-mind-off-dark-depressing-crap is underway. I'm an expert at this."

Awareness trundled through me as he walked us over toward the pool.

"Don't you dare." I smacked his ass twice, just to make sure I got my point across . . . not because it was the perfect excuse for me to cop a feel. Definitely not. "If you drop me, you're coming in too. It'll be like that swimming competition in elementary school, except I—"

Jace wasn't cowed by my threat, because the next thing I knew, my voice was trailing off and I was midair. The water seemed to rise around me, pulling me under.

It couldn't have been over sixty degrees tonight, and the pool certainly didn't have a thermostat, or at least one that was in good working order. It felt like plummeting into an ice bath, and my lungs twisted inside my chest. Pushing off the bottom of the pool, I resurfaced, gasping and spluttering.

"I can't believe you just did that! What part of trying to make the best of tonight means 'hmm, maybe I should throw my girl-friend into the pool'?" I lowered my voice to mimic him.

Tipping his head back, Jace laughed, and I hated that even at that moment, I couldn't deny that he had the best laugh. It was a deep, rich sound that had more goosebumps dotting my skin. "Wow. Was that supposed to be an impression of me?"

I fixed him with a death glare. Wringing out my hair only seemed to make that infuriatingly sexy smile grow wider.

"Aw. Look, I'm sorry, okay?" Jace pressed his lips together like he was desperately trying not to laugh again. Contrary to his words, he didn't seem the least bit apologetic. "If it's any consolation, you're cute when you're mad. And I was planning on joining you, unlike that time you pushed me in after the race. Still haven't forgiven you for that."

The memory drifted back to me, and I smiled slowly. When we were younger, we'd butted heads more than I cared to admit. I loathed sports, but occasionally, I'd participated. My only motivation was to try to wipe that smug smile off Jace's face. "I guess that was a bit harsh, huh."

"Maybe I shouldn't have been such a sore winner."

Jace and I exchanged a contemplative look, as if reaching an unspoken understanding. It was nice, being able to talk about our past this way. Not having to wonder or guess how we felt anymore. He just shared whatever thought was whirling around in that head of his, and vice versa. Everything was so honest and transparent between us now.

My fingers combed through my hair and then habitually shifted to my neck. "Where's my necklace?" I asked, my voice jarringly loud in the crisp night. "I was wearing it earlier. I can't lose it, Jace. It's the one Tom got me for my birthday."

"I know," he said, his features softening. "Don't worry, it's probably just in the pool." Jace extracted his phone from the front pocket of his jeans, placing it on the tiles as he crouched on his haunches. He peered into the dark water. "Stay still. I can't see when you're moving around like that."

As I slowly inched closer to him, a grin tugged at my mouth, and I didn't hesitate to grab the sleeve of his flannel shirt, hauling him into the pool with me. He came hurtling forward, landing with such a splash that it sent water spraying into the air and cascading over the ledge.

A second later, I heard him inhale sharply as his head broke the surface. "Really? I just told you I was gonna get in."

Satisfaction rang through me. "What can I say? Payback's a bitch."

"You had me going there," he admitted. He pushed a hand through his wet hair, and his biceps flexed beneath his shirt, which was clinging to him in all the right places. My mouth went as dry as a desert. "You didn't really lose your necklace, did you?"

"No." I quickly showed it to him. "The clasp is broken, but other than that, we're good."

"Thank God." Relief flitted over his handsome face. Then he frowned, suddenly serious. "Here, give it to me. I'll put it in your purse, just to keep it safe."

Jace held out his hand, and I passed it over.

The moonlight glinted off the silver chain as he turned to swim the short distance back to the edge. He dragged himself out, clothes soaked and dripping wet. Heading up the stairs to the deck, he grabbed my purse and tucked the locket inside. He brought it over to one of the glass tables by the pool, which I was grateful for. The last thing I needed or wanted was to lose it.

Then Jace dived back into the pool, clothes and all. He resurfaced beside me and shook out his hair, splashing me.

I laughed, shielding my eyes. "You're not planning for us to stay in the pool long, are you?"

His gaze slid to mine, and he surprised me when he answered with a shrug. "Why not? Once you get used to it, it's not so bad. Plus, it's colder outside of the pool now."

My heart skipped as Jace swam closer to me again. It was

almost like our bodies were magnets—there had always been this gravitational pull between us—and so, without even realizing it, I had swum closer to him.

His hand landed on the side of my hip. My pulse went frantic. The water flowed and rippled around us as Jace drew me against him and my legs instinctively wrapped around his waist. He bobbed down, lowering me with him.

The icy water lapped against my chest, and I was pretty sure I'd be numb from the torso down any minute now, but Jace really knew how to distract me, because the touch of his hands on my bare skin—the extra privacy we had—became my sole focus. The music and everyone else sounded miles away.

"Can I tell you something?" Jace murmured.

"Mm?"

"Do you know how nice it is"—he paused, considering—"to just be here with you now, away from everyone else? I remember all the nights I'd be drunk at these stupid ragers, trying to drown out what I was feeling. I never have to be that guy with you. When you're around, it's like . . . I don't know, like maybe I won't ever have to pretend anymore. I can just be. And I really like that feeling."

The heat of his proximity, the warmth of his breath on my shoulder when he spoke, made me forget all about the fact that I should be well on my way to freezing my ass off.

His eyes bore into mine, and I saw the tenderness in them, the depth of emotion, as if he was willing me to understand. As if he thought I didn't already. As if maybe he still didn't know, after all this time, exactly how I felt. The need to be with him felt bigger than my body.

I love you.

It was right there, on the tip of my tongue.

God, I was so tempted to say it, to scream it at the top of my lungs. I don't think I'd ever wanted to let those three words out so badly in my life, but I was afraid. Afraid it was too soon, that I'd scare him off.

"Do you know how much I like you, Jace?" I settled on saying, trying not to shiver. "As in, really, *really* like you."

A twinge of disappointment seeped in as I wished I had the courage to just tell him how I felt, but I hid it with a smile. My fingers slid back around his neck, and his arms squeezed me tighter.

His chin dipped down, his mouth grazing my ear. "I know, baby," he whispered. "I really fucking like you too."

nineteen

"What the hell?" Jace said, throat bobbing. "I swear to God, Hayles, you saw me put the necklace in your purse. I put it right there."

Panic clawed at me, piercing my gut. My necklace was gone, for real this time, and my brain emptied of anything to say.

How could it have just disappeared in the ten minutes or so we'd had our backs turned? And more important, why would anyone at this party steal *that* out of a purse, and not the cash stored in there, or my phone? I might've understood if they'd emptied it of all my possessions, not just the necklace.

"Shit," Jace swore. "I know how much that necklace means to you. I never would've put it in there if I thought that—"

Blinking back the sudden rush of tears, I touched his forearm lightly. "It's okay. It's not your fault." I felt ten kinds of stupid for crying over a necklace, but it was the last connection I had to my brother.

Leaning into Jace's side, I welcomed the heat emanating from him. Waves of shivers raced through me.

"Come on, we should go dry off in one of the bathrooms," he suggested, nodding toward the frat house.

Warming up far outweighed my desire to stand out in the cold air and speculate about who had stolen my necklace—and why.

Wheeling around, I made it halfway up the stairs before I sensed that Jace was no longer behind me. "Aren't you coming?" I asked, frowning when I saw he was still standing beside the pool, hands on his hips.

He shook his head, just barely. "In a sec. I'll ask around, see if anyone saw anything."

"You don't have to do that."

"But I want to." His tone dropped a level. "Bad shit always happens to us at parties. I'll be damned if tonight ends like this. If you go up to the second floor, there's a bathroom on the right. I'll meet you inside."

Nodding, I grabbed my purse and ventured back into the frat house—aka party central—and did my best to ignore the curious glances I earned. I knew I must have resembled a drowned rat when one girl covered her mouth with her hand, sniggering as I brushed past her.

The downstairs bathroom had a long line, which prompted me to follow Jace's instructions. I dashed upstairs, eager to towel-dry my hair and tend to my mascara-streaked face.

Sidestepping the random hamper of laundry abandoned in the middle of the hallway, I approached the first door on the right and tapped my fist against it softly. When there was no answer, I reached down and twisted the handle. Pushing the door open,

I was relieved to find that it was indeed a bathroom and not an occupied bedroom.

Propping my hip against the sink, I stared at my reflection and inhaled a wobbly breath. What was I doing? Even though I was miles away from home, I still felt lost. In some ways, I felt *more* lost now than I had before I'd started college. I should have known better. The shadows of my past would always catch up to me—no matter where I went—and when they did, when they tapped me on the shoulder and dared me to confront everything I'd tried to leave behind, I'd have to stop running.

Alone and feeling sorry for myself, I tried to push the night-mares—Levi's strangled pleas for help in the back seat—and my lost necklace out of my mind.

A knock sounded on the bathroom door before it opened, and Jace walked in.

"Hey," he said. "I couldn't find the necklace, but we can come back tomorrow. I'll mention it to Reese. I know it looks bad, but it'll show up, I'm sure of—" He stopped, noticing my expression. "Are you okay?"

"It's nothing."

A flicker of doubt danced in his eyes. "Bullshit. You look upset. Did something happen?"

Words climbed up my throat and, unbelievably, managed to escape past my lips. "The nightmare I told you about before. It wasn't about the accident, per se." I wrapped my arms around myself. All of me felt cold, thrown off-balance. "There was some-one else there. It wasn't just us in that car anymore."

Jace closed the door behind him, the music growing quieter again. I could feel him staring at me, but I couldn't bring myself to glance up from his scuffed brown boots. He took my hand in his and gave it an encouraging squeeze. When he spoke, he sounded as concerned as I felt. "What was different about it?"

"Well, you were driving. The usual. Then you warned me that someone was behind us. I've had this nightmare at least a hundred times, Jace, and you've never said anything to me before. Not once." I hesitated, swallowing thickly. "Anyway, I looked in the rearview mirror, and I saw him. It was Levi, he—"

Before I could continue, Jace was stepping forward, putting his arms around me for the second time tonight. I didn't want to depend on him so much, but it was hard not to.

"I'm sorry the nightmares are back." He sighed heavily, resting his chin on the top of my head. "You know I'm here, that I'll help you again."

"I know," I mumbled into his chest. "I love that you've always looked out for me . . . I just don't want you getting caught up in all this. It's bad enough we had to go through the accident together."

"Anything that involves you involves me," Jace said gruffly. I couldn't exactly argue with that. "What are you thinking? Do you want to go back and see Dr. Jensen?"

"I don't think so. Maybe if it keeps happening," I told him. "It's not like it was real. That's what's making it easier for me. At least this nightmare isn't a memory."

He nodded once, as if he'd been expecting that response. "Maybe you are okay right now, but I still feel like this is getting out of hand, Hayles. I'm trying not to think about it, but I barely slept last night. I'm not finding anything about this easy. I keep thinking about . . ." He paused, his Adam's apple bobbing. "That night at the lake. You remember, don't you? You said I was just being paranoid."

I did remember.

Jace's hand was on the stick shift, and the other was drumming a rhythm against the roof of his Chevy.

My playlist ended, about to restart itself. We'd driven for at least an hour and had been sitting in his car for an indeterminable number of minutes. The silence between us lengthened as I stared out of the windshield. It was dark down here, among the trees, and I could make out the silver hue of the water, filtering through the thick foliage.

His knee nudged mine. "Ignoring me again, Hayles?"

"Hm?"

"I asked you a question." A hint of a smile played around his lips.

"Sorry. I must've zoned out."

"No shit. Truth or dare?"

"Seriously? We're going to play that game?"

His answering chuckle brought out his dimples. "Sure. Why not?"

"It's just you and me, Jace. If you want to ask me something . . ." I trailed off, studying him closely. I didn't miss the concern that filled his sharp, pale gaze.

"Fine. When are you going to come back with me to the clinic?" he finally came out with it, voice rough. "I only ask because"—he cleared his throat—"you missed your last two sessions with Dr. Jensen. I'm worried about you."

Jace had quickly become my sanctuary in the swirling storm known as my life, but that didn't mean I had to like this new topic he'd raised. Going to therapy wasn't the problem. I think it was more everyone's confusion about why it still hadn't helped me find some kind of peace with the past.

I licked at my dry lips. "Nothing's working, okay? Time doesn't help. Talking about it doesn't help. I just—I can't keep forcing myself to talk about the accident, about Tom, just because that's what other people think is going to fix me."

There. I'd finally verbalized it. For months, this darkness had been a vast, wild, beating thing I'd tried to tame. To keep hidden. Especially from Jace. Now, all I wanted was to set it free. Maybe then it would stop consuming me.

"Want to go for a swim?" The words tumbled out of my mouth before I had the chance to curb them.

"It can't be more than fifty degrees tonight."

"So? Are you that much of a chicken?"

Jace shook his head. His expression was a blend of incredulity and unease, inching toward intrigued. "Okay. Let's do it."

"Good. Because if you had said no, it would've been my dare."

Fumbling with my seat belt, I didn't stick around to hear his reply as I headed into the darkness. Life felt exhilarating out here, which was new. Usually, it felt bleak, empty. The rush of adrenaline, the promise of bad decisions, was loud in my ears, overriding the voice of reason and logic. I never did this sort of thing—I wasn't spontaneous or fun. And if there was one thing I'd learned recently, it was that I should probably start living every day like it was my last. Hence the impromptu swim. Or maybe I really was just having a nervous breakdown. I prayed it wasn't the latter.

"Hayley!" Jace followed me. "Slow down. I can't believe you're actually doing this."

Beyond the soft dirt hill, there was an expansive black lake, and I wrapped my arms around my torso. Moonlight cast a spidery shadow on the dark water.

I hadn't come this far to turn back now. This moment felt pivotal, like an essential part of my growth.

As I shrugged off my nightgown and tossed aside my slippers, the soles of my feet found the slick lake bottom. It grabbed me by the ankles, slithering velvet that roped me in deeper.

Glancing at Jace over my shoulder, I smiled shyly. Once upon a time, I wouldn't have had the nerve to strip down in front of a boy. The material of my underwear was probably see-through, but I wasn't embarrassed. I was comfortable with Jace.

His eyes swept over my face, then trailed down my body, excruciatingly slow, and it was like being caressed by an open flame. An involuntary shiver skittered up my spine. He inhaled deeply through his nose, seemingly unable to speak.

I waded farther into the water. My blood ran cold and the hair on the nape of my neck rose, but I didn't retreat. After feeling numb for months, it was nice to finally feel something. Even if it meant catching pneumonia.

"Fuck. We're really doing this," Jace muttered.

The sound of him unzipping his jeans reached me, and I drew in a breath. The knowledge that he was shucking his clothes, too, had my flesh feeling feverish. Good thing I was about to plunge into what might as well be an ice bath.

Each step I ventured put distance between the pebbly shore and me. My hair disappeared under the surface of the water. My smile spread like honey. Soon, I was in it up to my heart, which replied in slow, slurred beats. I lay back, floating on my bed of black silk.

I turned my cheek to the surface of the lake and imagined my lips meeting with Jace's. I watched him, transfixed, as he moved closer, the water slowly rippling around him. My gaze roved over his broad, defined chest. The waterline just reached his waist—the cut V beneath his abs—and desire kneaded my skin. I forced myself to look away and spread out my arms as far as I could. Icy water lapped against my ears.

Staring up at the night sky, I continued to float and take in the stars twinkling above us. I wondered which star was Tom, convinced he was watching over me now. There were so many warring feelings, questions, inside me, and I did my best to silence them all.

Jace's hand bumped my leg, sending a jolt of sizzling heat through me, and I emitted a squeak of surprise. For a moment, I worried I might slip right under, but my feet easily found the bottom of the lake.

"Sorry," he murmured. "Can barely see where I'm going."

"It's fine."

Jace swam beside me, and I noticed his hair was darker when it was wet, almost black. The moon was reflected in those blue-gray irises that I adored so much.

In this sprawling body of water, I felt lighter—like myself again. Focusing on that and chasing the feel of the cool lake hugging my every movement, I submerged my head. Everything felt so peaceful underwater, quiet. Safe.

The next thing I registered, I was being dragged to the surface by two strong arms, and I gasped, feeling my chest expand.

"What the hell are you playing at?" Jace demanded, gripping my shoulders. He looked more scared than I'd ever seen him before— even out on that road, months ago. "I'm trying so fucking hard to be here for you, Hayley, but you're freaking me out. You're not acting like yourself."

"Jace." My voice sounded small, even to my own ears. I was thrown off guard by his confession, the anger and intensity clinging to him. "Hey, I would never do that. I'm just swimming, I swear."

"It didn't look that way to me."

Unsure how to answer that, I said nothing.

"Shit, sorry. Maybe I'm just paranoid." He let go of me and swam farther away. He dug the heels of his palms into his eyes. "Since the accident, I keep seeing things that aren't there."

"Seeing what?"

"For starters, their bodies."

Despite Jace's attempts to convince me otherwise, he still wasn't coping. My heart turned over heavily. "Why didn't you say anything? I'm here for you too. This goes both ways."

"I don't know. I just feel like disaster could strike at any moment now, and I'm always—" His head snapped toward the shore so fast, scanning the thick row of shadowy trees and shrubs directly behind the lake. "Did you see that?"

I shook my head.

We waited.

I didn't see anything. Everything was dark and eerily silent. Even the bats had stopped screeching, gliding in the sky above.

"I swear to God, I just saw someone. They were over there, watching us."

Following the direction his finger pointed with my eyes, I felt a wave of tiny goosebumps spread across my skin. There was another clearing, near where we'd parked.

"Stop it, Jace." I laughed shakily. "We're literally in the middle of nowhere. There's no one out here."

He turned to me again. This time, there was a different set of emotions carved into his features. "I'm telling you . . ." His voice choked off, and terror set its claws deep into my chest. "Someone was watching us. I know what I saw."

Even now, remembering that moment—the haunting conviction Jace had maintained the entire drive home and years later—generated another dull spike of fear. The bathroom walls felt like they were closing in on me.

"What about that night? Are you saying you think someone *else* is stalking me?"

His implication that what was happening on campus with Levi was secondary to the real danger I was in . . . it was almost too much to process.

Jace's jaw locked down tight. "I don't know what to think anymore," he replied. "I just know I want you safe."

• • •

Over the years, I'd perfected how to distract myself from my problems. It was a self-declared art form. Sometimes, I'd fall down YouTube's recommendation rabbit hole, work on another vision board for my dream house, or create playlists on Spotify for pets I didn't have. Other times, when things were particularly dire, I'd go for a jog, maybe attempt to meditate. Now that I had a boyfriend, I was interested in a different kind of physical activity.

Much to my frustration, Jace was the perfect gentleman when we got back to his apartment just before midnight. All the heady sexual energy only kicked up a notch when he'd suggested that I take a shower after our spontaneous swim at the frat house. Worse, he didn't plan to sleep on the couch tonight. My brain had instantly flooded with incoherent images of Jace and me together, naked, having all kinds of fun.

Nerves fluttered in my belly as he walked over to his dresser and asked, "Do you want some clothes to sleep in? A T-shirt or something?"

"Uh, yeah. A T-shirt would be good," I said, adopting a casual tone.

"Your toothbrush is in the holder from last time, and I'll get you a clean towel." Jace handed me one of his old T-shirts and brushed past me to open the linen closet in the hall. The innocent contact sent little zings of heat eddying through me. After rummaging around for a moment, he withdrew a towel and added it to the growing pile I was carrying.

When Jace's dark gaze locked on mine, my stomach ignited. His eyes burned with equal longing as they skated over me, lingering on my mouth. The atmosphere felt thick and heavy.

His voice came out hoarse when he spoke. "Is there anything else you need?"

You, I was tempted to say.

Instead, I just shook my head and fled to the bathroom, wildly aware of how loud my heart was thundering in my ears.

Adjusting the water temperature so that it was hot enough, I stayed under the spray for a lot longer than I needed to, reveling in the way it soothed my stiff, cold muscles.

Squeezing my eyes shut, I barely resisted the urge to drop my head against the tiles, feeling like death from sexual frustration might be in the cards for me tonight.

I knew Jace wanted to wait—he didn't want to rush this—but as much as I admired him for that, the anticipation was becoming a special form of torture.

When I was finished, I exited the steamed-up bathroom and saw that he was sprawled out on the bed, engrossed in his phone. He only wore low-hanging sweats, and I could detect the cut V just below his abs.

A little shiver coursed through me.

I had to remind myself for the umpteenth time that the horizontal tango was *not* on tonight's agenda, and that, considering everything that had happened lately, it was probably for the best.

I swallowed at the dryness in my throat. "Can you scoot over?"

He glanced up, his eyes traveling from the top of my head

down to my curled toes. "Damn. You look incredible in my shirt," he croaked.

When he reached out to toy with the hem, I inhaled. He slipped one hand beneath the material, his fingers tickling my thigh as they slowly skimmed higher.

I placed my hand on his shoulder to steady myself as I lifted my knee. He took hold of my thigh, guiding my legs until they straddled either side of him.

"God, I can never get enough of you." His raspy comment was almost my undoing.

When he pulled me into his lap, I was shocked by how much I could feel through the thin fabric of our clothes. He was hard everywhere that I was soft. Everything in me concentrated on this—the feel of his body beneath mine, the way he looked up at me. Then Jace was leaning in, capturing my mouth with his.

Need spiraled through me, pooling low in my belly.

His tongue gently parted my lips, and the kiss quickly turned deep and scorching. My palms slid up his taut sides, loving the indents of his chest, memorizing the many dips and planes. The heat of him surrounded me, crowded my senses, until I was sort of dizzy. Dizzy with just how much I wanted him.

Tunneling my fingers through his hair, I let out an audible moan. His hands skated over my hips, cupping my ass, and settling me firmly against him. The hard ridge of his erection rocked into me, and a shockwave of pleasure swirled. His hot lips left mine, trailing a blazing path down my jawline and my neck as he planted open-mouthed kisses, setting off another round of tingles.

Desperate to touch him—to get my fill—I reached down and tugged at the waistband of his sweats, slipping my hand into his boxers.

"Hayley," he ground out, his voice low, strained.

Before I could do anything, Jace caught my wrist.

"No. This isn't what I wanted," he started roughly. He drew in a ragged breath, as if his self-control was a taut band that was about to break. "Fuck, you have no idea how badly I *do* want this . . . it's taking everything in me to *not* go there with you, but I really think we should wait, take this slow and—"

"Are you just saying that because you think that's what I want? Because it's not," I pointed out. I wanted to make sure we were on the same page. I'd been fantasizing about losing my V-card to Jace ever since he'd been newly single, and that seemed like a lifetime ago now. "I don't want to go slow."

"Well, I do," he said with more conviction. "We've been through a lot lately, and our first time isn't going to be overshadowed by all the other negative shit going down. I don't want sex to become an escape for us, okay? I'm not into that. Believe me, wanting you is definitely not the problem." He bucked his hips up off the bed, his hard length pressing between my legs again as if to illustrate his point.

I dropped my forehead to his, working to snuff out the sparks of lust that were still firing through me. As usual, he was making a very valid point. "Okay. Sure. We can keep waiting."

Jace tucked a strand of my damp hair behind my ear. "Do you need me to put a shirt on, or do you think you can keep your hands to yourself for one night?" he teased.

My blood pounded in embarrassment, but I knew even a nun would struggle to hold on to self-restraint while sleeping next to Jace. He was devastatingly gorgeous to begin with, but when he was turned on and half-naked? He was a drool-worthy package I was itching to unwrap.

Half smiling, I wiggled off his lap and collapsed back against the pillow with a huff. "Man, you are such a jerk."

Jace's full lips twitched into a cocky grin and the bed shook with his quiet laughter. "Whatever, you still love me."

Something snagged my insides, like a perpetual knot was unraveling. Air left my lungs at an agonizingly slow speed, and it was like my mouth was no longer taking orders from my brain.

"Yeah, I do," I told him, the answer escaping before I could corral it. "I love you, Jace."

Holy shit.

I'd actually said it.

A frisson of fear surfaced as those three powerful words hung between us, and Jace and I froze at the same time. I could feel the weight of his gaze on me, even before I turned to face him. Both of us silently assessed each other, knowing that we were on the cusp of changing everything once again.

"C'mere," came his quiet response, his hand curling around the base of my neck. A second later, his lips enveloped mine. His hands cradled my face, his touch reverent. There was so much unspoken emotion in the gesture, it felt like he was giving me life all the while stealing my breath away.

With a low, approving noise, Jace deepened the kiss, and my bones melted, unable to withstand the intensity. I clung to his broad shoulders as he drew me against him, as if he didn't want to stop touching and kissing me.

This kiss felt different, filled with something far greater than desire and something fiercer than adoration.

"You mean everything to me too," he said throatily.

It sounded like he wanted to say something more, but the

deafening silence that dragged on and on threatened to wreck my heart.

To mask my disappointment, I flashed him a wobbly smile and burrowed deeper into his bed, pretending that the seconds that ticked by didn't hollow me out like a Russian doll. I stayed silent as I heard him get up and brush his teeth, the faucet kicking on.

The mattress dipped as he joined me again. He dropped a kiss to my temple and eased back onto his side, turning the light off. "Night, Hayles."

When he curled his body around mine, it thawed me a little. I couldn't deny that while spooning was a completely foreign concept for me, being held in his arms like this had never felt more right—almost as if we'd been doing it for years.

Jace's warmth seeped into me from behind, and his breathing grew steadier, fanning the base of my neck. A bittersweet feeling coiled my insides.

Snuggling in closer, I told myself that even though he hadn't said it back to me, he hadn't exactly hauled ass from the bed either. He'd tugged me closer and *kissed* me. That was a good sign, right?

When you considered our history, I was leaning toward yes. Maybe he just needed a little more time.

But no matter how many times I explained it away or tried to rationalize it, the heavy ache in my chest kept me awake until well after the stars had faded from the sky.

twenty

When I woke up the next morning, Jace was gone.

The side of the bed he'd slept on was empty, and the apartment was filled with a heavy, stretching silence, almost like last night had already dissolved into a distant memory.

My mind zoomed back to the moment I'd told Jace I loved him, recalling the catch in his breath, the way his eyes had left mine for a second. But before I could latch on to the rejection I'd felt for too long, he'd wrapped his arms around me and held me like he didn't want to let go. We'd fallen asleep with our bodies curled together, our limbs tangled, like two climbing vines that were growing together. Like two people who were well within reach of second chances and something better.

And actions spoke louder than words, didn't they? I needed to focus on that—on all the times he'd *showed* me he wasn't going anywhere. I needed to not make a big deal out of this.

But my body betrayed me and cold anxiety shlushed its way through my system.

Damn it. It was hard to make those insecurities permanently disappear, especially when they'd been building beneath the surface for years.

I wandered into the kitchen, the frazzled wires in my brain desperately trying to come up with some explanation. Jace had probably gone back to the frat house to find my necklace. Or to get us breakfast bagels from the café down the road.

I brewed myself a quick cup of coffee, needing my caffeine fix, and drank it while it was still scalding, hoping that maybe it would cauterize my gut. Rinsing the cup under the faucet, I placed it in the sink and told myself to just accept the facts.

Jace wasn't here.

And there was a good chance I'd scared him off, for real this time.

I think, deep down, I'd always had this feeling that I was on borrowed time with him, so in some twisted way, it made sense. As much as I was drawing conclusions and being irrational, the thought of losing Jace—the idea that I'd pushed him away by finally telling him how I felt—made me panic.

I'd never let someone in as far as I'd let him in. He'd broken through my emotional walls when my brother had died, rescuing me from the darkness when I'd been expecting to stay there forever. I loved Jace with everything I had, and maybe that should've terrified me, but there was no bargaining with my heart. I'd loved him for most of my life, and I knew I'd love him for the remainder of it, but he'd left without a text or a note. It was like last night had never happened.

When I heard the faraway sound of my phone ringing, I blinked in an effort to snap out of it. Trekking back into Jace's bedroom, I picked it up off the nightstand and saw that it was an unknown number calling.

I shouldn't have been nervous, or sick with concern, but I was. For some reason, my stomach dropped to my toes, and I forced myself to answer the call before it jumped over to voice mail.

"Hello?" I choked out.

"Hi, is this Miss Donovan?" a familiar voice replied, and I was surprised I could even hear it over the roaring in my ears. "It's Officer Bedford from the City Police Department. I'm calling regarding your complaint about Mr. Brooks."

I automatically clutched the phone tighter. "Yes, this is her. Is everything okay?"

"I'm afraid I have some bad news," she told me after a couple of beats.

I inhaled, sitting down on the edge of Jace's bed before my knees could give out. It was like I knew exactly what she was going to say before she'd even said it, and I braced myself to get this over with.

"Unfortunately, after reviewing your case against Mr. Brooks, we're unable to pursue the report any further due to insufficient evidence," she explained. "We don't have a witness who can corroborate your statement on the night of the attack, so it's a matter of your word against his."

Her words hollowed my chest, carving out any hope I had that maybe this semester wasn't going to be a constant uphill battle. As if having to juggle my classes, a new relationship, and the lingering grief of Tom's death wasn't enough. There just had to be a stalker thrown into the mix too.

"What I'm about to disclose is very sensitive. Not information that is public knowledge yet, but I feel it is prudent to let you know," she went on, lowering her voice. "Because of some fantastic undercover police work, paired with the unfailing cooperation of the university, we've been able to identify who has been behind the other attacks on campus." My pulse quickened. "Another girl was brave enough to come forward, and the car captured on surveillance is registered to Fred Zimmerman. I believe he's one of your professors. All the evidence points to him, not Mr. Brooks. Professor Zimmerman has since confessed to numerous incidents of stalking, harassment, and sexual assault, dating back to last year."

"Oh my God," I whispered, shuddering as I realized the man responsible for all the creepy attacks on campus was still someone I'd been in the same room with—emailed, stopped by his desk to ask for help, smiled at—over a dozen times. I wanted to throw up.

"We thought your case might have been related to the others— you do fit his usual victim profile—but it's not," she continued gently. "Mr. Brooks was able to provide an alibi for the other attacks."

The back of my throat burned. "What are you saying?"

"We've arrested the man responsible for scaring those girls, Hayley. As a result, your case against Mr. Brooks has regrettably weakened, but it's not impossible. You've done the right thing by taking out a restraining order, and we'll keep doing everything we can to keep you safe. You'll have the opportunity to explain every-thing to the judge in a couple of weeks." Thinking about facing the courtroom, the magistrate, and Levi only deepened my feelings of dread. "You were likely informed by the clerk already, but bring any eyewitnesses, messages, pictures, like the one you showed me from the football game, or videos you might have that are threatening or disturbing—really any evidence you have at all that will help convict Levi of breaching his protective order." There was a pause. "The least we can do is pin him for that. I suspect this will all be over soon." Her tone indicated that she wasn't happy about any of this either.

Lying back on the bed, I concentrated on not audibly crying. I hated that Jace wasn't here while I was having this conversation. But even more, I hated how easy it was to pretend that he was. His scent still clung to the sheets as I sank into them. My disappointment, mixed with relief and happiness for all the other girls, leaked out of my eyes in the form of tears.

"Okay," I finally said when I could talk, not caring if Officer Bedford had overheard me sniffling. "I understand. I just . . . is there really nothing else you can do at this point, until the hearing?"

She sighed. "I'm sorry, but until there is concrete evidence against Mr. Brooks—irrefutable proof that he attacked you at that party—my hands are tied here."

• • •

Remembering my last-minute plans to study with Eden in the library this morning, I left Jace's apartment to meet up with her. Although I was hardly in the right mindset, I was grateful for the distraction.

Still worried about Jace's whereabouts, I'd left him a voice message, texted him a couple of times. Nothing.

Apprehension gnawed at me the entire drive to campus, and I must have been giving off some majorly heartbroken vibes, because Eden hadn't brought him up once, even though she knew we'd left the frat party together last night.

"My brain has officially turned to mush," she declared, lowering her forehead to the thick textbook she'd been poring over for the last hour.

"Tell me about it," I almost groaned, leaning back in my seat to stretch out my stiff legs. I had two textbooks flipped open and a sea of handouts spread across the table in front of me.

The library was quiet, aside from the soft whirring of the heater nearby, the ruffling of papers, and the occasional blast of music whenever anyone with headphones set on the highest volume walked by.

"I mean, how are we supposed to remember all of this?" Eden looked as frightened as I felt.

I closed one of my books and leafed through the revision sheet that Assistant Vice President Briggs had organized. Professor Zimmerman's absence made so much sense now—not that I could talk to anyone about it yet. He'd been detained by authorities, and the higher-ups had been trying to draw a veil over everything for weeks.

"I don't know," I replied unhelpfully. "I guess we just keep going over everything and hope that at least half of it sinks in?"

"We're so screwed."

I couldn't argue with that, so I didn't. And even if I felt remotely prepared for my exams, it probably wouldn't have made a difference, seeing as the doubts about my relationship with Jace hadn't let up. They rattled around in the back of my mind, making it hard to concentrate.

"Uh, hey. It's Hayley, isn't it?" a voice spoke up out of nowhere, derailing my bleak train of thought. "What's up?"

I pulled my gaze from the handout I was holding, surprised to discover a complete stranger towering over our table.

My eyes flickered to Eden, catching her impudent grin that screamed "hottie alert."

He looked down at me expectantly, and I just stared back. Wasn't it obvious that we were cramming for our finals next week? Practically every freshman in my cohort was here, armed with caffeine and ramen noodles to try to make it through the hardest week of our education so far.

I smiled at him, trying to be polite. "Just studying," I said, gesturing to my sprawled-out flashcards, notes, and textbooks. "I'm sorry, do I know you?"

Eden let out a puff of amused laughter before schooling her face into a blank mask. Apparently she had no idea who this guy was either.

He scrubbed a hand through his shaggy hair. "No, we've never met. I'm Trevor." There was a pause. "Anyway, I have something to"—he dug his fingers into the back pocket of his jeans, tugging out a creased-up piece of paper that he dropped in front of me—"give you."

"Um, okay. Random much," Eden drawled, wearing an equally bewildered expression.

So, it wasn't just me.

This *was* weird.

Trevor shifted awkwardly, rapping the end of his pen against his denim-clad thigh.

Knitting my eyebrows together, I warily opened the folded note.

At least you know now, it's always better to keep your pretty mouth shut. Maybe it'll stay that way.

Icy tendrils of terror spiked through me, and I could feel all the color draining from my face.

The words on the paper blurred together, but it was the messy scrawl that had me sucking in a deep lungful of air. I'd seen it before. The note that'd been left in my textbook earlier in the semester flashed through my mind. I was sure if I retrieved it from my dorm and held the notes side by side, the handwriting would be identical.

Dizziness rushed me at a startling speed, and I let go of the note like it was a hot coal, watching as it fluttered back down to the desk.

Tearing my gaze up to glare at Trevor, I stammered, "Wh-who gave you this?"

Picking up on the fact that I was more than a little freaked out, he volunteered, "I don't know his name. I've never seen him before. He was just a guy. He had these intense green eyes and some wicked cool tattoos. He came up to me, pointed you out, and offered me twenty dollars to give this to you."

Green eyes? Tattoos?

I shook my head slightly, and a shiver rippled through me. This was not real.

Black dots danced in front of my vision, and I was conscious of my oxygen levels sinking while my pulse skyrocketed. I could feel the onset of a panic attack, creeping up on me around the edges.

Holy crap.

Was it only this morning when Officer Bedford had called me and said Levi was off the hook?

And he'd already contacted me.

"Sorry. Did I, uh, mess up?" Trevor asked, swallowing visibly. "You look like you've seen a ghost."

"No shit, Sherlock," Eden chimed in, huffing out a breath. "Whatever's on that note has obviously spooked her. Maybe next time you shouldn't be so willing to score some easy cash—there's usually a catch."

Concern etched into Trevor's features, which was kind of sweet, considering he didn't know me from Adam. He mumbled another unnecessary apology.

It wasn't his fault. For all he knew, he could've been bringing me a love note.

I tried to assure him that it was okay—that I was okay—but I couldn't speak. I was drowning in the anxiety I felt. It was a suffocating weight.

I needed to leave.

Shooting up out of the chair like someone had lit a fire under my ass, I clawed at my belongings, shoving everything into my bag.

"I have to go," I managed to get out. Reaching for my pencil case, I was trembling so badly that I nearly knocked over Eden's can of Coke.

"Whoa." She rose to her feet. "What's wrong, Hayley? You're scaring me."

I stumbled back. "It's fine. I'm fine," I lied to her, clinging to my last shred of composure. "I just can't be here anymore. I have to go. I'm sorry, I'll see you on Monday, 'kay?"

There was no response, and before I could question what I was doing, I snatched the piece of paper up and pivoted on my heel. I didn't miss the WTF look that Trevor and Eden exchanged, but by that stage, I was beyond caring.

As the fog cleared, I jetted into action mode, making a beeline for the automatic sliding doors.

This was beyond anything I'd ever imagined.

Stepping outside, I moved almost mechanically as I exited the library, my legs maintaining their fast-paced strides.

This handwritten note is another piece of threatening and disturbing evidence, I told myself. *It's going to be okay. They'll make him leave me alone.*

A cold gust of wind picked up, and I shuddered as I made my way across campus toward the parking lot. I didn't know where I was going, I just knew I needed to get far away from here. I inhaled a shallow breath, and the air smelled of damp earth and incoming rain.

I yanked my hoodie up and tucked some wayward strands of hair behind my ear, ignoring the unease that continued to unfurl in my belly. It was the same feeling I'd had the day Levi had been watching me across the quad, and the back of my neck prickled at the prospect that he was watching me again now. I could practically envision the smile twisting his lips as he stood somewhere in the shadows, knowing he'd scared the crap out of me.

Correction: I was fucking petrified, but the closer I got to my car, the less it felt like I was being followed.

And then it occurred to me that maybe it had less to do with my avenue of escape and more to do with the fact that the parking lot wasn't deserted like it generally was at this time of day.

My gaze zeroed in on Jace up ahead, leaning against his Chevy. Thank the good Lord.

Despite how upset I was, my first instinct was to run over to him, to tell him everything that had happened this morning, to have him hold me. There were no monsters when he was around.

He was still here, and he hadn't left me like Tom had—without warning.

My heartbeat and breathing were still erratic, but as I neared him, I realized he'd been crying, and Owen was with him. Comforting him. Jace was clearly tackling his own horde of demons.

The call from Officer Bedford and the note from Levi immediately took a back seat.

Owen's hand was clasped firmly on Jace's shoulder as he spoke low and consolingly. It was like I'd walked into the middle of a conversation I wasn't supposed to know about.

As if sensing my presence, Jace glanced over in my direction, and he seemed momentarily frozen, like he hadn't expected to see me here.

When his unsettled eyes locked on to mine, my heart turned to stone, plummeted, and crumbled at my feet.

It was the first time I'd seen him since last night, and he already looked different somehow, like he'd fought a storm overnight, and instead of finding shelter with me, he'd fled to hold his own.

An awkward silence fell, broken by Owen. "All right, man. I'll catch up with you later," he announced, drawing back and dropping his hand.

Normally, I'd be making a joke about their blossoming bromance, but any ability to make light of a situation had vanished. Instead, I just felt the crushing weight of Jace's stare and an ache deep in my bones, like I could barely move.

Owen pushed off the hood of Jace's truck, and when he brushed past me, he hesitated. "Go easy on him. He's had a rough morning." His dark-blue eyes met mine, and my mind scrambled to identify what they were brimming with. Guilt? Sympathy? I didn't know.

I acquiesced with a jerky nod. Mashing my lips together into a thin line, I attempted to keep my face stoic and not betray what I was feeling beneath the surface. Like the ocean, a current whirled inside me, stirring my thoughts until they were an incoherent jumble.

Before it became uncomfortable, I said, "What's wrong, Jace? What's going on? I woke up this morning and you were—"

"I know," he interrupted, wincing almost imperceptibly. "I'm sorry."

When he didn't say anything else, simply looked at me like he couldn't decide whether he should get the hell out of here or if he should help me understand, I asked, again, "Are you okay?"

Owen was out of earshot now—we were completely alone—and Jace's guard was up, locking me out like he had for so many years. Disappointment chiseled away at me. I'd thought we were *finally* past that, but it was like he'd done a total one-eighty, and something had thrown him off course.

He cracked his knuckles. "Yeah. I went for a drive."

"A drive?"

Jace's eyes were swimming in despair and regret and a million other things I couldn't quite put my finger on. "I didn't sleep much last night, and I . . . I needed to clear my head. I didn't think about where I was going, I just drove," he answered hoarsely, pulling his beanie down farther over his ears.

The wind whistled between our bodies, and the gap had never felt this far to bridge.

"Has this got something to do with your family? Is everyone okay?" This was not normal Jace behavior. I knew him well enough to know that.

He nodded, and I let out a quiet sigh of relief.

"Well, that's good to hear. I'm glad."

Silence. Horrible, nerve-racking silence.

"Does it have anything to do with what I said last night?" I asked. Any chance of pretending I was indifferent to his reaction was shattered by both the chill his words created in me and the way my heart felt like it was preemptively breaking.

When he didn't deny it, I just knew. I couldn't explain it, but

I think I'd known since the moment I told him I loved him that it would change everything again, and that I'd be forced to see this relationship for what it truly was. Almost like a kaleidoscope had finally stopped disarranging the picture of us together long enough for me to see the final image.

The sad truth was, I was only ever going to be the girl who believed she could love a boy enough for the two of them. But it was never going to be enough, not unless Jace was willing to fall with me. Not unless he was willing to make good on his promises—all the times he'd told me that I meant everything to him, that he was committed.

Anger simmered its way through me, but I wrangled it back, waiting until I'd at least heard whatever it was Jace looked like he was about to say.

After what felt like an eternity, he finally said, "I can't . . . I can't do this anymore, Hayley."

His words hung uneasily between us, and everything about this felt wrong.

Even though I knew what he meant, what he was saying, I didn't understand his thought process. And I didn't want to make this easy for him.

"Why?" I blinked, my mind spinning. "Why can't you be with me?"

"I just can't do this," he repeated, his voice softer. "This is too much—you and me. I thought maybe I was ready for something serious again, but I'm not."

Something ugly stirred inside me.

So, despite all the times he'd assured me he wanted to be with me and made it easier for me to believe him, now he thought he wasn't ready? What had changed since last night?

The only thing that was clear to me now was that I was drowning, being pulled under as a storm blew around me, thrashing the waters and wiping out everything I'd held true.

"I don't get it." My fists clenched and unclenched as I stood there, willing myself to focus on what he was saying. "You told me you were ready for the right person, that I was the right person," I said, further lamenting the fact that he'd either lied to me or that he'd had a change of heart—two possibilities I refused to accept. "What's really going on, Jace? You can talk to me, *trust* me. We can work this out."

A breeze blew up and knotted through my hair, momentarily distorting my view of him, but I didn't miss the way he grimaced. Aside from that, Jace was completely devoid of expression.

"That's just it. I . . . I don't want to work this out," he clarified. "I thought this was what I wanted, but it's not. I can't do this anymore."

And the kicks just kept on coming.

Frustration and fury flooded my system, and I clung to those emotions, latched on to them like they were a life raft.

"You really are a coward." I drew in a harsh breath, the air burning the back of my throat. "I may have finally said it out loud after all these years, but I think you already knew how I felt about you. I think you've always known," I went on accusingly.

The lack of surprise on his face was confirmation.

Shaking my head, I laughed bitterly.

I couldn't even justify why I was sticking around to continue this conversation, knowing anything he said now would only twist the razor-edged blade deeper into my heart, but my feet were rooted to the ground. I couldn't move. Hot tears stung my eyes.

"That's what I thought. So, what's really the problem, then? The fact that I'm in love with you? Or the fact that you didn't, and obviously can't, say it back to me?" I whispered brokenly. "The minute things get too real between us, you run. Hell, you run even when things are good."

It was his defense mechanism—how did I know that? For a long time, it was mine too.

"I never wanted to hurt you. Believe me, that's the last thing I ever want to do," he said woodenly, the generic remark grating on my ears.

I wrapped my arms around my waist, as if I could somehow shield myself from him, from the pain in the center of my chest that was threatening to break me in half.

"So just to make sure I'm not missing something," I croaked. "You told me you wanted to be with me, we finally got together, we were happy, and now, for no apparent reason, other than your inability to commit, you just can't be with me anymore?"

There was another stretch of silence. "I'm so goddamn sorry." He glanced down at me, swallowing hard.

He hadn't corrected me, and any hope I'd been holding on to eluded me now.

And then, to make matters worse, he added, "Listen, I want you to know that I'll still be here for you, okay? Especially while you have so much messed-up shit to deal with. And I mean, maybe one day we can eventually get back to being—"

"—back to being what? Friends?" Disbelief raced down my spine. This was not happening. "Wow. Okay. You went there."

He stared at me, eyebrows raised.

"First, I have zero interest in patching up a makeshift friendship with you, whether that's for the sake of Amelia, or to appease your guilty conscience." I stepped forward, closing in on him. He was the hurricane that was destroying everything we'd built, but I refused to be part of the collateral damage. I was more resilient than that. I would survive this. "And, second, as much as I love you"—his lips parted on a shallow inhale—"I can't promise I'll be here when you figure out that you've made a mistake, that what you're doing right now is a mistake. I want the record to state that this was *you* giving up on us, and that even though I'm walking away, *you* were always the one running."

Jace reared back at the harshness of my words, but there was nothing satisfying about it. I wished it didn't have to end like this, that the pain I felt wasn't flaring like wildfire as I watched us crash and burn. I wished Jace would shed the last wall around his heart. I wished for a million other things.

Myriad emotions flickered in his eyes, and like a reflex, he reached out before he could catch himself. He didn't touch me, but he might as well have. The heat from his palm, lingering by my arm, burned through to my skin.

Among all the anger and despair warring for my attention, there was a vast emptiness like I'd never felt creeping in.

As I tried to gather my thoughts, Jace opened his mouth to say something, but shut it quickly. Resignation settled into the strong line of his jaw.

Before he could tell me he was okay with that, or that he hadn't meant to hurt me—again—I was wheeling around and heading toward campus without looking back.

twenty-one

Having dealt with grief before, I could honestly say that the first stage had never been denial. Not for me, anyway.

Up until now, I'd never had any trouble processing the loss, or riding out the familiar swell of sadness. It would always twist my gut inside out, drag me into a deep, dark abyss. It was why, two years ago, I'd fallen into a state of depression so easily.

But this was different.

I'd never lost someone who hadn't actually died. More specifically, I'd never had to say goodbye to someone who already knew that it would result in losing *me*.

At least my brother hadn't chosen to leave. He'd been taken from me, and in a fucked-up way, I was only just starting to realize how much easier that was to accept.

After I'd made it back to one of the campus coffeehouses, despite having no strength in my legs, I'd parked myself on a bench outside and waited for the moment my addled brain would finally catch up, but there were too many things to process.

The empty, gaping cavern in my chest didn't even hurt. There was nothing left but cloying numbness. I'd become achingly hollow inside, not wanting to believe what Jace had done. More accurately, what he'd made me do.

He'd broken up with me, but I'd had to walk away from him, for good.

I knew I hadn't just said goodbye to the boy I'd loved since childhood, but also to my dream of leaving my small town behind, of escaping the past and writing a better future for myself *with* him. He'd always been included in my plans.

My parents were right; moving back home had been a good decision. I couldn't keep commuting here, living in fear—constantly suspended in limbo. What kind of college experience was that?

I'd attend my court hearing, take classes online next semester, and when the coast was clear, I'd come back and live on campus for my sophomore year.

Jace wouldn't be around anymore—he would've graduated by then—and the reality of what I faced dawned on me with horrific clarity. I had this odd flash of everything I would miss—the future Jace and I would never get. Just like that, it was gone, evaporating like smoke. And I made the mistake of imagining what our relationship would be like from now on.

Jace would probably get a photography gig across the country, and I'd go back to seeing him twice a year at Thanksgiving and Christmas. Eventually, he would bring a girl home with him, too, and I'd have to stomach the sight of them together, actively trying not to fall into the trap of wondering if that could've been us.

I didn't want to let him go. But I didn't want to keep holding on either.

I wasn't sure how long I just sat there as the chilly winter air danced over my bones, everything else in the world fading, but when I opened my eyes again, Eden was in front of me.

She plopped down, dropping her bag on the bench. For several moments, we sat there in companionable silence, watching as the darkening clouds rolled in overhead.

She didn't say anything for the longest time.

"Is this about what happened earlier in the library?" Eden finally asked, concern shadowing her eyes. "Or did something else happen?"

Fresh tears spilled down my cheeks, and I guess my face showed it.

She squeezed my hand. "Do you want to talk about it?"

It was such an unexpected gesture from a girl I was still getting to know. A friend who was quickly proving that you didn't always have to fight tooth and nail to get someone to open up to you.

Gratitude surged, snapping me out of my daze. "I wouldn't even know where to start," I admitted, my throat bobbing.

"It's actually quite easy," Eden said gently, her lips twitching. "You just start from the beginning."

It was so obvious.

I smiled thinly in spite of myself.

And so, determined not to make the same mistake Jace repeatedly had, I let someone else in—someone other than Amelia and her brother—for the first time since Tom had died.

I told her everything.

• • •

"It's official." Eden smirked, shooting me a sideways glance. The credits started to roll on her laptop screen, and we both straightened ourselves up on the couch. "Grant Gustin comes in a close second to Ryan Gosling for being totally drool-worthy. I mean, would you look at those dimples when he smiles. Is it weird that I just want to lick them?"

"Oh my God," I answered with a snort. "Yes. You're such a weirdo."

She laughed a little, shaking her head. "Don't pretend you don't have a soft spot for Barry Allen. He's, like, the epitome of a hot nerd."

"Okay, okay," I conceded, my voice laced with mock-defeat. "You've got me there. He is pretty cute."

Her eyes lit up, and I giggled.

We'd gone back to Eden's dorm room, which turned out to be on the floor below mine, and binge-watched five episodes of *The Flash*, a show I'd never seen that Eden was obsessed with. She'd had me at a socially awkward crime scene investigator turned metahuman. After everything I'd told her, she'd been determined to distract me and cheer me up.

"Are you sure you don't mind me staying here tonight?" I asked, feeling bad for imposing even more than I already had. Run out of my dorm *and* Jace's apartment, there was literally nowhere else to go. Unless I drank a gallon of coffee and drove back to my parents' place, of course. But I hadn't planned to go home until tomorrow. I wanted a night to re-evaluate everything and figure out what my next move should be.

"For the tenth time, I don't mind," she assured me, shutting her laptop. She stood, leaving for the communal kitchen to put our empty bowls in the sink. When she came back, a sudden vulnerability etched across her features. "It's been way too long since I've had a sleepover with a friend. This has been nice."

I nodded, knowing that if I started speaking, I'd bawl. With all this much-appreciated girly bonding, I knew I was nanoseconds away from bursting into tears again. And who wanted an emotional wreck sleeping on their dorm room floor?

Not Eden, I was sure.

I heard the faucet turn on and off as she got ready for bed. I hunkered down for the night in the cramped space between Eden's single bed and the wall, thankful for the air mattress she'd discovered in the storeroom we ransacked earlier. It was either that or becoming even closer friends with her couch. The mattress smelled musty but was otherwise clean. I lay back, trying not to think about the fact that this time last night, I'd been sleeping in the crook of Jace's arm.

Tracing a slow pattern on the cover, I convinced myself that I wouldn't be one of those girls who wallowed and dragged this out into a huge, messy breakup. The last thing I wanted was for it to end in friendship casualties because, generally, people took sides, and I couldn't bear the idea of losing Amelia or feeling super uncomfortable around Piper and Owen.

"I think, deep down, I knew it all along," I whispered tonelessly.

Eden gave me a quizzical look as she returned, her bare feet padding on the tiles. "Knew what?"

"That he'd hurt me. Even though he's the one person who truly makes me feel safe."

"Oh, Hayley." She exhaled, and her dark eyebrows drew together. "Don't say that. As much as guys can be such jerks, I think Jace's feelings for you are genuine. I know I hardly know him, but from what you've told me, from what I've seen, something's got him running scared. You just have to figure out what it is."

"You're right." My throat felt dry again. But scared of what, exactly? A relationship with me?

She climbed into her bed, shivering and yanking the sheets up to her ears. The heating system hadn't had any pressure for the last few days, and the building was dropping to freezing temperatures overnight. Awesome.

"I know you probably don't want to think about it, but I care about you, so I have to bring it up." I caught her worried expression before she could turn off the lamp. "If you don't want to go alone to your court hearing—I mean, I know your parents will be there, but I just want you to know, I'd come with you too. I'll be there, every step of the way, if you need me. Assholes like Levi don't intimidate me. You'd be surprised, but I've . . . dealt with them before."

The change of subject threw me for a loop. The mention of Levi's name had tendrils of disgust swirling in my belly, but they were quickly eclipsed by her kindness.

"Eden?" I murmured.

"Yeah?"

"Thank you for . . . well, thank you for everything," I said hoarsely. Somewhere in between the emotional catharsis outside the coffeehouse and just hanging out in her dorm, the vacuum of loneliness had been tugging at me a little less.

She was quiet for a few seconds. "Of course. You're always welcome to stay, just don't steal my Ryan Gosling pillow. That's my only condition."

"Okay, deal." I dissolved into laughter. I'd still thought she was joking about that, but then she'd whipped out a massive pillow with a printed Ryan Gosling on it when I'd first arrived, and my eyes had practically bugged out of their sockets. I needed one of those. "Night, Eden."

"G'night," she yawned, and her voice already sounded conducive to sleep as she rolled over.

Tangled in the blankets, I made a concerted effort to let sleep claim me, too, but even though my eyes were closed, my mind just wouldn't switch off. As I stared at the shadowy ceiling, my thoughts ran wild.

I shouldn't have given so much of my heart away at such a young age. It was a keepsake, and I'd handed it away carelessly. I was no less to blame than Jace. He'd always been so cautious and hesitant . . . and even though it had taken me a very long time to gather my confidence, too, I'd been all in. It was always me trying to bridge every gap and make it last.

That wasn't how a relationship was supposed to be.

I must have eventually drifted off, because I was woken up by the noise of my phone dinging, signaling an incoming message. I fumbled around groggily, trying to locate it in the dark.

I assumed it would be from Amelia, finally seeing all my "call me urgently" and "let's spend the entire weekend in bed watching Netflix" texts. But it wasn't.

It was from Jace.

I know it's none of my business anymore, but where are you staying tonight? You can come here if you need to.

My chest felt heavy and another surge of anger and disbelief rushed through me.

Yeah, there was absolutely no way in hell that was happening.

I'd sooner crawl through a mile of barbed wire than spend the night with the guy who'd taken a sledgehammer to my heart.

My fingers flexed around my phone. I contemplated ignoring him, but I'd never seen the appeal of playing games. And quite frankly, even if I did, there was no point. I'd already lost.

Don't worry about me. I'm staying at Eden's, I texted him back.

I decided to leave out the part where I probably would be finishing up at UD after this semester. He wouldn't have to waste any more time fussing over me. I'd be gone, and hopefully, whatever responsibility he felt he still owed me would be too.

Jace replied almost immediately.

I'm always going to.

I frowned, trying to make sense of that. He obviously still cared . . . still cared about me, and heat blossomed low in my stomach. Despite its transparency, his response seemed unusually cryptic and vague. I couldn't pin down why, but the more I replayed our conversation, the more something felt off about all of this—his behavior, the weak excuses.

Ugh. Just when I thought things couldn't get any more confusing.

I chewed the inside of my cheek as I read and reread his text. My mind spun like a revolving door, caught between wanting to demand more answers from him and not wanting to push it. Anything else he had to say would only leave me worse off.

Closure was overrated.

Hastily, I sent: *Good night, Jace.*

I let out a long-suffering sigh, my eyes adjusting again to the darkness that blanketed Eden's dorm room. I listened to my breathing, waiting for it to even out. Even though I was exhausted beyond measure, restless energy continued to pulse through my body, and I was tempted to whisper Eden's name, to find out if she was still awake.

Seconds later, my phone chimed again. Against my better judgment, I looked down at the glowing screen, holding my breath.

I'm sorry, Hayles.

Those words felt like a shot of electricity to my emotions, jolting cold logic back into them. The awful note of finality in his text wasn't lost on me, either, ricocheting around the dim recesses of my mind.

I was forced to see the truth in all its horrible ugliness.

He wasn't sorry enough.

twenty-two

"You look like shit," Amelia declared, holding the door a little wider so I could brush past her.

"Says the girl still in her pajamas at noon," I countered, my lips quirking. "And is that a Dorito stuck in your hair? What did you do, put your face in the bag?"

"Whoa," she muttered, lifting her hands in surrender but laughing as she did so. Then she combed a hand through her blond hair, grinning when she discovered said Dorito. "I never said I wasn't looking gross either. That's why you're here, isn't it? Strength in numbers and all that. Hey, so"—her voice lowered to a whisper—"I may have found a bottle of tequila left over from my party. Are you thinking what I'm thinking?"

"When in doubt, drink it out," I answered with maybe a bit too much vehemence. My devil-may-care attitude was a recent development, most likely the result of hitting rock bottom. Hence why I'd suddenly thrown my no-alcohol rule to the wind.

Wherever Amelia led, I followed, and vice versa. That was just part of the Best Friend Code—the unwritten rule of our friendship. Besides, I wanted nothing more than to escape everything that was Jace Hammond. Walking past his old bedroom hadn't exactly been the best start.

"You can forget about my brother," she said, as if reading my mind. Heading farther down the hall, we entered her bedroom. "And I'll try not to dwell on my impending homelessness. Deal?" Kneeling in front of her nightstand, she pulled out the bottom drawer and jerked the bottle of tequila upright.

I gave an enthusiastic nod, watching her as she took a big, long swig straight from the bottle. She winced, emitting a light cough when she came up for air. I'd never seen Amelia like this—so forlorn and off-kilter, so like *me*. Gone was my bubbly best friend who had the uncanny ability to put a positive spin on anything.

I sat on the edge of her bed, the mattress sinking a bit beneath me. "What are you planning to do about that, by the way? I mean, where will you go once the sale goes through?"

She glanced away, betraying all her uncertainties. "I'm still trying to work that out," she mumbled, shoving the bottle at me. "Still praying for a miracle. Jace only has a single-bedroom apartment, and his lease isn't up for another six months. So, despite his efforts, that's a no-go, and I'm fresh out of options."

"Maybe you could move in with me. You could stay in Tom's room," I told her, the suggestion flying out of my mouth before I'd had the chance to curb it. "I mean, I'd have to check with my parents first, but if you're desperate, that could be a last resort."

"I don't know. It wouldn't feel right . . ." She trailed off meaningfully, crossing her legs as she got comfortable beside me.

"At least think about it," I insisted. "To be honest, you'd be doing me a favor. I don't know how much longer I can handle his room being like a shrine. It's verging on creepy now. If you moved in, we could clean it out and give it a makeover. Something tells me Tom would've wanted that."

Amelia stared at me for a moment, scrutinizing my face for any sign of reluctance. "I'll think about it," she conceded, her expression softening slightly. "You know something I just realized? You don't talk about Tom with me anymore. Like, ever."

Her words surprised me so much that I almost dropped, and spilled, the tequila all over her comforter. Where was this coming from?

"I'm sorry. Maybe I shouldn't have said anything."

"No, it's fine. What you said is true . . . I don't—didn't—talk about him for a long time," I confessed. I swallowed some tequila to help my jittery nerves. The flames of liquor gave me second-degree burns somewhere between my throat and my sternum, and I scrunched up my nose. "I guess, for the most part, I felt like talking about it didn't really help. My sessions with Dr. Jensen were good because she gave me practical strategies, but talking about everything with her didn't make it any easier to deal with my grief. If anything, it made it hurt more. I still think about him every day." My heart squeezed. It physically hurt in my chest. "Tom was the golden child, but I couldn't even be jealous. He was the best person I knew, so selfless and nice to everyone, even me. I've made peace with the fact that I'll never know exactly what happened in the lead-up to the accident, and I'm certain that Tom wouldn't have let Derek drive if he knew . . ." My voice tapered off. I cleared my throat, trying again. "If he knew how much Derek had drinking. But I also can't help but think about the other family killed in the wreck, about the boy who lost his entire family and—"

"Your brother wasn't behind the wheel," Amelia interrupted, aware of where I was going with this. "Yes, he was drunk, but he didn't lie about it either. Derek did. He told people at the party that night he was okay to drive home. Everyone knows this, and I'm willing to bet that's why Derek's parents left town. They couldn't live here, not after what happened. If their son hadn't died in the crash, he would've gone to prison."

"Maybe," I acknowledged. "But that isn't the part that keeps me up at night, Millie. It was *my* fault too." Tears pricked my eyes, but I blinked them away. "If I hadn't fought with Tom, if he'd left with Jace and me, not Derek . . . God, it might've been so different. He might still be here."

"Hayley," she breathed. "You can't possibly blame yourself for what happened."

I shrugged uneasily. I didn't know how to respond to that because I *did* blame myself. I always had.

"The accident wasn't your fault." Amelia's hand covered mine. "You didn't cause it. You tried your best to save him. You have to know that. If you want to blame anyone, you should be angry at the real culprit—alcohol. And people who don't know their limits and make reckless decisions. It was an awful, tragic *accident*. A sequence of events you could've never predicted. Even if Jace had driven you both home, who's to say something bad wouldn't have happened, anyway?"

I glared down at the bottle of tequila we'd been passing back and forth, and I hated myself for using alcohol as a crutch—for trying to drown it all out with something that had the potential to ruin lives. I knew that better than anyone.

Her gaze followed mine, and she must have connected the

dots, because she screwed the lid back on and pushed the bottle underneath one of her throw pillows.

"I can't believe he's already been gone for almost three years, and it's, like, I know I can't keep carrying this guilt and grief with me, because it's suffocating everything good in my life, but it's so hard to let go at the same time." I turned my attention to my nails, picking at the flaking polish. I couldn't bring myself to meet her eyes, knowing what I'd find in them. Empathy. Awe. Pride. Surely Amelia knew, after nine years of friendship, that I loved her like a sister—that I trusted her more than I trusted myself sometimes. "I can't pretend that the less I bring him up, the less it will hurt. As much as I wish it did, it just doesn't work like that," I added quietly.

My parents and Amelia were right. I had to stop overanalyzing a horrible accident I could never change. I had to stop torturing myself with the past.

Amelia roped her arm around my waist, resting her head on my shoulder. "You know something? I'm really proud of us, Hayley. We're growing up. A couple of years ago, my emotional range didn't exceed anything beyond boys and online shopping, and let's be real, you were kind of an unfeeling zombie. No offense."

"None taken. I really was." I huffed a tired sigh. "It's stupid, but as much as I want to punch your brother in his annoyingly pretty face, I know he's mainly to thank for that. Even though I wanted to, I could never shut him out. We went through it together, and he was always there for me. He listened to me in the rare moments I wanted someone to hear what I had to say."

"That's not stupid. I mean, it makes sense. You both went through something super traumatic. And for other reasons that escape me, you love him. Duh."

The serious scale of this conversation was tilting into the red hazardous zone.

"Yeah," I groaned and dropped back against her bed. "Can we go back to the part where you were talking about me and my protective shell? That was an easier topic than me loving your brother."

The curtains of her window were half-opened, causing dappled sunlight to filter through, and it momentarily cast her face in shadow. She exhaled a breath, lying down next to me. "Do you actually want to talk about something else? Or are you just saying that?"

My tone wavered. "That depends. Am I still talking to my best friend?"

"As opposed to who?"

"His sister," I deadpanned.

"Oh, come on, that's not fair," she scoffed. "You know I won't be taking sides. I'm staying out of it, but that doesn't mean I can't still listen and be there for both of you."

I turned my head to study her, considering it, then cast my gaze back to her ceiling as if it contained the answers I so desperately needed. "Have you heard from him?" As the question left my mouth, I felt an immediate sense of regret. "Forget I just asked you that. I don't care." I *shouldn't care*, I silently edited myself.

"Do you think I'd still be lying here with you if I had? Nope. I'd have hijacked Dad's truck and driven to my brother's apartment just to kick him in the junk."

I bit back a grin. That mental image was kind of weird but highly amusing. "I thought you said you weren't taking sides?"

"Semantics." Amelia waved me off dismissively. "Even if he is my flesh and blood, he better watch out. He broke up with my best friend and broke her heart. That's all I need to know."

The air whooshed out of me at that statement, and I felt winded.

The memory of Jace standing in the parking lot, dishing out that final blow, hit me like an avalanche. I inhaled through my nose, feeling like someone had just ripped the imaginary Band-Aid off my heart—all the mental reinforcements that were holding the cracked pieces together. And God, it hurt like hell to hear the truth.

Not ready to unpack just how badly Jace had crushed me, I sat up and climbed off her bed. I wanted some space to clear my head, a moment alone to remind myself that I wasn't always going to be this pathetic, hollow version of who I used to be. I hadn't always been the girl who pined after Jace, and it was an identity I really needed to separate myself from.

"Shit, I'm sorry. I was just trying to lighten the mood. Don't go," Amelia whispered. There was a note of desperation in her voice. "We'll change the subject, or we can just not talk for a while. Whatever you need."

Wordlessly, I stretched out beside her again. For several seconds, I didn't know what to say. I settled on "The goal today is to *forget* about Jace, you even said so yourself. That's what I need right now, Millie."

She squeezed my hand in understanding, and I smiled, closing my eyes. A comfortable silence nestled between us, and I listened to the steady, powerful rhythm of my pulse, thrumming in my ears.

Amelia was right about a lot of things, but she was wrong about my relationship with her brother. Jace couldn't break me. Not when I was already kind of broken, never truly letting myself heal or move on from losing Tom—something I was determined to change. And so, we lay there, playing the silent game, both of us lost in thought.

• • •

The next morning, I was pulled from the arms of slumber when I heard nondistinct voices drifting upstairs. It took me a moment to focus on my surroundings, to remember where I was—Amelia's bedroom.

Feeling craptacular, I tiptoed over to where I'd left my backpack beside her desk, rifling through its contents until I located the bottle of ibuprofen I always carried on me.

Amelia and I had spent most of last night watching Netflix, devouring three bags of gummy bears, and devising a plan about how to tackle the fucked-up Levi situation. I felt wrecked, nursing an emotional hangover. I had a rip-roaring headache from crying after my best friend had eventually fallen asleep.

Those tears hadn't been wasted on Jace, though. They had paid tribute to my brother, releasing the buried grief I still felt about his death. About having to wake up in a world, day in and day out, where I couldn't talk to him or hug him when I needed to.

Hearing Geoff's booming voice again, I listened, picking up on a couple of fragmented sentences that were out of context.

"Is this the best decision for everyone . . . don't you think he'd understand . . . ? No, you're right."

As I lingered by her ajar bedroom door, my eyebrows immediately snapped together. Were Amelia's parents fighting about their decision to sell up and travel overseas? Suspicion blossomed. And who were they referring to?

The shouting became louder, and I cringed. That was probably my cue to leave.

Glancing back at the bed, I was grateful to find that Amelia had stirred. An agonized groan escaped her throat when she looked at the clock on her wall and discovered it wasn't even eight o'clock in the morning yet. I'd had the same reaction.

"What's that noise?" she asked groggily, kicking the covers aside and swinging her feet to the floor. "Are they arguing again?"

"I think so," I said unhelpfully, debating whether I should tell her what I'd overheard or just keep it to myself. Awash with conflicting emotions, I shook out four of the little painkillers and offered two of them to her, knowing she'd need it more than I did. She'd kept drinking the tequila, unlike me.

"Thanks. My water bottle's on the dresser." Amelia gave me a brief, tight smile, and motioned to her mahogany dresser and vanity. She crawled over to her nightstand to check her phone. "It saves us from having to venture out into that minefield." She let out a snort. "Don't worry, I'll sneak you out at intermission."

Curiosity got the better of me. "Do you know why they've been fighting?"

"Moving stuff, I think," she said vaguely, avoiding my concerned gaze.

I narrowed my eyes at her, wondering why she was acting so strange. The expression she wore was flighty, and her resemblance to Jace at that moment was eerie. Now that I thought about it, they both shared the same look sometimes—like I was trying to approach a cornered, wild animal that wanted to cut and run.

Telling myself it was none of my business, I forced my shoulders to relax. "Right. It can't be easy for them, leaving you and your brother behind."

She fidgeted with the blankets. "Yeah."

Not wanting to push her for more information, even though I was convinced that something was wrong, I let her weird behavior go. Resigned to deal with the pounding in my head, for now, I downed the painkillers and went to move away from her dresser. There was a folder sitting on top that I hadn't noticed earlier, and

I stopped in my tracks. A couple of loose documents stuck out. I leaned in closer, an icy ball of fear forming.

"What's this?" I asked, even though I knew the answer.

It was an itinerary planner, and there was a purchase invoice for a plane ticket to Bucharest, Romania.

My gaze flew to her, and I watched as all the color leached from Amelia's face.

"Uh, okay. Maybe there is something I've been meaning to tell you," she said, wringing her hands. "That's why my parents are fighting. I should have told you this yesterday. I was going to, but we were talking about you . . . about Tom. You're dealing with so much right now, and I didn't want to make it about me. I didn't want to risk anything coming between us." There was a pause. "You know you're my best friend, Hayley. Nothing will ever change that."

Already afraid of what else she might say, I felt myself tensing incrementally.

When I didn't respond, she stood and walked over to me. Her eyes were like two sharp-edged moonstones, shining in the bright morning light. It was almost like glancing at my reflection in the mirror, leaving me vulnerable and exposed. Every emotion I felt was a slideshow across her face.

"I have no plans to go to college, and my full-time job sucks. My constant whining about it attests to that." She expelled another quick, humorless laugh. "I didn't say anything, because I wasn't seriously considering it at first, but I don't know . . . I'm starting to think it could be good for me."

Understanding seeped in, and I felt light-headed, barely overcoming the urge to brace my weight on her dresser.

She was leaving.

"My parents asked me to come with them, and I'm thinking I might go."

In all honesty, now that she was explaining it to me, I knew I shouldn't have been all that surprised, but the idea of her moving away was still just as abhorrent and devastating.

"You're leaving me too?" I said without thinking. I watched as her expression crumpled, upset by my reaction. *Fuck*. "I'm so sorry, Millie. I didn't mean that. I love you, and I get that this is the right choice. I'm happy for you, but it's . . . too much for me. I—I can't do this right now," I told her, ignoring the guilt that burned like acid in my belly. "I need to go."

Grabbing my overnight bag, I practically ran from her room, realizing that Jace had *nothing* on his sister. This pain I was experiencing was wreaking havoc. There was no comparison. This loss went further, burrowed deeper, and something was breaking inside me now, tearing me apart.

"Hayley—wait!" Amelia yelled, rushing after me, but I was down the stairs like a bottle rocket, adrenaline surging through my veins. "It's not forever. I was only planning to stay with them for six months. I'll be coming back!"

It required a shit-ton of strength not to turn around when I heard her voice cracking as she pleaded with me to slow down, and I hated myself, because I couldn't. The pain was too intense, too relentless. It felt like I was on the verge of a panic attack.

Usually, I would've been reluctant to go home, but this time, I wasn't. Drowning in my inner turmoil, I hopped into my car and drove the short distance back to my house. I woke my mom up early by crawling into my parents' bed.

My dad wasn't there. He always took the boat out on a Sunday morning, spending the day fishing and shucking oysters down at the jetty. He said he felt closer to Tom as he stood out at the end of the dock before dawn. It probably had something to do with the fact that it was also where we'd scattered my brother's ashes a couple years ago.

I could remember the way I'd looked out at the ocean in sadness, the arresting sight of the dark cumulus clouds in the sky. The choppy water swelling up around me. And I could still remember wondering if I'd ever breathe normally again. Right now, I still had to work to draw air in and push it out of my lungs.

"Hayley?" Mom asked sleepily, her voice tugging me back to the present. "Is everything all right?"

"Why do the people you love always leave?" I let out a half sob, burying my face in between her shoulder blades. "First Tom, then Jace, and now Amelia's leaving me too."

"Oh, honey. Oh no." She rolled over onto her side, pulling me into her arms. Her warmth enveloped me, chasing away the cold that had set my teeth on edge, and her lips were soft when she kissed away the crease in my forehead. "I don't know, baby. Sometimes people are only meant to make our lives better for a short while. Sometimes they have to go."

That didn't mean I had to be okay with it. Or that it didn't hurt like someone had thrown another punch behind my thick armor.

"She's going to live overseas with her parents," I explained, her chest muffling the odd choking noise I made. "I can't lose her too."

"You won't," she insisted, her tone ringing with certainty. "You girls have been inseparable since fourth grade. That won't change. Yes, people leave"—she tucked a strand of hair behind my ear—"but not always. Sometimes, after you let them go, they come back to you."

"How do you know?"

"Because I lost you," she said softly. Her eyes were swimming with tears of her own, but her mouth was set in a determined, stoic line. "I lost your brother, and then you pushed me away. I thought you were never going to come back to me . . . but you did."

A part of my soul splintered and slipped away as I realized, too late, just how condemning and unfair my actions had been. The grief I'd been carrying with me for years now had nothing on the guilt I was feeling as her gaze searched mine, reaching in deep and scraping out painful memories.

"I'm so sorry, Mom," I whispered over and over, chanting it as if it had the power to erase all the times I'd kept her in the dark, or told her to go away when she'd tried to venture into the fortress I'd built in my bedroom and around my heart.

"It's okay, honey. I had hope that one day you'd come back to me, and that's what you have to do now," she said. "Trust that Amelia is making the right decision for herself. Hope that she'll come back home when she's ready."

I stayed silent, digesting her words. Somehow, she'd answered another question I hadn't even verbalized, and that admission alone felt like a bruise that still ached.

Did that mean I was supposed to trust that Jace had also made his choice because it was the only way forward that he saw right now? And, more important, was I supposed to hope that maybe one day he would come back to me too?

twenty-three

Winter break couldn't come quick enough.

For the last two weeks of the semester, I'd been a mess, barely keeping it together. My heart felt scorched and raw. I'd breezed through my finals, only because I'd spent every waking moment of my miserable existence studying. I'd thrown myself into my last few days of classes. Hanging out at the computer lab for hours, I'd second-guessed every one of my designs, and buried my nose in thick textbooks, trying to memorize all the history and theory we'd covered. Anything to keep me distracted. I'd been so determined not to fail, considering everything that had happened lately.

The court hearing was tomorrow.

I'd lost my boyfriend and said goodbye to my best friend in the same week, and it was lonely as hell.

Whenever I thought about it, it was like reopening a wound—a sucker punch straight to my chest. Amelia had pleaded with me to understand. Traveling and finding herself was something she needed to do. She promised that she'd be back from Europe in six months, that we'd still talk to each other every day, but that didn't mean letting her go was any easier.

When I'd gone with her to the airport, watching as she'd disappeared through the terminal, time had drifted to a standstill. Jace had said his goodbyes the night before as he'd had a final that morning. And it had dawned on me with terrifying clarity just how alone I was now. Amelia, Jace, and Tom—my three childhood sidekicks—were gone. I'd had to squelch the very real, plummeting grief.

Time was frozen, no longer flying by at warp speed. It had reverted to how it was just after Tom died, every minute stretching into what felt like an eternity.

But mostly, I'd been determined not to fail my finals because of Jace. I refused to let him affect me this much—to let my grades dip because of a guy.

I hadn't spoken to him since our breakup. Staying at home and commuting to school meant that I got to avoid him for the most part, but there were unlucky days. As if seeing him in Concepts in Design wasn't hard enough, he popped up around campus every now and then. He was always with Piper and Owen.

One morning, our gazes had collided for a fraction of a second, and the intensity and despair I'd seen in those blue-gray depths had robbed my breath. Sadness clung to him like a shadow, and the circles beneath his eyes had darkened. He was suffering, too, and it should've made me glad that I wasn't the only one hurting, but it didn't. Despite weeks of trying to forget about him, I still felt consumed by him. I still *loved* him.

The only silver lining to the mess that was now called my life was Eden.

The nights I couldn't drive home, she'd let me stay in her dorm, and whenever I would cry, she'd hug me tightly, staying until the tears dried. She'd witnessed some of my epic meltdowns, but never once did I glimpse pity or discomfort in her expression. Eden didn't judge me or tell me how to grieve, and in the quiet moments that hung between us, I sensed that she'd been through something similar before, or that she understood how I felt more than she was willing to let on.

She reminded me of the good things and helped me divert my attention from all the bad.

My world had been torn apart for the millionth time, and I was still trying to piece it back together, but there was no use in pretending that things would be okay. Sometimes certain things just didn't get better, no matter how much you wanted them to, and that truth was as bleak and cold as the weather.

I tightened my coat around me now as the chilly December wind picked up and made my way across campus for quite possibly the last time.

After winter break, I was going to take my classes online. I couldn't keep driving here every day. Aside from being impractical, I'd probably burned through enough fuel to fly ten fighter jets. And I couldn't stay in my dormitory, unable to remember a time I'd felt safe there.

I just had to accept that, in this reality, studying on campus wasn't a good idea. Not right now, anyway.

Keeping my head down, I made tracks for Thompson and wished that I'd arranged to meet up with Owen outside the coffeehouse nearby. I hadn't been to my dorm room since the morning Levi had ambushed me, and I hated that I was jumpy all the time, but I knew I had every reason to be on high alert.

There were things I needed to get from my dorm, and I'd asked Owen to help me carry some of the heavier boxes to my car. He'd jumped at the chance, and I'd been too desperate to question it.

Most students had headed back to their respective homes last Friday and walking through the grounds now was like journeying through a ghost town. When I swiped my key card and pushed through the glass doors of the redbrick building, I tried to ignore the way my muscles tensed.

The lobby was eerily silent, and as I scaled the stairs, I felt the hum of my phone vibrating. When I slid it out of my pocket, Owen's name popped up on the screen, and my thumb hesitated, hovering over the message.

Sorry, something came up. Gonna be late. See you around 6 pm.

Sighing, I walked down the hallway, and the sound of my Converse scuffing along the carpeted floor grated on my ears. Quickening my pace, I stopped in front of my dorm and rummaged around for the set of keys in my bag.

Slipping inside, I shut the door behind me and locked it again. Being back here, I was well and truly outside of my safety zone. I wasn't prepared to take any chances.

I tied my hair into a messy ponytail and got to work.

By the time I'd finished wrangling all my clothes from the closet and shoving my belongings into the recycled cardboard boxes, it was nearly nightfall. It had taken me just over an hour to pack everything away—the upside of having only been in the early stages of moving into my dorm room when Levi had run me out of it.

Then I started to carry the boxes out, balancing them in my arms as I traipsed back and forth between my dorm room and the top of the stairs. It wasn't until the third trip that I noticed some boxes had shifted a few feet from where I'd left them; one had even tipped on its side. Magazines, textbooks, and my New York snow globe were scattered over the carpet.

Unsettled, I stared down the deserted hallway, my brows knitting together.

"Hello?" I called out. "Is someone here?"

A beat of silence ticked by.

Okay. I was really losing it.

Blowing out a breath, I turned away and trekked back down the hall to my dorm. Retrieving my phone from on top of my dresser, I sent Owen a text: *Are you here? Did you move some of the boxes outside my dorm?*

Placing my phone back down, I bent to pick up the last over-packed moving box. I stepped into the hall again, using my hip to nudge the door open wider, and my gaze skimmed over the corridor, wondering why I still couldn't shake the feeling that something was seriously wrong. Then it hit me.

The door to the dorm room opposite mine was ajar and the early evening light spilled in from the open window as the cold draft rattled it. As the door swung back and forth, creaking on its hinges, my eyes zeroed in on something shiny sitting on top of the desk in the corner of the room.

Disbelief hurtled through me, and I almost stumbled to the side, the cardboard box teetering in my arms.

Before I could stop myself, I'd lowered the box to the floor and my feet were moving, carrying me inside the small, single dorm that looked almost identical to mine. At that moment, my curiosity was greater than the voice inside my head, telling me to wait until Owen arrived. Both impulses converged, making it impossible to think clearly.

The room should have been warm now that the heater was fixed, but the vent was closed, and the air inside felt damp and cold, sticking to my lungs. The space felt barely lived in, empty.

"What the hell?" I wondered out loud, and my fingers reached out, curling around the all-too-familiar locket that was coated with a fine layer of dust. Slowly turning it over in my trembling hand, I pressed my lips together as a small whimper escaped.

The engraving of Tom's words, the chip in the corner, the broken clasp—it was all there. It was my necklace. The one that had been stolen.

I lifted my gaze, glancing around the uninhabited room with a frown.

And then I registered it, like my brain had finally gotten on the same wavelength as my body and processed what I was seeing.

There were hundreds of photographs—all pictures of *me*. Some even featured Jace and Amelia. They were tacked up on the wall, concealing the chipped paint underneath.

I tasted bile, the acid in my stomach bubbling.

There were photos of me on campus, me studying in the library, and me eating lunch in the dining hall. There were photos of Jace and me kissing. There were even photos of me back home in Port Worth, of me in my bedroom. Photos of me *sleeping*.

I'd never felt so creeped out and violated. Just seeing all of them made me want to vomit.

My throat seized up when I realized that not all of these photos were taken this year. Some dated back to high school, well before I'd even graduated. I couldn't have been more than sixteen.

I swallowed back hot tears and the terror that was threatening to choke me. A particular photograph captured my attention. A dark image, obviously taken at night. Upon closer inspection,

I suddenly realized—really understood—what I was looking at.

It was a closeup of me, peering outside my bedroom window. It was the night of Amelia's birthday party, not long after I'd heard footsteps crunching over the front lawn.

A swaying rush of confusion and disgust rose in me. My mind raced a million miles a minute, trying to understand what was happening, to come up with a rational explanation, but I had nothing.

I hadn't even met Levi until I'd moved to Delaware, so how did he know where I lived? Why were there photos of me still in high school?

Another photograph caught my eye, and everything slowed down, my scope of vision narrowing.

It got worse.

It was Jace and me, wading in the lake together, all those years ago. His head was blurry, likely from turning, following the noise he'd sworn he'd heard from the shore.

I inhaled sharply, the realization pouring over me like a bucket of ice water: there really had been someone watching us that night, even back then.

Someone had been following me for *years*.

I jammed the necklace into the front pocket of my jeans, and I knew—I just knew—I needed to leave. I needed to call Officer Bedford, and get down to the police station. I was in very real, immediate danger.

But before I could move, I saw a familiar, dark figure in my periphery, and I bristled.

I wasn't alone. There was someone up here in this room with me.

A fissure of dread cut through me.

It was too late.

The hair along my neck prickled when a sound came from behind me—ominous footfalls puncturing the quiet. I heard the creak of the door closing, then the unmistakable click of the latch.

Someone exhaled a ragged breath, and when they spoke, their voice was hair-raising, dull. Worse, it belonged to *him*. "Since the day I woke up, all I've seen is you."

Levi's cryptic and downright creepy remark sent a shiver skating down my spine.

Was I dreaming? This was not real. But when I spun around and opened my eyes again, oh God, he was here. And he was blocking the doorway.

"Who are you?" The words spilled out in an agonized rush.

"You still don't know?" Levi stared at me for a moment. "Wow. That really hurts my feelings, Hayley."

More confusion swirled, and I watched him as he took another measured step toward me. I studied his face, those harrowing eyes, and tried to place where I might have seen him before moving to Delaware. We'd known each other at some point, that much was clear, but I still couldn't work out the connection. I'd been trying to figure it out since that day in the quad.

"I still remember the first time we spoke," he continued, his sick smile sliding into place. "I'll never forget it. You were sitting beside my hospital bed, the most beautiful thing I'd ever seen."

Hospital bed?

Oh my fucking God.

An old repressed memory tumbled forward, and I almost couldn't breathe as I remembered it—remembered *him*.

Suddenly it all made sense.

twenty-four

Against my better judgment, I was at Port Worth's Medical Center. I just couldn't stay away. Even though I knew I'd never shake the guilt—my constant companion since we'd cremated Tom—this felt like the right thing to do. What he'd have wanted me to do.

Courtesy of the nurse seated behind the front desk who'd directed me, I followed the short, narrow walkway until I reached the end—his hospital room. My feet stopped, and they felt rooted to the ground. What was I even going to say? Honestly, I hadn't thought that far ahead.

I inhaled a steady, calming breath. It didn't matter. I could do this. Just showing up was enough.

My heart was pounding loudly in my ears, a heavy drumbeat that drowned out everything else—the hiss of pain from an open door across the hall, the urgent voice over the intercom, calling out a code.

Before I could second-guess what I was about to do, I knocked on the door and crossed the threshold that separated me from the blond-haired boy who'd miraculously survived the accident that claimed his entire family. The same accident that had killed my brother and Derek.

I wasn't prepared for what I saw. It had been two months, but when I registered Aaron's scrawny, pale body, the bandaged limbs, black-and-blue flesh, and the hollowness of his cheeks, I fought for composure. He looked like a ghost himself, teetering on the brink of death.

My eyes darted to the chart hanging at the edge of his bed, and I recognized key words: internal injuries, head trauma, countless surgeries to correct broken bones. I swallowed against my suddenly dry throat.

He was asleep and hadn't heard me enter his room, no doubt used to people coming and going as they pleased. My fingers played nervously with the edges of my sleeves. For the first time, there was embarrassment, then uncertainty, spreading in my stomach. Maybe Jace was right. Maybe coming to see Aaron hadn't been the smartest idea. How would he react when I told him who I was? He'd probably hate me.

I'd come this far, though, and I couldn't turn back now. It would only add to the guilt that festered. Aaron deserved a visitor. An apology.

Slowly, I sank into the chair beside his bed, grateful to have an opportunity to collect my thoughts. To think about how I was supposed to start such a difficult conversation. This was something life provided no guidebook for, and I was completely out of my depth.

I gnawed at my bottom lip.

"Do I know you?" said the weak, disembodied voice, and I turned my head to meet deep-set blue eyes. Aaron was looking up at me so expectantly, but his expression was unreadable.

"No," I told him. "We've never met. I'm . . . well, I . . . uh, my name's Hayley."

Nothing.

My gaze stayed glued to him, studying his face, waiting for a reaction. "Hayley Donovan," I continued carefully.

The second he heard my last name, the puzzle pieces clicked together. Recognition settled into his features. He was completely immobile in the hospital bed, but he gulped visibly, his throat bobbing. He closed his eyes. Sympathy, followed by a pang of regret, fluttered through my belly.

"Do you want me to go?" I asked, glancing at the flat-screen TV on the wall. A muted commercial played, and the smell of his get-well-soon flowers tickled my nose. Honestly, I wasn't sure how I was still sitting here, so completely overwhelmed by my surroundings and yet numb beyond belief. Ever since the accident, I'd felt like I was in a daze, trying to shake off the vestiges of a bad dream, only to realize that this was just my life now. I could only imagine how Aaron felt. "I wanted to . . . I know it probably sounds silly, and maybe I shouldn't have felt like I had the right to come here and say this to you, but I wanted to apologize." I turned my attention back to him, willing my brain to find the words I desperately needed to take away his pain, his loneliness, his grief. There were none. "I'm so sorry for what happened. I know it's not enough, but I am. My brother would've been too."

His eyes snapped open, and I reflexively looked away. I felt like a coward, but I couldn't bear to look at him. I was so scared of what I'd see—the painful emotions I'd glimpse.

Touching my cheek, I was surprised to feel moisture there. I hadn't even realized I'd been crying.

I could feel Aaron watching me, tracking my movements. He

didn't say anything for a long moment, and I stood, realizing he probably wasn't going to respond. I hadn't expected him to accept my apology—to dole out his forgiveness so willingly—but no acknowledgment at all stung a little.

What I'd said earlier? I was wrong. The right words mattered so much, and I hadn't been able to find them. I'd come here on a whim, and it felt like I'd made a foolish mistake.

"It's Hayley, right?"

The sound of his voice halted me, stronger this time. I paused in the doorway and turned my head. His blue-eyed, curious gaze pierced into me.

"Yeah." I mustered up a tight smile.

He nodded infinitesimally, and then I walked out, accepting that that was the little closure I'd get.

I tried to block the memory out, but it kept flashing through my mind, and emotion welled up in my throat.

A part of me couldn't believe that Levi was the same person as the innocent, blond boy who had suffered so much at the hands of my brother's best friend—drunk, behind the wheel. But the more my brain went over it, the more it made sense, and that made me queasy.

"No," I croaked out, edging back until the solid wall was behind me. A vortex of fear ruptured in my chest. There was nowhere else to go. I was trapped. "Y-you're not . . ."

"Oh, but I am," he murmured, and his words slithered over my skin. "It's me. Aaron."

My voice trembled. "Why?"

"Why what?"

"Why are you doing this? You didn't have to *watch* me." I was certain my confusion—my disgust—was visible, even though I tried my best to hide it. "Why didn't you just talk to me? Like I came to you that day, in the hospital. Like—"

"A normal person? Is that what you were going to say? Be careful, Hayley," he advised, a sadistic smirk tugging on his lips. "I love you, but that doesn't mean I won't hurt you."

I swallowed the urge to dry heave before asking, "You love me?"

Instantly, I regretted the question. I didn't want to hear him proclaim that this sick, twisted obsession of his was love—we'd barely spent ten minutes together that morning in his hospital room—I was just trying to understand how it had become so fucking warped in his head, how he could justify his actions. You didn't do this to someone you loved—stalked and preyed on them.

"Of course I love you. We belong together. The accident took a lot from me, Hayley, but it also gave me you. Don't you see? It was a gift." A low, rough chuckle left him. "I was hoping you'd notice me that night at my party. I invited Jacc and his friends so you'd come. I wanted to meet you again, start fresh, but you're a lot smarter than I gave you credit for. You didn't make this easy for me." There was a pause. "That's good, though. Love is never easy. I get why you're putting up a fight, why you're making me work so hard for it."

My eyes stung, and a prickly feeling crawled around inside me, forcing me to acknowledge what was happening right now. I was paralyzed, and my limbs felt like they were held together by old, worn-down bones. I hadn't sacrificed so much this semester for it to end like this. I had to escape.

I needed to survive. I needed to run.

My gaze slid from Aaron and I quickly glanced around, hoping to find a way out of this room. If my dorm wasn't on the fourth floor, I could've climbed out of the open window. Ideas racked my brain, filling me with nothing but fraught hope.

If I could outmaneuver him for long enough.

If I could get to my dorm across the hall.

If I could just get back to my phone.

"I'm glad you told me, Aaron. I'm so happy you don't hate me. I thought you would, after everything." I smiled, but it was tight and fake. A fallacy I prayed he wouldn't see straight through. "Why don't we grab some coffee and talk some more?"

He blinked. "You really want to do that?"

Nodding slowly, I did my best to keep my fear contained. "You said so yourself, right? You love me. You don't want to hurt me. Let's get out of here and—"

"What about Jace?" he spat out his name venomously. "He won't stay away from you, from us, forever."

"Jace broke up with me," I told him soothingly. For the sake of this narrative, I was grateful for that piece of information. At least it was true. "He doesn't love me. It's over between us."

Aaron snorted and rolled his eyes. "Is it, though? I didn't give him a choice." He stepped closer, and I willed myself not to react—not to read too closely into his words. "And if we're going to be together, he can't be in the picture."

"He's not," I said. I was trying to convince myself, not just him. "It'll just be you and me, like that day in the hospital room."

Aaron's head cocked to the side, studying me, and I fought every urge to look away. A sliver of disgust wormed to the surface.

"It's just you and me now," I repeated, my voice conciliatory. One hand was braced on the wall behind me for support while the other rested on my belly.

A stretch of tense silence rolled out between us, and I focused on taking quiet, even breaths. On slowing my racing pulse. Pretending I wasn't scared out of my mind.

"You're lying," he accused, bitter anger permeating his tone. His words sank like lead in my stomach. "You're just telling me what I want to hear. I can see it, Hayley. It's written all over your face. I've watched you for years. Don't insult me. I know you, and you're looking at me like something gross on the bottom of your fucking shoe." Aaron shot forward. When he came into focus again, he was right in front of me. "You're never going to look at me like you look at him. Are you?"

I tried to regroup. I did. But he was so close, so terrifying. "Y-yes, I will," I argued weakly.

"If I can't have you, neither can he."

In one deft motion, the back of his hand struck my face. The impact drove the side of my skull into the wall with a sickening crack, and I cried out. An acrid, metallic copper taste filled my mouth and thickly coated my tongue, a result of my teeth puncturing my lip and the brute force of his assault.

Then his fist found the other side of my head and another streak of pain tore through me. The heavy thud of his knuckles smacking into my flesh, and the taste of blood, dripping out of the corner of my mouth, had a wave of nausea sweeping over me.

Losing my balance, Aaron's fingers knotted in my hair, yanking me upright by my ponytail. My ears rang from the relentless blows, and my scalp tingled, a sharp heat shooting down the back of my neck.

"Do you know how long I've been waiting for you to see me? *Love* me?"

I managed to lift my gaze up to his, determined to meet and hold his stare. His eyes were hollow and vacant, and I was convinced beyond a shadow of a doubt: Aaron was dead inside. I'd tried to reason with him, appeal to him, but it was all in vain. He was merely a shell of a person, deprived of a moral compass or a conscience. For whatever reason, he'd latched on to me, convinced himself that he was in love with me. He wasn't. He was obsessed, completely removed from reality.

"It doesn't have to be this way, Aaron," I whispered helplessly.

"Yes, it does." He barked out another short, humorless laugh. "I was stupid for thinking you'd love me back. The second we walk out of here, you'll be gone. Just like everyone else in my life. You'll leave me. You're never going to be with me."

Terror clawed at my stomach, gutting me. He'd given up hope now, and he wanted to kill me, or at least try. Everything I saw on his face confirmed it—from the haunted look that twisted his expression to the way his eyes had glazed over. Something horrible occurred to me at that moment: I was at the mercy of someone who'd become totally unhinged.

Adrenaline pumped through me. I had to move, to do something. Thrashing around in Aaron's arms, I tried to wriggle out from beneath his body, but I was immobilized between him and the wall. "I know what it's like to feel lonely, to lose someone you love. Don't do this, Aaron. Your family wouldn't want you to be this person."

Something flickered in his jade-colored irises, something that told me this was a seriously dangerous topic.

"Fucking shut up," he said through loud gasps. "Don't you dare talk about them. You have no right."

He momentarily loosened his stranglehold grip, but it was enough. Drawing my leg up and leveraging my weight, I rammed my knee with as much force as I could muster into his groin.

Satisfaction stole through me when he slumped over, emitting a shout of agony.

This was it.

My one shot at getting away.

His hunched frame writhed on the floor, and I sprang into action, pushing through the disorientation as I practically tripped toward the door. My heart lurched. Holy crap. I was going to do it. I could get to my dorm and use my phone to call—

Except, I didn't make it that far.

His hand snaked out, his fingers cuffing my ankle, and I went down like a ton of bricks. My palms smacked on the tiles, taking the brunt of my fall. When I tried to climb to my feet, to push up on my hands and knees, he settled his weight on top of me, restraining my body beneath his.

I squeezed my eyes shut against the rush of tears, and whatever blossom of relief I'd felt withered. Seconds ago, I thought I could somehow escape him, but now I didn't know if I was ever going to leave this room, if Aaron's face was going to be the last face I ever saw.

He grunted as we scuffled, and I tried to shove him off, but eventually, his strength won out and he flipped me onto my back with a bruising effort. Revulsion rolled over my skin.

Instinct kicked in, and I screamed. I might not have been strong enough to fight him off, but I still hadn't unleashed the deadliest weapon I had: my voice.

Aaron pierced me with a deranged glare and his hands fastened around my neck, completely undeterred by my struggling. "Shut the fuck up," he hissed again, his voice echoing around the room. "It's called winter break for a reason. Everyone's gone home. Nobody's gonna hear shit."

Surely someone was still in the dorm and could hear me. Thompson housed over a thousand students.

When I didn't stop screaming, his other hand clamped over my mouth, silencing me.

Desperation frenzied my movements, and I fumbled around in my pocket, withdrawing my necklace. It was the only thing I could defend myself with, and I wasn't sure what use it would be, or how I could inflict harm with it. But before I could even scrape together a plan, he was shifting his weight, pinning my arm down with his knee.

My fist tightened around the necklace, the cool metal digging into my palm, and I concentrated on that, not on the way Aaron was hovering above me, those eyes lethal and inches from my own. They'd always looked so haunting, so intense, and I realized they were colored contact lenses—how he'd changed his eyes from his natural blue to green.

"Please," I choked out. "Please, don't do this. You won't get away with it. They know you're after me. They'll come for you."

"You're right," he conceded. "But they'll come for Levi Brooks. Not me."

An icy spill of terror coursed through my veins.

His grip around my throat tightened, cutting off my oxygen supply. I couldn't breathe.

I focused on the old memory of Tom, the way his fingers had traced the engraving on my necklace.

I love you, sis, he'd said, emotion bleeding into his features. *I'll always protect you. Whenever you're scared or unsure, touch this locket, think of me, and I'll just know, somehow, that you need me.*

Tears spilled down my cheeks, falling onto Aaron's fingers as they continued to squeeze my neck.

I need you, Tom. Can you hear me? I need you now.

I needed my big brother to rescue me, to chase away the stars that were dancing in front of my eyes, but there was only silence. The knowledge that I was suffocating, that there was no one here who could save me, had fear tossing my insides back and forth.

I could only hear the choked, guttural noises that leaked out of my lips, and the sound of Aaron's erratic breathing, hot and foul on my face. This wasn't how I wanted to go.

God, I'm not ready.

In some warped way, there was comfort in the fact that I was tethered to Tom—holding the necklace he'd given me. Thoughts of my brother flitted through my mind, his face flashing back at me.

Just as the darkness started to creep in, beckoning me closer with its bony finger, I heard it. My name. That familiar voice. It sounded like it wasn't far down the hall, and it was enough to drag me back from the edge of consciousness.

"Hayley!"

I experienced a burst of hope inside my chest.

Oh my God.

It was Jace.

He was here.

I made a valiant effort to peel my eyes open again. To scream, as muffled as it was. Everything was blurry, like a dirty fingerprint had smudged my view. But I didn't need to see what unfolded next to piece together what was happening. The locked door groaned under the weight of what I assumed was Jace's boot. After three failed attempts, he kicked the door down, and relief crashed into me. All I wanted to do was cry. Then there was a lot of swearing. And Jace's footsteps, thundering heavily as they approached.

Either I was seeing things, or my ex-boyfriend was here, saving me. I prayed for the latter and refocused on him, closing in on us so fast. Without hesitation, Jace launched himself at Aaron, ripping him off me.

The throbbing pain lessened to a dull ache.

"Hayley," he said again, but it wasn't the use of my name or that voice that felt like someone was tossing me a lifeline. The pressure around my neck was gone, and I inhaled my first strangled, deep breath in what felt like minutes. Cold air rushed in, diffusing in my lungs. "That's it, baby. Breathe for me."

Jace was wrestling with Aaron, and he got one good punch in before Aaron's fist flew out, connecting with the side of Jace's jaw. I closed my eyes instinctively. I couldn't watch, still tasting blood in my mouth.

Slowly, I flexed my fingers on the hard, cold tiles, mustering what little strength I had to drag myself away from where they brawled. Snippets of static-filled sound penetrated the quiet ringing in my ears. I felt overstretched, every movement managing to feel both heavy and weightless.

Jace grunted, low and pained. Aaron laughed. And my skin crawled. I couldn't resist peeking, just in time to see Jace's fist collide with Aaron's face. There was this unmistakable crunching sound, and Aaron's head snapped back, blood spurting from his nose. Satisfaction curled through me when I realized that it was broken, when I heard him yelp.

"You're one twisted fucker," Jace growled. His grip on Aaron's sweater was turning his knuckles white, but he didn't let go. I was glad. Rage had morphed Jace's beautiful features into something dark and cold.

"I'll keep coming back." Aaron's eyes darted to me, then back to Jace. He smiled, showcasing bloodstained teeth. "There's nothing you can do to stop me. You've never been able to stop me."

The next thing I knew, my ex-boyfriend was stepping back, only to come at Aaron with a second full-force punch. Unable to suffer another direct blow, he crumpled, falling backward, and the side of his head hit the floor with a loud crack. It reverberated around the empty room.

My eyes zeroed in on Aaron's limp, unconscious body, and undiluted relief poured through me, making me shake with it. Everything started to fade out, a cold numbness trickling in.

The last thing I remembered was Jace's reply, his tone harsh and filled with conviction. "Nah. You won't be back. Not this time."

twenty-five

Someone was squeezing my hand, anchoring me as I drifted aimlessly between the darkness and a place where I wasn't quite lucid. My chest rose and fell in a slow, sluggish rhythm. The scratchy sheets cocooning me felt like sandpaper against my skin and the beeping sound of a monitor drilled through my temples.

"Hayles," a gravelly voice whispered. Strong, calloused fingers tightened around mine. "It's me. I'm here."

Jace.

"You're safe now," he reminded me, his thumb moving in slow circles. "I'm not going anywhere. Go back to sleep."

Even if I wanted to open my eyes, I couldn't. My body had been hollowed out, and I was lost in the pitch black, too tired to navigate a way out.

...

When I slowly blinked my eyes open, exhaustion rushed in. I'd been slipping in and out of consciousness, and it was hard to tell how many days had passed. Disorientated and groggy, I was having a difficult time processing anything, much less how I'd wound up in the hospital. The pungent smell of disinfectant, stinging my nostrils, had been my first clue.

I propped myself up against the pillows, wincing at the burst of fiery pain that shot up the back of my neck. Every small movement felt like someone had just shoved a hot poker straight through my spine, but I ignored it, shifting rigidly.

"Take it easy," Jace said, his voice pitching low. "The doctors don't want you making any sudden movements. Not yet."

He was sitting at the side of my bed in a chair that seemed way too small for his large frame. When our gazes locked, I inhaled deeply, feeling my lungs burn.

While it felt like I'd been sleeping for an eternity, I realized it couldn't have been more than a few hours. Not only was Jace still wearing the same clothes, but his face was also covered in fresh bruises, a stomach-churning canvas of blacks and purples—though some had begun to fade to yellow. His lip was busted, swollen and split open at the corner, but it was those crystalline eyes that completely and utterly wrecked me. They were glassy and bloodshot, filled with a world of unspoken emotion.

"Are you—?" I rasped, feeling a strange lump in my throat that I could hardly talk around. My voice sounded weak and hoarse. "Is he—?"

Jace stiffened, the muscles in his back tensing under the fabric of his gray sweater. "Levi—or should I say, Aaron—is in jail," he told me. "He's gone, and he won't ever be coming back."

Overwhelming relief swept through my system. I tilted my

chin toward the ceiling, my lower lip trembling. My vision blurred in and out, and I realized I was crying. A sort of calm settled over me; a semblance of happiness. There was justice, and while it would never erase all that Aaron had put me through, I could take comfort in that. I could take comfort in the fact that it was finally over.

"Did you know?" he asked.

Closing my eyes, I nodded. I knew exactly what—*who*—he was referring to. "Yeah. I realized who he was before . . . before he tried to kill me."

"The police know. They saw the photos in the dorm he was using to . . . watch you, the photos he'd taken over the last couple of years." Jace paused. "After the accident, he changed his name to Levi, his brother's middle name, and reverted to his mother's maiden name, Brooks. He never notified the authorities that he'd changed his name," he said, like this explained everything. "I don't know, maybe at first he was trying to start over, but grief can do fucked-up things to people. Sometimes they're not strong enough to see a clear way out."

I cast my gaze down at the white crocheted blanket, not wanting to see the flash of pity or reticence in his eyes.

Tom's best friend had killed Aaron's entire family. His parents and his brother had died that night. I couldn't even begin to imagine what that must have felt like: to go from having a normal life and a loving *home* to being alone, to having nothing at all.

I don't think I'd ever forgive Levi or wrap my head around why he'd felt compelled to do what he'd done, but I had only sympathy for Aaron. Having lost Tom, knowing the immense impact his death still had on me, it only exacerbated that feeling. The scrawny blond boy I'd visited in that hospital had looked so haunted and inconsolable. Aaron's smiling, carefree school photo had been plastered on the front pages of every local newspaper. There had been no rage or malevolence gripping him. Not back then.

"Your parents will be back soon," Jace went on. "They went to grab something to eat. I told them I'd stay with you. I, uh, hope that's okay." The vulnerability and uncertainty in his tone kicked me in my gut. Hard.

He looked so wary of me, like he could hardly bring himself to utter another word, but it felt like I'd been walking around in a fog for years, not hours, and now that I was coherent again, I wanted answers.

"How did you know?" I asked, ending our silence. I glanced down to make sure that I wasn't hallucinating. After weeks of missing him, trying to forget him, Jace was here, and he was holding my hand. He was careful not to touch the IV needle stuck there. "How did you even know where I was? We haven't spoken since that day in the parking lot."

Something indecipherable flickered across his face. "I arranged it with Owen. He gave me the temporary key card you'd organized. I was going to help you move out of your dorm, not him. I was coming to talk to you, because I was sorry, because I missed you, and I needed to . . ." Jace went quiet for a moment, and my stomach dipped. "But I got held up at the auction, dealing with the Realtor. I *knew* I had to leave Port Worth before three o'clock. I knew I couldn't be late, that everything rested on meeting you at your dorm this afternoon, and I couldn't even get that right. But then I got there, and I swear to God, Hayley, the world fucking stopped. I heard you screaming."

The memory of Aaron's ice-cold hands, clawing at my throat, came back to me. Even though I remembered every detail about what had happened tonight, it didn't haunt me. Maybe I was just so stubborn, so intent on not letting it. Or maybe it was because I'd already survived far worse and was almost desensitized now. Whatever the reason, I didn't feel broken when I probably should have. I prayed it wasn't just the initial shock, or the remnants of my adrenaline, staving off a nervous breakdown.

"I'll never forget what that felt like. The moment I realized you were in danger, how badly I'd fucked everything up. It was like being out on that road again, except this time, you were—" He couldn't finish that sentence.

"Jace . . ."

His shoulders shook, his body racked with silent sobs. He dropped his forehead to where our hands were joined. I'd never seen him like this before, and it made the cold knot of grief in my stomach swell.

"I know. But I'm still here," I murmured, letting go of his hand to thread my fingers through his hair. "Thanks to you."

"It's *my* fault, Hayley," he ground out, looking up at me. "I did this. I pushed you away, and more importantly, I wasn't there to protect you. I wasn't there to protect you when I said I would be."

I stared at him for a beat, registering the look of self-reproach he wore so well. I think I would've preferred being blamed. After all, I'd been the one foolish enough to wander into Aaron's lair.

"I thought I was never going to leave that dorm," I said, the harsh truth causing a shiver to race through me. "You *were* there for me. You saved me, Jace."

"Don't thank me," he whispered, drawing back. Self-disgust contorted his expression again. "I don't deserve your gratitude or forgiveness. When I got there, when I saw his hands around your neck, I wanted to kill him. It was more than redemption, the instinct to protect you. It was something dark and vile. Something I never want to feel again."

I recognized the violent anxiety in his eyes, rolling in like a storm cloud. This was guilt. Regret. Hate. Emotions I was so well acquainted with. After Tom's death, their fingers had mangled my gut, too, twisting and obliterating my insides. I hadn't had an appetite or been able to keep food down for days.

"I know this is a lot to take in," Jace continued slowly, cautiously, "and that the last thing you need is me complicating shit, but there's something I need to tell you. Will you hear me out? Can you do that?"

"Well, I'm not exactly going anywhere right now," I pointed out, my lips twitching.

A real, breathtaking smile appeared, but as quickly as that smile came, it vanished. His face darkened, brows furrowing together. Whatever additional smartassery I might have been able to produce melted away when Jace studied me. The intensity in his gaze was unparalleled.

"I shouldn't have broken up with you," he said, and I felt a very sharp, twisting motion in my chest. I'd been right that day in the parking lot. He'd finally figured out that he'd made a mistake, letting me go, but instead of feeling satisfaction, all I felt was sorrow. "Trying to walk away was where I went wrong. You need to know that I didn't end things between us for the reasons you think."

I sucked in a breath, my lungs expanding. Again, a twinge of pain stabbed me just below my ribs.

Aaron's words popped into my head, clear as day. *I didn't give him a choice.* Maybe I should've lingered on them for longer than I did, but my brain felt like it'd been knocked into the middle of next week. Trying to retain anything or have a conversation as emotionally charged as this one was proving difficult. Even though I still didn't know the full extent of my injuries, I could deduce that I probably had a concussion.

"I know better than anyone how close I came to losing you tonight, and I don't know if I can survive losing you again," Jace admitted, his voice gruff. "I know it's a jerk move, me saying all of this now, but maybe when you're up to it, we can talk more about us. The future."

As I held his gaze, I saw in an unguarded moment that passed between us what he wanted. Between the pain meds and everything I'd been through, I struggled to sort through the onslaught of emotions that flooded me.

I swallowed. "For now, for a while, I think I just need to—"

The hospital curtains parted, and Officer Bedford emerged, the lines softening around her mouth when she saw me. "Sorry to interrupt." She took a couple of tentative steps toward us. "I've been trying to hold off for as long as I can, but I'm afraid we're going to need to ask you a couple of questions, Hayley. For you to make a formal statement."

I tried to suppress the dread that followed. "Okay."

Her attention flitted to Jace. "Have you told her everything?" she asked, her demeanor professional and brusque, as always.

"No, not everything," he answered in a monotone. "She just woke up. I didn't want to overwhelm her."

"Good. That's good." She nodded curtly, sounding vaguely pleased. "Would you mind stepping outside for a minute, Mr. Hammond? I think we've got it from here."

Jace climbed to his feet and shoved his hands into the front pockets of his jeans. His face was blank, but the doubt and determination warring in his eyes told me that he really didn't want to leave. "I'll be in the cafeteria." Jace slid Officer Bedford a look, and a tense energy pulsed between them. "Fifteen minutes, okay? Then I'm coming back, and you're gone."

I was getting more worried by the second.

"Thank you," she said, lowering her notebook. "My colleague and I won't be long."

Jace turned to me. "See you in a bit." He smiled, but it didn't quite reach his eyes.

I nodded jerkily, desperately wanting to tell him to stay, but somehow resisting.

To my surprise, he placed his palm on the bed beside my shoulder, stabilizing his weight, and then he bent to kiss my forehead. His lips were warm and soft, like a whisper.

I shivered when he exhaled, the heat of his breath fanning my collarbone. Closing my eyes, I appreciated the calming effect he always had on me. The smell of him, light cologne, and the sharp fragrance of a pine-needle forest, always made me feel safe.

"I'm so sorry. I thought I was doing the right thing," he rasped into my ear. Something fluttered inside my stomach as I cataloged his words. The way I could feel his lips moving as he spoke. "I never meant for this to happen, Hayles."

Jace withdrew a second later. I caught him side-eyeing Officer Bedford one last time before he exited the room, slipping out the door and leaving the two of us alone, finally.

Snapping my attention back to Officer Bedford, I found her gaze steady on mine, and I inhaled a quiet breath. I needed to put this whole thing behind me. I needed to know that Aaron was going to rot behind bars. Surely my court hearing tomorrow was canceled. This went above a restraining order, right?

Then the door swung open again, and Reese, the guy Eden had introduced me to at the frat party, stepped inside.

I blinked, trying to sort through the many questions I had. "What are you doing here?"

Officer Bedford cleared her throat. "I feel like it's my duty to offer you an explanation. In fact, I think it's the least Officer Graves and I can do." She smiled slightly at that, glancing over at Reese, who apparently was a cop. "Officer Graves has been front-running an undercover investigation trying to take down who was behind the attacks all year."

I don't know what I'd been expecting, but it wasn't that. My brain felt like it was full of cobwebs and fog.

"You're a police officer?" My voice came out sharper than I'd intended. Technically, Officer Bedford had told me there was a heavy police presence on campus, but I hadn't guessed it would be him—someone I'd met at a frat party, of all places. His major in criminology had probably been the only truthful thing he'd shared. "Is your name even Reese?"

"Close. It's Rhett." He looked down at the hospital bedsheets, then back to me. "Ever since the attacks started at UD, my orders have been to figure out who was behind them, as well as to determine if any other unreported crimes were happening on campus," Rhett explained, crossing his arms. "While we, unfortunately, had another victim, I'm happy to report we've arrested and charged Professor Zimmerman. His position at the university has been revoked. Even after he gets out, he'll never step foot in another institution again."

Officer Bedford took over again. "After we'd identified the perp, only then did we start treating your attack as an unrelated incident. We thought Levi was our guy. We didn't know that he was Aaron, or that he had a personal vendetta against you, Hayley. We missed the connection here until it was too late," she disclosed. I felt like I needed a gallon of coffee to process everything they were saying. "But we've been doing everything in our power to keep you safe while we investigated your case."

I stayed quiet, sensing that she wasn't finished.

"When you filed for a restraining order, another undercover officer was assigned to protect you the same morning. Eden Lindy."

My stomach crunched in on itself. I wanted to be sick. Glancing up at the ceiling, I concentrated on my breathing, trying not to cry again. The room was spinning, the bright fluorescent lights out of focus.

"Eden?" I repeated numbly. "She's a cop too?"

I vaguely remembered our conversation from the frat party that night. *We go way back*, she'd said, when introducing me to Reese—Rhett, whatever. She wasn't joking.

The knowledge that the *one* person I'd thought, without a doubt, hadn't been caught up in all of this had played such a central part knocked me off-balance. Fortunately, I was already lying down.

I'd never suspected it. Never thought that Eden was anything more than a quirky freshman with a Ryan Gosling obsession. She really gave the term *undercover* a whole new meaning. I guess that was the point—to be so good at blending in that no one suspected you. And I hadn't. As much as the betrayal stung, knowing my friend had been in on it all along, I was relieved that there truly had been someone looking out for me. That she, of all people, had been protecting me, or at least, she'd been trying her best to.

"It's unfortunate that Aaron figured out who she was," Rhett continued, wearing one hell of a pissed-off expression. "After he attacked her, he was free to get to you."

I froze. The monitor I was hooked up to beeped faster, catching the spike in my pulse. "Is Eden okay?"

"Yes," he reassured me. "She's here. Just down the hall. I'm sure she'll be paying you a visit later when she's up to it."

I sagged back against the pillows, a profound sense of relief pouring through me. "What happens now? After I give you my statement, what will happen to Aaron?"

"He's got an impressive rap sheet," Officer Bedford piped up, and there was a lightness in her tone that I hadn't heard before. This was probably her favorite part of the job—locking the bad guy up and throwing away the key. "First-degree attempted murder charges tend to stick. Paired with the evidence we've gathered—eyewitnesses, campus CTV—we can also prove he was breaching his restraining order on multiple occasions. In other words, Aaron's going to be joining Professor Zimmerman in prison for a very long time."

Thank God for that.

This was clearly a big win for them—not just for me.

twenty-six

For the next few days, Jace never left my side. Even when my parents insisted he go home—take a well-earned night off—he remained stubbornly intent on manning the fort.

Despite his whispered, heartfelt confession that first night in the hospital, and all the times since then I'd felt him watching me closely, we'd slipped effortlessly into a platonic falsehood. Again.

I didn't know how to ask him what Aaron had meant when he'd said he hadn't given Jace a choice, and he never tried to broach the subject with me—or any topic of importance.

It didn't help that the hospital staff had stopped pumping me full of drugs. Now that the meds had worn off, I had trouble sleeping during the night. Everywhere was sore. It felt like even my bones were bruised. And when I did manage to drift off, I'd often be disturbed by the nurses doing their rounds, or by the weird noises that floated down the hall at an ungodly hour.

Tonight, I heard footsteps at the base of my bed. Peeling my eyelids open, I waited for my vision to adjust to the darkness. The lights weren't on, and the room was cast in a soft, dim glow from the hallway.

Jace wasn't back, but it felt like he'd only just left. He'd gone downtown to pick up bacon double cheeseburgers for us. To say I was grateful to be spared from consuming any more hospital food was an understatement. I think we'd both reached our quota.

Rising onto my elbows, I wondered why the weeknight nurse was being so unusually quiet.

"Sorry, I didn't mean to wake you," a familiar male voice said, and I squinted at the approaching figure. A sliver of light crossed Owen's face, and my shoulders relaxed. He was clutching a bunch of pink carnations, and he carefully placed them on the overbed table. "I'm just here to drop these off. They're from Piper and me."

Straightening up, I turned the small lamp on and leaned back against the pillows that were propped up against the headboard. "It's fine. I wasn't sleeping." The thoughtful gesture unleashed a rush of warmth. "Wow, they're lovely. Thank you, Owen. Tell Piper she has great taste too."

He nodded, a blush tinting his cheeks. "Have you had many visitors this week?" he asked, settling into one of the cushioned chairs.

"Yeah, a few," I told him, sort of smiling. "Eden was here earlier. She stopped by before they discharged her."

It hadn't been a long visit, and I still didn't really know how I felt about it all. Eden had apologized for deceiving me—I was convinced that also wasn't her real name, not that she, or anyone else, offered it to me. She'd told me that befriending people while you were undercover, people you were supposed to protect, wasn't smart—something they warned you about in the academy—but she'd done it, anyway. I knew she genuinely cared for me, and I'd

always care for her, but she was a twenty-two-year-old police officer from Philadelphia . . . not my close friend. And she was leaving. She was being sent to a different city for her next assignment,
and that was hard to take. Brutal, even. She would no longer be in
my life, and I'd had to say goodbye to her.

He shook his head. "I still can't believe Levi hurt her too."

Obviously, he had no idea about Eden's real identity or half
of the other shit that had gone down, and I didn't really feel like
explaining it all to him right now.

"Yeah," I agreed sadly.

An awkward pause fell.

"Is Jace around?"

"He's gone to pick up food for us," I told him. "He'll be back
soon. He's been here every night since . . . it happened."

Owen's dark-blue eyes returned to mine, and I battled the
overwhelming urge to fidget with the hospital blanket. Talking
about the attack with anyone who wasn't Jace, Amelia, or my
parents had a twinge of discomfort skating up my back. "Well, if
that's not a declaration of love, I don't know what is." Owen's hum
was all dry amusement. I was glad the subject had circled back to
his best friend. "It's always been easier for him to show how he
feels, rather than say it."

I sighed. He was mostly right.

"It's not out of guilt, you know," Owen considered. "It's
because you're *it* for him. That one girl we're all actively searching
for, whether we realize it or not. The girl who holds all the power.
The girl you spend your life with."

There was a beat, and then he revealed, "Honestly, I don't see
how Jace could've handled it any better. Yeah, he does dumb shit
sometimes, but he was trying to make up for it. As always, he was

just trying to protect you. I'm not making excuses for him, Hayley, because I would've done the same for the girl I love. And I'd do anything to keep my sister safe, too, even if that meant forgoing my own happiness. That's what being a big brother's all about." He noticed my quizzical look, and his expression became a touch uneasy. "Fuck. He still hasn't told you."

It wasn't a question.

I frowned. What was up with the abnormal number of secrets in my life? I was so over it. "Told me what?"

"A few months ago, Jace's phone stopped working, and he got a new—"

"I know."

"There was nothing wrong with his phone, Hayley. He kept it. He only needed a new number."

I blinked. "What?"

"Levi, or wait—Aaron . . . I'm still getting my head around that . . . had been threatening Jace. Trying to scare him off, to get rid of him, and to stop him from being with you, ever since you showed up at UD," Owen explained. "Jace tried ignoring it, changing his number. He thought, like me, that it was handled, until that day in the parking lot. You ran into us. We were talking about something. Do you remember that?"

"Of course." Jace had broken up with me. How could I forget?

"Jace woke up to a text message from Aaron, the morning after the frat party. Somehow, he'd gotten a hold of his new number. It was a photo of Amelia. He must've known that only threatening Jace wasn't enough to get him to do what he wanted. That sick fuck broke into Jace's parents' house and took a photo of her while she slept," he all but growled. "Aaron threatened her. He said if Jace didn't break up with you, he was going to . . ."

The fine sprinkling of hair on the back of my neck prickled. "What was he going to do?" I wasn't even sure I wanted to know where he was going with this, but my curiosity outweighed my reluctance.

"He told Jace if he didn't end things with you"—he tightened his right hand into a fist, his knuckles blanching white—"he was going to hurt her. Kill her. And after what he did to you, I can see it wasn't an empty threat. Aaron was hell-bent on isolating you from everyone who loves you. He wanted to be the only one left."

Another chill moved through me. The knowledge that Aaron had intended to go after my best friend, and that she'd been in danger, too, had terror resurfacing. Thankfully, Jace hadn't let that happen. And, with a burst of clarity, I realized just how wrong I'd been. How wrong I'd been about everything.

The night of the attack, Aaron had hinted at it. When I'd woken up in the hospital, Jace had tried to talk to me about it too. He'd said he regretted the way things had ended between us. I'd had a feeling—even that day in the parking lot—that Jace hadn't wanted this, but I'd dismissed it. It'd been easier to think this was just history repeating itself. To fall into my old pattern of thinking: that the happily ever after I so desperately craved would always be out of reach.

My brain snapped into overdrive, processing. The more I thought about it, the more I digested what Owen was saying, the more questions I had. A tiny flare of anger spiked, pushing down any lingering disbelief. I wished Jace had just told me himself, that he hadn't let Aaron blackmail him into ending things with me. We could've faced it, figured out our next step, together. He hadn't given me that chance.

And I wished Jace had taken credit for what he did that

night—saving Aaron's life. I was sure if he knew that Jace had been the one who rescued him, he wouldn't have been so quick to blackmail him.

"Jace wasn't going to go through with it at first," Owen said, as if he'd read my mind. "But the texts kept coming, and it got too much to ignore, so he went to the police. Showed them all the text messages. He was done, willing to lay it all on the line, if it meant that no harm came to you or Amelia. Officer Bedford explained that they'd assigned an undercover officer 'to protect you.'" He used air quotes over those last three words. "He put his faith in them. I think he thought if he appeased Aaron, he'd be keeping his sister safe as well until she left for Europe. It was a win-win."

That explained Jace's coldness toward them. Not to mention, I'd made him promise me that afternoon in the dining hall that he would stay out of it—to let the police do their job. As reluctant as I was to admit it, his latest string of decisions made perfect sense.

"I don't know much more than that; Jace only ever told me bits and pieces," Owen went on, and I swallowed dryly. "He probably tried to tell you, too, in his own cryptic way. But I know he didn't want this, Hayley."

My heart tripped about in my chest. Jace had been willing to sacrifice himself, his happiness—our relationship—to protect me. To keep Amelia safe as well. It didn't matter that I'd ended up getting hurt in the process. The intention was there. He'd walked away from me, yes. But he'd come back. As per usual, he'd shown up when I'd needed him most. He'd saved my life. Jace's recent actions lessened that anger pretty quickly.

"Jace did what most people would've done. What I wasn't brave enough to do for my sister," Owen admitted quietly. "I should've encouraged her to go to the police. I shouldn't have been so reckless and arrogant. I thought I could put an end to it, that I was enough to protect her from that monster, but I wasn't. She put her trust in me, and all I did was make it worse. Libby might be alive, but the sister I had . . . the bond we forged as kids, is gone. I still lost her that night, in all the ways that count. That decision will continue to haunt me for the rest of my life."

Emotion built at the base of my throat. Losing a sibling—or at least living with the guilt, knowing you'd played an instrumental part in something awful that happened to them—was something I understood all too well. "I'm so sorry, Owen."

"It is what it is." He shrugged one shoulder. All casual again. "We can't change the past, but we can vow to learn from it. Anyway, you understand what I'm saying, what I'm asking, don't you?"

I did. Owen wanted me to walk a mile in Jace's shoes, to forgive him and be thankful for being the person he was.

Wasn't that just the definition of love, anyway?

• • •

The following evening, I was discharged from the hospital with an astronomical health-care bill and a plethora of pain medication in tow. Per the doctor's suggestions, I wasn't driving myself home. Jace was.

My parents had been on standby, ready to make the round trip, but he'd insisted on giving me a ride. He was heading in that direction, anyway. The closing date on his family house was the day after tomorrow, and he had some loose ends to tie up with the new buyers.

After Owen's impromptu visit last night, Jace and I had only made small talk. I was still trying to figure out how to broach a real, meaningful conversation with him. I'd relied on one of his best friends to fill in the blanks for me, and I knew, right after Owen had left, that that had been a mistake. I should've summoned the courage to ask Jace myself. We'd grown up together, been to hell and back so many times. In theory, no subject was too awkward or off-limits. It almost felt like I'd betrayed Jace, talking about everything behind his back. And maybe that was stupid, but it was a hard feeling to suppress.

"You ready?" he asked, his voice coming from behind me. He crouched to pick up the small bag I'd packed, drawing my attention away from the empty hospital bed.

"Yeah," I whispered, turning around to face him.

My pulse sped up, hammering away at me until it was all I could hear. Every time I saw him now, it was the same reaction.

Jace was waiting patiently by the door, my tote bag slung haphazardly over his shoulder. His blue-gray eyes settled on mine, weighty, searching. He was wearing the same clothes as yesterday, and they were slightly rumpled, having been slept in. I wasn't sure how it was humanly possible, but even after days of disrupted sleep and massive doses of caffeine, Jace was even more gorgeous. His dark hair was a mess, sticking out in sharp pieces. His features were mesmerizing, but it was his vulnerability that really drew me closer.

Something was changing between us. It had been ever since I'd woken up, since the attack. I knew we couldn't undo everything that had happened in our past and that made it so much easier to focus on the present.

Heading down the narrow hallway, I thanked the nurses for all they'd done to assist my recovery. I gave them the edible hamper my parents had organized and told them to share the goodies in their staffroom. Slowly, we made our way toward the hospital parking lot. I was still weak, but there was something empowering about walking out of the hospital in one piece. I felt strong, healed, in a way that I hadn't before, and the irony wasn't lost on me.

The sun had set, and the air was cold, hinting at a fast-approaching winter. Thunderclouds rolled in low, their bellies full of rain, but it was so nice to be outside again, to feel the wind on my clammy skin.

Jace's Chevy was a chore to climb into at the best of times, and I had to tamp down a smile when he wordlessly followed me around to the passenger side. He placed his hands on my hips and, in one smooth motion, hoisted me into his truck. His grip on my waist tightened, and he didn't step back immediately.

Every cell in my body was aware of him, of his proximity. The warmth from his touch spread through me, thawing the perennial chill that had seeped in, and melting the layer of ice that had encased my heart lately.

"Thank you again for this," I murmured, staying there a moment longer, "and for everything else you've done for me."

His chin lowered, resting on top of my head, and he breathed into my hair. "You're welcome."

When Jace held me like this, it should've dredged awful memories to the surface. Memories of how close Aaron had been to breaking me beyond repair. But it didn't. Days later, there was nothing. Just the hollow ache of acceptance, the remnants of fear.

"Come on." His voice eased into the stretch of silence. He pulled back, and I glimpsed an ocean of sadness in his eyes. "We should get going. We've got a long journey ahead."

He was speaking the truth in more ways than one.

The newfound intimacy retreated as Jace put more distance between us, and we were suddenly worlds apart again. There had always been this intense pull for us to come together, but for some reason, we just couldn't get it right, like quiet ships passing in the night. Close, yet so frustratingly far.

With time, we'd become experts at this.

twenty-seven

Jace and I hadn't been on the road for long when the mother of all storms hit us. The rain was coming down so hard that I could barely see through the windshield anymore, and I felt the unmistakable swell of anxiety in my chest.

Usually, I loved thunderstorms, but whenever they touched down, I tended to be safely indoors—preferably huddled up in bed. Now, I was sitting in an all-metal vehicle, flying along the Route 1 highway.

I'd already had one brush with death this week and I didn't particularly fancy another.

"If you're just tuning in, folks, this nor'easter isn't letting up anytime soon, so try to stay off the roads tonight if you can," the radio host announced between songs, and I swallowed, pushing my hands down my thighs.

"Shit," Jace muttered under his breath. He sat forward, squinting as he focused on the road. "I don't think I can keep driving through this."

His admission caught me off guard, and I willed the knots in my stomach to untie themselves.

A deafening clap of thunder rumbled above us, so loud it literally shook the truck.

"Yeah. You're probably right," I admitted, pulling my legs up. Resting my chin on my knees, I tried to concentrate on the country music that was playing on the radio and not on the sharp streak of lightning that lit up the sky.

The farther we drove, the more cars we spotted spun out in ditches, or parked along the side of the highway, waiting out the storm—the smart thing to do. But at that moment, I didn't care that the sky had opened above us, or that we were right in the center of it. All I wanted was to get home, for the thick, gray clouds to part and the rain to cease, but it was incessant. Droplets beat down on the roof like thousands of tiny bullets, and I could barely hear Jace when he eventually turned to me.

"Did you see how far away the next exit is?"

"Uh, I think it's only a few miles ahead. Why?"

"We're going to have to stay the night somewhere."

I glanced over at him.

"I can't see anything." A muscle jumped in his jaw. "There'll be a place we can stay not too far from here."

While it was a completely rational explanation, the thought of spending the night with Jace in an interstate motel tore at my nerves. I could practically hear Amelia's voice in my head, too, calling me out for being a total chickenshit. Maybe she'd been right. For years, Jace and I had both been so paralyzed by fear, afraid to make the first move. This was an opportunity to fix that mistake.

Three very slow and agonizing miles later, we'd taken the next exit, venturing into the closest town, but every motel we passed had their NO VACANCY signs lit up, flickering in the darkness. Most of the streetlights were out, damaged by the storm, and our quest to find someplace to stay was becoming even more dangerous.

Jace's truck bounced roughly along the road, splashing through potholes that had formed deep puddles. Eventually, the strips of shops and Victorian-style buildings fell away, and we were surrounded by trees and vegetation again.

"Well, that was Middletown," Jace commented. In my peripheral vision, I noticed his eyes assessing me, then dropping to where I'd clasped my hands together.

"What do we do? If we keep driving this way, we're going in the wrong direction." Air hissed between my teeth. "Should we turn back?"

The forest was eerie and noisy. The storm thrashed the trees, and the wind howled, whipping up the fallen foliage. The distant rumblings of thunder were a reminder that we still needed to find somewhere to take cover. Somewhere we would be safe. That was something I always longed to feel, and the closest I ever got to it was when Jace was by my side. I reminded myself of that now.

After a beat, he spoke. "Hang on." He straightened in his seat, and I blinked, focusing on him, his shadowed profile. "I think I can see something."

As we carefully rounded the next corner, there was one last motel just up ahead, down a narrow dirt road. The wooden sign was hanging crookedly but I was willing to overlook that, because much to my relief, they had vacancies.

"This all right?"

Taking my silence for assent, Jace pulled into the driveway, following the winding gravel road until we reached the clearing. There were only two other cars in the guest parking lot, and

Jace idled the truck in the circular driveway, directly outside the reception.

Something flickered across his expression as he glanced at me. "I can spring for two rooms."

It hadn't really sounded like a question, more a statement, but the idea of sleeping alone in a dark, unfamiliar room, possibly seeing shapes out of the shadows, I just couldn't.

"No," I said, a little too quickly, and my cheeks flushed. "I mean, I just don't want to be alone right now. Can you—can we please share a room?"

His eyes betrayed nothing, but his hand stilled on the door handle. "No problem. Sit tight."

As I waited for Jace to check us into a room, I got out my phone, exhaling a pent-up breath. I quickly tapped out a message to my mom, knowing she'd be worried, especially when I didn't come home.

The storm has us staying the night in a motel outside of Middletown. See you in the morning. Love you.

My stomach flipped over as I read and reread the text I'd just sent her.

Jace and I were going to be stranded together all night in a cozy motel room, and I probably wasn't going to get a wink of sleep. I would be kept awake, but not due to recurring nightmares. I'd be lying next to him, having to clench my jaw around words. Words I could never take back. I'd be falling asleep beside the person I spent every minute loving, every minute missing.

My brain started to obsessively break down and sort through all the possibilities that brewed alongside the storm. Did this mean we would share a bed, as well as a room? Was this some form of divine intervention, Mother Nature showing us the full extent of her powers? Forcing us to finally confront the situation and talk about what really mattered. Spending the night together, it shot holes in the walls I'd meticulously fenced around me. It was going to be easier for Jace to break through, I realized. For him to find me again. Maybe loving him had been so easy before because I hadn't completely trusted it to last.

If we did get back together, it wouldn't be like it was before. That much I was sure of.

Countless moments later, he climbed inside the Chevy again with the room keys. "We're down just a bit farther." He was shivering, his hair and clothes soaked.

"Shit. You're drenched, Jace."

"There'll be a heater in the room or something," he said, shifting the gear into drive. "Don't worry about it."

When we parked, he grabbed the keys from the center console and turned to me. "I'll go up first and open the door. Can you make a run for it?"

"Yep." That shouldn't be too hard. It felt like I'd spent half of my life running away from things.

"Don't actually run, Hayles," he revised, hesitating. He smiled, an easy kindness that crinkled his face. "You're still recovering. Take it slow."

I waited for the signal, for the dim light to flick on in the room, and when it did, I braced myself. Shoving the passenger door open, I swung my legs around and inelegantly slid out of his truck, my feet finding the uneven ground.

Surprisingly, there was no pain. Amazing to think I'd been assaulted just under a week ago, and I was already starting to feel steady and strong again. I guess that was a testament to the human spirit. I wasn't as fragile as I'd thought I was, and maybe I had my past to thank for that.

The heavy rain fell on me, and in seconds, I was drenched too. Another crack of lightning split the sky.

I walked as quickly as I could toward the motel room, to where Jace was standing, the soft glow from the lamp illuminating his dark figure. I scaled the rickety stairs, my bones creaking in protest after days of nonuse. But still, there was no pain.

Stepping inside, I surveyed the room, taking in the small dining table, the floral upholstered chairs, and the antique four-poster bed. The interior reminded me of an old lady's house. Quaint. Outdated. The walls looked like they hadn't seen a fresh coat of paint in my lifetime, but it was kind of romantic, like it'd been an adorable bed-and-breakfast decades ago. More important, we'd found shelter.

"Here." Jace handed me the towel he'd retrieved from the tiny bathroom. His voice was rough. "Use this to dry off."

When I got a good look at myself, I saw that my T-shirt was dripping wet and transparent, clinging to my cotton bra. Of course. How cliché. I folded my arms across my chest, suddenly feeling shy. "Thanks," I mumbled, looking up at him.

With his gaze trained above my neck, Jace sat down on the bed, leaving me standing in front of him. There was uncertainty etched into his features, and then the familiar warmth and longing were back. Interest crossed his expression too. Sudden, extreme self-consciousness took root as his eyes cut into me, piercing and deep.

Wordlessly, I retreated into the bathroom, shutting the door behind me.

Peeling off my shirt and leggings, I wrapped the towel around my torso. I hung my clothes over the shower curtain railing, hoping they would drip-dry overnight. Even though I could hear Jace lighting the gas heater on the other side of the door, I knew it would take a while for it to permeate the two rooms.

Jace was crouched by the radiant heater when I emerged from the bathroom a few moments later. He was shirtless, his jeans slung low. Damn it. Forget the hospital food and sleep deprivation. This was the cruelest torture yet. All I wanted was to burrow into the crook of his arm, to tell him he was the most beautiful man I'd ever known. The only man I would probably ever love like this. Even my soul hankered for him. It was a greedy hunger that made me bite my lip. A hunger I never knew existed—until him.

Barely able to catch my breath, I tightened my grip on the towel, because if I was to accidentally let go, I would be standing there practically naked before him. And if I was being honest with myself, that wasn't what bothered me most. It was the thought of not being emotionally vulnerable after everything we'd been through.

Life was short. Too short.

Jace cleared his throat, jerking me out of my thoughts. "Uh, so, is this okay? Are you okay?"

It didn't bother me that he was asking such an impossible question, because it was Jace, and in this room, right now, I didn't feel compelled to lie, like I had to pretend.

He was either willing to love me unconditionally, or he wasn't. He could say goodbye ... but I was starting to doubt that he would. He could've left a million times over by now. Or he could grant me safe passage into his heart—where I would stay, where I could continue to heal. And I was ready to find out, one way or another.

It required tremendous courage, so it was a good thing I still had some left. "Not really." This was it. My last chance to talk myself out of what I was about to do. I waited. Nothing. I was doing this. "I'm scared."

The answering silence told me he understood. Maybe more than I'd ever realized.

Since Tom's death, I had been so scared of losing Jace. But I'd been equally scared of loving him, too, to the point of *trusting* him, trusting *in* our relationship. That was a different kind of love. Maybe, just like him, I hadn't been completely ready for it. I'd thought that I *had* been, but that prospect—having one hundred percent trust in anything—had once sent waves of crippling fear and terror crashing through me. Because that meant losing control. Now, there was just . . . stillness.

Real, lasting love couldn't exist without trust. I understood that now. Without it, it just wasn't strong enough. No wonder I'd been so willing to hear Jace's words and overlook his actions. The night I'd told him I loved him, I'd focused on the *"You mean everything to me, too,"* and not on the fact that he'd kissed me with unspoken meaning. The morning he'd broken up with me, I'd again focused on the *"I can't do this anymore, Hayley,"* and not on how I had been the one to walk away from him, to sling insults at him, while he stood there and took it all.

People left. Whether they chose to, whether they died. It was always going to end that way. And that wasn't even the scary part. The scary part—the part that hurt the most—was how far you were willing to let that person in before they left you. It was also what made it so painful when they did. And it had me preserving this last jagged piece of my heart. But I didn't want to live my life in fear anymore, even if it hurt in the end. I didn't want to hold back. And I had been, ever since I'd lost Tom. It took me almost dying to work that out. I hadn't truly been living.

I took a measured step toward Jace, my eyes sweeping over the heavy expression he wore. "I'm scared about what will happen if we do this."

He exhaled in a slow rush. "I get it. Believe me. But you shouldn't be scared. This goes at your pace, Hayles. Always."

Swallowing, I had to work up the nerve to keep going. It was past time for us to have this conversation. "I know . . . I know about the blackmail, about everything."

There was a pause. "I was going to tell you," was his answer to the question I hadn't even verbalized. One arm went up and he raked his fingers through his damp hair. "I just wanted to give you space. Like I said that night in the hospital, you've been through a lot, and the last thing you needed was me complicating shit. You said you didn't want to talk about our relationship, and I wanted to respect that, to give you time."

Ever the reluctant hero. Endearing, and totally selfless. But that wasn't what I wanted anymore. He wasn't a mind reader, though; I needed to tell him how I felt.

"Jace." His name came out as barely a whisper. I sank down on the mattress, still holding on to the towel. "When we had that conversation in the hospital, I thought you'd broken up with me because you didn't want to be with me anymore. Now that I know what really went down, that you tried to ignore Aaron's threats for so long, then went to such great lengths to protect me, to protect Amelia . . . it changes things. It changes everything."

For a beat, maybe two, he didn't react. He didn't say anything. "I always said I'd protect you, no matter the cost. Even if that meant letting you go, letting you think I didn't want to be with you anymore."

At that moment, it took everything in me to remember how to breathe. With him staring at me like that, uttering the words that had the power to change everything, again, it practically sucked the remaining oxygen out of the room.

The tiny spark of hope in my chest ignited into a ball of fire as I watched the last of his walls crumble around him.

Before I could guess what he was doing, Jace closed the distance between us, reaching me in two quick, purposeful strides. He kneeled in front of me, his hands flattening on the bed on either side of my legs. "I'm so fucking sorry, Hayley. I didn't know what else to do. I still don't know what I'm doing. Nothing makes sense anymore. All I know is I can't do this without you." He looked up at me, gaze resolved, and my heart clenched. "How can I make this right? Whatever it is, I'll do it."

His mouth was only inches away now, and the urge to lean down and kiss him was overwhelming. To wave the white flag in surrender—or, in this case, the towel. The sexual tension between us had always been a physical, pulsing thing, but when you removed every single emotional barrier, it was otherworldly.

"You shouldn't have broken up with me, Jace, or pretended like it was what you wanted. You should have told me everything. From the day it first started. I would've understood," I told him. My anger had burned itself out at long last, but that didn't mean I was just going to ignore the way he'd reacted. I needed to know it wasn't going to happen again. "This silent communication thing isn't going to work for us long-term. You need to be honest with me, always."

"I know." The line of his jaw hardened. "I wish I had."

I could only imagine the pressure he'd been under. Everything he'd been dealing with, carrying with him, paired with threats against his sister and me. I wasn't the only one ready for a break from all of it—for the crippling weight to finally be lifted.

"The thought that I might have lost you, it fucking kills me," he went on. "Officer Bedford assured me they would keep you safe. I just wanted you safe, Hayles. You know that, right? Because, I swear to God, if anything happens to you, I know it'll destroy me. It almost did."

I nodded, or at least I think I did. "There was a lot at stake, and I don't know what I would have done if something had happened to Amelia. You . . . you made sure it didn't."

"But something did happen. You got hurt"—he inhaled deeply, then exhaled—"and I wasn't there."

The silence hung again, and we stared at each other, absorbing those words.

How could I dispute that? Something awful *had* happened to me. But if Jace had never come for me, found me in that dorm room—if things hadn't unfolded in the way they had—I wouldn't even be here.

"It's normal to blame yourself. I've blamed myself for the last two years, ever since Tom left that night with Derek and not us, and I probably always will. But it gets easier," I whispered, needing him to hear that, to believe it.

Jace would endure whatever unfounded guilt he felt, and I wouldn't let Aaron—his misplaced "love" and attempt on my life—haunt me. We wouldn't let him take any more happiness from us than he already had.

My words must have cut through the darkness, through the doubt that had been digging its talons into Jace, because he leaned his forehead against mine, exhaling as if bone-weary. "Maybe we had to go through this. Maybe Dr. Jensen was right. When Tom died, I was there for you, but I could only be there for you as your friend. That was all I could offer you back then, because I was with Zoe, because it wasn't the right time for us. It's different now, Hayles. We're gonna get past this, together."

I'd never heard Jace talk like this before. It made placing my trust in this—us—as easy as breathing. Our relationship had transcended, taking on a maturity and depth that electrified me and calmed me at the same time.

He pulled back slightly. In the soft lamplight, his eyes stood out like two sharp-edged sapphires. "You were right that day in the parking lot. I made a mistake," Jace continued. "I shouldn't have kept the blackmail to myself or let anything—anyone—scare me out of being with you." A muscle in his jaw ticked. "I almost couldn't do it. But the cops wanted me to cooperate with their investigation, to let them handle it. And when you just accepted everything I'd said, I realized how badly I'd let you down by not being honest, by not telling you what you mean to me, sooner."

He moved his hand to my cheek, his palm warm and rough against my face.

"I stopped running from what I felt for you a long time ago," he confessed. "When I saw you again at UD, it was like I was seeing clearly for the first time. Why I never fought for my relationship with Zoe, why I couldn't help but feel like I'd been given an out when I discovered she'd been cheating on me"—he winced, as if he was only just admitting that part to himself, let alone me—"and why I wasn't interested in meaningless hookups. Not only are you so beautiful, but you challenge me and inspire me to be the best version of myself. You're a force to be reckoned with, but you're also the kindest and most forgiving person I've ever met. After all these years, you were bound to get under my skin. Yeah, it scared me at first, and the night you had the courage to tell me you loved me, I'm not proud of the way I reacted. It was like I saw my future barreling down the line, and I panicked like I used to, a knee-jerk reflex."

He thumbed away the tears that leaked from my eyes. "I'm not proud of the way I let you think I was indifferent after we broke up, that it wasn't torture seeing you around campus, knowing you thought I'd given up on us." There was a short pause. "But most of all, I'm not proud of the way I let you think I wasn't in love with you. Because I am . . . I am in love with you."

That was when everything stopped, my heart included. "You love me?"

"You know I do," he murmured, smiling crookedly. "All semester, I've been trying to find the words to tell you how I feel." The vulnerability in his voice was like a hook that drew me in, and I couldn't look away. "I love you, with all of me, and I always have, Hayles . . . it just took me a while to catch up. But I'll show you how much I love you, I'll spend every day proving it to you, with everything I have, if you let me. Will you let me?"

Warmth spread through me, his words stoking the fire that burned deep in my chest.

"Yes," I managed finally. "Jace, I—"

His mouth landed hotly on mine, and I opened up to him completely. Trusted him completely. There was no holding back anymore. No concern about falling apart if I let myself want this—want him—too much. He *loved* me, and the way he kissed me chased away any doubt. When his lips skated over mine, his tongue sliding into my mouth, my grip on the towel loosened. I pressed closer, craving more. Needing more.

Everything had changed. It was reminiscent of the two nights I'd told him how I felt. Except this time, he wasn't with Zoe.

He'd told me he loved me too. And neither of us were being threatened by Aaron anymore. We were free to feel the type of love that swelled so high between us, to be pulled down by the undercurrent.

Both of us were breathing hard now, drowning in each other.

His hands traveled down my body, deliberately slow, and goose-bumps broke out on my flesh when he reached the edge of the towel.

"I missed you so much," he said, his breath hot against my ear. His lips trailed along my jaw, down my neck, and back up in the most scorching, reverent kiss.

Within seconds, an intense, searing desire flared to life, but it was so much more than that, and I felt the shift within Jace too. The pain and sadness and loss didn't exist in that moment, and the way his hands managed to hold me steady and set me free at the same time was like a healing salve for my soul.

Here we were, our bodies sealed together, the sound of rain falling on the tin roof, the open land. Surrendering to each other and surrendering to the fight we'd been losing all year—for what felt like a lifetime.

I buried my fingers in his soft hair, seeking more of his mouth, more of his touch. Needing to feel every inch of him pressed against me.

Jace crowded my senses, the kiss growing deeper, and then he was lowering me onto the bed. I welcomed the warm solidness of him on top of me, the feel of his erection rubbing against the most intimate part of me. Jace made a pleased sound in the back of his throat.

A calloused palm slid up my thigh, over the flare of my hip, and then halted at the hem of the towel, which had slipped down significantly but still covered most of my torso. He was waiting for permission, and when I mumbled *yes* against his mouth, his fingers parted the material, revealing my breasts and cotton underwear.

"God, I could get lost in you," he whispered, tugging on my bottom lip.

I'm already lost in you, I wanted to say. *Finding more and more parts of myself. All the missing pieces you've been safeguarding.*

A fervent hunger swirled, surrounding us like a powerful tornado, and those two-toned eyes were worshipping me.

"We can stop. We don't have to do this."

I knew that. Having sex for the first time was a big deal. But so was finding the right moment with the right person. This was ours. We could wait, but that was the point. I didn't *want* to. I didn't need candles, champagne, or rose petals for it to feel special and meaningful with Jace. Life—love—was unplanned and imperfect, fueled by feelings that ran deep, that took over. I knew I wouldn't remember the minor details—what I was wearing, the flower-patterned bedsheets. I'd remember the feelings, the person. They defined the moment.

"I know. But I want this," I said.

"You've been through a lot. Maybe we—"

I silenced him with a long, slow kiss. As much as I appreciated how certain he wanted me to be about this, it wasn't necessary. I wasn't broken. I wasn't in pain. My injuries were healing quickly. The meds were out of my system, and the only thing I could feel right now was pure, undiluted desire.

Jace didn't stop me again. The tips of his fingers brushed my inner thigh, slipping under my thin panties, and I moaned, my belly fizzing with arousal. My hips arched up, shifting against him, as he eased a finger inside me.

Lust simmered beneath the surface, along with this weird, emotional bubble that encircled us. I squeezed my eyes shut, letting myself *feel*. Letting myself go. My mind was silent. Lightning struck outside, bursting and blending color behind my eyelids.

Jace's fingers drove me crazy, pushing in and out of me, and his mouth moved over mine, but still, it wasn't enough. "Please," I whimpered, grinding against his hand, seeking more.

Frenzied and fumbling, I reached for the front of his jeans, popping the button and tugging down his zipper. And then he was helping me, his hands shaking ever so slightly. Satisfaction shivered through me, knowing he was just as affected as I was, knowing he was being brought to the very edge, too, while still being held at bay.

"Hold on a sec." He backed away, digging into the front pocket of his discarded jeans. When he withdrew a small, silver wrapper, I bugged my eyes at him.

"You brought a condom with you?" As much as I could appreciate his preparedness, I let out a puff of amused laughter. "Wait. You *knew* this was going to happen?"

"No." His full lips curved into a half smirk. "But I hoped it would."

Jace wasted no time undressing me and rolling the condom on, and when there was no fabric between us anymore, the weight of him settled fully against me. His hard length rubbed against me there—right fucking there—grazing my opening and triggering a jolt of heat that spiraled down to my core. Nothing but need and want burned through me, kicking my brain out of the equation.

I felt his heart beating wildly under my palm, and his lips brushed against mine, pulling shallow breaths.

"Are you sure?" he asked gruffly, trembling from the restraint. His eyes narrowed, trying to detect even a flicker of hesitation. "We don't have to do this tonight."

My heartbeat thumped off-kilter, and I was swimming with equal parts anticipation and hope. "I'm sure, Jace. I don't want to wait anymore."

The sight of him positioned between my legs had my body on high alert. As he guided himself into me, a pinching pressure grew. Okay. I could manage this. My thighs involuntarily clamped on him when the burning sensation stretched further and increased, and just when I thought it was over—that his thickness was all the way inside me—he pushed deeper with one last thrust.

Shit. Shit. Shit.

It hurt more than I'd expected . . . but it wasn't anything I couldn't handle. I gritted my teeth, waiting for the sharp, stinging pain to subside.

Jace tensed incrementally, until he was utterly still inside me, not moving. "You okay?" His voice was guttural.

"Yeah. You're just . . . oh *wow*, that—" I gasped.

He pulled out slowly. Eased back in. The pain ebbed away to a dull ache, eclipsed by the friction.

His forehead creased with concern. "Do you want me to stop, Hayles? Should I stop?"

"No." I sucked in a ragged breath. "Keep going."

He rocked out again, and then back in, deep and full, making me whole again. I felt everything. It felt right in a way that nothing had ever felt right before—and I was so glad I'd waited, chosen this moment.

This was spontaneous. Fragile. Fleeting. *Real.*

He sat his forearms on either side of my head, his mouth

sweeping over mine again, and he instinctively started to move inside me. Jace was quiet and yet he'd never said so much. Every caress, every kiss, was like a vault opening, unsealing our secrets and reserving more memories between us.

Shards of pleasure rushed through my veins, and I moaned, trying to match him, rolling my hips up to meet him. Jace seemed to know what I needed, because he picked up the pace, increasing the intensity of his thrusts.

"Hayley," he rasped, exhaling a choked-up breath.

That one word—my name, his voice—anchored me. Prevented me from floating away on a cloud of all-consuming bliss.

Thunder rattled the window. Lightning flashed into the tiny room, filtering through the closed curtains and flickering across his face. A fierce ache pounded in my chest. The way I was feeling was overwhelming—hard to contain. I couldn't believe that, after nine years, Jace was mine. And he was making love to me.

We strained against each other silently, slowly, learning the curves and planes of each other's bodies. Jace watched me as I came apart in his arms, and then his hands cradled my face, and his lips captured mine, putting me back together again.

twenty-eight

In the darkness, as the storm raged on outside, Jace helped me to forget, to forgive.

The shadows that used to chase me, the memories that once haunted me, couldn't reach me anymore. Tom's death. Aaron's attack. My fear, guilt, and doubt. They were all things that had sought to destroy me over the years, but they hadn't. Whether I'd ended up in Jace's arms tonight or not, I was so much stronger than I'd ever realized.

His hands held their own memories, and as he'd traced my body—paying even closer attention to everywhere I was bruised—Jace gave me back something incredible. He gave me confidence. Confidence that I'd always be able to rebuild, no matter what life had in store for me. Confidence that I was worthy of his love—a slow, gradual love that wouldn't diminish. Confidence that even though I often felt trapped in my tragic past, it didn't mean I couldn't still reach for happiness, or forgiveness.

There was solace in the silence that drifted between us afterward, and I listened to the sound of his heart, thrumming beneath my cheek.

"Do you remember the first day you came over that summer?" Jace asked. His fingers swirled gently over my lower back. "We spent hours just listening to music and organizing my photo albums."

I nodded, my stomach dipping. It was something our therapist had recommended. *Try to find your normal again. Do something together that you used to do, that doesn't remind you of the accident.*

After a slight pause, he admitted, "You keep telling me that I saved you, but you were the one who saved me. You saved me, Hayles. And not just that day. Not just once."

I inhaled, thinking back to that summer. We were both so lost and confused, trying to make sense of Tom's death. Trying to piece together our shattered lives, forever changed after that night. Trying to find our footing in a world that was determined to keep spinning around, that didn't wait for anyone, especially those who were still trying to catch up.

"I could never go down a dark path, not when you were always there. That day, I remember you sat down on the floor next to me and closed your eyes, and you just listened. To nothing and to everything. Even though it was your brother who died, you still tried to comfort me," he said, and I stared into those blue-gray eyes as they melted me from the inside out. His chest rose on a heavy breath, and then his voice lowered, taking on a hushed tone. "I remember thinking, maybe one day, this girl will be mine, but only when I've earned it. Only when we can recognize what this is, so that we can honor it, so that we don't ruin it."

Something dislodged behind my rib cage, like an old, repressed insecurity wiggling free, and I knew, within those four walls, we'd found our freedom. Our truth. And it occurred to me then, at that moment, that life was filled with "maybe one days." There wasn't always going to be a guarantee, but I understood the importance of taking each day as it came. The importance of trusting that everything happened for a reason, unraveling in the way it did.

There was always a lesson to be learned, especially within all the pain, heartbreak, and sadness. After all, there was no light without a little bit of darkness. And I wasn't going to let my dark or frightening experiences consume me because without them, I wouldn't be here.

I wouldn't be with Jace.

I wouldn't be falling asleep in his arms.

And I wouldn't be held against him so tightly, my arm slung across the middle of his chest. I wasn't sure if there were two of us anymore—where he ended, and I began. I'd never felt this close, this connected, to anyone.

Emotion clogged my throat, and I struggled to form a worthy response. A response that conveyed just how much I understood, just how deeply my feelings ran.

I finally settled on saying, "I love you, Jace," and tilted my face up to kiss him.

His lips molded to mine perfectly, and we breathed one another in.

When that smile reserved just for me pulled at the corners of his mouth, and he whispered, "I love you too," I knew I'd also been given something else, something better: The promise of a future that contained the two things I'd wanted to feel for the longest time—hope and *trust*—and with Jace, the boy I'd loved for as long as I could remember.

epilogue

Six months later

Dearest Tom,

I can't believe it's been over three years since we lost you. Since I had to watch the one person I thought I'd never lose leave me. It didn't matter how much I prayed that you would stay, or how tightly I tried to hold on to you, just like sand between my fingers, you eventually slipped away.

A part of me left with you—my big brother, my protector, the person who promised to always keep me safe—and it's been so hard to define who I am without you anymore. It's been difficult to stand on my own two feet, and it's taken a long time for me to find myself again, but I finally have.

I've pieced myself back together, with the help of Mom, Dad, Amelia, and Jace. I think, in some way, even before you died, we were always destined to be a family. We've all had to learn to be resilient and brave in the midst of so much tragedy. And with Jace's parents still traveling, I think the three of us have been able to draw strength from each other even more.

I know I'm writing you a letter you can never read, and maybe that's strange, but Jace has been encouraging me to put my feelings into words—to say everything I've always wanted to. Perhaps he's right. Perhaps this is the chance for me to say one last goodbye, after all this time. I've held on to you, on to the overpowering sadness and misplaced guilt, for far too long. I know I need to let you, and myself, move on.

I'd like to think you've been watching over me since you left, and that you already know everything that's in my heart. That even though it's been over three years since we last spoke, you still listen whenever I feel like talking. And that even though you're gone, you still manage to be with me somehow.

Because if I look closely enough, some days I swear I can still see you, Tom. I can see that all around me is you. You fill the air I breathe, the sun that shines through my window every morning, and the flicker of hope I feel, burning from within. You might not be here physically anymore, but I know you are here in spirit. And now that I know where to find you, I can take comfort in the fact that you never left me. Not really.

You'll be glad to know Jace has continued to be there for me, especially in these last six months. The fallout of everything I've been through, the culmination of Aaron's trial, and hefty sentence for attempted murder, among other charges . . . it's taken such a heavy toll on me. Jace and I have been through so much together already, and we've come out of each challenge stronger than ever. I know I can always find him by my side in my darkest hours or in times of despair.

He safeguards my heart, and I treasure his.

So, I'm sitting here on my bedroom floor right now, writing this letter to you on top of an overpacked cardboard box, and I don't know when I'll be back here next.

Jace graduates next month, and he has a photography internship lined up in Oregon. After he submitted those beautiful portraits of me, Professor Martinez was willing to overlook the fact that they were late and nominated him for the Sony World Photography Awards, and he won. Being named Student Photographer of the Year was a real achievement. Lots of prospective employers thought so, too, which was how he was able to secure his dream job so quickly. Anyway, Jace asked me to move with him, Tom, and I think you already know what my answer was.

I told him yes, of course.

I'm transferring colleges and I start my sophomore year at Oregon State University at the end of the summer. They also have a great art program, and honestly, making it work with Jace is as important to me as studying design is. He wants to rent out this little Scandinavian-style cottage, and it's perfect. Seriously, I wouldn't be surprised if I've already pinned it to my House Inspo board. He says that's where we'll make our home. He wants to start building a life together, which is what I've always dreamed about.

I know it might seem like we're leaving everything behind, but I don't view it that way. I see it as a new chapter, not as an ending.

I might not see Mom and Dad for a while, and I'm kind of scared. Scratch that, I'm terrified. I'm going to miss the hell out of my best friend too. As it turned out, Amelia came home early, anyway. It wasn't a surprise to me or Jace, though. She'd wanted to give her parents their space to travel and be together, afraid of becoming an unwanted third wheel. And now, only two and a half months since returning, Amelia and I are going to be worlds apart again. But we'll make it work. We always do.

Leaving home is never easy, let alone adding nearly three

thousand miles of distance, but beginning a journey is something I believe we all long for.

It's nerve-racking every time I do this. Every time I pack up, move forward, and take another chance. But the last time I did this, it ended up being so much more than I could've ever hoped for. I made lifelong friends, I faced my fears, I overcame unexpected obstacles, and I found love.

After years of being patient, after years of waiting for something that I thought I'd never have, I finally found love with the boy I've always wanted to share it with. Despite all the hardships he and I have faced, we've healed together.

I can still remember the days you would glance back and forth between us, and your eyes would clear, almost knowingly, as if you knew long before we even did, that we'd find our happy ending in one another. I'd like to think you're proud of us now.

I'm leaving Port Worth for good in a couple of days, and I didn't expect it to be so bittersweet. I think I spent the last few years so focused on wanting to escape this small town that I didn't really appreciate everything that's happened to me here. All the sacrifices I've made, the mistakes I've forgiven and learned from, the sadness I've let go of, and the love I've felt. Everything that's shaped me into the person I've become happened in this sleepy small town.

As much as I'm going to miss it here, Port Worth will always be locked away in my heart—a special place I will remember and hold on to forever. It's where we grew up, and it's where I feel closest to you.

Even though I'm going to put this letter on top of your cremation headstone today, even though I'm going to drive away from our hometown tomorrow, I know you'll continue to follow me wherever I go. I know it's never really goodbye because I'll be reunited with you again, one day.

But, for now, I'm in safe hands, Tom, and you can be at peace with that knowledge. You can trust that I'll be okay. Because I am. For the first time in a long time, I'm okay. And when I'm not, I'll be sure to find some place quiet to confide in you.

I miss you every single day, and I will love you forever.

Hayley

acknowledgments

From posting my first chapter of *Maybe One Day* on Wattpad to holding the book in my hands eight years later, it's been such a life-changing journey, and there are so many people I must thank.

To my editorial team, Daphne, Deanna, Fiona, Shannon, and Delaney, for every reassurance, piece of praise, and your constructive feedback. I've had so many capable hands help me shape this manuscript, and I'm immensely grateful. To my Wattpad team over the years, in particular I-Yana, Samantha, Robyn, and Monica, for your hard work. Thank you for calling me back in 2019 to tell me you wanted to publish the first book I ever wrote. It was the best gift ever, and so aptly timed too—the day before my birthday.

To all the talented writers I've connected with and been inspired by since I first joined the platform (as a silent reader) in 2010, thank you. Thank you for giving me the courage to share my own writing. It's an honor to be a part of such a wonderful community. Whether we've spoken a handful of times or kept in touch over the years, thank you for your friendship and encouragement.

Most of all, thank you to my readers. Every single person who read, voted, commented, or recommended my book(s) to someone else. Without you guys, none of this would've been possible. Whether you're a new reader who's picking up *Maybe One Day* for the first time or someone who's rereading Hayley and Jace's story—thank you from the bottom of my heart for investing more than just your time. Thank you for taking a chance on this book and me.

My treasured inner circle of family, friends, and colleagues who've downloaded the app, pledged to buy my book, and kept my online handle a secret from many tech-savvy students, I appreciate you all more than words can say.

To Kell, for being there every step of the way. I'm so grateful our paths crossed back in 2016 (shout out to that group chat) as I gained an incredible writer in my corner. Better yet, one of my closest friends in the world. Thank you for letting me bug you with a million questions and send you excessively long voice messages (I really am sorry) with zero complaints.

To my uncle, Doug, a wordsmith in his own right. Thank you for loving me like a daughter and celebrating every milestone with me. To my grandparents, Jessie and Douglas, for their epic love story that lasted sixty-four years and inspired so much of my writing journey.

My parents, Anne and Paul, for everything. All the times I'd force you to listen to my stories growing up, especially when I went through the overly descriptive phase. I'd just discovered the thesaurus and naively thought that using as many big words as possible made you a good writer. It doesn't. Thank you for always encouraging my creativity and believing in me. I'm so lucky to have parents who created Wattpad accounts to champion my writing and bought me Pandora charms to commemorate *Maybe One Day*'s milestones—the 1 you gave me when it hit one million reads, and the 0 you added to my bracelet when it surpassed ten million. I think the fact that I still let you read everything—even the steamy scenes—speaks for itself.

Last, but certainly not least, my husband, Alex. I know writers don't always have to "write what they know" but it's no coincidence I finished my first book after you came into my life, and then I went on to write three more. Thank you for proving to me that all the moments we read about in romance books and long to feel one day are attainable and real. Thank you for not judging me when you got home to see that I'd hardly moved from my writing cave—or, more accurately, my spot on the couch—since you'd left. Thank you for everything you sacrificed or added to your workload so I could chase this lifelong dream. I truly couldn't have done this without your support.

about the author

Sarah Douglas started writing on Wattpad at the age of fourteen, and now holds a Bachelor of Education. Teacher by day and avid writer by night, she has accumulated over fifty-seven million reads online, been featured in *Cosmopolitan*'s online magazine, and worked with Netflix and Marriott Traveler. When she's not writing, you can find her playing video games, taking care of her many houseplants, or daydreaming about where she'd like to travel next. Sarah lives in Australia with her husband and two dogs. *Maybe One Day* is her debut novel.